Carriers

Patrick Lynch

CARRIERS

Mandarin

A Mandarin Paperback
CARRIERS

First published in Great Britain 1996
by Mandarin Paperbacks
and William Heinemann Ltd
imprints of Reed International Books Ltd
Michelin House, 81 Fulham Road, London SW3 6RB
and Auckland, Melbourne, Singapore and Toronto

Copyright © Patrick Lynch 1996
The author has asserted his moral rights

A CIP catalogue record for this title
is available from the British Library
ISBN 0 7493 1400 1

Printed and bound in Great Britain
by Cox & Wyman Ltd, Reading, Berks.

For
David and Pam
and
Sylvie

I should like to thank Dr Rupert Negus, Dr Helena Scott, Dr Marcus Matthews and Peter Sington for their invaluable help with the scientific and medical elements of this book. I should also like to give special thanks to Robert Winder and David Rosenthal.

Contents

God hath chosen the foolish things of the world,
and the things which are despised,
hath God chosen, yea, and things which are not,
to bring to nought things that are,
that no flesh should glory in his presence.

The Apostle Paul

The horrifying possibility that subtle changes in genes
of organisms of low virulence may endow them
with devastating new properties will almost certainly
turn out to be a common explanation for the
emergence of epidemics of new disease.

Prof Michael Levin
Darwin Lecture to the British Association
for the Advancement of Science, 1993

Prologue

The Chacra Mesa, New Mexico. Six years ago

'Vomit,' Jansen said, 'any splash – blood, excrement, anything like that – dry now mos' likely – just spray it.'

The guys with crew cuts, maybe from the same unit, exchanged a look.

'Use the paper to mop up. Triple-bag it, wash the bag with bleach, and get it into a hat box.'

He tapped the drum-like box between his knees. It was black and had a red biohazard sticker.

Everybody was soaked through. Six men in the truck. One black guy from Detroit. Ninety-five degrees, with the air conditioning dripping on a track stretched like piano wire back to the perimeter checkpoint. Corporal Robert Kinnel lifted his face into the stream of cooler air pumped through from the front. It would be hotter in the suits, if that was what they were using. Kinnel closed his eyes. Maybe it was just coveralls and a face mask. Look on the bright side.

'What are we wearing, sir?' he said, looking at Jansen's young face.

Jansen pushed sweat up into his white-blond hair.

'Full suits, soldier.'

Great. Blue suits. With a hose up your fanny to breathe through. Kinnel looked at the faces of the other guys. He had never seen any of them before. He wasn't even sure they were regular army. Apart from the little black guy they all kept their mouths shut. Kinnel would have liked to ask a few questions. He wanted to know if they had been flown in like himself. He wondered if any of them knew what this was all about. It had to be something dirty. A spill of some kind or maybe an explosion. But the Centre for Biological Warfare was at the RIID head-quarters in Frederick, Maryland, over two thousand miles away. Maybe they had centres scattered all over. Kinnel shuddered despite the heat.

'We spray, we fumigate, we seal off and we get the fuck out,' said Jansen.

There were three main buildings in the complex, the big-gest a low concrete structure without windows. Another truck stood waiting outside. Two uniformed technicians were stacking boxed suits onto a trolley. But they weren't the blue Chemturion suits Kinnel had expected. They were orange Racal space suits, positive pressure suits with a battery-powered air supply. Kinnel had been in a negative pressure lab where they kept BL–4 agents – hot agents like Marburg or Ebola that would burst you open, turn you to mush in a couple of days. The air was plumbed in through pipes. You clipped your hose onto the nearest manifold and just unclipped if you had to move on. If they were using Racal suits – fully portable with autonomous breathing apparatus – this wouldn't be that kind of lab. But if it wasn't that kind of lab what could have happened to warrant this kind of clean-up?

'We going deep sea shit diving,' said the little black guy, showing them his smile.

And if it was a lab working with hot agents they would have a system for disinfection. Press the alarm bell and down came the rain. Enough phenolic dis-infectant and whatever crawled out of the test tube stopped crawling. Why didn't they have that kind of

2

system here? Maybe they did. Maybe it wasn't working.

Kinnel followed Jansen into a cabin which had been set up against what looked like a fire door. Jansen explained how the suits worked, although the guys looked as though they already knew the equipment.

'You have positive air pressure. So if any of you busts the suit, the air will go out, not in. But you gotta close the hole right away, tape it shut, or you'll lose pressure. Your battery gives you clean air for six hours, but give yourself plenty of time to decon out. The techs have set up a modular decontamination shower in the airlock.'

'We got ourselves an airlock?' Kinnel shook his head in disbelief.

'Not a literal airlock, but we got a grey zone. It's beyond the insertion point.'

Insertion point. Kinnel bit his tongue, and checked the other guys' faces – Jansen was starting to get to him with his manual-talk.

'If you cut yourself or bust your suit, you go under the shower. You don't come back out if you haven't been cleaned. Understood?'

The guys nodded, already stepping into the surgical scrub suits that went under the Racals. Kinnel could see they were only listening out of respect for Jansen's rank, whatever that was. They'd been through this kind of operation before.

'And stay clean. I want you in pairs, watching each other's suits. If you get blood on your suit, or shit or soup – I don't care – clean it off. With a dirty suit or gloves, you won't see a hole.'

When they were in the scrub suits, Jansen rapped on the door.

There were two guys in coveralls standing next to a pile of Racals. Kinnel struggled into his suit, helped by one of the technicians. He pushed his head into the soft plastic

3

bubble of the helmet. Then he pulled on rubber gloves and held out his arms for a technician to tape the gloves to the sleeves. It was way too hot. Almost immediately Kinnel's bubble misted up. The technician flipped on the battery pack and filtered air rushed into the suit, inflating it. The mask cleared. Then the technicians tore four strips of tape from the wall and pressed them onto Kinnel's right forearm. The tape was for any emergency repairs that might be necessary, but to Kinnel it felt like a gesture. It felt like the guy wanted to reassure him. It made him nervous.

He stood listening to the steady roar of air, feeling his heart start to quicken. He didn't like not knowing what was inside the building. He'd seen plenty of corpses, but never people dead from chemical or biological weapons. All boiled up and twisted. Jansen opened another door and they moved into the airlock where there were two men already suited up, one of them carrying a spray unit with its four-litre reservoir. It was darker in here and warm in spite of the cool air supply. There was a decon module which didn't leave much room to move around. Kinnel felt his ears pop.

'We rigged up a unit that maintains negative pressure in the building,' shouted Jansen over his shoulder.

They shuffled forward until everybody was inside the airlock. The door closed. Kinnel tried to see the faces of the other men through their visors, but the gloom was deep now, the light thin, stretched like a skin on darkness, a fragile membrane they were about to penetrate.

Kinnel peered down into the stairwell, listening to Detroit scrabble at the light switches behind him, to no effect. His reedy voice cut through the roar of air inside Kinnel's helmet: 'What dumb son of a bitch sprayed the electrics?'

Looking down into the darkness, he could just make out two corridors to left and right. Where did they lead?

4

How many rooms were there? How many levels? They hadn't been told. At least *he* hadn't been told. The way the crew-cuts were trashing all the documents on the ground floor made him think maybe they knew more than he did.

Detroit was looking back up the way they had come. One of the other men dumped a drum of Clorox at the top of the stairway and walked away. Light or no light, the operation was going ahead. Detroit waved his arms: 'Hey! What the fuck . . . ? Hey!'

The other soldier didn't turn round.

'OK,' Detroit said. 'Stick around.'

He shuffled back up to ground level and away towards the grey zone.

Alone in the dark, Kinnel tried to control his breathing, hanging on tight to the rail. His head was buzzing and there was a dry metallic taste in his mouth. He wanted to keep moving, he wanted to get the spray unit off his back and out of this plastic-bag suit. Above all, he wanted to get out of this place, whatever it was. Sweat started to run into his eyes.

He was about to sit down when a single fluorescent strip flickered to life in one of the corridors below him.

Jansen clapped Detroit hard on the shoulder and pointed into the room beside him.

'Spray ceiling and floor, soldier, then make ready to fumigate!'

It was just a small study: a desk, potted plants, a plastic model of the double helix, a pipe lying in a marble ashtray. The contents of the desk and of a filing cabinet had been triple-bagged by the others and carted away. The drawers stood open.

'Sir, I left Kinnel in the . . .'

'What's that?'

Jansen brought his helmet close. His face was flushed

and distorted with impatience and the effort of trying to hear.

Detroit shouted, pointing back towards the centre of the building. 'Sir, my partner's in the basement area!'

Jansen pointed back into the room.

'Ceiling and floor, then get ready to nuke this sucker!'

There were dark red doors at the end of the corridor with a crooked X of hazard tape plastered across them. Kinnel looked back up the corridor. He couldn't get rid of the sensation that there was someone behind him, following him. Through the rush of air he thought he could hear footsteps. But he was still alone. The single fluorescent strip flickered on and off, throwing his shadow before him.

The doors were not locked. A padlock hung loose over a latch. There was no key. Kinnel took hold of the bar and pushed, noticing as he did so fragments of broken glass at his feet.

Jansen didn't like it. Most of the rooms on the ground floor were sprayed through, but there was still another level to tackle, and time was running out. In less than an hour they would have to evacuate and go through the whole decon procedure, because their batteries would start to fail. Even if the men changed suits and went straight back to work again – itself a violation of procedure – the change-around would add at least two hours to the operation, and that would mean working by night. Jansen didn't want that. Jansen's orders were to get it done and get out. He went quickly from room to room, checking on progress, checking that there were no mistakes. They should have given him a bigger team. They should have given him more back-up. They should have given him more of everything.

'Hey, you,' he said as Detroit went past him. 'Where the hell is Kinnel?'

They had turned it into a makeshift ward. Two beds, two saline drips, one fallen on its side, radioelectro-cardiographs, sinks full of used hypodermics and old dressings, no windows, no way out. Beside each bed the naked, cinder-block walls were spattered with dark blood, as if the patients, whoever they were, had been finished off with shotguns. The sheets that had covered them were still on the beds, twisted and purple-black. The haemorrhaging had been massive, uncontrollable. It had reached into the brain, judging from the violence of the convulsions, bringing delirium before death.

Kinnel took a deep breath and stepped inside the room. Shattered glass was strewn everywhere. At least one of the patients had managed to clamber out of bed before collapsing by the door. Kinnel could make out his progress from the dark smears he had left behind on the cement floor. Had the door been locked? Kinnel looked down at his feet. Was this the spot where the patient had died, begging to be let out, begging to be heard? But why hadn't the patients been taken to a hospital? Why had they been shut away down here?

Kinnel adjusted the nozzle on his Envirochem spray and made his way towards the sinks. That was the place to start, then bag all the moveables for incineration and nuke the place with formaldehyde. If they weren't done in one hour, they would have to come back. And Kinnel didn't want to come back.

PART ONE

Corpse lily

1

Manhattan. July 16th. Three years from now

She was on her back, naked in the middle of the floor, her heels touching the border of the Turkish kelim. Up here on the twentieth floor it was cooler than down on the street. A light breeze ruffled sheets of paper scattered near her head.

'Holly?'

She stirred, drawing an arm across her face against the sunlight. Richard Meyers walked across the room and put his attaché case on the sofa. There was a carton of orange juice on the coffee table. He drank a little, then stood looking at her for a moment. Making a list of some kind, she had gotten green marker pen on her left breast, just beneath the nipple, and there was another trace near her mouth. He smiled. It was a fine sight to return to after the rush hour traffic. It made him feel like stripping off himself.

For a woman of thirty-six Holly was in great shape. The twins, Emma and Lucy, were twelve years old now and she'd had no other children. That had to be one reason. And then there was all that rollerblading she did in the park. It was on her face you saw the difference. There were faint lines around her eyes, and on either side of her mouth where she smiled. And there were one or two strands of silver in her thickly growing, dark hair. Richard pulled off his tie and draped it over a chair. He had seen her old wedding photographs, taken thirteen years earlier, but she was if anything more beautiful now. There was a completeness about her, an identity. The girl in the wedding pictures, smiling sweetly through painted lips, her hair teased into an elaborate perm, lacked all that. He had missed almost half her life, it was true, but he could not help believing that the best was still to come.

'Holly?'

She pursed her lips, and took a deep breath. Richard leaned across her and picked up the empty glass that was inches from her right hand, a half-melted ice cube in the bottom. Then he noticed the Polaroid photograph.

It was partly hidden by her hair. Careful not to disturb her, he separated the dark curls and drew out the picture.

All the windows in the apartment were open. The breeze lifted strands of hair on his damp forehead. Down on Columbus a squad car went past giving a single warning whoop. Holly took her arm away and laid it next to her body so that Richard paused for a second, waiting for her eyes to open. But she was sound asleep.

There were six people in the picture: three children, including Emma and Lucy, and three adults behind them. They were on a veranda surrounded by spangled green foliage. Richard recognised Holly's ex-husband, Jonathan Rhodes, and there was a woman next to him who had to be Christina, his latest girlfriend. Next to them stood a kindly looking Indonesian woman in a long yellow dress with a crude flower pattern print. She wore a white scarf around her head in the Muslim fashion. The other child was probably this woman's daughter. She stood directly in front of her mother in a green T-shirt and baggy knee-length trousers. She looked about twelve. Everyone in the picture was smiling, their faces coloured gold in the late afternoon sun. Both Emma and Lucy wore colourful batik shirts that Richard had never seen before.

The picture had to have been taken at the research station in Sumatra, where Rhodes was posted. Dr Rhodes was a botanist, and had spent most of his adult life in one tropical country or another, mapping out the huge variety of plant species in environments perpetually under threat of destruction by settlers, ranchers or logging companies. Among the thousands of undiscovered species lay the basis for new life-saving medicines, a fact recognised by the pharmaceutical companies that employed him or sponsored his research. It was important work – a race against time, Holly said – to which Jonathan had dedicated himself unstintingly. Everything else had taken second place. Holly was philosophical about it now, but she'd clearly had some bad years, especially when Emma and Lucy were very young. She was always having to choose between dragging them off to remote and even dangerous parts of the world, or staying behind in Washington for months on end, waiting for her husband to come back. Needless to say, her own career as a journalist – a promising one – had fallen by the wayside. Jonathan's new girlfriend, Christina, ten years his junior, was another botanist. Maybe she would fare better.

'Richard?'

Holly was squinting up at him, her dark eyes seeming to absorb the light.

'Hello there.'

She drew her legs up.

'The air conditioning broke down.'

'So you thought you'd take all your clothes off.'

She smiled, holding the end of her tongue between hard, white teeth.

'Here I am working my butt off and you're lounging around in your birthday suit getting a tan. I just hope no one out there's got a pair of binoculars.'

She took the photograph from him.

'See the little girl? Her name's Indah. Her mother's

13

the housekeeper. She's the same age as Emma and Lucy. So they've got a playmate. Speaks pretty good English, Jonathan says.'

Richard sat down, his suit trousers snagging against his thighs. He pointed at the picture.

'What's that Lucy's holding?'

Holly looked at the football-sized fruit in Lucy's hands.

'It's a durian, an indigenous fruit. Apparently it's absolutely disgusting – like onion-flavoured ice-cream, Jonathan says. And the smell's even worse. You're not allowed to take them on public transport because of the stink.'

'Onion-flavoured ice-cream?'

'Lucy has a passion for them. Can you believe it? She can't get enough. They make her eat it out on the veranda.'

'I'm not surprised. When did it arrive?'

Holly rolled over and put the loose pages of the letter together.

'It came this morning. Only took a week to get here. They're all having a great time, apparently. Anyway, Jonathan says he'll meet us at the airport when we go out.'

Richard nodded and took another swig of orange juice. Somewhere along the line *if we go out* had been transformed into *when we go out*. In the beginning, before the twins had gone, Holly had been as hesitant about the idea as he had. But two weeks without her children had changed that: she missed them and she worried about them. Their tentative plans for a holiday alone together had been shelved. It was clearly going to be Sumatra or bust.

It had been Jonathan's idea, of course. For some time he'd been trying to persuade his ex-wife to let the twins spend a month or two with him abroad. Until then he'd only ever seen them when he was back in the States, but now that they were almost in their teens and anxious to travel, Holly hadn't felt either willing or able to stand in their way. Besides, as Jonathan put it in one of his carefully crafted letters, it would do the children good to experience other cultures and ways of life. Judging from some of the types Emma and Lucy were hanging out with in school these days, Holly had to agree. And so it was arranged: the twins would spend six weeks with their father and Christina in Sumatra. Jonathan even managed to get the flights paid for by Westway Pharmaceuticals out of his generous sponsorship budget.

Six weeks alone with Holly! In the two years Richard had known her the most time they'd had together was a week in Vermont the previous fall. Six weeks seemed an impossible luxury. It wasn't that he didn't get on with the twins – there was no way he could have sustained his relationship with Holly if they hadn't taken to him – but they were old enough to know, to feel, that he was not in any sense their father. Between them there was still a respectful distance that prevented them from being a family, even though they were now all living under the same roof. He wished, as much for Holly's sake as his own, that this could change, but he had no idea how or whether it ever would.

It was only once the dates and the flights had been arranged for the twins that Jonathan suggested that he and Holly fly out too, a little later. Once again everything was couched in terms of what was good for the children. The world was full of screwed-up kids whose mothers and fathers hated each other – that was what he'd said – and it would be good for Emma and Lucy to see for themselves that their parents could still get on. Now that so much water had flowed under the bridge, and now that they'd both made new lives with new partners, there was no need, as he put it, *to preserve the old barriers*.

It all made perfect sense, of course – everything Jonathan did made perfect sense, Holly said – but Richard

15

couldn't help feeling uncomfortable about the whole idea. Maybe it was the adult thing to do, but there were a lot of unknowns. For one thing, how was Holly going to react once she got there? She could be pretty scathing about her ex-husband, but Richard sensed a lingering something for him, a residue of deep feeling that was more than just nostalgia or respect. When confronted with evidence of these feelings, he felt deeply insecure.

Rhodes was a hard act to follow. The work to which he had dedicated himself was so damned *admirable*, the way he'd gone about it, from Peru to Cameroon to Indonesia, so skilled and energetic. Dr Jonathan Rhodes was everybody's ideal man-in-the-field. He may have been a lousy husband and a half-baked father, but he was out there saving the planet, not sitting in an air-conditioned tower block in downtown Manhattan, shuffling electronic money around with the sole objective of *making a turn*. And then, how was Holly going to get on with Christina? Jealousy was a funny thing. It could surface in the most unexpected places at the most unexpected times. Richard knew that only too well.

'Are you sure you really want me there?' he found himself saying.

Holly looked up.

'Of course. Don't you want to come?'

'Sure, sure I do. But, I don't know, I just thought if you and Action Man are going to be patching it all up, maybe you'd prefer it . . .'

Holly had grabbed a towel from the armchair and was tucking it around her with sudden haste.

'Richard, we're not patching anything up. Don't be ridiculous. That's all history now. Of course I want you there.'

'OK, OK. I just thought I'd – '

'Well don't *think*.'

She sighed. For a moment they looked at each other.

16

Then she came over and knelt down on the couch beside him.

'You don't think I want to play gooseberry while Jonathan carries on with his fancy woman, do you? Besides, I want him to see I've done better than him.'

She ran her fingers through his thinning brown hair. He was five years older than her, with an ex-wife, a teenage son (both in Los Angeles) and a passable degree of expertise in corporate finance. Next to Dr Rhodes, he didn't feel like such a great package.

'So when do you want to go?' he said.

'I called Malaysian Airlines. There's a flight to Singapore on the third of August with an immediate connection to Padang.'

Richard frowned.

'The third? That's only a fortnight away. There's no way I can get away until at least the tenth.'

Holly put her hands on his shoulders.

'Honey, that's OK, isn't it? It'll give me some time to sort everything out at the camp.'

Richard looked into her dark eyes. What did she mean, *sort everything out*? If she really was looking to patch things up with Jonathan it would be a lot easier without him around. On the other hand, they had been divorced for seven years and Jonathan had a new woman. Could that really be what was on her mind?

'You know,' she said, 'make sure they have running water, and plenty of cold Budweiser. You never know, where Jonathan's concerned.' She kissed him on the mouth. 'Talking of which, how about a beer?'

Richard let himself be led through to the kitchen, where Holly opened the refrigerator and took out two Buds.

'Did you have a hard day?' she asked.

Richard shrugged.

'You know how it is. Sometimes I think I should have a telephone grafted to my ear.'

17

She pulled open one of the cans and handed it to him, together with a tall glass.

'I've been reading about Indonesia, about Sumatra. You know they have people there, the Minangkabau, they're Muslim, but they have a matrilineal society . . . and there's all the animals and insects. Did you know they have 40,000 species there, around 10 per cent of the world's population, and Sumatra has the biggest variety of mammals in the world. Elephants, orang-utans, even tigers.'

'Snakes,' said Richard, 'spiders, scorpions. What's the Indonesian for snake? Excuse me. I have a snake attached to my ankle.'

'There are no snakes in the camp. They're frightened of vibrations. They keep the vegetation cut back around the compound.'

She came and stood close to him, resting the cold beer against her face.

'It sounds beautiful,' she enthused. 'Rafflesia Camp. Jonathan named it after a flower that grows in the forest there, which was named by Sir Thomas Raffles, the great naturalist and explorer. The biggest flower in the world. It's huge, I mean, like, two feet across. Can you imagine? We can go for walks in the forest. Take photographs. They have a hollow where you can swim, and a beautiful veranda. Imagine, just sitting there at sundown.'

'I thought you divorced Jonathan to get away from all that. Bugs, malaria, typhoid.'

Holly hesitated for a moment and then pulled open the second can.

'I divorced Jonathan to get away from *him*.'

Richard sipped at his beer, watching as Holly placed one foot on top of the other. She gave a shudder.

'You should get dressed,' he said.

'What's the matter, Richard?'

She was holding her head on one side. Richard put

his beer down and pulled one of the plastic chairs out from under the table. He sat down.

'Nothing,' he said. 'It's not rational.'

'So what?' she said. 'Tell me.'

'I'm just not crazy about the idea of you and him . . .'

'And Christina. Don't forget about her.'

'Whatever. I said it wasn't rational.'

'You don't like the idea of us being together for a while?'

Richard shrugged.

'I guess, no. I mean maybe he wants to give it another shot. Maybe this Christina woman isn't anything serious. Have you thought about that?'

Holly sat down opposite and looked into Richard's face. He was tired. He worked too hard these days, she had said so many times. But it made no difference: he was determined to see that she and her children wanted for nothing. After eighteen months of going out with her he had even got himself promoted.

'To tell you the truth, yes I have. You can never tell with Jonathan. Everything he wants to do, even if it's just buying a hamburger, has to be justified rationally, explained. But this time, I think he is sincere. I told him a while back about Emma and Lucy, I mean the trouble they were having at school – '

'For God's sake. They aren't the first kids in the world to skip a class or two.'

Holly reached over and touched his arm.

'I know. And that's all behind them now, thanks to you. Having you around's made all the difference to them, I've told you that. But I think it got Jonathan to thinking. I'm sure he's building bridges for their sake. He thinks they need to feel he's there for them.'

'And what if he's got something else in mind?'

Holly looked down at her knees.

'Then he's wasting his time. Seven years with him was

enough.' She looked up again and he felt the pressure of her dark gaze with an agreeable soft jolt. 'But it's worth doing, isn't it? I mean, if it makes any difference at all for Emma and Lucy, it's worth trying.'

Richard smiled, taking in her face for a moment.

'Of course, of course. Don't listen to me, I'm paranoid. Comes with the job.'

There was a long silence as they looked at each other in the cool light. *Of course, if you were to marry me*, he thought about saying. But no, the moment wasn't right. She would tell him she wasn't ready yet, just as she had two months earlier and two months before that. And then he would feel low for the rest of the evening, just as he had both times before. Of course, they had talked the subject into the ground, talked it to death. But the funny thing was nothing had changed really. That was the problem when your vocabulary was more enlightened, more sophisticated than your feelings. You could talk about *substitutes* and *tensions* and *sublimations* as much as you liked but words were not spells. They had no magical power to ward off the old demons of jealousy, and fear. All Holly's reasons made sense – just like Jonathan's suggestions – but they left Richard feeling just the same as he had before. All he knew was that the children held the key. Where Holly was concerned they always had. And it wasn't just the intensity of a mother's love. Holly had had to overcome some sizeable obstacles to have children, biological obstacles. She had never gone into the details with him, shutting him out on this as she did on so many matters relating to her precious, difficult years with Jonathan. But something – some frustrating and arduous fertility treatment, Richard guessed – had made the arrival of Emma and Lucy, some twelve years before, seem all the more special.

Richard showered and went into the bedroom to change. Without the air conditioning it was stifling in the bedroom, and he started to sweat. He pulled on a cotton robe that Holly had bought him and sat looking at the wall.

The deal he was working on was still there. The moment he relaxed, all the figures, all the problems lit up in his head like the board at the Stock Exchange. He was in the middle of bringing to market an unlisted software company run by a bunch of computer prodigies – nice guys but a little crazy. There was no way the deal could be tied up by August third. And he knew Holly wouldn't wait. She wanted to get down there straight away. That was the way she was where the girls were concerned. She was like a kind of love-seeking missile. But it was their love she sought, not his. And then there was Dr Jonathan Rhodes. From the other side of the world he still had the power to change their lives, to make things happen the way he wanted them to. He still had power over Holly.

Richard looked at the pattern on his robe. In spite of himself, he wished they did not exist, not the girls, not their father. He wished they had never existed.

2

Jambi Province, Sumatra. July 24th

Lieutenant Amir Salim might have returned from his first patrol in the interior if he had listened to Sergeant Sidharta.

'We're in Jambi here,' Sidharta said, planting a nicotine-stained finger in the middle of the map. 'That's someone else's province.'

Lieutenant Salim wiped the sweat from his eyelids and squinted back the way they had come. The red earth of the track was barely visible beneath the clumps of prickly grass and razor-edged weeds. Tall rubber trees reached across the gap on either side, as if trying to knit up a wound, masking the sun. The scars on their trunks were several years old, he noticed – the rubber tappers long gone.

'So?'

'So it's not *our* province, sir. Not our responsibility.'

The jeep came to a halt behind them. One of the men jumped out of the back to take a leak. The rest sat peering into the forest gloom, keeping a firm grip on their rifles. For the first time in Lieutenant Salim's experience they looked wide awake despite the heat and humidity.

'Our base is the nearest,' he said, reaching for the map.

'But we should report to the command in Jambi,' said Sidharta. 'If it's their province, it's their problem.'

Salim didn't respond. Nearly two months on Sumatra and this was the first time he'd been more than five miles from barracks. It was certainly the first time he had taken a jeep beyond the highlands. He was not going to turn around because of a dotted line on an out-of-date map, still less because Sergeant Sidharta was letting his imagination run away with him. It would have made him look foolish.

Salim traced their route from the Trans-Sumatra Highway, trying to match it to the instructions he had been given by the police in Padang. The map had been drawn up fourteen years earlier, and the pattern of minor trails had clearly changed. In Padang he had asked the police to come with them to be sure they went the right way, but they'd made a lot of excuses about duties in town. At the time he had assumed they were just lazy like most of the locals, but now he was beginning to think they were a little scared too. He himself had never taken much notice of the rumours, but maybe they did. In any case it hardly mattered. If the position he had been given was correct, the camp could not be more than a few miles away. If the trail went on veering in the wrong direction, they would just have to retrace their steps a little and look for another. If that didn't work, they could always go cross-country. They still had a couple of hours' daylight.

The whole thing had started with a radio operator at the main post office on Aziz Chan Street, a wiry little man called Djamil. Every couple of days at 1300 hours Djamil made contact with Rafflesia Camp, speaking in his broken English to the leader of the project, Dr Jonathan Rhodes. When necessary Djamil could patch Rafflesia through direct to Washington, but more usually he just passed on messages or reported on the contents of the Rafflesia PO box.

Two days earlier Rafflesia camp had failed to reply.

Djamil had tried all the frequencies and there was nothing, just a strange whispering interference on the central band. it was not the first time he had had trouble getting through. The Minang Highlands stood between the coast and the camp, and when atmospheric conditions were wrong a signal could sound like it was being blown down a hosepipe. So Djamil decided to do nothing and to try the radio again the following day.

At eleven o'clock the next morning he had appeared at the offices of the Bank Dagang Negara asking urgently for the manager, a man who spoke good English. According to Djamil, a man – he wasn't able to say whether it was Dr Rhodes or not – speaking English, but in a way, in a tone, he could hardly understand had called in from Rafflesia camp. Djamil had tried responding with his few broken phrases, but without success. The manager reluctantly left his post and went back with Djamil to the post office. By the time they got there Rafflesia Camp had once more fallen silent. It was then that the police were alerted, and through them Salim's company at the Bayur barracks.

At the time Salim had wondered whether he was not over-reacting, assembling seven men and two M38s to carry them. His commanding officer, Colonel Azwar, who was bedridden with dysentery, had simply told him to find out what was going on. He didn't seem to think it could be anything serious. But as they travelled through the highlands the following morning, past scores of squalid slash-and-burn farmsteads gouged out of the upland forest, Salim had begun to wonder.

He had seen this kind of haphazard resettlement once before, on Timor, where his father, then also a colonel, had been stationed. When there was competition for land and livelihoods, sooner or later people got hurt.

The government in Jakarta saw the forests of the outlying islands as nothing more than wilderness, virgin land into which they could export the excess population from Java. Thousands of people were lured from the shanty towns and turned, by way of an official piece of paper, into farmers. The only problem was the tools and the grants they were promised never materialised. So they were left to wring a living from the meagre soil any way they could. And as they penetrated deeper into the interior, striking outwards from along the roads like infection from a cut, they began to compete with the people who had made the forest their home.

The government had tried to evade the problem through 'Forest People Integration' projects, designed to settle the Kubu Indians on conventional farms, but these had been a failure. The Kubu had listened politely to all the official lectures about the benefits of the modern way of life, picked up their hunting spears and walked away. These days the concrete houses built by the projects were occupied by more Javanese immigrants. And now there were stories going round the bars of Padang of attacks on new settlements, of poison arrows and disappearances in the night – and witchcraft, of course. They still believed in all that sort of thing, these people, even if they never came out and said it.

Sergeant Sidharta crunched the gears as the jeep tore its way through young bamboo. A big flying beetle smacked against the windscreen, its body catching under the wipers. They seemed to be moving south again – the right direction, Salim reckoned – although it was not easy to read the dashboard compass with all the jolting around. The track grew darker, looping between the trunks of emergent hardwoods which pushed the canopy up to two hundred feet over their heads. Salim was about to tell the sergeant to slow down when they found themselves in a narrow clearing, a blue sky above them. They had come out onto another trail, a wider one, properly cleared. Tyre tracks were baked hard into the surface. It was the trail they had meant to take from the Muaratebo road. They had turned off too soon.

They found the Rafflesia Camp about four miles further on, the words painted on a sign nailed to a gatepost.

The compound had been there for two years or more, so the police had said, but even so Salim was struck by how neat and orderly it was. There was a handful of buildings arranged around an expanse of short grass in the middle of which stood a tall mango tree covered in netting, and a large straggling banyan. The buildings were of wood, some painted white, others a plain grey. They were built well off the ground and some of them had verandas. Flowering shrubs grew in between them. It reminded Salim of the garden around the governor's residence in Padang, where he had been invited for cocktails at the start of his posting. This was civilisation – well-kept, everything in its place.

Except the pick-up. It stood by the side of the track, just outside the gate, its bonnet sunk into the low mesh fence that surrounded the compound. The driver's door stood open. There was no sign of blood.

'Get fallen out!' shouted Sidharta, without waiting for Salim's order.

The soldiers jumped down, their rifles at the ready. Salim took out his automatic and climbed out with them, looking for any sign of movement. Without the noise of the engines it seemed very quiet, as if the jungle was holding its breath, waiting for them.

Salim walked over to the pick-up. There was nothing inside but a steel towing line and some cans of fuel in the back. The driver had veered off the track, but it was hard to see why. There was no sign of damage and the tyres were sound. *Maybe he had been forced off the track.* Salim leaned inside the cabin again, checking carefully for bullet holes. He found nothing but a faint brown smear on the inside of the glass, about eighteen inches

26

above the top of the wheel. There was a fine speckle in the smear like chewed coffee beans.

Impatiently he waved Sergeant Sidharta towards the buildings, stooping to pick up a small pink tracksuit top which lay on the ground a few yards away. He examined it. There was no sign of tearing, of a struggle. It was clean and smelt faintly of citrus. The police had told him there were children at the camp – two, maybe three. They hadn't been too sure.

Sidharta wasn't taking any chances. He sent one man around the back of the nearest hut and two more to scout out the perimeter fence. They looked ridiculous, sidestepping clumsily around the grounds, pointing their weapons at bushes and shadows. They looked like the useless, half-trained conscripts they were. Salim tucked his automatic back in its holster and marched towards the largest building.

He thought at first it was music, a shifting hum that could have come from a radio. On the veranda he stopped to listen, but immediately the sound seemed to recede. He felt something tighten inside him. He looked over his shoulder. One of the men by the fence was just standing there, staring at him.

He went to the door and rapped twice. No one answered. Dr Rhodes and his crew were no longer at home. Had they left or had they been taken? Salim turned the handle and walked inside.

The flies swarmed around him, bumping against his face as if trying to drive him out. He swiped them away, spitting, brushing them from his tightly compressed lips as he advanced into the foul-smelling interior. He saw plain furniture, a table with empty glasses on it, dyed fabric hangings from Sumba, books on a shelf. In the opposite wall was a narrow passage with doors along it. A square of sunlight lit up a far corner. As he approached he began to hear a crackling, whining sound cutting through the insect din, and then a voice – snatches of a sentence.

'Hello? Is there . . .'

The voice came again. It was distorted, constrained, echoing off the ionosphere on a short-wave radio signal. Someone was calling. Maybe it was Padang, or Dr Rhodes himself. Salim pushed open the nearest door, searching for the set: there were two beds, camp beds, the mosquito nets slung untidily across four parallel lines of string. By one of the beds lay a pair of children's slippers, made to look like giant mice, with ears and whiskers. He hurried on to the next room.

And then he was staring at them, his hand pushed against his mouth. They were women. He could tell that from the long hair that spilled out from under the sheets, sheets that had been dragged over their corpses to hide them, to soak up all the blood. One of the women was blonde, a westerner. There was blood smeared on the walls, and a pool of blood and what looked like bits of flesh on the floor. Behind one of the corpses there was a splatter on the wall as if a shotgun had been used. The hum of the flies seemed to intensify. Someone was calling from outside. Sidharta – calling his name. And he knew from the voice that there were more dead in the other buildings. *There were children.*

He walked slowly towards the nearest bed, avoiding the upturned chairs, his boot crunching against broken glass. Then he took the corner of the sheet, and lifted it.

3

The fall had broken its neck for sure. Ahmad swore, spitting out a stale pellet of tobacco leaf. It didn't matter how quick you were, or how big a dose you used, sometimes they still managed to reach the upper branches before the drug got into them. Then they would come crashing down through the trees and land in a heap of fur and broken bones. He looked down at the body and rolled it over with his foot, just in case the animal was alive after all. A pig-tailed macaque; an adult female, its coat a smooth fawn colour. Dead.

He knelt down, searching for the dart. At 2,000 rupiahs each you couldn't afford to waste them. The way the animal had thrown its head back he was sure he had hit it at the side of the throat. It had spun round, shrieking in fright, before scampering up a tree trunk between fronds of clustered bromeliads. But there was no dart there now. It had been whipped out by the fall, or by the monkey itself. Ahmad cursed again. Two hours crouching in an ant-infested hollow, and nothing to show for it but a 2,000-rupiah loss.

He picked up the monkey by its feet and carried it away. There was a chance he could sell it for fur if the right traders were in town that week. But he would have to get back there before the flies started in. He put the body in a sack and carried it down to his boat, together

29

with the empty cage.

It was late afternoon and he was beginning to think his luck had run out. He rolled a cigarette and looked over the river at the dark forested hills. The muddy, dimpled waters of the Hari slid by on their way down to Muaratebo where he too would soon be going. Until today he'd had a good run: nine macaques and a *bilou*, the sleek black gibbon whose dawntime song, it was said, could move a man to tears.

Maybe it was the *bilou*. Maybe that's what had made the forest turn its back on him. He didn't normally go after them. They weren't the kind of animal you could sell by the crate-load, only one by one, when some fat cat in Jakarta or Medan wanted a birthday present for his kids. The big traders in Singapore weren't interested in them – or so Bacelius Habibie, his Muaratebo buyer told him – and on top of that it was illegal to hunt them. But that wasn't what bothered Ahmad. It was more the question of luck.

According to the local Kubu Indians, the *bilou* and man had once been one and the same. Only when the trees became too crowded did their ways part, the *bilou* of the ground becoming men. That was why the *bilou* were never hunted. They were cousins. They could walk upright. If you killed one in cold blood it was like killing a man. His spirit could come back to haunt you.

Ahmad spat into the river. On the whole he didn't take much notice of the Kubu and their like. Most of the Indians he knew were scroungers who skulked around the streets of Muaratebo selling fake charms and getting drunk whenever they could afford it. But there were others, who lived the old life as their ancestors had all the way back to the beginning of the world. They might be stubborn and godless, but they understood the forest. He had never had a chance to sit down and talk to them about it, of course. He rarely saw them, even in the uplands. But then again, that only served to prove how much they really knew. Because they were there all right.

All the way back up the river the *bilou* was in Ahmad's head. He tried to direct his thoughts to Muaratebo, to the hospitality he would soon be enjoying at Madam Kim's, but the *bilou* kept coming back, like one of the forest demons that could crawl in at your ear.

'But I didn't kill it – only caught it,' he said. His voice sounded small, foolish. The listening forest drifted by on either side of the boat.

It was getting dark as he came round the last bend of the waterway. It was then he saw it: a boat, moored just below the little jetty he had built from dead wood and bailing twine. The *bilou* was not finished with him yet.

He cut his engine and steered close into the bank so that the overhanging trees would hide him. In the past three months thieves – Indians or maybe just hungry farmers – had come to his shelter twice, stealing tins of food and even damaging the roof. This time he would catch them; show them his precious Remington hunting rifle which went with him everywhere in the forest in case he had to stop something bigger than a monkey. He would show them he was not a man to be toyed with. He took up his paddle, manoeuvring the boat gently so that water did not break against the bows. As he drew closer he caught glimpses of the shelter but there was no one in sight. He could hear them, though. It sounded like they were searching among his things.

He left the boat wedged among the branches of a fallen tree and stepped ashore, one foot splashing in the water. He paused for a moment, listening. But they were too intent on going through his things. The monkeys which he kept behind the shelter started to get restless. If they were messing with his animals . . . He took out the Remington.

He moved as far as the big palm where he normally tied up. The ground was slippery underfoot, but the cover was good and he could see up into one corner of the hut. As soon as they appeared he would shoot. Put a round into the branches overhead. Then he would reveal himself. He took another step forward. It occurred to him that they might also be armed.

He was just lining up his sights when the inside of the shelter was suddenly lit up. They had found his torch. The beam swung left and right and then fixed itself on the ground. Ahmad drew back the bolt and took aim as a pale figure began to emerge, the torch beam dancing around it, throwing shadows across the trampled ground.

Just as his finger tightened on the trigger he heard a piercing scream come from behind the hut. There was a brief commotion, and a dark shape came darting towards him, leaping up onto the trunk of a tree. He toppled backwards, his foot slipping on the mud as the macaque – one of *his* macaques – disappeared into the cover of the forest.

He cursed, raised his rifle again, and found himself looking straight into the face of the thief. At first he couldn't believe his eyes. The thief saw him and stared back, except that it was not a thief.

For the first time that day, Ahmad smiled.

4

The noise of the jeep brought Salim to his feet. Buttoning his trousers, stumbling through the spiny shrubs that crowded against the perimeter fence, he jogged over to the grey tents which they had pitched in the shade of a banyan tree. It was just after one o'clock.

They had been stuck in the compound for two days waiting for the 'experts' from Jakarta to arrive. When Salim had found what was left of the bodies he had called the Bayur barracks, asking for instructions. The men had been shaken up by what they had seen, and the two-hour wait for a reply had seemed like an eternity. But eventually the radio crackled to life. The order had come back from Colonel Azwar that they were not to touch the bodies. They were to secure the perimeter of the compound and set up camp inside the fence. A team of 'experts' was being flown in.

'How long will it take?' Salim had asked. 'We only have rations and water for three days.'

It would take as long as it took.

Nobody had seemed to mind the fact that he had taken his unit across into Jambi province, but even so Salim couldn't help feeling exposed. 'Experts' from Jakarta: the idea that they had organised planes, helicopters and God knows what else, had put together a team of specialists, and all on his say-so, made him uneasy. For all he knew

33

the people had been attacked by the local Indians. That was certainly the view taken by most of the men in the unit, including Sergeant Sidharta. The corpses were in such a bad state it was hard to tell, but the amount of blood splashed on the walls and the floor did seem to indicate an attack of some kind. If it turned out that they had fallen foul of some local tribesmen he would look very foolish.

The men had lined up by the front gate under Sidharta's watchful eye. Such a display of military efficiency was unusual, but Salim could see they were more than anything relieved. Two days of rice and noodles and nothing to do was getting to them. Let the experts take control, that was what they were thinking. Get back to the relative comfort of the barracks. Get the hell out of the forest.

The insignia on the jeep identified it as coming from the Bayur barracks, but the four men inside were all strangers. Salim squinted in the harsh sunlight at the leader of the party, a small man with short black hair. He had the pale skin and supercilious expression of an upper-class city dweller. As the man climbed out of the jeep, Salim saluted, bringing his dusty boots together with a dull thud.

'Salim?'

The stranger's voice was soft, and informal. Salim held his salute.

'Lieutenant Amir Salim, sir. At your command, sir.'

'Dr William Angarrayasa. Stand easy, soldier. And dismiss your men.'

The men broke up, some of them going back into the shade of the tree where they were cleaning equipment, two returning to the repair of part of the fence which had been damaged by a falling palm branch. Salim was offered bottled water by the doctor. He wore no indication of rank. He was an 'expert', and from Jakarta. That was enough, it seemed.

Having drunk from the bottle, Salim returned it. But the doctor shook his head, keeping his delicate hands in his pockets. His eyes moved over Salim's face.

'Keep it. We have supplies for you and your men.'

Supplies. Salim frowned, but there was no time for questions.

'When did you arrive?' asked the doctor, removing a pristine handkerchief from his pocket.

'Two days ago, sir.'

'We were told that the alarm was raised by a radio operator in Padang.'

'That's right, sir.'

'When was that?'

'The same day we set off, sir.'

'And how do you feel, Lieutenant?'

Salim blinked, his eyes wandering across to the other men, who were occupied in getting equipment from the back of the jeep. Two of them looked more like soldiers than scientists. Probably an escort.

'Sir?'

'How are you? You look well enough.'

'Fine, sir. Thank you, sir.'

'Have you had any problems?'

'No, sir.'

Did he mean problems with the natives? Perhaps the men were right after all.

'There has been no trouble here, sir.'

'No animals? Monkeys? Rats, maybe?'

Again Salim frowned.

'No monkeys, sir, nor rats that I've seen. There were a lot of flies, sir.'

The doctor appeared to think for a moment.

'Any trouble with the flies? Anybody bitten?'

'None of the men has said anything, sir.'

The doctor smiled.

'Good. Now I want to see the bodies.'

35

'Certainly, sir.'

Salim started to lead the way, but the doctor made no move to follow.

'I'm sure we can find them ourselves, Lieutenant. The bodies are where you found them, isn't that right? You haven't moved them at all? Haven't touched them?'

'Our instructions were to leave them alone, sir.'

'Quite right.'

And then Salim was surprised to see one of the men come forward and give the doctor a respiratory mask. This man and the doctor both slipped the masks over their heads. They exchanged a few words. Then rolling what appeared to be surgical gloves over their hands they went up the path towards the building, leaving the other men standing by the jeep. For the first time Salim noticed that these men were carrying assault rifles.

Watching the masked scientists walk towards the buildings, following their hard shadows, Salim got the feeling something was wrong.

A stripe of sunlight ran from the window across to a wall hanging. Breathing steadily, Angarrayasa took in all the detail, already planning his report. Not many flies now. Was that important or not? He mustn't jump to any conclusions. Observe, interpret. Above all he must keep control of the situation. The man Salim seemed sound enough, but he was not sure about the others. They would have to be very careful how they proceeded. The situation could get ugly.

Sudradjat Ruru came into the room behind him. He was carrying the microcassette.

'No sign of damage to the building from the outside. If it was an attack I think it must have been a surprise.'

Angarrayasa crossed the room and entered a narrow passage with doors off it into what he assumed were bedrooms. Ruru followed. Angarrayasa pushed open the first door. Two camp beds. Mosquito nets thrown across string. A child's novelty slippers. Where were the children?

'William?'

Ruru's voice boomed through the wall from the next room.

Blood on the walls. On the floor. And what looked like a pool of blackening faeces by the side of the bed. The only sound was the hiss of their breathing in the masks.

'Women,' said Ruru. He stepped forward, and slowly drew back the blood-spattered sheets. A handful of flies lifted from the bodies. His breathing accelerated as he struggled to control himself. Angarrayasa blinked as Ruru snapped in the record button and began to speak.

'Two subjects uh . . . women. One white, one Indonesian I would say. Call them A and B. Maybe in their thirties. Difficult . . . difficult to say. Flies . . . and, flies and maggots complicate the . . . uh . . . Extensive, extensive petechial rash, and blisters, I think . . .' He moved closer, his eyes drawn to something on the breastbone of the white woman. Trying to be a good scientist, trying to be exact. 'My God, it's . . . this is – Spontaneous bleeding from the eyes, ears. Bleeding from mouth and nose though it's hard to . . .' He could see it now – hardly able to believe his own eyes: 'The tongue – subject A has lost the surface˙ . . . the skin of her tongue. The skin of her tongue appears to have been . . . well . . . vomited out. Complete. On her breastbone . . . uh, bleeding from the uh . . . the breast . . . correction – bleeding from the nipples. No sign of trauma, no major lesions. Correction. Correction. The left hand of subject A is missing two fingers. So much blood. Difficult to say what . . . It looks like . . . is that? –' Ruru pointed to what looked like scraps of flesh between the white woman's legs.

'Placenta?' said Angarrayasa. But Ruru was shaking

his head, squatting down to look at the bloody ruin. His words came more slowly now.

'Subject A . . . appears to have . . . defecated the . . . the lining of the gut.'

Angarrayasa touched Ruru on the arm. Ruru looked at him through the mask. Eyes fixed, terrified.

'We'll take specimens,' said Angarrayasa. 'There's a limit to what we can see like this. I don't think we should cut them up.'

He dropped the sheet back over the women and turned away.

From the shade of the banyan tree Salim watched the men come out of the building. They walked to the jeep and reached out white plastic packs. Nobody spoke. They didn't remove the masks. The two men with rifles looked on, impassive. Salim was trying to work out why they had come from the barracks with their own escort instead of using local soldiers. Was it a question of trust?

Ruru prepared the blood films in the room with the two women and the drifting flies while Angarrayasa moved on to locate the other corpses. Working silently, concentrating on his gloved hands, knowing there was only a thin barrier of latex between him and the same horrible death if the corpses were still infectious, Ruru fixed the films in buffered formalin for fifteen minutes, then washed them in buffered water at pH 7.0 three times. Then he stained them.

He was placing them in the hermetically sealed containers when Angarrayasa came back into the room.

'Two corpses in the same condition. A man and a boy, maybe twenty years old, Indonesian I think. But no sign of the children. I understood from the Padang police that there were children here.'

'Did you see the slippers?'

Angarrayasa nodded, deep in thought.

'And there's the truck in the ditch just outside the camp,' said Ruru. 'Could they have driven it out? Maybe crashed it and walked off into the jungle.'

'I don't think they were big enough to do that. If they did, they must be dead by now.'

He looked back along the passage to the entrance.

'We need to search the forest.'

Salim came out of the shade of the banyan tree to meet the two masked men, but they ignored him, going on to where the jeep was parked. Salim watched them step out of their clothes, stripping naked. They threw the clothes and shorts together in a pile with the surgical gloves. Then one of the soldiers squirted lighter fuel over them and ignited it. The respirators were placed in a plastic bag which was itself sealed.

The naked men washed themselves with a pinkish liquid which they got out of a fuel can. There was a powerful smell of disinfectant.

When he was dressed again, Angarrayasa walked across to Salim.

'Lieutenant, I need your men to conduct a search of the forest. I want you to work within a radius of about a mile around the camp.'

Salim swallowed hard.

'I believe there were children here,' said Angarrayasa. 'I think they walked out of the compound. I don't think they got very far.'

'Perhaps the Indians took them, sir.'

Angarrayasa looked at Salim. The flat nose and prognathic mouth. He was sweating profusely. It occurred to Angarrayasa that he had perhaps underestimated Salim's intelligence. The man was trying to get him to say something about what had happened, deliberately provoking

39

him with a pretence of ignorance. The two men were silent for a moment.

'Perhaps,' said Angarrayasa, his face perfectly expressionless. 'Organise the search as you think fit. You can start immediately.'

'It will take at least a day, sir. The jungle here is – '

'I don't care how long it takes, Lieutenant. Start the search immediately. There are another two hours to nightfall. You can make a start at least.'

When Salim and his men had left, Angarrayasa gave instructions to the two soldiers to prepare a meal of rice and chicken. He told them to set up camp on the path, next to the jeep. Then he turned to Ruru.

'So what is your opinion, doctor?'

Ruru tugged at his bottom lip for a moment.

'Well, it looks like a haemorrhagic disease of some kind.'

'You don't think they were attacked?'

'There's nothing to indicate an attack. I think they picked something up out here. God knows what.'

'What about a vector?'

'Monkeys maybe. Salim said there were monkeys here when they arrived. Ebola was isolated in macaques imported into the USA from the Philippines in the late eighties. Ebola virus is the prevalent cause of infection among macaques in Southeast Asia. So – '

'Well the lab will be able to confirm that one way or the other,' said Angarrayasa. 'What are the chances of infection?'

'Usually with this kind of thing – I mean if we're talking about a virus of some sort – transmission is through contact with blood, pharyngeal excretions. No question of aerosol transmission if they were already dead when the men got here.'

'Salim said nobody had touched the bodies. And it

doesn't look as though they've been disturbed.'

'There is something which is worrying, though.'

'What's that?'

'Someone cut those fingers off the white woman.'

'But why would they?'

Ruru shrugged.

'I don't know. For a ring, maybe. Maybe the white woman was wearing rings.'

'Salim?'

'Maybe. Maybe one of the other men. Gets up to take a leak in the middle of the night. Goes into the building to steal the ring. But the body has swollen. He can't get the thing to budge. He cuts it off. Throws the fingers away in the bush, and keeps the ring. Maybe even thinks to wash it. But he's had plenty of contact by that time. I mean if whatever it is is really hot.'

'Maybe he kept the finger.'

Ruru started to chuckle, making a high-pitched feminine sound.

'Let's try to be positive,' he said.

'None of them looks ill,' said Angarrayasa.

'If they are going to get sick, it'll start tomorrow. The normal incubation period for control purposes is from three to twenty-one days. They'll wake up with a fever. Headache. Generalised aching. Gastrointestinal disturbances. Nausea, vomiting, diarrhoea maybe.'

'And then?'

'A few days into the illness, and they'll get a rash. With Marburg and Ebola the throat and conjunctivae get inflamed and there are small transparent lesions like tapioca granules in the soft palate. Then they start to bleed with a paradoxical combination of blood clots and haemorrhaging. The clots lodge in the brain, liver and spleen, and the haemorrhaging accelerates until the body cavities fill up with blood. Death comes some six to

41

seven days after the first symptom, either from a massive stroke, or from shock.'

Angarrayasa looked at the ground. He no longer felt like joking. After a while he looked back up.

'So what are we going to do?'

'Well, it's difficult. These viruses are killers. They'll kill in over 80 per cent of cases, even with hospitalisation. We'll have to keep them together inside the compound,' said Ruru. 'We can't risk any of them running off. If they develop symptoms we'll just have to watch and wait. Keep the sick ones separate, maybe. We can explain that infection can only happen through contact with bodily fluids. Explain that they'll be OK as long as they haven't touched the bodies.'

'But there are seven of them.'

Angarrayasa looked across at the tent under the banyan tree. He called out to the soldiers who were just finishing their own tent.

'Take the weapons and ammunition,' he said. 'Do it quickly.'

'What is it?' said Salim, forcing his way between the men, who had come together around a dark object on the floor. A pre-twilight gloom was oozing out of the forest. Salim switched on his flashlight. One of the soldiers stumbled backwards. The man appeared to be kneeling, the shirt pulled tightly across his back. It was a westerner. Tall and well built. Salim could see a blackish trail coming from his right ear. He gave the man a push with his boot and what was left of Dr Jonathan Rhodes rolled over. They were quiet for a moment.

'He looks the same as the others,' said Sidharta.

In the distance a bird called. Salim looked up at the sky. The clouds were turning pink and gold. They had perhaps twenty minutes to get back to the camp before it was dark.

'Nobody touch the body,' said Salim, still looking up. 'We'll come back to him tomorrow and bury him then.'

'When are we leaving?' asked one of the men.

'When we are ordered to do so,' said Salim, his voice hardening. He looked at the circle of faces. They all looked scared. 'Now let's get back to the camp.'

They walked quickly, almost jogging along the paths they had cut. Night seemed to swell between the trunks of the larger trees. Salim was trying to think about what might happen next. By the time they reached the camp, they were soaked through.

Angarrayasa was standing next to the jeep with one of the soldiers, both men holding their guns in the ready position. Salim noticed that the soldiers returned his stare. Until now they had avoided looking at him. Suddenly he had become an object of their interest. He came to a halt in front of the little expert.

'We found a body sir. A man. Dr Rhodes, I think. He ran the camp.'

'Good work, soldier,' said the doctor. He held out his hand. 'Now I want you to give me your pistol.'

5

At lunchtime the Lisboa was packed with investment bankers talking shop over plates of steaming squid or – the Lisboa speciality – *bacalao* in a thick olive oil sauce. Holly was pleased to see that despite the low-cal high-fibre times some of the bankers were really getting into it, taking off their jackets and rolling up their shirt sleeves, enjoying the heavy food. Richard, however, looked edgy, and Holly felt a little squeeze of guilt for having made him leave the office at lunchtime. He normally ate a sandwich at his desk despite being top dog in corporate finance at Barnes-Winthrop.

'God, Richard. Your hands are shaking.'

He looked at the menu he was holding. The edge was trembling violently. He held his right hand out straight. There was a distinct tremor.

'I OD on caffeine at the office,' he said with a shrug. 'We've got this slick espresso maker – you know, all chrome and levers? Peter Brassens – the partner I report to – is always grinding up beans.'

'In the office?'

'In his little galley kitchen. He's a coffee nut. Honest to God. You go into his office and there's this smell. He's got all these packages.'

He signalled for the waiter, and they both ordered big seafood salads. Richard was even avoiding the bread

44

– Holly noticed – watching his waistline. It occurred to her that it might be the prospect of meeting Jonathan in a few weeks' time that was making him count the calories.

'So what was your big idea?' he asked.

Holly looked down at her food for a moment.

'I got another letter this morning from Jonathan,' she said.

Richard stopped chewing for a second and then forked a big fat prawn, waiting to hear what was what before saying anything. Holly gave him a little smile. He was so jealous. She hated to see him uncomfortable, but got a kick out of his little fits of pique nevertheless: it showed the strength of his feelings.

'Confirming the arrangements for August third,' she went on. 'He's going on about how beautiful the forest is and so on, and he said I should be sure to bring out my old Nikon and a macro; said there's so much stuff to photograph. That's when I had the idea.'

Richard smiled.

'Well I know you'll get to it eventually.'

'To what?'

'To this great idea you had, the reason I came down to have lunch. Not that I mind having lunch with a beautiful woman.'

'Ooh, Mr *Smooth*y.' Holly reached across and touched the back of his hand. 'The idea is I take my camera down to the camp.'

Richard looked disappointed for a moment. He dabbed at his mouth with a napkin, watching her.

'Well I figured that's what you'd do anyway.'

'Wait. I'll take down my Nikon and take some real pictures. That's the idea. Then I'm going to write up Jonathan's whole project as a feature.'

'A feature. What for?'

'To sell, dummy. It's exactly the kind of material they're looking for in the big travel magazines.'

45

'Well great. Go for it.' Richard smiled warmly, stirred by the sight of Holly's excitement. 'As long as I don't figure in any of the pictures.'

'No, nobody. None of us. Just the forest and the camp. Maybe a couple of shots of Dr Jonathan Rhodes and that flower I told you about, the rafflesia.'

She said Jonathan's name ironically, putting Dr Rhodes up there in ironic lights, but her interest in Rhodes, her *involvement*, was clear for Richard to see. All he could do for a moment was eat.

'God it'll be so beautiful out there,' Holly said.

They ate for a while in silence. Then Holly was asking him about news on the deal with the software writers. Richard answered monosyllabically. The coffee arrived, and Holly could see that he was anxious to get back to earning money. It annoyed her sometimes that he couldn't keep his mind off work for more than a few minutes.

'One of the children's sick,' she said.

That got his attention.

'Nothing serious. Jonathan says it's like a cold. Lucy went down with a headache and a bit of a cough. That was a week ago, though. She's probably OK now. Can you imagine – catching a cold in such a warm place?'

6

Muaratebo, Sumatra. July 27th

Bacelius Habibie flapped a plump hand at the mosquitoes which had come under the eaves of the big house to get out of the rain. They never bit him – something about him, his odd lemony smell perhaps, put them off – but their whining was more than he could stand in the heat and humidity. It had been raining since mid-morning, rain that fell in a dense drifting curtain, hiding the frangipani and hibiscus that filled his garden, but the rain brought no freshness or relief. He stood for a long time, looking out, one hand raised against the dancing mosquitoes, his flat feet pushed into broken canvas shoes, his immense belly rising and falling gently under a long white shirt which all but hid his blue sarong.

Then the rain slowed and stopped. It was as if someone had closed a faucet. Habibie sighed. Water gurgled in channels it had cut in the red earth which spread out around the house. It ran past the porch, and sluiced down off the grass roof, dripping, splashing. Habibie's plump hands disappeared under the shirt and worked away at loosening a knot there. Eventually he was satisfied. He let out a deep, resonant belch, and shouted: 'Wayan!'

There was no reply. He drew a deep breath.

'Wayan, curse you!'

A small boy with a flat face and almost oriental features came skittering around the side of the house.

'Tuan?'

'My umbrella, boy. Quickly.'

Wayan plunged into the house and reappeared almost immediately, holding a green-handled woman's umbrella. He fussed trying to free the clasp, but he was not quick enough and Habibie's surprisingly hard hand smacked against his ear, making his head ring.

'Aay!'

'Give me that thing.'

In his master's grip, encumbered today by a bandage on the left hand, the umbrella flared open with an authoritative pop and a spider dropped out onto the polished veranda. Habibie regarded the spider for a moment, and then slopped down the steps and onto the moist red earth of his garden.

There were still one or two spots of rain. They thumped against the taut silk of the umbrella like balls of wet cotton wool. Habibie went to the bottom of the garden ducking beneath the frangipani trees. If he hadn't been holding the umbrella, he would have rubbed his hands together.

The hangar was an impressive structure with concrete uprights supporting a zinc roof. There was a large truck and, stacked in one corner under a tarpaulin – the fruits of his latest transaction.

The monkeys were in their new steel crates. The transfer from the hunter's makeshift wood and wicker crates only took a half-hour, but straight away the merchandise looked more valuable. As indeed it was. The animals would be transferred once more at Jambi airport to crates owned by the carrier. The monkeys were silent, sitting huddled at the back of their cages, the red splash marks of the hunter's dye showing faintly luminous in the gloomy, water-charged air.

A large male sat watching him out of the shadows. Habibie extended his bandaged hand.

'D'you see what you've done?' he said. The monkey

scratched at its neck. It looked passive enough now, but when Habibie and Ahmad had been transferring it to the bigger cage it had taken a bite out of both of them. Snap, snap! Quick as lightning. Wayan had fetched disinfectant to clean the wound, and Habibie had emptied almost the whole bottle on his. You could never be too careful with animals coming out of the forest.

Habibie watched the big male for a moment, calculating the margin he was going to make this time. Ahmad the hunter was perhaps dirty and he certainly had the morals of a Balinese dog, but you could rely on him to call regularly, his merchandise was rarely damaged, and he was *very* cheap. Twenty dollars per monkey, which Habibie could sell at a minimum of one hundred and fifty dollars apiece, simply because he had friends at the airport, who themselves had friends who supplied a company in North America who in turn . . . Friends were everything to Habibie. When drunk, or otherwise sated – Wayan propped up in bed beside him smoking a clove-scented cigarette – he would talk at length about the importance of friendship. Drawing Wayan close, he would whisper: 'A rich man without friends is a pauper, Wayan my boy; a poor man indeed.'

The monkeys were sold for experiments – part of the 16,000 imported by the USA every year – though Habibie had no idea what these experiments might entail. It was just as well. For all his truculence, Habibie was a sentimental man, and if he had seen the tumours and sores the monkeys would be obliged to wear like corporate logos for the rest of their new careers he would probably have cried.

'Sit tight, my little friends,' he said, waving to the silent animals. 'I am just going to visit an acquaintance of yours.'

Brushing the heavy heads of flowers as he walked, he made his way out of the front gate to his Mercedes saloon.

The road into Muaratebo wound down hill, following the kinks and bends of the river. The houses were set well back off the road, and it wasn't until you got nearer to the centre that you saw there was quite a considerable settlement here. Forty thousand people. The main street was itself very busy with endless streams of noisy motor scooters often carrying whole families, the minibuses which served as transport between the scattered towns of the coastal plains to the east or uphill towards the Trans-Sumatra Highway, and the towns of the rugged western coast.

Habibie honked his horn and slowly made his way towards a cluster of buildings near the river just above the main conurbation and the ferry. He was looking for a low building built with blackened timbers and roofed with old corrugated iron and bits of asphalt. It was a building he knew well, but which was unfamiliar during daylight hours. The truth was, it depressed him to go there at this time of the day.

After nightfall the interior of the unprepossessing building was almost glamorous: the velvet dark, with its smells of flesh and woodsmoke, lit here and there with coloured spirit lamps, seemed to enfold you like a gloved hand. There were some fairy lights in a garland around the bar where Jon, the young Javanese barman, made him the banana daiquiris he loved.

But at this time of day . . . The girls looked pathetic with their painted mouths and scraps of dresses, and the older women – some of them actually missing teeth! – well they didn't bear looking at. How a man was supposed to feel amorous in such conditions was beyond Habibie's understanding. And as for the *lady* who ran the establishment . . .

He parked the car in the shade of a coconut palm and opened the door. After the air conditioning it was like stepping into a kiln.

It was Ahmad who had insisted he come at such an ungodly hour. Of course Ahmad was the kind of man who would revel in the company at any time of day. Habibie had had the misfortune to see Ahmad after one of his long stints in the jungle. That a man should have appetites was something Habibie understood well, but the ferocity of Ahmad, the way he slobbered and fawned over the youngest girls, some of them no more than children actually, was appalling. He hurt them. Seemed to enjoy hurting them. And when he was blind drunk, and lashing out, draped in one of his frightful silk shirts, well, it was an ugly sight.

And why had he insisted on early afternoon? Because it was the only time he was lucid, the brief period in which he was just starting to recover from the previous night's debauchery, and not yet ready for his first drink of the beckoning evening. It was the only time Ahmad could talk business. 'What business?' Habibie had asked, as he counted out the dollar bills for the consignment of monkeys he had received only that morning, but Ahmad had not been willing to share his secret. He had only leered, treating Habibie to a view of the tobacco-brown stumps in his twisted little mouth.

The sun was beginning to break through the clouds, but inside the brothel a kind of permanent twilight existed. Ahmad sucked on a clove-scented Salem and blew smoke against the window as he watched Habibie waddle through the sunlight and shadow. What a sight with his umbrella! What a tub of guts. Ahmad stood on one leg and then another. He had to keep his wits about him, but the bottle of rum he had already started was making him feel a bit wild. He knew that underneath the mountain of flesh there was a nimble enough mind in Habibie, but he felt that what he had to offer him was so special, so unusual, it might just tempt the great Tuan Habibie to forget reason for once. For things that Habibie really liked, like his little pet Wayan for example, he was ready to pay top dollar. Everybody in town knew that.

7

Marshallton, Delaware. July 31st

'Get outa there, Carl, whaddaya doin'?'

Larry Spalding shrugged apologetically as the driver looked back at him from his cabin. The cages were all loaded and it was time to move out: sixty *cercopithecus aethiops* bound for a testing lab in Massachusetts via Dulles airport.

'Carl? The man wants to get going.'

One of the doors at the back of the truck swung open and Reiner appeared, his pristine white lab coat dazzling in the mid-morning sun.

'Just saying goodbye? Jesus. Let's move, huh?'

But Reiner didn't move.

'I er . . . I think there's a problem here,' he said, his shoulders still hunched over so as to keep from banging his head. 'The air-conditioning unit – '

'What?'

'It's not working.'

The driver gave the gas pedal a couple of squeezes. The stink of fumes filled the asphalt forecourt.

'Carl, just get down and shut the doors, OK?'

'Without air conditioning it'll get like an oven in here. *And* there's no proper ventilation. Federal regulations say the temperature mustn't rise above – '

'I *know* what the regulations say, Carl,' said Spalding, struggling to keep his voice down. 'But that's not our

53

problem because this is not our truck.'

Reiner adjusted his glasses.

'But as the consignors, we're also responsible for over-seeing the conditions of transport. If these animals – '

'If these animals aren't got outa here right now then where are we gonna put the next batch, huh? Have you thought about that?'

Reiner looked down at his clipboard. It was true: they needed Room D that afternoon for forty-eight *Macaca nemestrina* due in from JFK.

'Of course, if you wanna explain to Dr Aldiss how we lost a major customer and screwed up all the schedules, you go ahead.'

The engine growled again.

'Almost there!' Spalding yelled over the noise, showing the driver a grease-smeared palm.

Reiner tucked the clipboard under his arm.

'I guess it is just a couple of hours,' he said. 'How bad can it get?'

He jumped down and stood watching as Spalding banged shut the doors and secured them with the external bolts. One of the monkeys let out a solitary shriek. Then the truck rolled out of the forecourt and away towards Interstate 95, its hydraulic brakes hissing as it passed the gates.

'Right, instant coffee time,' Spalding said, checking his watch. 'That rich, smooth taste that says quality.'

'I hope it will be just a couple of hours,' Reiner said. 'Otherwise we'd have to talk to someone, don't you think?'

Spalding turned back towards the loading bay.

'Yes, Carl, you talk to someone.'

Reiner followed him back inside without saying any-thing more. When Spalding started with one of his jokes and slogans (Reiner never knew whether or not they came from real commercials) it meant he wasn't going to talk about work, no matter what. After three months at Farrell Research Supplies Reiner should have known better than to try. As it was, most of the guys had him down as nerd because their idea of humour didn't crack him up, and if he tried being serious at the wrong time people just shook their heads and rolled their eyes and said *oh for Chrissake, Carl*. It got to him at first, and it still did sometimes, but the truth of the matter was that nobody worked at the Primate Quarantine Facility out of a love for animals (in fact it had to be a genuine disadvantage). Even those, like him, who had degrees in veterinary medicine were just looking to make what they could and get out. A newcomer wasn't going to make himself popular by asking a lot of questions about procedures and regulations, even if he was just being curious.

Not that the facility itself was out of line. Built only five years earlier on the site of an old carpet factory, it conformed to all the recommendations and bristled with expensive machinery. At full capacity it could hold over five hundred primates, each one in its own wardrobe-sized nylon-mesh cage. There were ten different quarantine rooms of differing sizes, the largest of which could hold up to a hundred animals. Each room had its own independent air-filtration system to minimise the risk of cross-infection, with temperature and humidity regulated by computer. Natural light was also provided through the twin-layered glass roof (psychological tests had shown that some primates suffered increased stress if kept for prolonged periods under artificial light, even when care was taken to mimic the day–night sequence). Gone were the days when the animals were kept in stainless steel cages in windowless bunkers. Besides the quarantine rooms themselves, the facility was equipped with an autopsy theatre, a full diagnostic laboratory and a staff canteen, where assistant supervisor Bert Levy, thirty pounds overweight and gorilla-hairy, now sat holding an extra-large polystyrene cup of Hearty Beef instant soup.

'Cheer up, Carl,' he said as Reiner wandered in. 'There'll always be a place for you in green monkey heaven.'

A slick of brown fluid clung to his upper lip. Reiner turned to the drinks machine and punched the Coca-Cola button.

'We know how it is,' said Spalding, taking a seat opposite Levy. 'Just when you think you really got to know the little critters they just up and leave you. It hurts the first time, son, but you'll get used to it.'

Levy's laugh sounded like a barking seal. Reiner pressed the Coca-Cola button again. In the display window the words SORRY! FRESH OUT appeared in flashing green letters. He opted for an iced tea and pushed his way through the swing doors, leaving Spalding to embellish any way he wanted the story of Rookie Reiner and the busted air conditioner.

The quarantine rooms led off from either side of a long straight passageway which ran the entire length of the building. As he walked towards Room D, his footsteps loud on the painted cement floor, he could hear the chattering of the monkeys and their long, whooping calls. Thanks to the breeze-block walls it sounded as if the animals were far off, the way it probably sounded in the jungle, Reiner liked to think – a sound of the wild. But he knew that was not true. Such a density of population could never occur in the wild. It was unnatural, just as the animals' cries were unnatural, a response to circumstances for which evolution had never equipped them. Still, Reiner could not help feeling that it was special, a taste of something exotic, something you didn't normally come across in the greater DC area, that you didn't see advertised on TV. *That rich, smooth taste that says quality.* It was something real.

It was hot and humid in Room D. The empty cages had

already been hosed out and the heating was turned up high to dry them out. The animal smell was strong. He checked the clipboard again. Forty-eight *Macaca nemestrina* – the pig-tailed macaque, if he wasn't mistaken – arriving via JFK at 1330 hours on TWA Transport Flight TW 1077. Place of origin? He turned over the sheet. *Sumatra, Indonesia*.

The short-haul flight from Jambi touched down at Changi airport at 0900 hours local time, just ninety minutes before TW 1077 was due to take off. The crates were unloaded by fork-lift and stacked in a transit hanger on the southern periphery, where they were signed for by a Singapore customs agent called Kedar Rajaratnam. Rajaratnam had done a lot of work for Farrell Research Supplies over the years, and he was used to the complexities of handling animal cargoes. With his usual efficiency he had cleared all the necessary paperwork several days in advance, and had even laid on contingency plans for temporary quarantine should there be some kind of hold-up (customs officials, he had learned, were highly unpredictable people who enjoyed discretionary powers any military dictator would envy. The most important thing a customs agent had to do was get to know them.) All the same there was not much time. As he awaited the arrival of Lieutenant Kim San, he took the unusual step of calling up the handling office in advance and telling them the cargo would be ready for loading in twenty minutes.

He was having a cigarette outside when the jeep pulled up. Kim San was not in it. Instead, a sergeant he had never seen before stepped out onto the tarmac. He was a short, muscular-looking man with a fleshy, pock-marked face. Rajaratnam got a bad feeling the moment he saw him.

An incoming 747 drowned out their cursory introductions. The Sergeant was called Nyak Lin, but Rajaratnam only learned that from the name badge over his left breast pocket. He was too old to have just joined the service, and that meant he had to have been transferred from the docks. The officials who worked the docks were all bastards, especially when it came to dealing with ethnic Indians, like him.

'You got species authentication?' said Sergeant Lin, as he unfastened the main chain on one of the crates.

'It's on the veterinary certificate,' said Rajaratnam, pulling a wad of papers from a document wallet.

'What certificate?'

'They need a certificate before they can leave Indonesia. I've got a copy.'

Sergeant Lin scoffed theatrically, as if Indonesian certificates weren't worth the paper they were written on.

'I'm talking about authentication at *this* end.'

Lin was talking through his arse, but the agent's first rule was: *never make a customs officer look stupid*.

'Well these macaques are going to the States, you see, Sergeant. They have pretty strict controls over there. If it was some Third World place they were headed for, it would be different. And since this is only a transit stop . . .'

The side of the crate swung down and landed with a crack on the floor. The animal inside the nearest cage jumped, retreating to the far end of its cage, its brown eyes blinking at the light.

Sergeant Lin squatted down to take a closer look, screwing up his face at the pungent urine smell.

'Hey, this animal's bleeding,' he said.

Rajaratnam bent down beside him. There was a circular red smudge on the monkey's flank.

'That's dye, Sergeant,' he said. 'The hunters use that to identify the animals they catch. So they don't get mixed up later.'

Lin looked unconvinced. He put his face up against the wire and stared at the animal.

Rajaratnam was getting worried. He had to get his cargo loaded in the next half an hour or there was a good chance that the captain of TW 1077 would refuse it. That meant a whole morning phoning around the airline offices, trying to get another slot, which wasn't going to be easy at such short notice. He just hoped Sergeant Lin wasn't going to insist on that local certificate. Technically speaking, there was no way he could, but *technically speaking* didn't mean a whole lot in the customs business.

Meanwhile Sergeant Lin stared, unaware that in doing so he was flouting monkey etiquette in a way that couldn't go unanswered.

'Sergeant,' said Rajaratnam, 'I don't wish to hurry you, but – '

'What the . . . !'

Sergeant Lin suddenly leapt back, covering his face.

'Agh! Shit!'

He slipped, landing with a thump on his back.

Kra, kra! Kra, kra!

The animal barked and hurled another handful of fresh faeces from the far end of the cage. Rajaratnam watched, horrified, as a lump the size of a sugar cube attached itself to the hem of Sergeant Lin's immaculately pressed trouser leg.

It was a quarter-past eight and most of the staff had already gone home. Reiner sat waiting in the canteen, nursing a cold cup of coffee, slowly turning the pages of *Time* magazine. Head office had called that afternoon to say that the macaque consignment had been held up at Singapore, but would be coming in on another flight five hours later. Arrangements for two and a half hours' overtime had been made, and Reiner had been one of the volunteers. He hadn't had any plans that evening, and –

though he hadn't admitted it to anyone – he was curious to see the animals. They were a species unfamiliar to him. Most of the macaques at the facility came from the Philippines, about fifteen hundred miles further east.

The truck finally arrived at ten minutes after nine. Reiner and Spalding had to unload the cages by hand because there were no fork-lift drivers left on site. It took them almost an hour to get all the animals logged in and down to Room D, especially with Spalding looking at his watch the whole time and complaining that he wasn't getting paid for this. Finally, at ten o'clock, the macaques were ready to be moved into the main cages.

'That's it. I'm outta here.'

Spalding's lab coat was already screwed up in his hand.

Reiner looked up from the protective gloves he was struggling to put on.

'But we have to transfer the monkeys.'

Spalding turned to go.

'Someone can do that in the morning, for Chrissake.'

Reiner went after him.

'They've been twenty-four hours in there. We have to move them! You're not supposed to – '

Spalding kept walking. His voice echoed back up the passage.

'They got feeding holes. Just give 'em a squirt of water and leave it.'

Reiner watched the other man disappear into the shadows at the far end. A few seconds later he heard something that sounded like: 'Good-night, Carl.'

He walked back into Room D and shut the door behind him. You weren't supposed to handle the animals on your own, in case one of them bit you and you needed help. But that was one regulation *he* was going to have to break. He knelt down by the nearest cage and peered inside. An adolescent – he couldn't tell the sex – lay curled up at one end, silent like most of the others, dazed. He tapped the wire gently with his index finger. The animal stirred.

'Don't worry, little fella,' he said. 'The worst's over.'

8

Muaratebo. July 31st

Sami was kneeling on the bed, her head propped up on her elbows, staring at the television on the dresser. She winced as Ahmad thrust into her. The prong in his iron belt buckle was jabbing her in the back of the thigh.

'Hey!' she said, but Ahmad took no notice. Encouraged, he carried on, grinning at Segma, who sat in the corner of the room painting her nails. She gave him an approving nod and smiled, the brilliance of her pink lipstick offset by the dull yellow of her teeth.

After a few more thrusts Ahmad paused for breath. Over his head a big moth was doing circles round the 40-watt light bulb. On the fuzzy ten-inch screen a pack of hyenas were ripping apart a water buffalo, dragging great strips of flesh from its flanks. But the animal wasn't dead. It bellowed and kicked its legs helplessly. *The hyenas must eat quickly. News of a kill spreads quickly.* The commentator's voice was young and eager – some city boy from Kuala Lumpur. Ahmad wrinkled his nose. It wasn't one of the Japanese sex videos Madam Kim had been boasting about, that was for sure. Sami jumped as the moth banged against the screen and settled there.

Suddenly Ahmad wanted to be finished with her. He took a firm grip on her hips and speeded things up so that the iron bedsprings shook, picking up on the movement and exaggerating it. The bedstead banged against the plywood walls. When at last he pushed Sami away and slumped onto his back he was beginning to feel dizzy.

Segma put down her bottle of nail polish and came over to him. She was not one of the main attractions of Madam Kim's. She was more than twice as old as a lot of the girls and skinny, but Ahmad never left her out of his monthly sex blow-outs. She was more attentive than most of the others, and the way she handled her men, as if they were little boys out for their first screw, felt good sometimes.

Sami reached for a pair of lime green panties and pulled them up under her cocktail dress with an urgent wriggle. She was in a hurry. It was pay day on most of the palm oil plantations and business was going to be brisk. She could turn ten tricks a night if she kept off the whisky, maybe more. She was sixteen years old and popular, in spite of her ugly snub nose and the rash of angry spots on her chin.

'See you later,' she said, letting the elastic snap against the flat of her stomach. Ahmad did not try to stop her. He didn't want her again anyhow. He wasn't sure he wanted anyone, not until the ceiling stopped sliding about. She closed the door with a bang.

Segma was slowly rolling down his trousers, which were caught around his thighs. She got to work with the tissues, humming softly as if she were doing the dishes or sweeping the floor. From downstairs came a loud thump-thump-thump of western music, followed by a lot of yelling. The first of the plantation workers had arrived. Ahmad sighed. He preferred it when things were quiet, when he could take his pick and take his time. It gave him something more to reflect on when he was stuck out in the forest for weeks on end. It was the difference between a good meal and something wrapped in newspaper from the market.

Suddenly he felt Segma's bony fingers grabbing at

him. He heaved himself up onto his elbows, the dirty printed sheet sticking to the hollow of his back. Segma sat smiling at him.

'I knew you weren't finished yet,' she said, keeping a firm grip on him with one hand and unbuttoning the front of her dress with the other. 'Not you.'

Her thin pointy breasts exposed, she climbed over him, pulling up her skirts in folds around her middle. It was hot in the room, stiflingly hot, and the thump-thump-thump from downstairs seemed louder. It vibrated in his guts. He felt a trickle of sweat run down his temple.

'I want a drink,' he said, his voice little more than a whisper. 'Get off me.'

He pushed her away. She toppled off the bed and landed on her side. Two empty beer bottles rolled away across the floor.

'Ahmad,' she said, her voice thin and whining, 'where are you going?'

He turned and headed back down the passage. It seemed to tilt slightly as he walked. He still felt a little dizzy. And now he had a headache. It had crept up on him, but now it throbbed behind his temples, pushing hard against the back of his eyes.

9

Riau Province, Sumatra. August 2nd

Moving through the dawn light the big males made little noise, alert to the sounds around them, listening for predators or rivals. The smaller females with their recently born offspring – twelve babies had survived the first months of infancy – and one or two younger males emerged in groups of two and three from a dark keyhole-shaped cave set in a bluff composed of a jumble of volcanic rock and schist. The cave entrance was almost totally obscured by the knotted roots of a juniper tree.

And just as quickly as they had appeared they were gone, moving upland to feed until twilight brought them down again. Soon all that was left were the sounds of the jungle, the squeak and pop of heating vegetation, the ceaseless rustle of insects, the call of birds high up in the forest canopy.

As the morning wore on the shadow of a huge ketapang tree moved like a sundial until it fell directly across the mouth of the cave. And as it moved on it was as if a piece of the shadowy fabric snagged in the juniper roots to remain there for the rest of the day. The temperature climbed.

But it was cool immediately inside the cave, the light failing after a few metres, and the air was sharp with the smells of the mineral salts which saturated the rock. Once the baboons had gone, bolder animals would come there to lick the cool salty surfaces. But the intruders rarely moved more than a few metres into the cave. It was too dark, and foul smells were carried on the air which seemed to issue from deep inside. Even the baboons, who knew the site well, who felt at home there, rarely went too far in. But a man with a flashlight, taking the trouble to squeeze along the narrow passageway, ready to risk the odd cut on the sharp crystals embedded in the rocks, would have discovered that the cave was in fact a complex of caves, going deep into the foundations of the forest.

He would discover that twenty metres into the system of passageways the cave opened out and the air whirred with the wings of the fruit- and insect-eating bats which roosted there, themselves supporting a colony of biting flies, ticks and mites. The air was virtually unbreathable with the stink of faeces and urine. And in the midst of all this stink and darkness, as if by magic, the pure water of an underground stream made a brief, bubbling appearance, describing a short loop before disappearing back into the rock.

It was the smell of water, mingled with all the other smells, which brought the pig-tailed macaque to the cave entrance that afternoon. It had been moving through unfamiliar forest for days and was half-starved and dehydrated. It paused at the cave entrance, sniffing the air, confused by the mixture of animal smells, the smells of salt, and, like a thread of silver, the smell of fresh water. It took a step forward and listened intently. It was marked on its muzzle and neck with the bites of other primates. On its hindquarters there was a big red blotch which, had it been a bite, would surely have proven fatal. But it wasn't a bite. It was dye; a mark of ownership.

10

Muaratebo. August 3rd

'Make him leave!'

Sami slammed her plate against the table, sending peanut sauce across the bare wood.

Madam Kim chewed on her bottom lip and became very quiet. Underneath the table Sami clenched her fists and prepared to make a dash for the door. But Madam Kim surprised her. Speaking in a level voice, obviously struggling to control her anger, she came and sat down opposite.

'He can't leave until he can walk, now can he?'

Sami watched her for a moment, trying to work out why she was being so reasonable. Could it be that she was scared?

'Why don't you call the doctor?' said Sami. 'He should go to the hospital.'

'And who is going to pay?' said Madam Kim, managing a smile.

Sami said nothing. Ahmad had been a good enough customer, had put enough money into Madam Kim's pocket to expect better treatment – that was what she was thinking. But to say as much would have been to invite one of Madam Kim's clubbing blows – delivered open handed maybe, but your head rang for hours afterwards. And with the headache she had already, Sami could do without that.

She watched Madam Kim scoop peanut sauce from the table with her dirty finger and lick it off. It wasn't just a question of money. Sami realised that. Madam Kim had a horror of officials. The idea of government people, even if they were only hospital employees, filled her with loathing. And no wonder. If they saw the condition the girls were in they would close her down quicker than you could say HIV.

Still licking her finger, Madam Kim scrutinised the young girl in front of her. She didn't like to see Sami so thoughtful. Or any of her 'staff', for that matter. She smiled, showing the gap between her front teeth.

'Sa-mi,' she said in her wheedling singsong. 'Sa-mi. You have always been happy here. I have always treated you like my own daughter. Just look after him for a little while longer. I'm sure he'll get better soon enough. He'll soon be the smiling Ahmad we have known all these years. Then he will leave. Then you can take a holiday.'

An hour later Sami was outside Ahmad's room. She put down the jug of water and leaned against the wall. It seemed unfair that just because she was the youngest she should have to do all the dirty work. Especially as, strictly speaking, she was no longer the youngest in the house. Since Ahmad had become sick, Madam Kim had refused to come anywhere near his room and so she was the one who had to bring him water.

For two days he had kept to his bed, refusing food, only drinking and drinking, his face burning with fever. Then he had started to shout at her, claiming that she was the one who had given him whatever it was. When the shouting got really bad Madam Kim turned up the music downstairs. He had even tried to strike her. But the violence didn't last for long. He would quickly sub-side into silence or start whining, start complaining about the crumbs in his bed. And there were no crumbs. The sheets had been changed on the dirty foam mattress after he had made a mess in there. But even with clean sheets he wasn't satisfied. He'd slowly work himself across to the edge of the bed, pull back the sheets, and start making this pathetic sweeping gesture, 'sweeping the crumbs out of the bed', he said. Sami felt sure it was the drink. Madam Kim's *arak* had destroyed his mind.

All day he had been quiet. Sami had been busy in the afternoon with some of the men who were digging a well near the village. They were nice. They were clean compared to the plantation workers and one of them – he'd had an aftershave smell like a westerner – he had given her an extra big tip. If it hadn't been for the headaches she had been getting on and off all day she would have almost enjoyed it. And now she was getting a fever. She put the back of her hand to her head.

Segma slouched along the corridor with a client.

'Cleaning the pig?' she said as she went past.

Sami snorted. It was fine for Segma to joke. She didn't have to go in there and face Ahmad, she didn't have to put up with the smell. And if anyone had given Ahmad a disease it was Segma. She never cleaned herself before or after. It was a wonder she never came down with anything herself.

Sami watched Segma disappear into one of the rooms, and then stood away from the wall.

'Aay!'

She clutched at her head as a blinding pain stabbed into the back of her eyes. She had never felt anything like it.

Inside the room Ahmad stirred. Had someone cried out? The room was almost dark. Ahmad stared up at the ceiling, and the stationary fan, blinking his eyes which felt full of grit. He tried to move, but he could hardly raise himself up on one elbow. With the greatest effort he shuffled across to the edge of the mattress. Then he started to sweep at the crumbs which seemed to fill the bed no matter how much he cleaned.

The light snapped on.

'Aaargh!'

He covered his face with his hands. He cried out for the girl to switch it off, but she just stood there staring at him.

'Cleaning the bed, Ahmad?'

Ahmad collapsed onto his back, covering his eyes with his arm. It was stifling in the room. He wanted to get up. It would be better on the bare wooden floor. There would be no crumbs there. It would be cooler. He rolled away from Sami, and from the light, and pulled himself onto the floor, falling in a knot of sheets on the other side of the bed.

Sami brought her hand to her mouth.

It was the first time she had seen it. She walked to the foot of the bed to get a better look. Ahmad's back was covered in a speckled purple rash. There were what looked like bruises, and now that she could see it – she took a step forward, horrified, but fascinated too – it looked like little beads, little white grains like tapioca, all over his skin. Her foot touched the bucket which had been put in the room for him to go to the toilet. It was half full of watery faeces streaked with blood.

Sami felt the vomit rush into her mouth as she ran from the room.

Just after two in the morning Madam Kim came into the room, a handkerchief covering her mouth. She was followed by Sami and Segma and two other girls. The last of the clients had left and the house was quiet now. The generator was switched off after twelve and the girls were carrying oil lamps which threw streaks of shadow across the woven rush walls. Madam Kim held her big flashlamp, cradled like a baby. She wasn't going to waste batteries on Ahmad unless she had to.

Ahmad hadn't moved from where he had fallen. Sami had tried to lift him but he was too heavy for her alone, and he was wedged behind the heavy bed. Madam Kim had refused to take the other girls from their work *just to lift a drunkard back into bed*. When Sami had said he might suffocate or choke, Madam Kim had simply replied that that would be better for everyone concerned. That had been six hours ago. Sami had refused to go back into the room on her own. She was starting to run a fever herself, and looked pale. She had yet to notice the beginnings of a rash at the base of her spine. But Madam Kim had shown no mercy, forcing her to work hard all evening as punishment for being such a difficult girl. Luckily the men had been so drunk or so stupid, they hadn't noticed they were screwing an invalid. They had banged into her, the rhythm of their thrusts pounding in time with the headache which felt like it would crack open her skull.

It was hot in the room. They were listening to hear if he was breathing, the flames from their lamps burning straight up in the bad-smelling air.

'Is he dead?' asked Segma, her dark eyes staring into the shadowy corner. All they could see was Ahmad's back. The little grains were clearly visible in the flickering light of the oil lamps. And underneath, the blotchy rash.

There was a muffled noise, as if Ahmad was trying to swallow.

'Please.'

'He's asking us to help him,' said Sami.

'What's that on his back?' asked Madam Kim, looking at Sami's scared face.

'I don't know. He says it feels like there are bread-crumbs in the bed. I think *that* is what he is feeling.'

She pointed in disgust at the strange white spots.

'But he looks like he's been beaten,' said Madam Kim. Sami shrugged.

'Pl. . .ease.'

Ahmad's voice sounded muffled, far away. It made Sami shiver.

'Well I suppose we should try to get him back into bed,' said Madam Kim, trying to sound businesslike though she too was disturbed by what she saw.

They stood for a moment longer, listening to Ahmad making his funny swallowing noise. Then Madam Kim walked to the foot of the bed. She looked down at Ahmad's feet. He was moving his feet as if walking in a dream.

'Sami! You get on the bed. You too, Segma. We'll try to pull him up together.'

'I'm not touching him,' said Sami, backing away towards the door.

Madam Kim rounded on her.

'You'll do as you're *told!!!*'

Her voice boomed in the small room. The little flames jerked and flickered.

'I clothe you, I feed you, I give you a place to sleep, and what do I get?' Sami cowered against the wall as Madam Kim advanced, her free hand raised. Crack! She struck down against Sami's raised arms, striking her shoulders and head.

'You'll do as you're told, you'll do as you're told!' screamed Madam Kim, keeping time with her blows, until Sami fell to the floor, sobbing. The other girls watched, terrified.

'Ala. A-la. Please, plea . . .' came Ahmad's feeble voice.

Madam Kim put her hand into the back of Sami's dress and pulled her to her feet.

'Now. You and Segma get onto the bed. Pull him up. I'll grab his feet. You two – ' she turned to the other girls who were trembling in the doorway. 'You hold the light so that we can see.'

Sami and Segma handed their oil lamps to the others and then climbed onto the bed. Sami tried not to touch the stained bedding with her hands. She shuffled forward on her knees to the shadowy hole where Ahmad was wedged.

'Give us some light. How are we supposed to – '

Madam Kim snapped on her flashlight, pointing the beam into the shadow. Ahmad's back was marbled with the flecks and blotches of a petechial rash. In spite of the stink of the bed and the sick man, Sami could not help thinking of raspberry ripple ice-cream.

'Grab hold of his arm.'

Sami and Segma hesitated, then both took hold of Ahmad's right arm and pulled. He twisted a little, so that they could see his hairy armpit. He felt hot and dry.

Suddenly it was all too much for Madam Kim.

'Filthy, filthy man!' she screamed, reaching down and giving a furious yank at Ahmad's skinny leg. But he was really wedged against the wall. The momentum carried her forward. Her legs shot out from under her and she fell heavily to the floor. In spite of her splitting headache, Sami couldn't help laughing. The beam of the flashlight jerked back and forth under the bed.

'You girls, you . . .' Madam Kim struggled to get her breath. 'You girls. Help Sami and Segma.'

The laughter seemed to make the situation seem less frightening. Madam Kim clambered to her feet and the other girls put their candles down on the floor. They climbed onto the bed and shuffled to the edge so that they were looking down at Ahmad's horrible back. He was wearing dirty cotton shorts. One of the girls reached down and got hold of the waist cord. The other leaned forward until her head was almost on the floor, and put both hands around Ahmad's right leg.

'Pleeease.' Ahmad began to cough. It sounded like he was choking or vomiting. There was a splash of something on the floor. The smell was terrible.

'Now,' said Madam Kim, raising her voice so as to drown out the nasty noises the man was making, and taking hold of Ahmad's ankle again, 'after three. One. Two. *Three!*'

All the girls heaved, pulling Ahmad up out of the hole, hauling him over onto his back. Sami was trapped underneath, the horrible rash pressed against her screaming mouth. Madam Kim screamed too, seeing that he was blind, that his eyes were full of blood, that there was blood coming from his nose and mouth, that there was blood streaming from his nipples. She screamed and brought her hands to her face so that the torch beam snapped up against the ceiling. And in the confusion of shadow and light, with the girls struggling to get away, kicking and shrieking, Ahmad was wrenched up into an arc, vomiting black fluid across the bed.

At dawn only Madam Kim and Sami were left in the room. The other girls had gone to their beds, having scrubbed themselves clean in the *mandi* at the back of the building. Ahmad was still covered in vomit and blood, but he was not dead. His face looked like a wooden mask in the candlelight. His blood-filled eyes stared at the opposite wall as he struggled to breathe. He was dying inside, focal necrosis spotting his liver and kidneys like pins marking the outposts of death's empire. As the sun came up his kidneys failed. He suffered a massive stroke at seven in the morning, and when his sphincter ripped open, sending the lining of his intestine across the blood-soaked sheets, he was already dead.

11

'But what if they aren't?' said Richard, watching Holly's suitcase disappear behind the heavy plastic flap. Holly grabbed him by the lapel.

'Honey, they'll be there. It was all sorted out in Jonathan's letter. He's going to drive up with the kids and meet me at Padang airport.'

'But he also said he was going to phone to confirm.'

'It was all in the letter. He didn't need to confirm the confirmation.'

'But he said he'd call.'

Holly stared into Richard's eyes, chafed red by another day under neon light. His anxiety was infectious. Jonathan had said he'd call. Failing to do so, he'd made everything seem more tenuous. She was about to fly across the globe, after all. It would have been nice to know there was somebody expecting her at the other end.

'Yes but you know how it is out there. He says that there are times when he can't even communicate with Padang. They probably got a lizard in their radio or something.'

Richard tried to smile, and Holly had to kiss him. He was trying desperately to be reassured; not wanting her to worry but at the same time unable to stop himself worrying.

'Well, yes. I guess.'

'Look, he probably called already. When you get back there'll probably be a message on the answer machine.'

He stood back a pace and looked around at the bustling crowds of people.

'Jesus. Maybe we should have gone down to the Caribbean.'

Holly felt a flash of irritation.

'Well if you don't want to come, you can always – '

'I'm kidding.' He took her in his arms now and she could smell the coffee on his breath. 'I'll be down on the – when did we say?'

'The 12th. And you'd better be, mister.'

They held each other for a moment.

12

Marshallton, Delaware. August 4th

Standing in front of the empty cage, Carl Reiner struggled to suppress the feeling that something bad was happening in Room D. The death of a monkey in quarantine, *Macaca nemestrina* O14 in this case, was not an unusual event. When you moved an animal from one part of the world to another you inevitably exposed it to new microbiological environments to which its immune system was not adapted. When Europeans and native Americans first started coming into contact with each other, epidemics were often the result; a bacteria or virus that gave a Mayan Indian laryngitis could kill a Spaniard, and vice versa. That was what ecosystems were all about. Yet there was something about this, about the way all eight monkeys had fallen sick at the same time, within hours of each other, and just the look of the dead animal, that felt – it wasn't easy to find a word for it – *unnatural*.

But then again, everything at the quarantine facility was unnatural. What did he expect? His concern for the welfare of the animals, which itself bordered on the unprofessional, to judge from his colleagues, was growing into a distaste for the whole quarantine set-up, the whole trade. And now he was letting these attitudes interfere with his work. The events in Room D were straightforward, and the procedures for dealing with them were well established. What he *felt* didn't come into it. Professionals used their heads. Professionals, he reminded himself, had student loans to pay off. He closed the cage door with a bang and stuck a KEEP VACANT tag over the lock.

Things had started to go wrong three days earlier. The Indonesian macaques had settled in well enough. Within a few hours of arrival they had become physically active, moving around their cages, chattering excitedly when food came along, eating their full ration. But then suddenly eight of them had stopped eating. The neat stacks of monkey biscuits, which were normally finished off before anything else, were left untouched. Reiner noted the fact in his log, but that was all. For monkeys, just like their human cousins, stomach upsets were a common accompaniment to travel. It just took a little time for the soup of benign bacteria in the intestines – the gut flora – to adapt. Then it would go back to work digesting anything that the host's enzymes couldn't, and the invading microbes would be devoured.

It was not until the next day that Reiner started to be concerned. The same eight animals began to show signs of bronchial infection, coughing and wheezing. The oldest of the males, O14, seemed all but immobilised. A mild form of dysentery also set in that day. Reiner made sure there was plenty of liquid on hand to reduce the risk of dehydration, and cleaned the cages out every few hours. He did not get much help because most of the ancillary staff were off on holiday. The task was complicated by the fact that some of the monkeys became aggressive when disturbed. One of the females bit through Bert Levy's heavy rubber glove and almost drew blood.

Then, in the afternoon of the previous day, a Sunday, O14 went into shock and died a few hours later. Reiner had found it the next morning, slouched back like a music hall drunk, its head propped up against the back wall. It seemed to have fallen from the top of the cage, and there were traces of blood around its mouth and nostrils. But the thing that struck Reiner most was the taut, staring expression on the animal's face: the eyes wide open, yet sunken into the skull, the teeth visible between parted lips. He had never seen anything quite like it before, at least not at vet school.

Reiner did not wait for Bert Levy to arrive. He picked up his clipboard and walked slowly down the room checking each of the cages in turn. Most of the macaques seemed in prime condition – better, in fact, than many of the primates that were brought to the facility after capture in the wild. They certainly had plenty of abdominal and subcutaneous fat on them, which was a pretty reliable sign. There were still only seven macaques that were sick, and they showed no obvious deterioration. Three had begun to eat, and all were taking water. Whatever it was that had infected them, it picked off the old first.

Reiner was almost finished when he heard Bert Levy's heavy footsteps outside. Some of the monkeys started making a noise when he came in, jumping around in their cages. Maybe the smell of all that food Levy ate was seeping through his pores. Maybe the monkeys thought it was their turn.

Levy's voice bellowed down the room: 'How's it going, Carl?'

The monkeys all jumped. Some of them started shrieking, and in a moment the whole room was alive with movement. Reiner *hated* the way people did that, carried on as if the animals weren't there, as if they were just a row of items, merchandise. There was no respect.

'Everything checking out?'

Reiner turned: 'You shouldn't come in here without a surgical mask. We've got sick animals here.'

'Sure stinks. That's a fact.'

'Go get a mask, will you?'

Reiner was surprised at the hardness in his own voice.

But he was right. The safety procedures weren't there for fun.

'Oh for Chrissake, Carl,' Levy said. 'Some monkeys got the shits, so what?'

'One of them died.'

'One of them always dies. At least one. You gotta stop taking it personally.'

Levy swatted him on the shoulder. Reiner ignored it.

'We shouldn't take chances until we've done the necropsy and we know what we're dealing with.'

'Necropsy?' Levy smiled in disbelief. 'Who said anything about a necropsy?'

Reiner went back to work. O36, a young female. Apparently healthy. Levy studied him for a moment. Then his gaze shifted to the animal opposite.

'OK, OK' – he started fishing in his lab coat pocket – 'I got the mask. Now. You want some help or don't you?'

He tied the green rectangle of fabric across his bulging features. It did not look big enough.

'I'm almost done,' said Reiner. 'Just six more to check.'

Levy took the clipboard.

'You tryin' to do me out of a job? Now what do we have here?'

Reiner waited while Levy scanned the data. The man spent so much time in the canteen it was easy to forget that he had once done a doctorate in simian dietetics at Montana State, and had almost ten years' experience of working with primates. In fact, one of Reiner's teachers at Ohio State had spoken highly of him, called him 'one hell of a sharp guy'. Clearly being at Farrel Research Supplies had taken the edge off that old sharpness. It was good money maybe, but it was also business, just business. Reiner was beginning to understand that.

'So, you see a pattern?' Levy said after a few moments.

'Well, we have broadly similar symptoms and very uniform timing.'

'Why do you say that?'

'Well, one day they were eating, and the next day they weren't.'

'Yeah. But what if another one stopped eating today, or tomorrow?'

'Well then I guess . . .'

Levy smiled, pulling the green mask tight across his mouth.

'Then you'd have *ir*regular symptoms, right? There are forty-eight animals in here.'

'Forty-seven.'

Levy shook his head.

'That's right, Carl. One died. And you say these symptoms are regular?'

'O14 was pretty old,' Reiner objected, 'one of the oldest of the batch.'

'*The* oldest?'

'Well I . . . I'm not sure.'

'According to the log there are at least three animals here that must be as old as O14, and they're all fine, so far.'

Reiner sighed. At least they were talking like vets for a change.

'So you think there's nothing to this? Just stress-related symptoms and a one-off case of flu?'

Levy looked down at the clipboard and then handed it back.

'What do *you* think?'

'I've been working on the assumption that there's a bacterial or viral infection at work, and that it's contagious.'

'That's why you want a necropsy done on O14?'

'I thought it might be as well to know what killed it. I don't know, I just feel . . .'

Reiner stopped himself. There it was again: *feel*.

Levy was walking away slowly down the line of cages. A few yards down he stopped.

'This one of the sick ones, O29?'

Reiner didn't have to check the log.

'Yes. Male, about two years old. I'm especially worried about him. Still has dysentery and the water uptake's low.'

Levy peered into the cage, keeping a discreet distance from the wire. The animal sat in the far corner, its muzzle twitching, its teeth half bared. For a moment Levy's eyes narrowed. He stood still, as if trying to remember something.

'You realise,' he said, quietly as if to himself, 'that if we did a necropsy of every primate that died in our care we'd need our own private army of surgeons?'

'We have Dr Maynard.'

Levy stood up straight again and carried on walking.

'This is August. Maynard goes fishing in August. In the Catskills. Along with Mrs Maynard and all the little Maynards.'

'And Dr Aldiss?'

'Dr Aldiss hasn't used a scalpel for years, at least not on anything dead. These days Dr Aldiss is on the executive career path. The Farrell fast lane.'

Reiner went over to where the other man was.

'But if we do have a virus in here, something contagious – '

Levy stopped again.

'This one, O22?'

'Yes, that's a sick one. A three-year-old female.'

Levy was thinking now. Reiner could sense it.

'You see, what Aldiss would say is, just look at the distribution. One animal is sick at one end of the room, another seven cages down, another on the other side of the aisle, and the others in between are all fine.'

'So?'

'So if the animals were infecting each other – endangering each other, let's say – you would expect the disease to spread from cage to cage. This distribution is about as random as you could get. That suggests that the health of the animals depends upon the individual. Not on some external agent.'

Reiner had been thinking about that.

'Unless this group of eight animals was exposed to infection well before they got here, and are expressing the symptoms ahead of the others.'

Levy shook his head.

'In which case we just have to wait and see if the others get sick too, don't you think? That's what quarantine's for when you get down to it.'

Reiner fell silent. Levy's was the voice of experience, he knew that. And he was right. Quarantine centres weren't hospitals. The point was to keep the animals there until you knew they weren't carrying anything and then send them on their way. If they got sick, you let the disease run its course.

'So you think Dr Aldiss will refuse a necropsy?'

'Yes, at least until Maynard gets back from fishing.'

'But that's weeks away.'

'Unless there's some evidence that links these eight macaques, and separates them from the others, I can't see why he'd want to go to the trouble. These things cost money.'

Reiner thought about it. He had to admit, his main reason for wanting a necropsy was simple curiosity. He wanted to *know*. But then, knowledge wasn't the motivating force behind Farrell Research Supplies, a division of the Lancing Corporation. The motivating force was money. No wonder a scientist like Levy had lost his edge.

'And if the other seven die?'

Levy didn't answer. He was staring at O22, his eyes screwed up over the rim of his mask. A little dribble of sweat ran down his temple.

'Will we get a – ?'

'Wait a second.'

Levy kept staring.

'Bert?'

'Wait a second. Wait a second. Where's the next one? The next sick one?'

'Er . . . Er, it's . . .' Reiner hastily consulted the log. Levy was suddenly excited about something. 'It's O20, two cages down.'

Levy was there in a second.

'Bert, what is it?'

'And this one?'

'Er, O19. She's clean. What are you – ?'

Levy's voice was hushed.

'Jesus, there it is. Right there.'

'What? What is?'

'Carl, my friend.' Levy turned to look at him. Reiner had never seen him so serious. 'I think you just got your necropsy.'

Dr Stephen Aldiss pulled a Kleenex from the box he always kept on his desk and started rapidly polishing the thumbprints off his glasses. He had driven down from a meeting in New Jersey that afternoon and looked tired. Reiner and Levy sat opposite.

'You're quite sure it's dye, Bert?'

'Absolutely. I've seen it before, or something a lot like it. The hunters use it to identify their animals when they're captured in the wild. Saves arguments in the marketplace.'

'And all the sick animals have this mark, this red mark?'

'All of them.'

'And O14 too,' Reiner added.

'O14?'

'The dead one. I checked.'

'So you think this group of eight infected each other with something before they got mixed in with the others?'

'Seems likely,' said Levy. 'And the one hundred per cent infection rate makes me worry.'

Aldiss nodded slowly.

'OK. You've seen the animals. What do you think, Bert?'

Levy pursed his lips and looked down at his knees. Then he looked up again.

'I think we're looking at a virus. Quite possibly SHF, or some Indonesian relative.'

Reiner stared. Simian haemorrhagic fever – SHF for short – was as near as damn it a worst-case scenario. It was highly contagious, and could wipe out an entire primate colony in a matter of weeks. There was no cure. The monkeys died from a combination of pneumonia and internal haemorrhage, sneezing and coughing up blood. And now he remembered: O14 had been found with blood around its face. Levy must have seen that. And there was another thing. The haemorrhaging sometimes damaged the blood vessels in the brain, causing changes in behaviour. Levy must have remembered that bite one of the infected females had given him on the hand. Yet he had said nothing about SHF until now.

For a moment Aldiss's polishing stopped.

'Bert, one of the reasons our customers have been switching from *Macaca fascicularis* to *Macaca nemestrina* is the reduced prevalence of SHF. *Nemestrina* aren't swamp dwellers.'

'I know,' said Levy. 'Primary rain forest is their habitat. And it may yet prove that this is a milder strain of the disease, or something completely different. We've only had one fatality so far.'

Aldiss sighed. In his pale grey lightweight suit he looked every inch the hassled forty-five-year-old executive – except that he was a scientist and he was only thirty-eight.

'We can't take any chances. If you're right we'd better know straight away. Damn! Why did this have to happen in August? I haven't handled a scalpel in years.'

'You could always call someone in,' said Levy.

Aldiss shook his head.

'No thank you. If we have to slaughter the whole batch I don't want it in the local newspaper. Things are bad enough as it is. Quite bad enough.'

Reiner and Levy exchanged a look. There had been rumours about the Lancing Corporation and their attitude to the whole trade in laboratory animals, at least as far as primates were concerned. The new chief executive was apparently very touchy about public relations. Maybe that was what Aldiss's meeting in New Jersey had been all about.

'I'll let the diagnostic staff know,' said Levy. 'When do you want to do it?'

Aldiss stood up and started loosening his tie.

'Soon as you can find me a scalpel, I guess.'

13

Sitting at the bamboo bar Wayan looked radiant in the
afternoon light. He had put on a western-style jacket
which Tuan Habibie had bought for him one drunken
afternoon from a market stall, and the soft caramel star
of a frangipani blossom drooped on his lapel. As Madam
Kim entered the room he smiled broadly. She realised at
once that he had come on serious business, his master's
business. And that meant money.

'Well, Wayan,' she said sweetly. 'This is an unexpected
pleasure. I hope you will forgive us if we have been a little
slow in coming to greet you. Things have been . . . very
busy.'

Wayan inclined his head graciously.

'No doubt your favourite client was keeping you up
till the small hours,' he said, with a knowing grin which
Madam Kim thought more than a little insolent. 'Such
appetites that man has.'

Favourite client. Who could he mean other than
Ahmad? And the way he was looking at her. That little
brown cut of a smile pushing into his smooth bronzed
cheeks. He was toying with her. Did he or his master know
what had happened? How could they know? Unless Sami,
Segma perhaps . . . unless one of the girls had told him.

'Yes, yes, Ahmad,' she managed to say. 'Such an
appetite, as you say.'

Wayan looked at his ridiculous flower, pushing at the petals with his fingers.

'Is it . . . do you think, too early to wake him?'

Madam Kim felt the blood rising into her sallow cheeks. But she refused to own up, especially to Habibie's boy. What went on at the Dancing Agung was none of his business. If he had something to say he would just have to say it. She would play along. It would give her great pleasure to see Wayan's expression when he saw Ahmad's bloody smile.

'No, no. Not at all. Unfortunately my girls seem to be asleep. We will have to go ourselves and wake him.'

How did he like that! Not very much, by the way he swallowed and fidgeted on his stool.

'Come, come, madam. I think we both know it would be rather hard to wake him this morning.'

So he did know! Madam Kim gave a little dry laugh, and was about to speak, when he said: 'I came by the dock on the way down. I noticed that Ahmad's boat was gone. And with it Ahmad, presumably.'

Madam Kim walked behind the bar and poured herself a large Scotch. She drank it, her eyes fixed on the boy in his silly western suit. What would he come out with next?

'Then why do you come here asking for a man who has already left?'

Wayan squirmed on his stool.

'You must forgive me, Madam Kim. It was just a joke. And I wasn't entirely sure . . . After all, some fool might have taken it into their head to steal Ahmad's boat, though I can't imagine why they would.'

'But all you had to do was ask.'

Wayan held up his hand. He was beginning to adopt the mannerisms of his fat master, Madam Kim noted, except that he didn't have the brains to go with them.

'Madam, madam. Whether or not Ahmad is here

is really beside the point. The reason I came . . . the reason I wanted to talk to you . . . Well it concerns a transaction Ahmad proposed several days ago to Tuan Habibie.'

Madam Kim's eyes glittered over the smeared rim of her glass.

'He had been thinking about the . . . uh, merchandise, and says he thinks maybe he was a little hasty to refuse. He is in Jambi now, selling off his monkeys, but he called up this morning and asked, me to come down. When I saw the boat was gone I thought it was perhaps too late. Is it?'

Wayan suddenly looked less certain of himself. And no wonder. He had given too much away. Madam Kim suppressed a smile. So Habibie had found a buyer in Jambi. He'd gone to all the trouble of calling up that morning and sending Wayan down in his best jacket to reopen negotiations. She finished her Scotch, taking her time now. It was going to be inconvenient, getting rid of Ahmad, but perhaps his death wasn't wholly undesirable – if she could make a little profit on the side.

'No, Wayan. It isn't too late. When Ahmad left he said I should make whatever arrangements I could. He left the . . . the *merchandise*, as you so nicely put it, he left it with me.'

Wayan heaved an almost comical sigh of relief.

'Tuan Habibie told me to . . . asked if I would take a look. Before making a down payment, I mean.'

Wayan followed Madam Kim up the stairs, holding his handkerchief against his mouth and nose. The smell of the place was much worse than he remembered it. It was a heavy smell, a smell of putrefaction. It was hard to believe a whorehouse could smell like that. The smell of sin, he thought, as they reached the landing.

They turned into a passage that led down to a single

door at the end. Madam Kim rapped on doors as she went past, shouting out to her girls.

'Wake up you lazy sluts! You dirty bitches. There is work to do.'

She smiled at Wayan over her shoulder.

'They spend most of their time in bed, and they *still* can't get up in the morning!'

They reached the door and Madam Kim fumbled for the key.

'We used to do laundry here in the old days. But I use it to store things now.'

She found the key she wanted and pushed it into the lock. Wayan could hardly breathe. The stench of the woman was so bad, and he felt constricted in his suit. It had been a bad idea. But then again, he had wanted to make a good impression. His heart was pounding and behind his back he gripped at his slim brown fingers.

Madam Kim was about to turn the key. She paused and looked at Wayan's face, which was glistening with sweat. She was going to set the price very high.

'To look only, OK?'

Wayan nodded and the door swung open revealing two enamel sinks and deep shelves on which there were scraps of bedding. Madam Kim drew in a sharp breath. The merchandise had gone.

14

Padang, West Sumatra. August 4th

Seventeen hours in economy class and suddenly she found the energy to be nervous. As the aircraft banked, showing her a view of the Bukit Barisan mountains swathed in billowing grey clouds, Holly felt her stomach squirm. Ten thousand feet below her children were waiting. Maybe they were even at the airport itself, where Jonathan had said they would try to meet her. How would she react when she saw them all together? Lucy and Emma had grown to accept their separation, but had never understood. When they were older they would see. They would understand how hard it was being the wife of Doctor Jonathan Rhodes.

The FASTEN SEATBELTS sign came on. One of the stewardesses hurried past, jogging a businessman's elbow, waking him up. A plastic cup rolled out into the aisle, spilling a trail of ice-cubes. They were banking the other way now. The mountains were gone. Through the window Holly could see only grey sky.

She looked down at one of the Polaroid photographs Jonathan had sent her. The children stood either side of their father, holding fishing rods and grinning at the camera. Were they grinning for her, as she had thought at first? What had Jonathan said to make them smile? She studied their faces for some sign of falseness, of pretence. Instead she began to see for the first time the faces of the women Lucy and Emma were one day going to be. Instead of openness, curiosity, Holly could see knowledge, a view of the world, certainties. It came home to her that in a few short years their childhood would be over.

She thrust the photograph back into her bag and closed her eyes for a moment, trying not to think about it, trying also to shut out the idea of Christina, Jonathan's new partner. Beneath her the landing gear locked into place with a thud. They were lining up for the final approach. Down below lay a rolling expanse of untidy fields and patches of forest, some sunlit, some in shadow. There were roads stretching away into the distance, a railway, power lines, clusters of single-storey buildings with rusty iron roofs, and, on the horizon, the blue-green sea. Holly watched it roll past, her gaze shifting from detail to detail: washing strung out across a yard, a herd of oxen being driven down a track, a man lighting a bonfire. It was a new world, a fertile, burgeoning one. Holly felt herself relaxing again. It was a good place to make a new start with Jonathan. As the wheels thumped against the concrete runway a handful of passengers burst into applause.

The tiny arrivals hall was packed full of people and luggage. Holly stood for a moment, searching the crowd for a familiar face. A huge woman in a sarong pushed past her, dragging two shopping bags and a colossal suitcase tied up with string. Holly stumbled, almost losing her grip on her luggage.

'Taxi? Taxi, lady?'

A skinny young man in a printed T-shirt already had a grip on the handle of her case.

'No thank you,' Holly said. She had to pull it back from him.

'Taxi thirty dollar.'

Holly ignored him, pressing on through the crowd.

How far was it to the town? Jonathan hadn't said in her letter. It didn't matter anyway. He and the children were probably waiting outside.

Another taxi driver, a short stout man in his forties, was standing by the door with his hands in his pockets.

'Taxi?' he said, sullenly.

Holly shook her head and pushed open one of the doors.

The heat and humidity hit her like a wave. Though the sky was mostly overcast she could feel the sweat prickling through the skin on her back and shoulders. Her cotton blouse felt clammy. She put down her case and looked up and down the road. There was a small car park opposite the terminal with two rows of wooden shelters for shade. Beyond it lay an untidy expanse of hoardings, power lines, streetlights and clumps of ragged palms. Beside her six yellow taxis lined the pavement. The driver at the head of the line looked back at her and threw a cigarette butt into the road.

Holly checked her watch. She was maybe twenty minutes late, but that was all. She had the time zones right, she was sure about that. Jonathan had said that if he was delayed getting to Padang for any reason, she should go straight to the Pangeran Beach Hotel, which was on the right side of Padang for the airport and the most modern in town. If it rained too much, he had explained, some of the roads on the other side of the highlands could become almost impassable, and there was a small chance that all the vehicles might be tied up, especially if one of his superiors turned up from the pharmaceutical company. But none of that was very likely; at least that was the way it had sounded.

Holly went back inside the terminal building and put her case down near the door. It was stupid to worry in a place like this. She would wait a while and then go on. The big woman in the sarong was making a scene in the middle of the hall. One of her shopping bags had split and people were stepping on the contents. Outside, a camouflaged lorry went by full of soldiers.

The skinny young man came up to Holly again. His T-shirt read *Luky Bar* in faded pink letters.

'Taxi, lady?' he said, holding up two fingers. '*Twenty* dollar.'

The reservation was still there, but it was three weeks old and had not been confirmed. After fretting at her computer for a couple of minutes the woman at reception had demanded a credit card before handing over the plastic tag that would open the door to her room. There were no messages.

An hour later Holly was sitting in a damp towel on the end of a double bed, staring out through double-glazed patio doors at a view of the sea framed in palm trees. Cold air cascaded down from an aluminium grille high up on the wall, making her shiver. She picked up the phone and dialled. Snatches of conversation cut in, first loud then far off, before an even hiss took hold, followed by the familiar American ringing tone. She tried to imagine the phone itself, on the bedside table.

'Hello?'

Richard sounded croaky, annoyed.

'Richard, it's me.'

She thought she could hear him yawn – or was it a sigh? The faint echo on the line made it hard to tell.

'Oh hi. Hi, honey. How are you?'

'Fine. Fine.'

'How was the trip?'

'Fine. No problem. What time is it there?'

She heard him breathe against the mouthpiece.

'About ten to five.'

'Sorry. I just wanted to be sure and call you while I was still in Padang. It's not so easy from the camp.'

'Sure, sure. You going up there right away?'

Holly hesitated. A lone Chinese man in a purple printed shirt and flip-flops went by outside, holding a rolled-up beach mat and a complimentary cocktail.

'No, not right away. But pretty soon.'

'Oh. So what's it like?'

'Hot and steamy, except in my hotel room which is like an ice-box.'

'I like the sound of that.'

He yawned loudly.

'It's beautiful, though. I mean, from what I saw on the plane.'

'I can't wait. So, you met up with Jonathan OK?'

Holly tried not to sound tense. There was no point in worrying Richard when there was nothing he could do.

'No, but they'll be on their way. It's been raining I think, so maybe the roads out there . . . Jonathan said that might happen.'

'Sure. Your guidebook says the hills above Padang get five metres a year. You should have packed an umbrella.'

Holly traced the outline of a big flower on her bedspread.

'So everything's OK? No big snakes and spiders?'

'No. But I found a gecko living on the bathroom ceiling.'

'Nice. It'll kill the roaches.'

'It's three inches long and sort of beige. Just sits up there over the air vent – ' Richard was yawning again, trying to hide it this time – 'Anyway, you'd better go back to sleep. I'll try and call you from the camp.'

'OK. No, wait. Call me before you set out. Just so I know you're on your way. Any time, OK?'

'OK. I will. Don't worry.'

'I'm not worried,' he said. 'Everything's going to be fine. I know it is.'

She smiled. He wasn't just talking about the trip.

He was talking about the children, about her and him.
He must have been thinking about it while she'd been
away.

'I hope you're right,' she said.

'Sure I'm right. I have this feeling.'

PART TWO

Third space

1

Aspen Hill, Maryland. August 7th

Lieutenant-Colonel Carmen Travis allowed herself a quick glance in the hall mirror as she collected the keys to the station wagon.

'Don't forget your caps,' she called out. 'I don't want you guys getting too much sun.'

Some of her fine brown hair had come loose at the back. She hastily opened the barrette and tucked it back in, but it still didn't look right. She had decided to have it cut short three days before, wanting to get rid of the last inches of an unsuccessful perm, but the new 'sensible' cut had brought out something dowdy in her. It made her look all of her thirty-nine years and more soldierly than she generally liked. She drew in her cheeks, and leaned in towards the mirror, scrutinising the tiny wrinkles around her blue eyes.

Joey came running out of the kitchen, his pitcher's cap reversed like a breakdancer.

Carmen pulled back from the mirror and turned.

'Peak to the front, young man,' she said, turning it around. 'You can have it the other way when we get an ozone layer.'

Oliver appeared a moment later, yawning theatrically.

'Can't I ride down later, Mom? I'm still sleepy.'

Carmen opened the door.

'We've already discussed this, Ollie. When Joey's old enough to ride along with you – '

'I can ride – ' Joey protested.

'*Without* stabilisers, then you can both go down on your bikes. Until then you go down to the Ryans' in the car, OK?'

'Ow-kay,' said Oliver, and walked out onto the driveway, dragging his feet.

It was less than ten minutes' ride to the Ryans' place, an elegant two-storey house in the Georgetown style with a good-sized lawn at the back and roses growing all around the porch. Andy Ryan was an old college friend of Carmen's husband, Tom, and worked at a law firm in Washington. Julia Ryan did charity work, part-time. During the school vacation Carmen often left Oliver and Joey with the Ryans, who had two young children of their own. Julia Ryan said it was no bother, and Carmen and Tom made sure they returned the favour whenever the Ryans wanted to take off somewhere. The only problem was that Carmen had to leave the kids before nine if she was going to get to Fort Detrick in time for work, and, with the exception of Andy, the Ryans were not early risers. Carmen dreaded interrupting their breakfast time.

That morning the house looked as quiet as ever. Carmen climbed out of the station wagon and walked slowly up the pathway with Joey and Oliver in tow. She felt self-conscious in her uniform. Although she was in pretty good shape, army slacks were not designed to be flattering, and the artless cut only seemed to exaggerate the breadth of her hips. Besides, in a cosy place like this any kind of uniform looked like an intrusion from a harsher world.

Carmen was about to press the buzzer when Julia Ryan opened the door.

'Hi there! Come on in.'

She was tying a length of shimmering blue material

into her abundant brown hair. She wore a white roll-neck sweater, a long black and green skirt and a beautifully embroidered waistcoat. Carmen took off her sunglasses and smiled up at her.

'I hope we're not early, Julia,' she said, ushering Oliver and Joey inside. 'It's just that I've – '

'Of course not. Scott'll be dressed in a minute and – ' she looked up the stairs – 'Michelle? Are you getting up?'

There came a faint childlike whine from somewhere overhead. Julia rolled her eyes in mock despair.

'We could really use some military discipline around here, that's for sure,' she said, smiling at Carmen. 'Have you got time to stay for a coffee? There's some on already. Real dark and strong.'

They went into Julia's newly fitted kitchen and made small-talk for ten minutes while Oliver and Joey half-heartedly kicked a soccer ball back and forth in the yard. Scott Ryan wasn't Oliver's best friend in third grade, and Michelle was little more than a baby, but they still had to be better company for the boys than some professional minder. The army had crèche facilities in the area – government standard prefab huts in the middle of a disused parade ground – but the boys hated going there. So the Ryans it had to be. And Julia Ryan was very nice, very understanding. Her father had been in the military for a while, and she'd spent a part of her childhood on an army base in Germany. All the same, Carmen couldn't help wondering if she wasn't missing something, carrying on at Fort Detrick while her kids were so young. Everyone encouraged her to do so – Tom, friends, the people at the Institute itself – but the one lot of people who never got asked were Oliver and Joey, because what did they know about grown-up things like careers?

'Tom'll come by and pick them up around six,' she said, as they were crossing the hall again, 'if that's OK.'

'Sure thing,' said Julia with a big smile. 'We'll be here.'

At five to nine Carmen was back in the station wagon, heading up towards the eastern slopes of the Appalachian Mountains. The road took her through rolling farmland and oak forest, over the Monocacy River and then on to Frederick, where Fort Detrick was located. It was a very quiet road, yet beautifully surfaced and marked out with solid white lines. Carmen often felt a guilty pleasure gliding along that smooth asphalt in the mornings, watching the dairy cattle behind their neat wooden fences, looking at the yellow sun on the hills. It felt like she ought to be sharing it with somebody.

Fort Detrick was a secured area of some twenty-five acres, fenced off with razor wire and patrolled by guard dogs. At its heart lay a huge windowless block, around which were clustered a handful of smaller buildings. The block served as headquarters for the United States Army Medical Research Institute for Infectious Diseases (USAMRIID), where Carmen was head of the pathology division. People inside the military called this place 'the RIID' – rhyming with *lid* – or sometimes simply 'the Institute'.

USAMRIID's main field was biological warfare. Established nearly half a century earlier, when fear of Soviet capabilities had been running high, USAMRIID's task was to conduct research into how military personnel could be protected against biological weapons and naturally occurring infectious diseases. Although staffing levels these days were a fraction of what they had been, USAMRIID was still one of only two organisations in the country equipped to handle the full range of known human pathogens. Its laboratories were all sealed, with independent, filtered air supplies. The special biocontainment laboratories, where the most dangerous samples were studied, were kept at negative air pressure, so that in the event of a leak air would flow into the room and not out. All work in these laboratories was conducted inside pressurised space suits.

The sentry at the gate smiled at Carmen as she handed over her ID. His submachine-gun was tucked neatly into the small of his back – almost out of sight.

'Morning, ma'am.'

Carmen smiled back and waited while he ran her card under the UV scanner. Even under the pure blue sky the RIID was ugly, an ugly concrete box half-buried in the ground, blind except for the nest of antennae clustered around one corner of the blast-resistant roof.

'Thank you, ma'am.'

The sentry handed back the ID and saluted. Carmen waited for the gates to go up and drove inside.

Dr Marcus Gaunt replaced the receiver and checked the clock above the electron microscope. Provided he left the facility before five he would have plenty of time to make it home for supper with his family. And he was confident he would not be staying late. There was no reason to, for a change.

During the last few days, since Stephen Aldiss's call to head office, things had been pretty hectic at Marshallton. The possibility that simian haemorrhagic fever had established a foothold in the facility was something that had to be taken very seriously. If confirmed, it could have meant the slaughter of virtually the entire primate population there – some 320 specimens. SHF, in most of its forms, was airborne, carried through the air inside tiny particles of moisture. A cough, a sneeze, even a breath, could send millions of such particles into the atmosphere. Even with the advanced ventilation systems installed at Marshallton, it would be extremely difficult to stop the virus spreading through the facility. The chances were it would infect the quarantine workers too, if it hadn't already. And while they would be unlikely to suffer symptoms any worse than a bout of flu, they would have to keep away from any of the other primates for three weeks at least. Replacement staff would have to be drafted in for the duration, and they did not come cheap. As it was, the rosters had to be completely rearranged to ensure that staff who had worked near the infected animals in Room D did not work anywhere else.

Aldiss had done the necropsy himself the same day. By the time Gaunt set off from New Jersey *Macaca nemestrina* O14 had been opened up, its internal organs removed, swabs taken from the throat and nasal cavity, and its carcass sent to the incinerator. By the time he arrived at Marshallton, Aldiss's report was waiting for him. It did not look good. The diagnosis continued to point to SHF: for one thing, the animal's spleen and kidneys were enlarged – a classic symptom – and there were lesions consistent with mild internal haemorrhage. Gaunt's task was to isolate and identify the viruses themselves, to confirm or refute the provisional symptomatic diagnosis. He did not waste time.

Immunofluorescence presented the quickest and simplest option, and the lab at Marshallton was fully equipped for it. Before Gaunt even arrived the resident technician, Wesley Southern, set to work preparing a series of tissue cultures. He took a small sample from O14's liver and ground it up with a pestle and mortar. Then he did the same with a sample of spleen. He also took cell samples from the throat swab, giving him three different sets of infected material. In each of them, among the millions of cells and the billions of cell particles, tiny clusters of the virus lay hidden, too small and too few to be spotted. The point of the tissue cultures was to breed the viruses in such numbers that they at last became distinguishable to biochemistry and the electron microscope.

Playing host to each group of viruses were MA–104 cells – kidney cells cloned from those of an African green monkey, a standard and commercially available medium for the investigation of primate viruses. The cells sat at the bottom of rectangular plastic culture flasks the size of aspirin bottles. Living carpets one layer deep, under an optical microscope the layers of cells looked like walls, each cell a flattish brick.

Gaunt's first task upon arrival at Marshallton was to prepare the samples of infected material as 10 per cent solutions in Eagle's minimal essential medium – a fluid containing enough salts and nutrients to sustain living cells and microbes, but not enough for them to multiply. With Dr Aldiss still pacing up and down the lab like an expectant father, Gaunt, protected with mask and goggles, carefully pipetted 25 cubic centimetres of the solution into each culture flask with its carpet of MA–104 cells. After absorption for one hour at 37 degrees centigrade, he added a cocktail of richer nutrients mostly made up of foetal calf serum. With the caps screwed on tight, incubation began immediately. If the virus that had killed *Macaca nemestrina* O14 was simian haemorrhagic fever, the cells in the culture would start dying four to five days later.

Exactly what it was that made viruses become active was still a puzzle about which there were plenty of theories, but no clear answers. A virus could lie dormant for years – generations – and then suddenly go off like a land mine left over from some half-forgotten war. But the conditions inside the culture flasks were designed to be so ideal that any primate virus would become active and seek to replicate immediately. Once the resulting damage was detectable the culture would be exposed to a series of fluorescent antibodies, each corresponding to a different primate pathogen – one of them being SHF. If the pathogen in question was present the antibodies would attach themselves to the infected cells and glow under ultraviolet light. No glow would mean they had the wrong virus.

Gaunt was fascinated by the strange, oblique relationship viruses had with organic life. No more than a tiny capsule containing one or more strands of DNA or RNA – the material that has made up the genetic code of every organism in the history of the planet, from dinosaurs to fruit flies – the virus contained the software – the genetic code – for making a copy of itself, and that was all. They required the living, metabolising environment of the host cell to switch themselves on, and were otherwise inert, to all intents and purposes dead. Some of them, through adaptive evolution, had developed the capacity to find their way deep into the nucleus of the host cell where they could lodge in the cell's own genes, forcing the cell to replicate the virus over and over again. For Gaunt, the most interesting question was whether viruses were by-products of organic life or had existed before it – a question he had had plenty of opportunities to raise with his colleagues at Marshallton as they waited for the virus from Room D to surface.

Stephen Aldiss had spent a lot of time in the lab since Tuesday, but his visits were becoming less frequent and the reason was clear: no other monkeys in Room D had died. In fact, most of them were beginning to show strong signs of recovery. A normal outbreak of SHF would have claimed half the animals there already. As Gaunt had been quick to point out, incubation periods could vary a lot, but the fact that the infected monkeys were not getting any worse was encouraging. It might be that the virus in question was a milder strain of SHF, or that *Macaca nemestrina* as a species was, like *Homo sapiens*, better able to resist the SHF virus than *Macaca fascicularis*, its swamp-dwelling relative. Either way, it was looking less likely every hour that wholesale slaughter would be necessary. In fact, Gaunt reckoned, with a little luck he might be able to leave the whole episode behind him by the end of the week. Wesley

Southern was perfectly capable of tying things up without him.

At that moment Southern was standing by the incubator, carefully sorting out the tissue cultures for their daily examination. Twenty-three years old and pretty smart, he had watched and noted everything Gaunt had done at Marshallton with a diligence that the older man found rather flattering.

'All ready for Series One, Dr Gaunt.'

Gaunt was in an indulgent mood.

'You take a look, Wesley,' he said. 'I'll do the log this time.'

He picked up the clipboard and waited patiently as Southern positioned the first flask under the microscope. The Series One flasks all contained cultures of cells from the infected liver of O14. With the naked eye all that could be seen was the rosy pink of the foetal calf serum, which drained away to one side as the flask was gently tilted, bringing it into line with the focal plane of the lens.

'So. Any change?'

Southern seemed to be taking a long time getting the cells into focus. Dr Gaunt looked at him over the top of his glasses.

'Observations?'

'I . . . I'm not sure. I mean, yes. It's all . . . Jesus, it's . . .'

Gaunt resisted the temptation to move Southern aside. The kid had to learn somehow.

'Just tell me what you see, Wesley, OK?'

'Yes, Dr Gaunt.'

Southern changed the focus again. He was moving the focal plane into the uppermost level of the culture, sliding the dish upwards at the same time, so that he could look into the pool of serum. Then, unsteadily, he moved the dish back again.

'It looks . . . just dead, sir. I mean it's just *ripped*

to pieces. Half these cells are clean off the plastic.'

Gaunt sighed, disappointed. *Ripped to pieces* was not a recognised scientific term.

'All right, let me have a look.'

He stepped up to the microscope, plunging the focus down to the back of the flask with a single twist of the dial. In laboratory conditions SHF would not normally cause visible damage to the culture for another day at least. When it did the cells took on a shrunken look, the cell walls angular, some squashed into thin lines. The carpet of cells in this culture looked as if it had been blasted through with buckshot. Whole sections were simply gone – *ripped to pieces*. Thousands of dead and dying cells had come free from the bottom of the flask, floating away, clouding the serum. Cell death had been sudden and violent. Gaunt frowned. The lab suddenly felt hot.

'What is it, Dr Gaunt?'

He stood up.

'Bacterial contamination, I should think,' he said. 'Probably pseudomonas. Easy enough to tell.'

Southern nodded. Pseudomonas was a harmless soil bacteria which had an annoying habit of turning up in laboratory cell cultures and ruining them, in spite of all the precautions. Such contamination was a routine event – one of the reasons why a group of identical cultures was always created instead of just one. Gaunt tapped the side of his nose. There was always one easy way to tell if stray bacteria were responsible for a mess like this: the smell. When bacteria multiplied they gave off an odour. Viruses did not. In pseudomonas' case, the smell was like grape juice. Gaunt prided himself on being able to identify types of bacteria just from the smell they made. Some people had a nose for wine; he had a nose for microbes.

'Shall we check the other flasks, doctor?'

'Let's just finish up with this one first,' said Gaunt.

Here was a lesson Southern was not going to pick up from any textbook. Gaunt slid the flask out from under the microscope and unscrewed the cap.

'Now, if I'm not mistaken,' he said, swilling the contents around and raising the flask to his nose, 'we'll find . . .'

There was no smell at all.

Gaunt repeated the action, but there was still no smell, not even a trace. He replaced the cap. The cell culture had been ravaged by a virus after all, and the virus was not SHF. He checked the other cultures one by one. All of them showed a similar level of damage. He could not remember seeing anything quite like it. After fifteen minutes' careful logging he stood back from the microscope.

'I'm going to take a closer look at this right away. We'll try out the immunofluorescence later. Are you up to speed on EMS preparations?'

Southern nodded.

'Good. We'll take a sample from the first batch. Just drain off some of the fluid.'

The only way to get a look at the viruses themselves was to get them under the electron microscope. Southern pipetted a sample of the milky serum from one of the cultures and placed it in a test tube. This he then span in the microcentrifuge, giving them a concentrated button of dead and dying cells at the bottom. This button, no bigger than a crumb, he removed with a small wooden spatula, sterilised and soaked in plastic resin. It was cross-sections of this sample, sliced with a diamond knife, that would be going under the scope. Advanced computer software would enhance the image, strengthening definition and even adding false colour if required. The first part of the picture was building up on the big computer screen ninety minutes later.

To Southern it looked like one of those satellite photographs of Earth they published now and again in glossy magazines, a rain-forest landscape of winding rivers, lakes and marshes, littered with unfamiliar shapes. He was looking at one corner of a single cell, the cell wall a dark, blue-green arc across the screen. Dr Gaunt sat peering at it, manoeuvring the picture around with the mouse.

'I don't see anything here,' he said and decreased the magnification, yanking the image several screens to the right at the same time. Southern saw another cell wall go by and what looked like a part of a nucleus, a dark fuzzy-edged mass. Even this close up it was easy to tell they weren't looking at healthy tissue, with its order, its comforting repetition. This was a graveyard, a chaos of discarded and ruptured cells, and they were picking through the bones.

Gaunt held the picture still for a moment and then moved it again.

'Nothing there.'

The image moved again, and again. It was starting to make Southern feel dizzy.

'No. Damn. This is going to take a while. Needle in a haystack, I'm afraid.'

He changed the magnification again and swept down. Two twisted mitochondria loomed up, their surfaces seemingly lacerated, torn open. Southern pulled up a stool.

'Dr Gaunt, you want me to prepare another sample? If I get going maybe I can have another ready . . .'

The image had stopped moving. Gaunt was leaning forward against the screen, his glasses lifted away from his eyes.

'Ready by five . . . Dr Gaunt?'

Gaunt hit the mouse button twice more, doubling the magnification each time. It was then that Southern saw them too.

*

The first Carmen knew about the problem at Marshallton was when her commanding officer called her into his office at half-past two that afternoon. Major-General Rob Bailey was a lean man in his late forties with a good head of hair, a straight, rather pointed nose and penetrating brown eyes. He had only been in command at Fort Detrick for three months, having transferred from an advisory post in the Pentagon. Although not as well liked as his predecessor, Colonel Seyfarth, Bailey was respected for his quiet, efficient style and a good command of detail.

He was looking at one of her old reports when Carmen came into the room.

'Take a seat, Carmen,' he said. 'You've done quite a bit of work on *filoviridae*, one way and another. Is that right?'

Carmen shifted in her chair.

'Yes, sir. The Ebola group mostly. That was a few years back.'

Bailey smiled and closed the report.

'Why did you stop?'

Carmen paused for a moment to consider what the question implied. Bailey watched her.

'Well, for a while there was concern about the direction in which the Ebola virus might be mutating. Some strains became airborne. But in the event these proved harmless where humans were concerned. So the urgency kind of went out of it.'

'Yes, I see.'

'Has there been some kind of – ?'

'Outbreak? No. Nothing like that. But something has turned up, and I think it might be worth looking at. You don't know Dr Stephen Aldiss, by any chance, do you?'

Bailey started writing something down on his jotter pad.

'No. Should I?'

'No, just wondered. He runs a primate quarantine

operation a little ways from here. I was at college with him.'

'Primate quarantine?'

'That's right.'

Bailey leaned across the desk and handed Carmen a scrap of paper with the address and telephone number of the Marshallton facility.

'It was at a primate quarantine unit that the last Ebola outbreak occurred.'

'I know.'

'That one was airborne, sir.'

'Right again. And so's this, probably, whatever it is. The cultures they've got don't look too pretty, and they've got some electron shots to match.'

'But there's no evidence of human infection? No casualties?'

Bailey smiled.

'If that were the case, I'd be down there myself. There's been some sickness and one death among the primates. All the same, the lab data looks interesting. That's why I want you to go and make an assessment right away. Just in case.'

Carmen folded up the scrap of paper.

'Right away, sir? I'm supposed to be – '

'I promised Dr Aldiss I'd help him out. It'll probably turn out to be nothing more than some exotic strain of flu, but you never know.' He planted his hands on the desk and smiled at her. 'Call me when you get there, would you? Oh, and take full precautions if you handle any hot material. Better safe than sorry, OK?'

Carmen paused for a moment as she drew the door shut behind her. She heard Bailey pick up the phone.

During the long drive back towards the coast Carmen had plenty of time to think through her old work on filoviruses. It had been her first major project after finishing the RIID's pathology training programme some seven years earlier – a relatively high-risk one. Handling BL–4 pathogens was like handling high explosives. However thorough the procedures, however careful and systematic you were in your methods, the fact remained: the more you were around them, the greater your chances of dying.

Looking back, Carmen wondered if she would willingly work on filoviruses again. Even now, years later, it was hard to recall that period in her life without a shudder, without feeling that she'd put at risk everything she and Tom had built together. In the third year of their marriage they had lost their first child, Annie. A cerebral embolism had killed her when she was only eighteen months old. She had gone to sleep one night just like normal and the next morning Tom had found her lying there, cold and pale. Carmen had sincerely believed that grief would kill her, that her own life was over just as surely as her daughter's, but then, just weeks later, she had discovered that she was pregnant again. She and Tom had wanted another child. It was something they had always planned on. But Carmen could not welcome her discovery. She couldn't help feeling that her unborn child was trespassing on her grief, on Annie's memory, stepping too quickly into her first-born's shoes. Even when Oliver was born, something of that feeling had stayed with her.

In the circumstances the normal thing would have been to turn down the BL–4 work flat. That was what everybody at the Institute had expected, and they had only informed her of the opportunity out of respect for her rank. But she had surprised everyone. Even with Oliver inside her she had thrown herself into the work with an almost ferocious dedication, returning to it swiftly after he was born. Day after day she had clambered in and out of space suits, endured the tedium of decon procedures, chemical showers, disinfectant drills, for the privilege of cutting up bloody lumps of traumatised tissue, for the privilege of staring at death through the eye of a microscope. Looking back on it, Carmen struggled to understand her compulsion. Behind the quiet devotion, the measured protocols of scientific enquiry, had she been harbouring a death wish?

She had quit the BL–4 labs just around the time when Oliver started to talk. By that time the dark clouds were gradually lifting. Tom's small animals veterinary practice in Bethesda was taking off at last, and she could feel the two of them growing closer again, day by day. They took to holding hands as they watched TV or pushed a shopping trolley through the local grocery store, the way they hadn't done since they were sweethearts at vet school. Life, her own life and those of her family, began to feel precious again, more precious than ever.

The lab suites at the RIID were divided into four different levels, according to the lethality of the material handled in them. The most dangerous pathogens of all – lethal viruses for which there was no vaccine and no cure – were kept at biosafety level 4, stored inside samples of animal tissue and blood serum frozen to minus 70 degrees centigrade. Among these viruses was a group known as the filoviruses or *filoviridae*, because of their peculiar, thread-like appearance.

The filoviruses, Marburg and Ebola, had first emerged some thirty years earlier from the tropical rain forests of Africa. Their precise origin was unknown, but their effect on primates, and man in particular, was very well documented. The most significant thing about the *filoviridae*, from the military point of view, was their extraordinary killing power. Some 88 per cent of people exposed to one of the group – Ebola Zaire – died, making it one of the most dangerous viruses ever discovered. As the basis for a weapon of war or mass destruction, that was a pretty good starting point. It was for this reason that Carmen and her team had spent nearly two years working inside space suits at biosafety level 4, trying to come up with some way of treating a filovirus infection. Their efforts had not been rewarded.

They had run through the full range of immuno-fluorescence tests by the time she reached the lab at Marshallton. As Dr Aldiss explained to her, none of the enzymes they had tried out on the infected cell cultures were responding, which ruled out SHF and most of the known primate pathogens.

'I think there's a chance we've got something new here, Colonel,' he said as he handed her a surgical mask. 'At least, it's new to us.'

Inside the lab a stout middle-aged man with a rather red face and glasses introduced himself as Dr Marcus Gaunt, followed by a young black man called Wesley Southern. They seemed proud, elated at what they had discovered. Only Aldiss showed any signs of anxiety.

'We're preparing some more samples for the EMS right now,' said Gaunt. 'We'll have more pictures before the day is out.'

'Could I take a look at what you've got so far?'

'Of course.'

Gaunt went to the computer and punched in some numbers.

'There you are,' he said. 'These look like the culprits. Cute, aren't they?'

Carmen had to stifle a curse. The picture was homed in on a region of cell wall, jagged and uneven, blistered along the outside edge. Inside it, coiled up like piles of thick black rope, lay the heaviest concentration of *filoviridae* she had ever seen. Ebola, Marburg, whatever the hell it was, she knew it was something she never wanted to see outside the confines of the RIID – outside the confines of a pressurised lab suite surrounded by two yards of concrete.

The possibilities crammed into her mind. She struggled to remember what General Bailey had told her: there was no evidence of human infection. A primate had died, that was all.

She turned to Dr Gaunt and forced a smile.

'That's a very impressive picture. I'd like to have my people take a look at it.'

'Of course,' said Gaunt. 'We can copy you a disk.'

'I'd also like to go over the veterinary data,' she said, turning to Aldiss. 'In particular your belief that this virus may have been airborne to some degree.'

Aldiss nodded.

'That's only a supposition. I tell you what. Why don't you talk to the man on the ground, as it were?'

There was a phone on the bench. Aldiss pressed a button. A dialling tone rang out.

'The vet office is 8672,' Southern volunteered.

Gaunt dialled the number. Larry Spalding picked up the phone at the other end. His voice sounded loud in the quiet of the diagnostics lab.

'This is Dr Aldiss here. Is – '

'Oh hi there, Dr Aldiss. How you doin'?'

'Fine, fine. Is Carl Reiner there? I wanted to go over something with him.'

'Carl? Er, I'm afraid not, Dr Aldiss. He took the afternoon off. Said he wasn't feeling too good. Is it something I can help you with?'

2

Padang, West Sumatra. August 7th

It hadn't rained since morning, but it looked like it might. The air felt pressurised.

'It's the ice,' said Graham Willis. 'You can be as careful as you like with the food. You can buy bottled water. But, at the end of the day, when you've been working your backside off in this heat, do you have the strength, do you have the moral fibre, to refuse ice in your Scotch?'

Iwan, the pocket-sized barman, looked confused.

'I take ice, Tuan?'

Willis shook his head, and held the glass up, enjoying the play of electric light on the white chunks swimming in his drink.

'No, no, no.' He took a sip and smacked his lips. 'Because in my case, Iwy, as far as I personally am concerned, I do not have the strength or the moral fibre. And if that means a touch of Bali belly, or the local – '

At that moment Holly Becker entered the room. Willis watched her walk through to take a seat on the veranda. She was wearing a print dress and canvas shoes. Willis hadn't seen a western woman for the whole six weeks he'd been in Padang; it was all knotty little Australian businessmen with attaché bases, or bow-legged Japs, or the dreamy locals, and to see such a beautiful white

117

woman – well, it made an impression. And she really was something. Thick, dark hair pulled back in a purple velvet bow, and the most beautiful eyes he had ever seen outside of a fashion magazine. Big dark eyes, with thick lashes.

He turned to register Iwan's reaction, but the little barman had already gone, weaving his way through the tables to offer his services.

Willis watched open-mouthed as Iwan, whom he had assumed to be more of a listener, started to talk to the woman like he knew her.

'Everything OK, Ibu? My brother come in jeep?'

She looked tired. Tired and dejected. It seemed to take her a moment to register what Iwan had asked. Then she nodded and asked him to bring her a coke.

Back at the bar Iwan winked at Willis as he opened the bottle.

'Er, Iwy – '

But before Willis could get in a question, Iwan was gone again.

'No good? No find friend?'

She took a long drink before answering. Thirty-five. Maybe older. Willis took in the long athletic legs. Not much of a tan, so he assumed she'd just arrived. She lifted her hair off her neck. Little damp curl there like a question mark. Willis licked his lips.

'The road was blocked,' she said. 'Your brother drove me up to the highway, but the turning was blocked.'

'The rainy is it?'

'No, it wasn't the rain. From what I could see the track looked OK. Muddy, but OK for the jeep. There were military there. I don't know.' She sighed. 'Anyway they wouldn't let us go down. We were just near the Hari river. Your brother said that was the way down to Rafflesia Camp. Then we took the highway along to the Jambi turning, but that was blocked too. And that's an asphalt road.'

118

'Miri – ?'

'Soldiers. Army.'

'Yes. Yes.' Iwan put his head on one side and smiled in the dreamy way that was familiar to Willis by now, a look that got his back up like nothing else. He slid off his bar stool.

'Oh, oh,' said Iwan, smiling. 'Well. Maybe try again.'

'Excuse me.'

Holly looked up.

'I couldn't help overhearing. Did you say you'd had some trouble getting down into Jambi province, to Muaratebo?'

She looked at Iwan and then back at him. Big hypnotic eyes.

'No, not Muaratebo, exactly. It was on the Hari river just above Muaratebo, I think. At least that's what my map says. Rafflesia Camp.'

Willis nodded slowly, thinking.

'Oh yeah, that's right. There's some sort of research facility down there, isn't that right?'

She seemed to perk up.

'You know it? Maybe you know my . . . Dr Jonathan Rhodes.'

'No, I've never been down there.'

He stuck out his hand. Stage two. Physical contact.

'Graham Willis. I'm in resort development. Doing a little preliminary assessment. I know the area pretty well.'

There was another pause. Then the woman said:

'You're Australian.'

'That a problem?'

She smiled.

'Not necessarily.'

Keep talking, thought Willis. Keep it flowing.

'I was interested to hear what you had to say about the roadblock on the Jambi road. I've been hearing stories about a situation not far from Muaratebo. Mind you, there are always stories. You have to take everything with a pinch of salt around here. In fact, a shovel-full would be more like it.'

'You said a situation. What do you mean?'

'Some kind of disturbance. Indians, I think. You know there's been some trouble with the Kubu up here. They're unhappy about what the government is doing to their land. Cutting down the trees. Clearing the forest. Mining. Japanese capital behind a lot of the development. There's been some trouble with settlers too.'

She looked interested, concerned. He decided to keep going on the same tack.

'Yeah, you probably know how it is. Urban overspill from Java. Government skims off the crud and drops it in the jungle. It's another way of getting the Indians out. People come from the slums. They all want to be farmers so they come over here with a hoe and a few seeds, hoping to make a living.'

'But what about Muaratebo?'

'Well – do you mind if I – ?'

'Of course, please.'

Willis sat down and made himself comfortable. After three months on the assignment he was very knowledgeable about the highlands, about what they represented to the politicians in Jakarta – he had to be. And here was a pretty woman to be his audience.

'Well of course I haven't had a chance to get up there myself recently. But if the military are blocking the roads, presumably it's because there's been trouble down – '

'Could you get down there if you wanted to?'

This woman – he still didn't know her name – was really eager. Willis had a vision of himself driving a jeep along jungle trails. The woman next to him. Damp T-shirt clinging to her back. Of course, they'd need a guide. He rolled his head around, considering. Giving it his consideration.

'Well, I think for someone who really knows the forest there's probably a way through. Some of the jungle trails, some of them real old – trails cut by the Kubu themselves or trails widened by the rubber tappers and the companies working the forest – some run parallel to the road for a few miles and then disappear. Might be just fifty yards between you and a big trail, and you'd never know. You have to know where to get off the road.'

'And do you?'

'I have a friend who does. He's half Indian himself. Knows the jungle like it was a shopping mall. Course you'd have to pay. Hundred dollars for the jeep and driver. And I don't know if you'd want to be alone in the jungle with this guy.'

He shook his head doubtfully. The woman was clearly disappointed. He hesitated, long enough for it to look like he didn't really want to say what came next.

'On the other hand, I suppose . . . I suppose I *could* come along. We have to have an idea of the political situation in this business. Tourists scare easy. I hadn't exactly planned on it, though.'

The woman was no longer looking at him. Willis took in her breasts. It was all very encouraging. Then suddenly she was looking straight at him. He felt his face go hot.

'I have to get to Rafflesia Camp. I have . . . relatives there.'

Willis frowned.

'Doctor Rhodes. He's not your . . . ?' Holly blushed, and Willis brought his boots together under the table. 'Your husband.'

'My ex-husband.' She looked around the bar room for a moment like she was lost. 'Look, it's a long story. The fact is . . . the fact is I flew over from the States to see my children – they're staying at the camp. They were supposed to meet me at the airport a couple of days ago. I've been trying to get through on the radio, but haven't had any luck.' She brushed a mosquito away from her face. 'Iwan's brother drove me up there today. I was hoping to get through that way. But the road was blocked and now you say that the Indians . . .' She gave a shudder, and sipped at her drink.

Willis took a chance. He put his hand on her shoulder. Only for a second.

'Look I'm sure your kids'll be OK. You have to realise it's not like home out here. For a start the military do whatever the hell they want. If they feel like blocking the road, they block the road. And if there is something happening over at Muaratebo, it'll probably be some spat between settlers and Indians. Probably something happened in the marketplace. Somebody asks too much for a chicken, and before you know it somebody gets his throat cut.'

She nodded. These were probably the first words of comfort she'd had since she arrived.

'People running these research stations are often real close to the indigenous populations. More often than not that's the whole point of what they're doing. Corporations trying to develop pharmaceutical products, instead of just going out and collecting leaves or roots, they talk to the Indians, get an idea of what they think the plants can do for whatever it is – rheumatism, or eczema, or whatever. Then they orientate their research according to the folk-lore.'

Willis took a sip at his drink. The woman was looking at him now, trying to weigh him up. He wished he hadn't put on his batik shirt. Taken the wrong way, it could look a little seedy.

'So you don't have to worry about Indians.'

She was still looking at him.

'Rafflesia,' he said, trying to change the subject. 'The smelliest flower in the world.'

She looked puzzled now.

122

'How do you mean?'

'I was just thinking about the name of the camp. Guess that's why it stuck in my mind. Tourists come out here wanting to take shots of this great big flower. Then when they find out about it, they sort of change their minds, start looking for orchids.'

'Find out what?'

'The way it smells. It's an incredible thing. It imitates the texture and smell of decaying flesh to attract the flies it needs to pollinate.'

'Flesh?'

'Yeah, like rotting flesh. They call it the stinking corpse lily. You can smell it from fifty feet away. Evolution I suppose. The thing only flowers very rarely and it doesn't live for long. Comes up like a big dirty soufflé. I suppose it needs the maximum number of insects in order to improve its chances of pollinating. And if there's one thing that'll attract a lot of flies it's a dead body. Hellish thing, nature, don't you think?'

3

Carmen lifted the orange from the heavy teak bowl and looked at the underside. The dusting of green mould gave off a faint smell. It didn't matter how much she insisted, the kids never ate enough fruit. Little Joey wouldn't even eat one piece a day. So at the end of the week one of her jobs was to go round the house picking out fruit which was either unappetising or downright rotten, and throw it in the garbage can. She looked at the tiny threads of corruption which were spreading over the skin then looked at her face in the mirror. Despite a cold shower she still looked a little puffy around the eyes. The Marshallton case was taking its toll. She had slept badly the night before, coming down to the kitchen at four in the morning to drink a glass of water. Tom kept telling her to slow down, insisted on trying to massage the tension out of her shoulders, but it didn't work. And at breakfast Joey and Oliver – who you could always rely on for a frank opinion – had told her she looked awful.

What she had seen of the monkeys at Marshallton had made her uneasy, but it was the thought that people might soon be suffering the same fate – that she might be suffering the same fate – that really disturbed her. She had spoken briefly to Carl Reiner on the telephone. He was being held in an isolation unit at the Taylor Trust, a small private hospital near his home. He was trying to put a brave face on it and Carmen had gone along with him, reassuring him as best she could. He clearly had no idea what it was that had put him on his back. Probably just as well. A bug, he called it; said he'd picked up a bug from the monkeys.

But it wasn't a bug, it was a virus. And now she had to go and talk to Bob Bailey – tell him what she thought they ought to do. She turned away from the mirror, leaving the bad orange by the telephone.

It was hot in Bailey's office in spite of the fan.

'It gave me a jolt, sir – seeing it outside the lab. The screen was just packed full.'

'I saw the pictures, Colonel.'

Major-General Robert Bailey lifted the napkin from a carafe of water and proceeded to pour two glasses.

'Of course, sir – thank you.'

Carmen accepted the drink and leaned back in the hard wooden chair. She was never quite sure what he was thinking. Bailey had been wearing a uniform long enough to find a woman's presence in situations of professional parity disconcerting, and coming from the Pentagon, where the few women he would have seen were either wives with time on their hands or daffy secretaries, it would be understandable if he had a hard time taking her seriously. But Carmen thought that maybe there was something else.

When she had first come into the RIID, like everyone else she had been given a course of vaccinations for lethal agents – yellow fever, Q fever, Rift Valley, botulism – and had expected to work in the lower-level biosafety levels. But then Annie had died, and everything had changed. Biosafety level 4 was beyond any protective vaccines. At BL–4 the only thing between you and death was a space suit. Yet she had dived into it as if she were reaching into the grave, as if the grave might bring her somehow closer to her dead child. She had never really explained to Tom what her work involved, the risks she took daily, but everybody at the RIID knew about them. Looking back on those days she sometimes wondered about her frame of mind. Had Annie's death left her in some way unstable, reckless? Had other people at the RIID asked the same question?

Sitting opposite Bailey, sipping at her water, she wondered whether he was one of those people. Did her behaviour back then still have some influence on his attitude toward her? Had it all been noted down in some psychological report she had never seen, that she was not fully in control of her emotions, prone to become irrational? She bridled at the thought. She was over all that now. She was fully in command and she wanted Bailey to know it.

'I read your report,' he said, starting to shake his head. 'There's one thing that . . . You say that some of the animals are recovering?'

He fixed her with his piercing brown eyes.

'Apparently so, sir. Carl Reiner – '

'The sick man?'

Carmen nodded.

'The attendant who was working with the animals when the problem was first spotted – he kept a log. It's very clear. They run a very tight outfit over at Marshallton. The animals were numbered and there was no doubt about which were developing the symptoms.'

'But it is possible that different pathogens were active?'

'Yes, sir.'

'So some of the monkeys could have been sick with something other than – '

'Yes, sir. But I had our people take blood samples from all the animals that had developed symptoms and they are all infected with the virus. There's no doubt about that.'

Bailey frowned and brought his hands together in front of his face.

'So what are your conclusions, Colonel?'

'Well if we were going on the symptomatic data we'd have to suppose that these monkeys, this species – *Macaca nemestrina* – we'd have to suppose that they were resistant somehow.'

'And what about the attendant . . .'

'Reiner.'

'Yes. What's happening to him?'

Carmen sipped at her water. She didn't like to think about it.

'It doesn't look good, sir. He came down with a fever two days ago, as far as we can tell. It's too early to call with any certainty, but my guess is he's developing a viral haemorrhagic fever.'

Bailey's pale fingertips separated in front of his face and then came together again. He pushed air through his nose. A little impatient now.

'Colonel, if it was Ebola, any known strain of Ebola, then you wouldn't have monkeys making a recovery. Ebola will kill them every time.'

'I'm not saying it is a strain we've seen before, sir. In fact the necropsies have shown things we haven't seen in any of the recorded cases.'

'Like what?'

'As well as the enlarged kidney and spleen, all the dead monkeys had an inflammation of the lung lining.'

Bailey stood up.

'Really?'

'That's right.'

Bailey was quiet for a moment. Carmen watched him as he took out a cigarette and lit it. His manner had changed. He was pensive now.

'And Reiner seems to be developing the disease very rapidly. It's too early to say, sir, but I think the disease may be even more fulminating than Ebola. As if the virus reached extreme amplification at a quicker rate.'

Then Bailey was talking through his smoke, shaking his head. Denying something to himself, though she couldn't say what.

'We've sealed the quarantine station. We've isolated anyone who came into contact with these animals.' He flashed a look at Carmen. 'Now all we can do is pray for the poor sons of bitches in hospital. The one thing . . .' He walked over to a chart on the wall, his hand held to his mouth. 'The one thing in all this that I . . . that we can be thankful for is that the press hasn't got hold of it.'

Carmen couldn't believe what she was hearing. Was that all he was concerned about?

'Sir?'

He turned to look at her, his eyebrows raised.

'What is it, Colonel?'

'One of the attendants noticed that the animals which were first to develop the symptoms were all blotched with some kind of marker dye. Apparently the hunters use it to identify their catch when they get crated up.'

'Are you saying the sick monkeys all came from the same hunter, the same place?'

'Maybe. It should be possible to find out. We know they came from Sumatra. It shouldn't be too hard to find out where exactly.'

Bailey nodded.

'Talk to the liaison people at the World Health Organisation. They're the ones with the resources for that kind of thing.'

Carmen sipped at her water. They were sitting in one of the world's most sophisticated microbiology facilities. Bailey seemed to read her thoughts.

'There's no way I'm going to send any of our people in. The Indonesians don't take too kindly to Uncle Sam sticking his microscope in where it's not wanted.'

'What about Marshallton, sir?'

Bailey thought for a moment.

'What do you think, Colonel? I have to say I don't have a great deal of sympathy for people who make a living out of the suffering of dumb animals.'

'Are you saying we should close them down, sir?'

'No, Colonel. I'm asking you what you think we should do.'

'The way I see it, sir, the trade in these animals is going to continue. Science wants it that way and so does industry. We have to have quarantine centres to filter the flow. These people at Marshallton weren't negligent in any way. Maybe a little too focused on the bottom line, but then it is a business. They're not trying to run a zoo. They were just unlucky is my guess.'

'So what are you saying, Colonel?'

'I think we should kill the remaining animals in the room where the disease has spread. Learn all we can. Then let them reopen in a couple of months' time.'

'If they can. It's gonna play havoc with their cashflow.'

'And at the same time notify the WHO and see if there is any way we can stir up some enthusiasm for an investigation into the source of this thing. With the WHO's backing we might even be able to make a contribution ourselves.'

Bailey gave her a look.

'I have a lot of respect for the WHO, sir. But it seems to me the work we've been doing in the RIID, the techniques we've developed, along with all the back-up – well, it would be a shame to miss an opportunity to use it.'

4

Padang, West Sumatra. August 9th

Graham Willis's hotel was at the north end of Dobi Street,
a jostling thoroughfare in the middle of town full of motor
scooters and goods trucks belching diesel. As she climbed
out of the taxi Holly wondered why Willis preferred it to
the modern comforts of the Pangeran Beach.

'I go up there now and again, just to see who's in
town,' he said as they sat down at the bar. 'Look over
the clientele. But this is where it's at.'

He raised his glass and took a sip of whisky, casting
a faint look of disapproval at Holly's Coca-Cola. Holly
looked around the room. There were two westerners
sitting in the corner: a man in his twenties with a beard
and an unironed T-shirt, and an old man who must have
been eighty or more. Apart from some young couples at
the Pangeran Beach they were among the first westerners
she had seen in Padang.

'They mostly come out of the woodwork a little later,'
Willis said. 'After dark. This is the favourite place for
foreigners. The nearest thing they have to a club.'

An old-fashioned wood and wickerwork fan went round
and round over their heads. It made a pleasant change
from the arctic air conditioning at the Pangeran Beach.

'It's nice,' she said. 'Authentic.'

'And discreet, too, more to the point,' Willis said, giving
her a significant nod. 'Not like the people at your hotel.'

Holly was puzzled: 'What do you mean?'

Willis smiled and took another mouthful of whisky. Holly noticed that he had on a spotless khaki safari jacket, a contrast to the gaudy batik shirt he'd been wearing the last time. It looked like he'd had a haircut too.

'In places like this the authorities like to keep tabs on foreigners, especially if they aren't – how can I put it? – ordinary. Who aren't obviously holidaymakers.'

'But I'm – '

'On holiday, I know. But a young woman, on her own. You could be a reporter or something. They're incredibly sensitive about all that sort of thing. Interference in their internal affairs, they call it. Imperialism. Westerners telling them not to cut their forest down, not to build this or that dam or factory because it'll damage the environment, telling them how to treat their Indians, lecturing them about human rights, nagging away about democracy and freedom. You know.'

Holly frowned. It wasn't at all like the places she had read about in the glossy travel guides, full of smiling people in colourful ethnic costumes.

'But I thought they wanted western visitors. I thought they wanted to encourage tourism.'

Willis smiled.

'Some of them do. The finance ministry, the trade people, the business community. They want the money. The dollar is the one thing about the western world they can't get enough of. But not everyone's so keen, least of all the military. And if they are going to have lots of foreigners crowding in they want to keep an eye on them. Anything odd has to be reported. They're very co-operative about that at your hotel.'

'And that's why we're meeting here.'

'You got it.' Willis drained his glass. 'I'm ready for another. You?'

'No thanks. But let me.'

The barman was an Indonesian with a deeply lined, weatherbeaten face. He nodded at her formally and brought over the bottle of J&B.

'You should join me in something a little stronger, you know,' Willis said. 'Out here in the tropics it helps you keep a sense of perspective.'

'It just makes me fuddled.'

'Exactly,' said Willis, raising his glass. 'Try making sense of these places and you go loopy. Cheers.'

Holly watched Willis drink. A bead of sweat ran down his throat and disappeared beneath his collar.

'So have you spoken to your friend?'

Willis put down his glass.

'Uh-hu.' He leaned towards her slightly. 'I told him about the problem, and I think with a bit of luck he'll help. But it's not going to be cheap, I'm afraid.'

'He knows the place? Rafflesia Camp?'

'He knows where it is. That's the main thing. But people are getting pretty jumpy. Apparently . . .' A couple of official-looking men walked past holding briefcases. Willis watched them go by. 'Apparently something *is* going on. Someone was talking to the troops at the Bayur barracks the other day. A platoon of their men went up country a couple of weeks ago and they haven't come back.'

'Do they know why?'

Willis shook his head.

'I don't think anyone knows anything, to tell you the truth, but they're going crazy up there speculating about it. And there were these guys came in from Jakarta, apparently. Some specialist team, I don't know. All very secretive.'

Holly swallowed. She had read Jonathan's letters over and over, looking for some hint about what might have gone wrong. He had warned that the roads became very difficult when it rained, and the radio communications

132

were sometimes tricky because of the mountains. But real trouble? The possibility was never even mentioned. If anything had happened to the children she would never forgive Jonathan.

'Can your friend take me up there?'

Willis nodded.

'I think so. Just give us a few days to get it organised. But I'm afraid you're not going to see much change from five hundred bucks. Like I said, people are getting nervous. There might have to be a few back-handers passed around, if you don't want anyone checking up on you.'

Holly nodded. It was most of her holiday money, but what did that matter? Richard could always bring more. *Richard*. She had almost forgotten that he was coming out to join her. She had to call him to let him know what was happening.

'I'm anxious to go as soon as possible, Mr Willis,' she said. 'I want to see my children.'

'OK then. But be ready to clear out at short notice. And one other thing.'

'What's that?'

'Call me Graham, will you?'

The moon was already shining on the ink-black ocean by the time Holly dialled New York. Twelve hours behind, Richard would be at the bank, high up on the fortieth floor of a glass office block, looking down on the Woolworth Tower and a hazy skeleton of the Brooklyn Bridge. He hadn't seemed so far away the first time she had called him from Padang. She had only been away for twenty-four hours then. Such a short time shrank the distance, made it seem unreal. But now it felt as if they had the whole world between them. It felt the way it really was.

The line in Richard's office rang once and then she heard his voice, echoing, distant.

'Hi, Holly. How are you, honey?'

There was someone else in the room. She could tell. She heard Richard mutter something to them, accepting a cup of coffee maybe.

'I'm fine. But I'm still in Padang.'

'Padang? I thought you were going up to the camp.'

'I am. But I haven't heard anything from Jonathan yet. Or anyone. I'm getting worried.'

There was a rustle on the line. Richard was shifting the receiver.

'Tom, do you mind if I call you back in a couple of minutes? I've got . . . OK. I'll just be . . . OK, thanks. Sorry, honey. You say you still haven't heard from them? What the hell is going on?'

'Don't get upset. There must be some problem. I tried to get up there the other day and the road was blocked. There's something happening on the other side of the mountains but no one seems to know what it is. I've been in – '

'Wait, wait, wait a second. Something happening? What do you mean? What's happening?'

He sounded anxious, as if she was about to go off and do something stupid. She could not help feeling irritated.

'I don't know. Like I said, no one knows. There's just a lot of soldiers around up there, and some of the roads are closed off.'

'My God, near the camp?'

'On the way, yes. But that may be nothing to do with it.'

'But you're OK?'

'I'm fine. I'm just worried.'

'Well have you talked to the police?'

'Of course, Richard. They don't know anything either. They didn't even want to know. The point is I've been talking to a guy who knows his way around here. He has a friend, a local, who can get me up there. We'll use small roads where we have to.'

A loud hiss drowned out most of Richard's reply.

134

Suddenly Holly remembered what Willis had said: they were very co-operative with the authorities at her hotel. Maybe they were listening in.

'Honey? I'll be there in a few days. Just wait for me, OK?'

Richard's voice was urgent. Clearly he did not like the sound of her plan. It had to seem pretty crazy from where he was sitting in Lower Manhattan. But this was her children they were talking about. If there was danger, then it was danger for them, not just for her.

'Richard, look. I think it would be better for you to hold off for a while.'

'What?'

'It's just that with all this . . . I think it would be better for you to stay put at least until I can find out what's going on. Don't worry. This guy – he's called Graham Willis – he said it would take a few days for them to get everything sorted out. As soon as I know what's what I'll give you a call.'

'For Christ's sake, Holly.'

'I'll call you anyway. I'll call you tomorrow at the same time. OK?'

The sound of thunder awoke her with a start. On the far wall a shadow was moving. She sat up, watching, listening. The wind had picked up. She could hear it whistling over the roof, shaking the trees. From outside came a dull wooden thud – a beach chair blowing over, a shutter breaking loose. There was going to be a storm. She thought about the rain, about a narrow track through the jungle, jeeps sunk up to their axles in mud. The jungle had been in her dreams. She had seen her children running barefoot along the forest floor, patches of amber light flashing across their pale skin. What had they been running from? She sighed and let herself sink back into the bed. Beside her the green luminous hands of the clock read half-past three.

Then the thunder came again, except that it wasn't thunder. It sounded like someone pounding on the perspex doors that led to the veranda. Against the wall, the moon threw the shadow of a man's head, his arm raised.

'Holly?'

She wasn't sure she'd really heard it. The sound was swallowed up by the noise of the wind. She rolled over and hit the light switch. The sudden brilliance hurt her eyes.

'Who is it?'

There was no answer. She drew back the covers and walked slowly towards the veranda. She felt unsteady, as if still in the dream.

'Holly?'

She knew she had really heard it this time. She ran to the window and pulled back the curtains.

'Richard?'

He was standing right outside, one hand pressed against the glass, his eyes screwed up against the light. It was Willis. She stood for a moment staring at him, trying to make sense of what she was seeing.

'Open up!'

Willis pointed down at the door handle. Holly hesitated, then pulled it open. The wind flapped against the hem of her nightdress. Suddenly she felt exposed.

Willis stepped inside and slid the door shut behind him.

'Sorry about the intrusion, but I didn't want to walk in the front.'

His voice was breathless, urgent.

'What do you mean? What's going on?'

Willis looked her up and down. Instinctively she folded her arms.

'I mean, if you want to get up over the mountains

without everyone knowing about it, this may be your last chance. Telee wants to go now.'

'Now? But you said – '

'I know, I know. But they're tightening up all the checkpoints and Telee's scared. He wants to get moving while the going's good.'

'Can't it wait until morning?'

Willis closed the curtains behind him.

'Listen. If you just check out of this hotel tomorrow morning every soldier from here to Jambi'll probably be looking out for you. You'll just get turned back like the last time, and Telee could get into trouble. If we go now no one will know who's helping who, OK? Just hurry and get dressed.'

'But the hotel. Won't they – ?'

'They'll charge your credit card, don't worry.'

Holly sat down on the bed and reached for the phone.

'I said I'd call my . . . my husband, and – '

Willis took a step towards her.

'Tell him what we're doing on that phone and the deal's off. Remember what I told you about this place.'

Holly looked at the receiver and slowly replaced it.

A few hundred yards from the hotel a pair of headlamps flashed from the shadows of the palms. It was Telee, waiting behind the wheel of a battered Toyota pick-up. Holly was surprised to discover that he was young, no more than twenty-five and dressed in jeans and a camouflage vest. The way Willis had talked about him she had expected somebody older, a tribal elder or something. He looked her over without smiling. Holly climbed in the back.

They passed an old black and white sign that read TABING. Up ahead Holly could see a few points of light, a small town or a village. Telee was driving fast, the occasional gust of wind pushing against the side of the truck. He swerved, the rear wheels scattering gravel.

'Take it easy, mate,' said Willis under his breath.

The points of light were drawing closer. Above the trees to their right the stars were hidden by a faint yellow glow. Telee began to slow down. Willis leaned over the back of his seat.

'We're stopping here for a second. Stay in the truck, OK?'

A hundred yards away in the beam of the headlamps Holly caught sight of a wooden pillbox, and outside it a couple of men in uniform. One of them held up his hand and took a few paces towards them. He had a rifle slung over his shoulder. Telee drove the truck to the side of the road and thrust out a hand towards Holly.

'I'll take care of it,' Willis said. 'We can settle up with Mrs Becker later.'

5

Riau Province, Sumatra. August 10th

The pale brown type was almost invisible beneath a confusion of contour lines. Squinting at the old logging map one night, Dr Peter Jarvis had noticed that there were letters strung out along the escarpment about six inches from the red line representing the Pekanbaru road. Drawing the map closer to the single flickering bulb he had discovered that the letters formed one word: CAVES.

Two days later he was still edging his way towards the escarpment along tracks that had not been used for twenty years. But for the map, no one would have known that the tracks were there at all, except perhaps a few forest Indians. His guides, Agga and Rulek, were deft with their parangs, but there was no hope of taking a Land Rover all the way up there until the Forestry Department agreed to clear the way with some heavy machinery. Jarvis didn't want to think about all the patience and diplomacy that would involve – if it ever came to that.

'OK, let's give it a rest for a minute, shall we?' he said, ducking a huge flying beetle as it came humming towards him from out of the shadows. 'No sense in killing ourselves.'

Rulek lit a pair of cigarettes and handed one to Agga, who took a drag and then dabbed the end against a leech that was clinging to the underside of his arm.

'How much further to the escarpment?' asked Jarvis.

Agga squinted at him: 'Uh?'

'To the rocks? How far to the rocks?'

Rulek nodded, pointed over to the west.

'There,' he said, making a loop in the air with his finger. 'We go round there. Soon, soon.'

Jarvis nodded positively. *Soon.* Nearly two months on Sumatra and he hadn't yet found a single person who knew the meaning of that word. He would not have minded all that much – after a few years in Africa he was used to it – but for the fact that he had to get back to London in less than a week. The Research Fund Committee at the Natural History Museum was due to make its provisional allocations on August 18th. His project had its supporters on the committee, but without a proper presentation and all the details it wasn't likely to get the cash it needed.

Jarvis drained his aluminium water bottle and tucked it back inside his rucksack. Water was the key to it. The terrain in the area was perfect, a mixture of primary and partially degraded rain forest. It was an ideal place to study the long-term effects of forestry and the rate at which the forest recovered after logging. And there was a bonus: the band of limestone strata that ran all along the upper slopes. Many of the broad-leafed trees which populated the rest of the forest would not grow there, making way for a different set of species. These in turn provided habitats for entirely different populations of insects and animals. A permanent field station here would offer two ecosystems for the price of one. But there could only be a field station where there was a source of fresh water. There were supposed to be springs near the old logging camps, but these had proved either contaminated or impossible to find. The caves were his best hope.

Jarvis checked his watch. The humidity had gummed up the mechanism somehow and it had stopped again. He reckoned it was about two o'clock. In a little over an hour they would have to turn back – another precious day wasted and nothing to show for it. He hoped for once that soon really did mean soon.

Rulek was fiddling in the packet for his second cigarette.

'All right,' said Jarvis, moving ahead. 'Let's get on with it.'

He pushed his way past a giant fern, his baseball boot crunching against the dead wood of a fallen branch.

'Keep an eye on the time,' he said, looking back over his shoulder. 'We don't want to have – '

He was interrupted by a loud noise almost directly overhead, a call. It sounded like a monkey. The call was answered from further off: whoops and shrieks like the sound of a Victorian madhouse. They were baboons. Jarvis knew the sounds they made. The plantation workers nearer the coast trained the animals to gather coconuts, keeping them on chains as long as the trees were tall. He looked up into the canopy. He could hear the branches shake, hear the shiver of the leaves, but he could see nothing. He felt an instinctive stab of fear.

'Interesting,' he said out loud, moving on. 'Monkeys have to drink, don't they?'

Agga was aiming an imaginary rifle at the treetops, following the sound.

'Pow! Pow, pow!' he said, pulling the trigger and grinning. 'All dead. All dead.'

The entrance to the cave was difficult to spot beneath the tangle of tree roots, but Jarvis had an idea where to look. From the other side of the ravine he could see that there was water. Most of the escarpment was bare rock, clumps of grass and bushes clinging to the crags. But at one point the vegetation seemed to cover everything, brimming over, its tendrils hanging down over the harsh limestone surfaces. It was a sign he had come to recognise. The big colony of primates in the area was another. Even as they crossed over he could hear them barking and

141

chattering. The threats – or were they warnings? – seemed to get louder and more urgent as they drew closer to the rocks.

The cave mouth was tall but narrow and there was a drop on the other side of about five feet. As he lowered himself down, the other end of his rope tied around the trunk of a huge mahogany, Jarvis shone the torch around beneath him, searching for a good foothold, trying to establish the extent of the space around him. Above him Agga and Rulek stood peering down into the darkness, whispering to each other as if afraid that someone inside the cave might overhear them. Jarvis had asked if either of them wanted to follow him in. Both had said no.

His boots hit the ground with a crunch. The floor of the cave was covered in splinters of rock, flecked with animal droppings. The sound hummed around him, the walls closed in on either side. Jarvis turned around carefully, pulling his khaki sun hat tight around his head. The sky above cast a pale light upon a hard diagonal of limestone, which stood directly in his path. He had to stoop to shine the torch past it.

'OK, Dr Jarvis?'

It was Rulek, his head poking down into the darkness.

'So far so good,' said Jarvis. 'Just wish I had a proper hat.'

'You proper hot?'

The torch beam disappeared into a black void a couple of feet from the cave floor.

'Just wait there,' Jarvis called back. 'I'm going to take a look down here.'

He crouched down and peered through the gap. The torch beam seemed stronger now that his eyes were getting accustomed to the dark. He caught a glimpse of another pale wall of rock about twenty feet away.

'There may be another chamber here,' he said.

'What do you say, Dr Jarvis?' Rulek sounded a long way off already.

'Never mind.'

Jarvis lowered himself onto all fours and crawled into the gap. The air coming from the chamber was cool, but tainted with an acrid smell like ammonia. And there was – he snapped the torch off for a moment – light, so dim as to be almost indiscernible. But it was there. It had to be coming from another cave entrance nearby, perhaps somewhere above him. He switched the torch back on and edged forward. The rock beneath him felt cold and hard against his bones.

He seemed to crawl for several minutes, the walls on either side twisting first left then right, closing in on him, sometimes catching a hip or a shoulder. He did not dare to try and stand up in case he banged his head. Every few yards he stopped and listened, hoping to hear the trickle or the drip of water, but everything was silent. Looking back down along the length of his body he could no longer see the light of the cave entrance, or hear Rulek's voice. In fact, he could see nothing at all.

He gripped his rope and gave it a tug, just to reassure himself that it was still secure.

'Still with me back there?'

They were too far away to hear him. He felt his breath quicken, drawing more deeply on the tainted, tomb-like air.

'Come on, come on,' he muttered. 'Get on with it.'

Without the rope what he was doing would have been idiotic, he knew that. People had got themselves disorientated in caves no bigger than a dining room and never been able to find their way out again, even when their torches didn't die on them. Once you lost the light of the entrance you were in serious trouble. If only he had spotted the caves a few weeks earlier he could have organised a proper team. If only there had been time.

And then suddenly the narrow passageway opened out. He knew it not from the sight but from the sound. His every move, the scrape of his boot, even his breathing echoed gently far above him. As he listened he became aware of something else, not so much a sound as a kind of gentle pressure on his eardrum. Rolling onto his back he pointed the torch beam directly above him.

'Shit.'

It was just as he feared: the roof of the cavern, some forty feet above, was alive with bats, black shadows circling and circling, their sonar shrieks too high-pitched for human hearing. They had their own entrance to the cavern, that was for sure, and their droppings meant that any water there would most likely be contaminated. Where there were bats the water was always unsafe.

Jarvis groaned. He would have to find another cave further along. There was still time for that, and the very fact that there *were* caves meant that there had to be a usable source of water somewhere. Maybe that would be enough for the Research Fund Committee. Maybe the *exact* location of the source could wait. A decent hydronomist could probably find one in half an hour. He looked up at the bats again. They were big, wingspan nearly a foot across he reckoned, maybe more. He tried not to be afraid, to think what species they could be.

'Too small for fruit bats.'

One of them swooped down low, close enough to make him cover his face. He could hear its wings flutter past. Then the fluttering grew louder. Were they drawn to the light?

Suddenly he wanted more than anything else to get out, to get out of the darkness. He didn't belong in this place. He tried to turn but there was no room. The rocks pushed in on both sides. He heaved himself forward into the chamber, just looking for enough space to turn himself around. But the ground beneath him was suddenly gone. The torch fell from his hand as he scrambled for something to hold on to.

'Jesus!'

The torch landed with a clatter and a splash. His fingers scrambled against the serrated rock edge, tearing his nails. He peered over the ledge and saw the torch lying no more than four or five feet below him in a shallow pool of water. It was still working, the beam lighting up a cloud of tiny insects that hovered over the surface. The thought of feeling his way back to the surface without it was unbearable. Keeping a firm grip on the rope he climbed down towards the water, afraid that any second he would be plunged into darkness. He tried to feel his way among the rocks but they were sharper here, crystalline, like knives. He felt them stabbing against his knees, his arms, his hands, but he didn't care. All he wanted was the light.

As he gripped the handle of the torch and carefully lifted it up, he hardly noticed the swirls of blood he left behind, mingling with the clear water.

6

Carmen Travis stopped on her way out of the bathroom and listened. She could hear the clock ticking in
the hall downstairs and Tom's regular breathing coming
from the other side of the bedroom door. Eight o'clock
on a Sunday morning and everyone was still asleep, lying
in as usual. She yawned and tiptoed down the passage into
the spare room where she had laid out her uniform the
night before. She would be gone by the time they woke
up, halfway to Frederick or maybe further – maybe deep
inside Fort Detrick itself, working inside a space suit
beneath the cold white lights of a BL–4 containment
suite.

She got dressed and went down into the kitchen.
Today was meant to be the big fishing expedition, and
she was going to miss it. Tom had got everything ready,
right down to the bait, the junior fishing rods and the toy
sailboat for when the boys got bored. And he had taken
care to find a good shallow spot so that there was no
danger of Joey falling in. She had been afraid she might
not be able to make it, but it was not until General Bailey
called with the news that Carl Reiner was dying that she
knew. Tom had been understanding; 'Orders are orders,
I guess,' was what he'd said. And she was glad, because
she hadn't wanted to explain all about the emergency and
what she was going into the Institute to do. It had kept her

146

awake most of the night, and that was enough worrying for both of them.

She turned the radio on low and went to the fridge for the remains of Saturday's chicken and the big slab of Emmenthal. Even if she couldn't make the fishing expedition itself, she could still make the sandwiches. She put four slices of bread in the toaster – that was the way the kids liked them – and got busy picking at the carcass with the kitchen knife and a fork. The meat was a little stringy, and clung to the bone. She had to pull most of it off with her fingers.

'Mom, can I – ?'

Carmen jumped.

'Oh!'

Joey was standing in the doorway, his little frame lost inside his oversized pyjamas.

'You startled me, sweetheart.'

'Can I have some juice?'

Carmen took a tumbler from the cupboard.

'Help yourself. And don't spill.'

Joey shuffled forward, pulled open the fridge door and took hold of the big two-litre carton of orange juice with both hands. Carmen watched as he carefully poured out half a glass-full, breathing noisily through his open mouth.

'Well done,' she said and went back to the sandwiches. Joey drank in silence. In the background the radio was playing an old soul number Carmen remembered from her teens.

'Why aren't you coming fishing, Mom?'

Carmen put the knife down. So he'd heard. Or had he just worked it out somehow, the way kids did sometimes without having to be told?

'Sweetheart, you know I want to. It's just my job. I've got to . . .'

'What?'

'To work.'

'But *why*?'

Carmen thought for a moment. She felt terrible letting him down. It was only a day's fishing, but to kids it was the kind of thing that could take on real importance. She knew that.

'There's a problem, Joey,' she said. 'Something unexpected. And I've got to help sort it out right away. I'll be back this evening. And when you get back from the fishing trip you can tell me all about it, OK? And in a couple of weeks we – '

'*What* problem?'

'Just . . .'

Carmen hesitated. Joey deserved an explanation, a good one, not just any old thing, and yet there was no way she *could* explain. She squatted down opposite him.

'Some people, Joey . . . Some people are getting sick, you see? And we don't know how to make them better. So we have to try and find a way to help them, before . . . before more people get sick as well. Do you see?'

Joey nodded slowly, thinking about it. Carmen ran her fingers through his hair. He was growing up so fast. Then he looked at her and said: 'Will you get sick too, Mom?'

Carmen laughed, more from shock than from the need to reassure him.

'Well of course not, sweetheart. Of course not.' She wrapped him up in a big hug. 'It's not like that at all.'

Reiner had been certified dead at two o'clock that morning. His body had been triple-bagged by a RIID team and driven in an unmarked ambulance to the Institute. By half-past three it lay in a freezer at minus 70 degrees centigrade. Carmen found a copy of the hospital report on her desk. There was also a voicemail message from General Bailey, instructing her to perform an autopsy immediately. She called his office, but Bailey had gone out early on some other business. She was about to pick up the phone again when it rang.

'Colonel Travis?'

Carmen recognised the voice, but couldn't place it.

'Speaking.'

'This is George Arends. I'm helping you out this morning. General Bailey's orders.'

Lieutenant-Colonel George Arends, head of the veterinary medicine division. Carmen knew him now.

'Helping me out?'

'With the autopsy. I'm going down to the staging area in half an hour with Major McKinnon. We'll wait for you there.'

'Is the body – ?'

'It's coming out of the freezer now. Have you had a chance to look over the hospital report?'

'I just got it.'

'Well you might like to take a look. It'll make it easier when we start cutting.'

Arends was a pathologist like Carmen, one of the oldest and most experienced in the Institute. In fact he had been in the pathology division up until a year after her own arrival as a resident, but the fact that he had been assigned to the autopsy unsettled her. True, it wasn't every day they cut up a corpse infected with a BL-4 pathogen. It was risky. But there were plenty of good people in her team, not just Major McKinnon. They did not need to call on another division for their third man. What did Bailey mean by it? Did he think she needed an old hand to back her up? And what did Arends mean by *easier*?

'I'll be down in thirty minutes, Colonel,' she said and hung up.

She went out into the corridor and got herself a black coffee, then sat down at her desk. The report was short

149

and brutal. It gave the date for Carl Reiner's admission, and registered the developing symptoms from onset of extreme amplification of the virus to the very end. Carmen sipped at her coffee, her eyes following the lines of text, frowning at the burgeoning disaster they described.

Almost immediately after Reiner's admission his lungs began to accumulate a watery mucus and he developed acute respiratory distress syndrome. At the same time he developed the petechial and maculopapular rashes that characterise infection with filoviruses. For a couple of days he complained of acute headaches and then lapsed into a semi-comatose state. He bled from the puncture sites of hypodermic injections administered by hospital staff. Two days before his body finally gave out, his pupils dilated and remained fixed, indicating brain death. At least he wasn't around to suffer the final horrors, thought Carmen. During the agonal state subcutaneous pockets of blood had developed, a condition referred to in the report as third spacing; third spacing as opposed to first where the patient bled into the lungs, and second where there was bleeding into the stomach and intestine. What was left of Carl Reiner on the ninth day of his illness was bleeding into the space between the skin and the subcutaneous flesh. The report said there were places where the skin appeared to be separated from the underlying flesh. Carmen drained the dregs of her coffee, starting to understand why Arends had wanted her to read the report: better to be prepared. Carl Reiner's body was not going to be a pleasant sight.

As she rode the elevator down to four levels below surface, she couldn't suppress a growing anxiety. In all the years she had been working with BL–4 pathogens she had never been that close to the victims, and she had never had to dissect one; Arends, she knew, had. He had been a member of the first RIID team into Zaire after the Ebola emergency, for one. All the same, the idea that she wouldn't know how to handle herself, that she might come unstuck somehow, was unfair. Her record was second to none. She felt she had done enough to earn Bailey's trust.

The elevator door opened noiselessly, interrupting her thoughts. She went quickly down into the featureless white corridor to the locker room and undressed, showering for the second time in two hours, this time with a harsh carbolic soap instead of the blue lavender-perfumed gel which Oliver had given her for her birthday. As regulations demanded, she put away the clothes she had arrived in and went to a sterile cabinet where a long-sleeved scrub suit, a surgical cap and a pair of white socks were waiting for her, all of them bathed in strong ultraviolet light. The socks were several sizes too big – men's socks in fact – and as she walked slowly towards the door, taking care not to slip on the polished linoleum, she could not help thinking of Joey shuffling across her kitchen floor in his oversized pyjamas. She wondered what he was doing right then: squabbling with Oliver in the back of the station wagon, probably – or were they all still having breakfast, listening to their dad explain about how to outsmart a fish? It seemed like a different world, a warmer, more welcoming one. And yet it was only a few short miles away from the quarantine facility at Marshallton, from the virus that had erupted inside the body of Carl Reiner. Just a breeze away, in fact, and part of the same world, the only world there was.

The security sensor by the entrance to the grey zone read her card and checked her for clearance. After a moment the red light at the top of the panel turned green. The locks retracted and the door slid open with a hiss. Once it had closed behind her, another identical door, twelve feet further ahead, slid open. Containment Suite 7 lay on the other side, a negative-pressure BL–3 staging area just two doors away from the hot zone itself. Arends and McKinnon were there waiting, dressed as she was in the green cotton scrub suits. There was a continuous hiss from the air extractors.

The two men stood up. Major McKinnon was Carmen's number two; blond, thirty-two years old and a little overweight. Arends was in his mid-forties, a lean man, taller than average, with thinning black hair and a deeply lined face. Carmen didn't know much about him. People said he was the quiet type, kept himself to himself.

They did not salute or shake hands. There was a tacit understanding that once you passed through an airlock at the RIID you left military formalities behind. Shaking hands was simply a violation of safety procedures. All physical contact between staff was prohibited except in emergencies.

'I hope I haven't kept you waiting, Colonel,' Carmen said.

Arends smiled. For the first time she saw that he must have been handsome when he was younger.

'No problem. In fact I was glad of a chance to . . . go through a few things with Major McKinnon.'

McKinnon was flushed and sweating. Carmen could see a patch of dampness on his forehead. Had he been reading the report? She tried to seem relaxed.

'It's good of you to come and help out, Colonel,' she said. 'I understand you've had a lot of experience in this area.'

'Not recently, I'm happy to say. But I've had my share.'

'Has General Bailey given you all the facts, sir? He told you what we're dealing with?'

'In outline. I read the hospital report, of course.'

Carmen opened a drawer and took out three sealed packets of surgical rubber gloves.

'It's a filovirus, for certain,' she went on. 'Possibly a new strain of Ebola.'

'But for the respiratory inflammation. That's an unusual symptom for Ebola.'

152

'At such an early stage, yes.'

'And aerosol transmission, not just transmission through fluids. That's suspected too, as I understand it.'

'Suspected.'

Arends nodded slowly.

'I can see why it's got you all so worried.'

Carmen handed Arends one of the packets.

'We're not worried, Colonel,' she said, glancing at McKinnon. 'Not yet. We're just covering our bases. In case.'

Arends took the packet.

'I'd be worried,' he said. 'I already am, down here.'

'We're fully versed in the procedures, Colonel,' said Carmen, struggling to put on the gloves. 'All my team have had practice at working within them. We've never had a single case of – '

'That's very reassuring,' Arends broke in. 'It's just that in the theatre, with a recent victim. It's not the same as . . . Let's just say it's the kind of thing you *can't* practise. There are emotional responses to deal with.'

Carmen tried to smile.

'Of course, Colonel. And we're glad to have an old hand with us. Shall we get going?'

They sealed the inner surgical gloves to the sleeves of their scrub suits with adhesive tape and collected their space suits from another ultraviolet-lit cabinet. The suits were Chemturions made of bright blue plastic with a soft plastic helmet and a clear, hard faceplate. At the base of the helmet was a valve into which an external air supply could be connected. Attached at the wrists of the suit with a gasket were another pair of rubber gloves, heavier ones this time. Carmen stepped into her suit, pushed her arms through the sleeves and pulled the helmet over her head. Suddenly the sound of the staging area, the air extractors and the hard, echoing walls was lost. All she could hear

153

was her own breathing. Carefully, so as not to let it snag, she zipped up first the inner steel zipper and then the outer, nylon one.

She looked up at the others. They were standing opposite, their hands by their sides, their faceplates already steaming up, especially McKinnon's. She realised that her own helmet was misting up too. The whole room looked like it was disappearing beneath a thick white fog. Arends gave her a thumbs-up and gestured towards the grey zone leading to the BL–4 suite.

They walked in single file through the first door, which was blazoned with a brilliant red trefoil, the international biohazard symbol. The walls of the airlock were tiled, like a public swimming baths or an abattoir. There were drains running all along the floor and a trough of Envirochem disinfectant on one side, big enough to stand in. Once Carmen and the others had gone, a chemical shower would sterilise the space through which they had passed, ensuring that no organisms flowed back from the hot zone into the staging area. The same procedure would be repeated once they returned, this time with the team inside their suits. As she reached for the button that opened the second door, an image formed in Carmen's mind. It was Oliver and Joey, casting their lines onto a stretch of sunlit water. She could hear them laughing, and Tom's calm, cheerful voice.

The hot zone wasn't much different to any other part of the Institute except for the yellow air hoses that hung down from the ceiling. There were enough of them so that you could go anywhere in the room and have your own air supply, although you had to take care when working in a team not to get the hoses tangled. Carmen walked over to the steel cabinets to the right of the door and connected one of them to her helmet. The air entered the suit in a roaring rush that made it hard to hear, but it cleared her faceplate in a few seconds. As the mist evaporated, hard ceramic and steel forms came into view: the glazed white walls, the steel sinks, the necropsy table with its three high-resolution TV cameras suspended above it.

The cabinets contained pairs of smooth rubber boots, more pairs of surgical gloves and boxes of necropsy tools and specimen containers. Unlike in a conventional theatre the containers were all plastic. Glass was too dangerous, because if it broke, the glass slivers were sharp enough to puncture protective clothing, as well as the skin of the person wearing it. Five or ten virus particles suspended in a microscopic droplet of blood or lymph was enough for a fatal infection, and a droplet like that could slip through a hole the size of a pinprick. If anyone received a cut inside the hot zone they were immediately consigned to a special isolation hospital at the RIID known as the Slammer. The regime in the Slammer was as rigid as in the hot zone itself, and you stayed there, visited only by doctors and nurses in space suits, until it was proven beyond doubt that you were clean, or until the time came to carry you out in a triple body bag.

Just such a bag was lying on the necropsy table at the far end of the room, the human form within barely discernible beneath the layers of thick plastic. Carmen pulled on her yellow rubber boots over the soft feet of her space suit, and then put on latex rubber gloves. Maybe it was the air flowing into her suit, but her mouth felt dry. She lifted up her triple-gloved hands and flexed them gently. You could not tell from the outside that they were trembling.

'OK?'

Arends was shouting, but his voice sounded muffled and far away. Carmen took a moment to register it. She gave him a nod. They walked one by one to the necropsy table and took up their positions: Arends on one side, Carmen and McKinnon on the other. At three corners of the table were plastic trays half full of Clorox bleach,

155

placed there to rinse the blood off their gloves. Above them the small red lights on the side of the TV cameras indicated that they were on and recording. Carmen put the box of necropsy tools down on a trolley and set out the gleaming steel instruments side by side. When she was done Arends reached up to the top of the bag and slowly pulled down the zipper. The thick grey plastic parted to reveal more plastic, creamy white this time, like a shroud. Now Carmen could make out the line of the body – the breadth of the shoulders, the hips, the curve of the jaw. But it still did not seem like a person. It seemed almost too solid, too heavy, like something carved out of stone, like a monument.

The innermost bag was black, with a fine nylon zipper running around three sides. Arends seemed to hesitate, his gaze fixed on the shiny surface of the plastic beneath which the contours of Reiner's face were partly visible. Carmen wondered why he did not unzip the bag. Out of the corner of her eye she saw McKinnon edge away from the side of the table.

'Colonel?'

Arends looked up at her and nodded. He turned to the tray on his right and dipped both his gloves in Clorox. Then he turned back to the zipper, drawing it all around before carefully pulling back the plastic flap.

Carmen heard McKinnon curse as the upper torso came into view, and felt her heart start to race. At autopsy the bodies were usually naked, but Reiner had been bagged still wearing the hospital smock in which he had died. It clung to his bloated chest, stained purple by a huge bloom of congealed blood. The jagged, blackish wounds where the skin had torn were clearly visible below the armpits and around the elbows. But it was the face that held Carmen's attention: the open eyes, crimson slits without pupils or whites, and the mouth, frozen into a crooked bloody-toothed smile – or was it a sneer? She knew that it was just the effect of the virus, lesions in the brain leading to involuntary muscular contractions. Reiner – Reiner the person – had been long gone at the death of his body; no sneering would have been possible. Yet she could not help feeling that the corpse was mocking her, mocking them all, their powerlessness to help him, or themselves. She continued to stare, trapped breath roaring in her hood. It was as if his face was a hole and she was falling into it. There was something . . . There was a puffiness about his face. The flesh seemed to be drawn tight against the sharp bridge of his nose, drawn down as if the earth wanted him, as if gravity wanted him and could not wait for him to be buried. Then she remembered. It was the collagen. The virus had attacked the connective tissue under the skin. Like Ebola Zaire this virus had a particular liking for collagen protein; Ebola's furious replication turned collagen to a pulpy mess, and this virus did the same. Brain death and death of the connective tissue that enabled expression. Carmen stared and stared. The annihilation was so complete. She had to force herself to look away. She picked up a scalpel. She wanted to get it over and done with. She wanted to take her samples and get out of there.

It took a while to cut the smock away. Six hours in the freezer had hardened the bloodstain into a crust, yet it was important to discover exactly where the lesions were. Arends watched Carmen intently as she worked, only stepping in to help when she signalled for him to do so. Twice he held up his hand to prevent McKinnon from helping roll the material away before he was asked. Carmen knew why: it was her small pointed blade. Already stained with infected blood it was now the most lethal object in the room. It only took one slip, one accidental jab. Incredibly, the history of viral haemorrhagic fevers was littered with accidental needle sticks and scalpel cuts. She knew she had to concentrate, be slow, absolutely methodical, but knowing why – *seeing* why, seeing it lying there in front of her – made it harder.

'OK there, Carmen?'

She looked up, surprised to hear her first name. Arends's face was obscured by a reflection on his faceplate. She couldn't see his expression.

'Yes, fine,' she shouted.

He nodded and pointed towards the nearest tray of Clorox. She looked at her gloves. There were smears of dark blood where her fingers had come into contact with Reiner's body. She put down the scalpel and rinsed both hands. McKinnon immediately did the same. When she picked up the scalpel again Arends was removing the last fold of the smock from the upper torso. The blood beneath was a brighter red, the lesions concentrated around the nipples. The surrounding skin was disfigured by a maculopapular rash, the surface puckered into granules like tapioca pudding. It barely looked human.

Carmen glanced up at the cameras, taking a breath as though about to dive. They were sucking up every detail, making it unnecessary for anyone to record the findings verbally. All of that would be done later in front of the monitors. It was an arrangement designed to minimise the amount of time spent in the hot zone. Arends stood back, his arms at his sides. It meant they were ready for the main abdominal incisions, after which the internal organs would be removed.

Making clean incisions was tricky. There were blood blisters everywhere, especially around the intestinal area, and they ruptured as the blade went through them. In places the skin had come clean away from the subcutaneous tissue. Reiner was a dead bag of blood. Not even of blood. His blood had been devastated by the virus so that it was no longer red cells and serum, but a mess of histo-junk, a purée of virus and cell-wrecks.

Getting through the muscle was relatively easy – Reiner

had been a thin man even before he fell sick – and once that was done the scalpel was disinfected and set aside. Arends opened up the chest cavity with the rib cutters and from then on they worked wherever possible with surgical scissors, the ends of which were rounded to reduce the danger of an accidental cut. Carmen took samples of tissue from the liver and spleen, both of which were enlarged, and placed them on glass slides, the only glass objects allowed in the hot zone. Her work was hampered by the sheer volume of blood inside the body cavity. The intestines themselves were full of it. Carmen found lesions at the base of the stomach and took a third set of samples from there. She left the lungs until last, partly because it was clear that they were largely filled with blood and would need to be drained. It was just as she had expected. *Macaca nemestrina* O14 had been the same, according to the report from Marshallton. Before reaching for a new scalpel Carmen indicated for the cameras the dark discoloration caused by the haemorrhage. So far it was the one unique aspect of the way this filovirus worked: it attacked the lungs of its victims first, whether monkeys or men. The coughing that resulted looked like part of the virus's strategy for self-propagation.

What happened next was deeply disturbing. Suddenly Carmen could take no more. Afterwards she remembered the moment like a convulsion, but a convulsion that happened inside, as though her soul or psyche had convulsed. It was too much. Too much ruin and death. Something deep in her seemed to reject it, and no matter how she clung to her training and experience, and her will to succeed, there seemed to be nothing she could do. She was incapacitated, and the loss of control was almost worse than her sense of revulsion. She put down her scissors and placed her blood-smeared gloves hands into the pan of Clorox, hoping to win a few seconds' respite. She tried to control her breathing, sucking at the dead air in her suit in whooping gasps. She was going to pass out; she was going to fall. The thought that she *might* fall, might just keel over in the BL–4 suite terrified her. She looked up at Arends. He and McKinnon had stopped working. Arends was saying something to her but she couldn't hear. She pinched her hose, to slow the rush of air into her suit.

'. . . left to do,' she heard him say. 'I'll finish up here, Carmen.'

She looked from Arends to McKinnon. McKinnon was nodding. She rinsed her hands thoroughly in the Clorox, unclipped her airline and walked away from the abyss that had suddenly opened in Carl Reiner's entrails.

With a hiss the hot water showers came on, filling the grey zone with steam. Carmen kept her eyes closed the whole time, and tried to focus on Joey and Oliver and Tom, forcing herself to imagine what they were doing at that very moment, what the sun was like on the water. But the picture kept breaking up, as if the suit wouldn't let her mind out, as if even her imagination was trapped inside. The shower shut off abruptly. The steam slowly cleared and was replaced by a disinfectant mist. Carmen stood in the trough of Envirochem and carefully scrubbed her plastic boots with a brush, saying their names now, saying Tom's name over and over again. Finally another water shower came on, rinsing away the disinfectant from their suits and from the walls. From start to finish the decon cycle had taken five minutes.

Inside the staging area Carmen unzipped her space suit and stepped out of it. And it was like stepping out of her fear, as if she were shrugging off death, death's dirty pelt. Her head buzzed and the floor seemed to drop away beneath her, as if an elevator had fallen between two floors.

She came to with Arends looking into her face.

'Carmen?'

He tapped her cheeks, bringing her round. For a moment she didn't know where she was. She looked around at the walls of the staging area.

'What . . . ?' Then realisation flooded in. She had fainted. She gripped Arends by the sleeve. He lifted her up from where she was slumped against the wall, and helped her to a stool.

'It's only the fear,' he said. Still she clutched at his sleeve, looking at him, appalled by what had happened, above all by her failure to cope. He stared back with a grave expression that nevertheless seemed to hide a smile in it somewhere, a warmth.

'Jesus,' said Carmen.

And Arends's smile seemed to show through a little more. Carmen felt herself relaxing.

'That's right,' he said. 'Just give it a minute. It's only the fear.'

7

Major-General Bailey had the air conditioning on max so it was actually cold inside his office.

'I appreciate your coming down on such short notice, Colonel. I know how busy you are.'

Carmen nodded deferentially, though she was a little thrown by Bailey's warmth. First Arends and now Bailey. Everybody being nice to her, like she was an invalid. She prayed that neither Arends nor McKinnon had said anything about her walking away from the autopsy. Of course it was all on the television monitors anyway. But she wasn't sure how much of what had happened was visible. Bailey looked tired. Like he had been up all night.

'I heard about the autopsy,' he said, and Carmen tensed up. *Heard what?* 'Sounded like the body was a real mess. I really appreciate your work on that.'

He didn't know.

'Just doing my job, sir.'

Bailey smiled some more, keeping his serious brown eyes on her all the time. Carmen waited. Now that he had her there it looked as though he didn't quite know what to say. Finally, after a lot of fidgeting around, he put together a few preliminary remarks.

'Now Colonel, I wanted first of all to thank you for the way you've handled this Marshallton business. I was very sorry to hear about Carl Reiner, and I understand that a gentleman . . . Bert Levy is it? It looks as though he might be developing the same . . . uh, the same problem.'

'That's right, sir.'

'The reason I wanted to talk to you this afternoon . . . well, I actually want you to talk – '

The phone rang, making Bailey jump. He stabbed on the conference button so that Carmen could hear who was on the other end of the line. It sounded like his secretary, Linda.

'I have the Pentagon on the line, sir.'

'Put him on.'

There was a click and then they were both listening to a very slow version of 'Greensleeves' on some kind of electronic glockenspiel. Bailey smiled sheepishly.

'He's put me on hold.'

He who? thought Carmen. There was an embarrassing pause, with Bailey hunched over his desk listening to 'Greensleeves' as though it were some kind of coded message, and Carmen looking hard at her flat shoes, trying to work out what was going on.

The music continued. Bailey looked up and tried a nervous smile.

'As the senior officer with hands-on knowledge of the operation, I wanted you – hello?'

A smooth voice filled the intercom.

'Robert?'

The bone seemed to go in Bailey's neck and his head was flopping around in a kind of super-friendly relaxed manner.

'Hello there, General. Good to hear your voice, sir.'

There was a rumbling, rasping noise on the other end of the line. It sounded as if the General, who-ever he was, was trying to get comfortable in a noisy leather chair. Bailey smiled at Carmen, and pressed on.

'I have Lieutenant-Colonel Carmen Travis here with me, sir. The Colonel has been – '

'Carmen?'

Carmen sat up in her chair. Surprised to find herself on first-name terms with this unnamed person.

'General!'

'Carmen, I don't know if Robert explained to you, but I take an interest in what you guys get up to down there in Maryland – not just from the budgetary point of view, and . . . I've been particularly interested in this Marshallton thing. Bob's been sending through your reports and making all kinds of crazy recommendations. So I thought we should all get together.'

The voice stopped and there was more of the squeaking sounds. Bailey was staring at his blotter. He looked tense now.

'I understand, sir,' said Carmen, drawing a look from Bailey. Something in his expression seemed to be saying *for Christ's sake be nice.*

'So I'll get straight to the point. The way I see it this is all about containment. It's fortunate that this thing has turned up in circumstances that make that a possibility.'

Carmen kept her eyes on Bailey. Why had she been called into a discussion that should have been between him and the General? Where did she fit in?

'I'm not sure I understand, sir.'

There was a silence. Carmen thought she heard a sigh.

'Well, the problem is focused on Marshallton, am I right?'

'As far as we know, sir. There is the possibility of infection through secondary contacts, but we believe we have isolated all the parties at risk.'

'What about the facility itself? I'm talking about the monkey house.'

'Yes, sir. Well we have sealed it shut. There are some RIID people running it now, all of them protected.'

'Well, look Bob, there's somewhere I think we can do something. I want you to nuke the whole facility.'

Bailey sat up straight.

'Lieutenant-Colonel Travis already – '

'But sir, they have air conditioning that makes it virtually impossible for cross-infection to take place. At the most we would have to kill only – '

'I want you to kill all the animals in there, Colonel.'

Bailey pressed his lips together.

'If this thing does get into the press I want the RIID to be seen to have acted promptly and definitively.'

Carmen shifted in her seat. All anybody ever seemed to think about was the press.

'What about the airports, sir?' She sounded recriminatory. Bailey nodded. He seemed to be encouraging her.

There was a silence.

'What do you mean, airports?'

'Well sir, these animals came into the country through the airports. It's too early to be precisely sure about the cycle of this infection, but I think there is a risk that some of the monkeys were infectious while in transit.'

'Where did they come through?'

'The sick monkeys all seem to have come from the same place, somewhere in Sumatra. They came through Jambi airport, then Singapore and then Washington.'

There was another long silence. If the General was sitting in a squeaky chair, he was sitting still now.

'Have you had any reports?'

'Of what, sir?'

'Of outbreaks. Have you had any reports from any of those places?'

'No, sir.'

Well listen, Carmen.' There was the faintest note of sarcasm in the man's voice now. 'It seems to me that if this thing is as contagious as you suggest – I mean if it is actually capable of transfer in aerosol form – I think that by now we would have heard something from our little brown friends in Indonesia.'

He was sounding like a racist hick. Carmen's response was to get cooler, harder.

'It may be, sir, that there has been some kind of incident, but that they don't know what they are dealing with. It may be that the officials want to keep it quiet to protect tourism, to protect trade.'

'Come on, Colonel.'

So she was no longer Carmen; just another soldier.

'It's what happened in Africa, sir.'

'What's that?'

'It's what happened with HIV. For a long time the officials didn't want to admit what was happening because of the impact it would have on the economies of those countries.'

There was a sharp, rasping sound.

'Are you saying they have an epidemic in Indonesia, that they have people bleeding to death in the streets and nobody knows about it?'

Bailey was looking straight at Carmen now.

'No, sir. What I'm – '

'Because I think that would have to be some kind of over-reaction.'

Bailey was shaking his head. Who was he disagreeing with?

'What I'm saying is that this thing, this virus may just have taken a toe-hold,' she said: 'But each day's delay will be disastrous. This thing will not spread like . . . it works exponentially. It will spread like . . . like a plague.'

Carmen heard a cup click into its saucer.

'So what are you saying we should do, Colonel?'

'I'm saying we should notify the World Health Organisation, and we should get a team down to Sumatra to see – '

'That's what I thought.'

'Sir?'

'I was expecting you to come up with something like that. Bob? What do you think about sending a team down there?'

Bailey worked a finger into his collar and tugged.

'I think we need to be advised by the Indonesian government, General. Or at least wait for an invitation from the WHO.'

'But the longer we – '

'You don't seem to understand how things are down there, Colonel. We are talking about the biggest Muslim community in the world. We are talking about two hundred million people all praying to Mecca.'

'I don't see what religion has to do with it, sir.'

'Well Colonel, if we give the Indonesians a reason to tighten their links with the ayatollahs it may have a lot to do with it.'

'But I thought they were a moderate nation, sir. And industrialisation has made them, if anything – '

'Well you don't have to believe everything you read in *Newsweek*. Trust me on this. There are plenty of people who would like to see us fall out with the Indonesians. And I'm not talking just about the towel-heads. Our Japanese friends would also love to see us trip over our big feet out there. And you can take it from me that now is not the time for us to be pointing the finger at the Indonesians because of some little hygiene problem they may be having.'

Some little hygiene problem! Carmen couldn't believe what she was hearing. Bailey also seemed astonished.

'But, sir – '

'So for the time being we're going to wait and see. I want you to continue the surveillance of the infected people, and I want that Marshallton facility nuked.'

The line went dead. Bailey waited for a moment and then put down the phone.

'Well, we gave it our best shot, Colonel,' he said.

Driving home in the dark, unable to stop yawning, it seemed to Carmen that she had been used. For some reason, maybe to do with his past career in the Pentagon, Bailey hadn't felt like putting the interventionist view to the General. When asked directly what he thought they should do he had advised caution and yet his demeanour, the way he had reacted when she was explaining how serious this whole thing was, seemed to point to his agreeing with her entirely. It was hard to fathom. The only possible explanation was that he had wanted the interventionist case to be put but had felt unable to put it himself. Because he knew it was not what the Pentagon wanted to hear?

She pulled off the freeway and onto the road leading to her front door. She wanted to be relaxed and ready to partake of her family, but she could not get Marshallton or Carl Reiner out of her head. And to make matters worse, now, instead of doing something useful, like setting up an investigation into where this thing had come from in the first place, they were going to spend time and taxpayers' dollars on destroying a building full of harmless monkeys.

PART THREE

Muaratebo

1

North of Muaratebo. August 13th

They had been waiting by the side of the road for twelve hours – since first light in fact. Waiting for new instructions. All they knew was that a roadblock had been set up in the night, and all the trucks carrying food and medical supplies had to wait. One of the big transports had driven off the road and dumped supplies out the back. Now soldiers were setting up some kind of canteen as if they were all in for a long stay. Standing by one of the trucks a young man with the flattened features of the indigenous Sumatrans watched a Chinook pass overhead, going north. As it dipped beyond the trees he turned his attention back to the road, and to the group of young soldiers, conscripts by the look of them, who had been policing the traffic. What he saw made him step out of the shade.

'What is it?' asked his driver, who was sitting on the step of the cab smoking a cigarette.

The young man, an officer with responsibility for three of the trucks, kept his eyes on the men.

'The soldiers.' He pointed. 'They're armed. Those are Kalashnikovs.'

'So?'

'They didn't have them before. Half an hour ago all they had was batons.'

'So somebody's been handing out guns. So what?'

'But why do they need assault rifles?'

He stared hard at the armed soldiers, some of them barely seventeen by the looks of them. They looked jumpy as if all they wanted was an excuse to fire off a few rounds, cut down some of the straggly banana trees growing close to the road. The Kalashnikovs were serious weapons, and the young officer had first-hand experience of what the 5.4 mm rounds could do to human flesh. It really was like a war zone. It made him nervous.

'Well as long as they don't point them over here,' said the driver.

The officer climbed into the cab and closed the door. Both men were watching the soldiers through the fly-spattered windscreen now. It was even hotter in the cab and there was a disagreeable, clinical smell from the supplies. The driver scratched at his leg. Black smoke drifting up from the south hung in a pall over the jungle. But he couldn't stay quiet for long.

'Maybe that's what happened to Salim,' he said.

The officer lit a cigarette and pushed the smoke out in a long sigh, reluctant to go over the story again. A Lieutenant Amir Salim and a detail of soldiers from the Bayur barracks had disappeared while on a patrol in the Jambi area, and since then all anyone in Padang could talk about was what might have happened to them. Some said it was natives. Kubu Indians.

'Got caught in the crossfire,' said the driver. He didn't want to let it drop. The officer just smoked his cigarette, squinting out at the black smoke and every now and then checking on the armed soldiers. The only thing he knew for certain was that there were civilian casualties in Muaratebo and he was part of the relief operation.

How these casualties had been produced was hard to say. He had been told the supplies were for a natural disaster, but nothing more specific than that. Looking at the plume of smoke made him think of fire, but it

172

didn't look like the forest was burning, and anyway it was all too wet for that. It looked as if the town itself was burning, but he couldn't think of a natural disaster that would cause the town to burn.

And why the roadblock? The armoured vehicles? The Chinooks? Which enemy were they preparing for? It seemed unlikely that the Kubu could have tooled up sufficiently to warrant that kind of response.

'I'm hungry,' said the driver.

The officer stirred in his seat.

'We'll have to see . . .'

He fell quiet. He was looking at a boy and an older woman; his mother, by the way she was holding him. They came walking out of the trees away to his right. He wouldn't have seen them if he hadn't been looking in that direction. Their torn, smoke-soiled clothes blended in with the earth. As soon as they cleared the trees they came to a halt. They were about fifty yards from the cab. The officer froze, his cigarette posed at his dry lips.

'Have to see what?' asked the driver.

The boy and his mother took another step. The young officer could see they were looking at the mess tent and the sacks of food which had been thrown from the back of the lorry. They were obviously famished. It came to him that they must have made their way through the jungle up from Muaratebo. Refugees. There were no other settlements nearby, and even Muaratebo was twelve kilometres distant. It must have taken them days to come through the densely growing forest. The boy staggered. Immediately his mother reached to support him. They had dirty black hair and their skin looked burnt, blotchy. The woman appeared to be bleeding from the nose.

'Have to see what?'

The officer glanced across at the soldiers on the road. Then he turned the door handle. He was stepping down from the cab when the first shot split the air.

One of the jumpy conscripts on the road had fired off a single round. The officer turned to see smoke twisting from his raised weapon. He was pointing directly at the refugees and shouting. Several soldiers raised their weapons. Others came running back from positions along the road. The officer felt his heart lurch. They were going to shoot the refugees.

The driver said something he didn't hear and then he found himself shouting, walking jerkily towards the refugees, calling out over his shoulder as he went.

'Don't shoot, they've come from Muaratebo. They have come . . . they need help.'

A voice rang out from the road.

'*Stand still!*'

The officer half turned and then froze, his face running with sweat now, the lit cigarette still burning between his fingers. The boy who had fired off the first shot was coming towards him, his assault rifle pointing at his chest. He looked terrified. The officer could see his finger on the trigger. He could see the bitten nail and a piece of abraded skin by the ragged cuticle. Everything was coming through to him with crystal clarity but without making any sense. It made no sense at all. They were here to save these people.

Shouting broke out from the road. The soldiers were gesticulating. Two of them took aim. The officer span round to see the refugees, running now, stumbling over the broken ground back towards the trees, the woman screaming. The burst of fire was short. It cut into them, ripping into their bodies with a hard thwack, punching them forward. The dull earth was splashed red. Suddenly they were bundles of rags. The boy, maybe ten years old, opened and closed a grimy hand.

Then the officer was stumbling forward, hardly aware of his feet striking the uneven ground. As he tripped and stumbled, taking for ever to reach the broken bodies, he saw faces looking out from the forest. It brought him up short. There was another burst of fire from the road. A warning this time. The branches of a tree exploded into splinters and there were rapid zipping sounds of impact as the bullets ripped into the foliage. He was three feet from where the two bodies lay. He stepped forward and went down on one knee. He touched the woman's neck. It was warm, pliant. Her mouth opened and a small pink bubble formed on her cracked lips. The faces in the forest were watching, waiting to see what the officer was going to do next.

'We are here to help,' he called out to the faces.

A small boy came forward so that a ragged banana leaf was touching his shoulder. An old woman also came out of the trees; she had a hand pressed to her temple, and looked to be in pain.

'Help us,' she said.

There was a stir of movement as the people came out from their hiding places. They all looked sick and tired. Their clothes were torn and grimy. Some of them were carrying bundles of possessions. Refugees. That was all.

'Please,' said the little boy.

A shout brought the officer's head round.

'Stand away!'

He rose to his feet.

'You don't . . .' His throat was parched and he had to swallow. 'You don't understand. They're refugees. They've come from the town.'

He pointed towards the plume of smoke over Muara-tebo.

It was so quiet. The forest, the trucks on the road, the soldiers, the people in the trees, everything seemed to become still, as if all sound had bled from the air. The officer felt his heart throbbing in his throat. He had got some grit in his eye, and blinked to try to dislodge it. The soldiers took aim. Hard light moved on the barrels of the Kalashnikovs. The officer blinked again, trying to see all this as clearly as it was possible to see.

2

Jakarta. August 13th

'It looks well established, but my boy grafted it onto
the tree only last summer.'

The Minister turned away from the camellia tree on
which a white orchid was nodding, its roots apparently
suspended in mid-air.

'But that is the way it is here. We have such a climate,
such soil. Our volcanic origins, you see. They say you
could plant a walking stick in the earth and the following
spring it would flower.'

Hasan Afiff Suharto turned from the orchid and looked
at Mr Bob Wheeler, the American ambassador in his
white suit. Suharto took in the clumsy hands, the blue
eyes set in the big red face. The comical baldness. Even
after forty years of dealing with westerners, Suharto was
still able to find them amusing.

'But of course you did not come here to admire my
garden, Mr Ambassador.'

Wheeler stiffened.

'No, sir. The truth is we have been hearing – '

Suharto waved his delicate brown hand dismissively.

'Rumours, rumours. Not that I am denying that there
has been some problem in the Jambi region. But the
suggestion that the situation is somehow out of control
is . . .'

Suharto's voice tailed off as he approached the stone

177

idol which seemed to be protecting the small banyan tree growing almost under the straw eaves of the big house. He removed a decaying frangipani flower from the idol's clenched hand.

'There was never any suggestion from our people that your government had lost control, sir.'

Suharto turned and looked at the American for a moment. Wheeler disliked the man's mocking expression. It didn't help to know that the guy was only Minister because of his family connections. The ministries in Jakarta were full of such people. You'd think the Indonesians had a patent on nepotism.

'Then you did come to admire my garden. I'm deeply flattered.'

'Actually, sir,' Wheeler took a deep breath, 'I actually came to offer our assistance, if – '

'– we should require it.' Suharto smiled, showing his small, discoloured teeth. 'It is of course very kind of you to think of our needs, but as I'm sure you must know the World Health Organisation is giving us all the help we need.'

Wheeler nodded deferentially.

'They have some great people in the WHO, sir. I'm sure they'll – '

'So am I, Mr Ambassador. Now, as far as you are concerned, as far as the people of the United States are concerned, I can categorically state that there is no danger of any . . . em, *epidemic*. The airports in the region have been closed for the time being, the military are helping the affected population and it is only a matter of time before the WHO gets to the bottom of the matter.'

They had reached the veranda. Suharto lowered himself into a cane chair, and Wheeler did likewise. They looked out at the garden for a moment. There was so much vegetation you couldn't see the surrounding wall. Wheeler found it oppressive.

Then there was a young boy wearing a blue sarong and red sash. He came onto the veranda carrying a slim mobile telephone. Suharto gestured for him to come forward and took the phone. Wheeler got to his feet immediately.

'I'll just take a turn – '

But Suharto put out his hand, and Wheeler sat back down. Wheeler knew very little of Indonesian, but he could tell by Suharto's tone that he was talking to a superior, and that the subject was of considerable importance. The conversation seemed to go on for ever. At one point Suharto sat back in his chair, a frown puckering the skin into fine wrinkles between his dark eyes. He shot Wheeler a glance, and Wheeler went back to his contemplation of the garden.

Five minutes later Suharto put down the phone and smiled. He looked embarrassed.

3

Carmen looked out through the patio windows at Tom clowning around in his chef's apron. The smoke of the barbecue caught spokes of sunlight thrown through the branches of the big maple tree. Carmen watched, thoughtful. Even from a distance she could see the silver in Tom's curly brown hair. It brought home to her how long they had been together. She remembered how he had looked when she first met him – on the poultry course, of all places – part of the veterinary programme at the George Washington vet school. He was showing the Ryans a small bottle of herbs, giving some kind of explanatory talk, hamming it up. Carmen watched him, smiling. Despite the greying hair, he still looked youthful. His rear was still as tight and sexy in his faded blue jeans as when she had first noticed him in med school all those years before. He said something to Julia Ryan and they both laughed. The Ryans were sitting in sun loungers, plates of food balanced on their legs while Scott Ryan and Oliver poked at the beefburgers on the griddle with their forks. Carmen lifted her hand and waved to Joey, who was looking straight at her, serious faced, Tom's chef's hat perched comically on his head.

The barbecue had been Joey's idea. He wanted to reassert a proprietary claim over his mother, was the way Carmen saw it. With Marshallton wrapped up, she had been spending more time with the family and Joey wanted it to stay that way. So today was barbecue and tomorrow they went swimming. Together. After her panic in the BL–4 suite, Carmen had given a lot of thought to her two boys and to Tom, to the life they lived together. It had been the thought that if she became infected with Carl Reiner's blood she would never be able to kiss her children goodbye that had changed things for her; the realisation that the virus might rupture her cell walls, but before that happened it would break her heart, and the hearts of each member of her family. It had thrown into relief the relative importance she gave to her career and her home, and in the moment of terror, she had felt that everything about her life was wrong. There was no way she was going to resign from the RIID – work meant too much to her for that – but she knew that it was important to reconsider everything, to question the fairness of her continuing to risk her life with BL–4 agents. Joey was watching her through the window, making sure she wasn't about to slip through his ketchup-stained fingers. Carmen smiled.

She was blowing him a kiss, kissing her fingers and then pressing them against the glass when Bailey came on the line.

'Colonel Travis?'

'General?'

'Sorry to bother you on your day off, but something's come up that . . . well I think it requires your attention.'

Carmen lowered her eyes, and Joey immediately set off across the grass towards the window.

'We've just received a report from the Jakarta embassy notifying us of some kind of epidemic . . . some kind of outbreak in Indonesia.'

'Sumatra?'

'That's right.'

'Shit.'

'As in "hitting the fan", yes. There is very little detail so far. It might not even be . . . you know what. The Indonesians figure they've got the situation under control, but they've called in the WHO and now the WHO is asking for the RIID.'

Joey was at the window. He had removed the chef's hat and was pressing his nose against the glass, wanting to get her back to the barbecue.

'I thought they weren't very open to American intervention.'

Carmen pressed her finger against Joey's nose, but he could see by her face that she wasn't with him. She was on the phone. He stood away from the glass and watched her, scowling.

'They're not. That's what makes me think that the situation maybe isn't as under control as they say. In fact I have it on pretty good authority – unofficially, you understand – that there may have been another Ngaliema-type scenario.'

Carmen closed her eyes. In 1976 there had been an Ebola outbreak in Kinshasa focused on Ngaliema Hospital. President Mobutu sent in the army, giving orders to shoot on sight anybody trying to escape the area.

'So what do you want me to do, sir?'

'Carmen, it's a hell of a thing to ask you, but I know how keen you were to test the RIID's resources in the field, and . . . well . . . this is your chance. I've already spoken to Major Leigh.'

'Right.'

Carmen swallowed hard. She felt like destiny or God or something else big and obscure was looking straight at her now, and smiling. She looked up, but Joey had gone back to the barbecue. All she had to do was say no. Bailey would understand. Christ! She was a woman with a husband and kids. He couldn't expect her to go into a situation more dangerous than anything she might encounter in the Institute. There the pathogens were either in dead bodies or bottles and you had a suit to protect you. What would it be like in Sumatra with the virus out in the open? Bailey's voice droned on.

'Carmen, I want you to head a RIID team – go out there and find out where the hell this thing is coming from.' Carmen looked at her family standing in the slanting sunlight, as she listened to Bailey's tight, formal voice on the phone. 'Then I want you to go find out how we put the stopper back in the bottle.'

Carmen, her eyes squeezed tight shut against the garden and her two boys, heard herself accept.

'I appreciate your placing so much confidence in me, General.'

4

General Bailey had put Major Leigh in charge of the inventory, and Carmen was grateful for that. She didn't know Leigh well, but had seen him around Fort Detrick – a big man with cropped hair and green friendly eyes set high in his long face – and had heard good things about him. He was a veterinary surgeon and one of the few people available with experience of working inside Racal suits. Having Leigh shoulder some of the burden meant she had time to see Tom and the boys in the morning before she left for the Institute. Tom had offered to quit the office for the afternoon and come down to Andrews air force base to see her off, but military departures were usually unceremonious and hurried affairs, and she told him that she preferred to say goodbye at home. She didn't admit it, but she didn't want the rest of the RIID team to see her cry either. As the only woman in charge of seven men, that mattered.

It hadn't been easy, breaking it to the family so suddenly that she was going away, especially since she couldn't say when she would be back. Nothing quite like it had ever happened before, and she was worried about what the boys would think. They were both old enough to know that parents split up sometimes – it had happened to at least one of Oliver's friends at school – and that it was something they often tried to disguise with excuses. So she went into as much detail about the whole thing as she could, without making it sound too scary. Medical detective work was how she described what she was going to do, and Tom obliged with a joke about packing a raincoat and a magnifying glass. Oliver had asked a lot of questions – Carmen could see him telling all his friends about it – but Joey hardly said a word, angry and upset about having lost to the RIID again. He only cheered up a little when she started to tell him about all the different kinds of monkeys they had where she was going, and that she would take him to see them when he was old enough. Joey liked monkeys.

A staff car came to pick her up at a quarter before nine. It was a still, golden morning, the chatter of bird song and the distant pulse of a lawn mower the only sounds. Carmen climbed in the back and wound down the window so that she could wave at Tom and the boys, who were standing together at the end of the driveway. The car was about to move off when Tom flipped open the mailbox.

'Here!' he shouted, running over. 'There's some stuff here for you.'

He handed her a postcard and a slim manilla envelope marked *Private and Confidential*. Then he leaned in through the window and kissed her.

'You take care, now, OK?'

'I will,' she said. 'Don't worry.'

Tom smiled and banged on the roof of the car. A few moments later he, the children and the house were disappearing from view behind the ranks of hedgerows, street lamps and acacia trees. Carmen stayed looking out of the rear window until they were through the traffic lights at the far end of the road.

The postcard was from Oregon where her sister Isabel and her husband were on vacation. On the front there was a picture of a grizzly bear on its hind legs, on the back a breathless account of the scenery and the weather and the white-water rafting they were trying out for the first time. That was the thing about Isabel: she gulped life down as if it wasn't going to last the season. More now than ever, it struck Carmen as a good way to live.

She watched the streets of Aspen Hill roll past, Isabel's card in her hand. She still hadn't figured out why, when she was on the point of withdrawing from BL–4 work, she had accepted Bailey's assignment. It was as if she were two distinct people – a soldier and a mother. She knew it was the soldier who had just said goodbye to her children, the strong person who didn't want to have them worry while she was gone, and she felt bad about that. They should worry. Christ knows, she was worried. And still it wasn't too late to back out. But if she did she'd be finished at the RIID, she knew that. Not that they would dismiss her, but the trust would be gone, she would no longer be given responsibility. Maybe that wasn't such a bad thing, she thought. It would almost certainly get her out of BL–4 work, which was, after all, what she wanted. Except that someone else would have to do it in her place, someone probably less experienced, less qualified – someone who might fail.

She looked at the card in her hands, at the grizzly bear. It was her pride that was the problem. She just couldn't stand failure. And since success came easier in the professional sphere – all you had to be was *professional*, it wasn't like being a mother where you had to be so many things – that was where she felt most comfortable. Sometimes she wished she could change herself, make herself care about different things. She had ridden roughshod over her parents' wishes in joining the military in the first place. They wanted her closer to home in Connecticut, they had wanted her to be a surgeon like her father. But she had been attracted by the promise of front-line research, work in the field, above all the state-of-the-art technological back-up that only the military could guarantee. Sometimes she hated herself for that. Sometimes she just hated herself.

They were halfway to Frederick before Carmen remembered the envelope. She had thought at first that it was just another piece of junk mail, or something routine from the bank or the insurance people. They nearly always marked their correspondence PRIVATE. But as she looked more closely she began to have doubts. For one thing the sender had used a stamp, not a franking machine. And there was something in the way the address had been typed, unevenly, with a couple of the full stops punched right through the paper, that looked odd. It was not something that had been reeled off by a laser printer along with ten thousand others. She checked the postmark: it said Washington, DC. She tore open the envelope.

Major Leigh had done a good job with the inventory. Besides all the regulation protective gear, testing and communications equipment, which the Institute had in abundance, he had managed to get his hands on a brand new capturing array which they would use to collect samples of insects and other arthropods. It used a new dieldrin-based aerosol system, and was said to be quicker and more effective than the traditional blood-and-wire traps – if a little less environmentally friendly. The array was packed away in two large metal cases, each one the size of a small refrigerator. Leigh had also whistled up a set of hunting rifles, for bringing down primates and larger mammals. Detailed maps and satellite scans of Sumatra were being sent down later that morning, together with all the relevant zoological studies of the area, courtesy of the Smithsonian. Meanwhile an air force cargo plane was on its way from Midway Island to Jambi with three Jeep Corporation four-wheel-drive Cherokees in its belly and one metric tonne of combat rations.

Carmen spent the best part of two hours going through the list with Majors Leigh and McKinnon, paying particular attention to the scientific equipment and supplies. She wanted to be able to do as much analytical and diagnostics work as possible in the field, without having to fly samples back to the States or anywhere else. General Bailey had put in a request that the authorities in Singapore be brought in to assist in the mission because they had the best laboratory facilities in the area, but as yet he had received no response. The Indonesians were touchy about involving a neighbouring state in what they still insisted was an internal matter, and the Americans couldn't ignore Indonesian sensibilities for fear of being shut out themselves. For just this reason it was agreed that the RIID team should be as self-sufficient as possible.

At half-past eleven Carmen signed the order for the transfer to Andrews. A few minutes later a call came in from Bailey. He sounded hurried, brusque.

'I think we have everything we need, sir,' she told him. 'I just hope we can carry it all. I understand it can get pretty wet out there this time of year.'

'We've received assurances that you'll get full co-operation from the local military,' Bailey said. 'That's your first port-of-call.'

'Brigadier Sutami. I have his details, sir.'

'Good. He's in charge of the quarantining operation so he might have some useful information. He's also been responsible for liaison with the WHO. I'm afraid what we're getting through the diplomatic channels is . . . patchy.'

'No need for undue concern? Situation fully under control?'

'That's about the size of it.'

'And is it, sir?'

Bailey hesitated.

'We've had no more reports on the shooting incident

I mentioned but that doesn't mean . . . I'm afraid you're going to have to find out for yourself, Colonel. I know that the WHO want to concentrate on dealing with the epidemic, so I guess it's pretty bad. They don't feel they can commit resources to tracking down where this thing started. So I think you'll have a free hand there.'

There was less than an hour remaining before she was due to leave for Andrews when George Arends finally showed up in Carmen's office.

'Sorry it took so long to reach me,' he said. 'I was preparing the material for the primate EPD programme. Didn't want to hurry it.'

Carmen understood. The primate epidemiology or EPD programme was a vital part of the campaign against the Muaratebo virus, as everyone was now calling it. It would involve infecting a range of primates with the virus and seeing when, if and how they themselves became infectious. With a virus this lethal the carrier only had a limited period to infect others, so long as the corpse was not disturbed. If the exact time and duration of that period could be established, it might help the field team trace the spread of the virus back to its source. But before the programme could begin, precise and controllable doses of infected material had to be prepared inside a BL–4 containment suite. Down there no one hurried anything.

'There was just something I wanted you to look at before I moved out,' Carmen said.

'I'd planned to see you off anyway,' Arends said, pulling up a chair. 'This is one hell of a job you're taking on.'

'And there's something else, something I wanted to say.' Carmen looked down for a moment, trying to find the right words. 'I wanted to say how much I appreciated what you did in the lab the other day. When I – '

'You let me finish up. Gave me a chance to demonstrate

to the cameras now neatly I can tie off a duodenum.'

'You know what I mean.' Arends smiled. 'Christ, Bailey congratulated me for my good work.'

'Damn right. It was good work. You do a hell of a job here, Colonel. And as for . . . as for what we talked about – the fear, that's something we all have.'

'Doesn't make you walk away from the job though.'

'But I dream about it. Wake up in the middle of the night with blood *inside* my gloves. And you never know when it's going to get a hold on you. It's not something you can control, Carmen. Remember when they isolated Ebola virus for the first time in Zaire, when that CDC team flew out there? They were stopping off for supplies in Geneva when all of a sudden one of the doctors just refused to go any further . . .' Arends raised his eyebrows. 'Refused. Can you imagine the embarrassment, the *shame*? The guy couldn't go on. In the field trained professionals run – they *run* to get away from the disease. These are primitive responses, deep responses.'

Carmen smiled. She had been thinking all morning about who she could talk to, and Arends was the only name she could come up with. Now she was glad she'd called on him. The warmth she had seen in the staging area was not an illusion. It helped her to hear him talk.

'Well, it sure felt primitive in the BL–4 suite,' she said. They both laughed.

'But there was something else. This.' She showed him the envelope: 'I received something in my mail this morning.'

She slid it across the desk. Arends looked at her for a second and took it. There were just two pieces of paper inside, and they were photocopies. You could tell that from the uneven black margins down one side. Several sections of the text had been blacked out with a thick felt pen, especially near the top of the first page. Arends looked at them for a few seconds and frowned.

'This document's classified. Or rather, the original is.'

Carmen nodded.

'And this came in the regular mail?' He looked at the front of the envelope. 'Nothing with it?'

'Nothing. Have you read what it says?'

Arends held up the first page again.

'Well, it's a military report of some kind. Name and unit's blacked out . . . there, I guess. Likewise who the report's for. Reference and serial numbers'd be up there somewhere. Can't see them either. You got a date, or year at least: 1988. That's it. Whoever sent this to you doesn't want you to know where he got it, I'd say.'

'The person that wrote it's called Jen something. You can see the bottom of the letters on the left there: J–e–n. Must be Jenkins or Jenson, or something like that.'

'Yeah, I got it.'

'But look what the report's *about*.'

Arends wetted his lower lip and started reading. After a few lines he suddenly sat forward, concentrating hard. Carmen let him read. She wanted to know if maybe she'd missed something, got the wrong end of the stick somehow. After a minute Arends looked up at her again.

'A decon job, right?' she said. 'Biohazard level 4, the works.'

Arends nodded.

'No question. They really nuked this place. What's it called?' – he flipped back to the first page – 'Willard. Sealed it like a tomb.'

'Ever heard of it?'

'Willard? No, never. Should have done, though, by the sound of it.'

'That's just what I thought. A major decon job like that, almost certainly in the US somewhere, nine years ago. Looks like someone's been digging in our patch.'

Arends squinted at the top of the first page again, this time trying to see through the thick black lines.

'CDC? Maybe a civilian show?' he said.

'They keep us pretty well informed, don't they? Besides, that report's got military written all over it.'

Arends nodded.

'Special Forces, in fact.'

'What?'

Arends pointed to one of the blanked-out corners of the first page.

'You got a pair of brackets and two words between them. There's an *l* and there's a cap *F*. Special Forces. What else could it be?'

Carmen sat back slowly in her chair. There were voices outside her office. One of them belonged to McKinnon. For a moment she thought someone might come in. But the voices went on past. She let out a sigh.

'I suppose we should report this to General Bailey at once,' she said. 'There's clearly been a serious breach of security somewhere.'

Arends didn't respond. He watched her, waiting for her to reach for the phone. Carmen picked up the receiver and got ready to key in the numbers. She felt sure he was going to say something, but he didn't. He just sat there. She hesitated.

'You don't think I should?' she asked.

Arends shrugged.

'There's been a breach of something, that's for sure.'

Carmen frowned.

'So you think I should report it, right?'

Arends shifted in his chair.

'Perhaps. In time.'

'In time? What do you mean, in time?'

Arends folded his arms. She had seen it down in the hot zone a few days before: he was one very cautious guy. Calm, methodical, risk averse. Maybe it came from handling those deadly microbes all day.

'Well, it's just that if you inform General Bailey,

he will have no choice but to inform someone at the Pentagon. And then there'll be an investigation. And if that happens then the person who sent this photocopy to you may get found out.'

Carmen's finger was still poised over the number pad. 'So?'

'Well, I can accept that this . . . information probably doesn't help us at all with our filovirus. I mean, it doesn't look likely, does it, given what we know so far?'

'No, it doesn't.'

'But suppose it *does* help, in some small way? I mean, you have just been assigned the job of investigating Muaratebo's development in Sumatra and this classified document arrives in your mail. Maybe it's just a coincidence. But maybe not. Maybe someone is trying to tell us something, trying to help. Do we want this person to go on helping us – assuming he or she can – or do we want him to stop?'

Carmen replaced the receiver. If she was going to commit a serious breach of military regulations for the first time in her career, she wanted to get the reason for it straight.

'What are you saying exactly?'

'What I'm saying is very simple. This virus – the truth is, we don't know what it can do. We don't know for sure where it came from, we don't know how to stop it, we don't even know if it *can* be stopped. Now, we're all putting a brave face on it, keeping calm, and that's the way it should be. But when have we ever had to deal with a virus like this that's airborne before? I mean a human pathogen even half as hot as this one? You have to go back centuries. You have to go back to the goddam Black Death. So what I'm saying is, if there's someone out there who's trying to help us . . . Well, I think we should just be grateful, don't you?'

5

Jambi Province. August 15th

It was just five or six yards square of flattened earth and a few broken twigs, but Willis was certain they had found the site of the Kubu camp.

'They were here all right,' he said, unscrewing the top of his blue aluminium water bottle. 'Probably moved on a few days ago. Bloody typical.'

Telee reappeared from behind some bushes carrying an empty cigarette packet and a torch battery.

'There you are,' Willis said. 'Proof.'

Holly was still out of breath from the climb. They'd had to leave the pick-up on the other side of a stream and scramble up the tangled slopes on the other side. It had been hard work in the mid-morning heat, like doing aerobics inside a sauna. Holly's T-shirt was wet with sweat and her jeans were smeared with red earth. Willis handed her the water.

'How long, you reckon?' said Willis.

Telee turned over a few dead leaves with his foot.

'Two day,' he said, risking a few words of his pidgin English.

'But they'll come back, won't they?' Holly asked.

Willis shrugged.

'You just can't tell,' he said. 'The Kubu don't like staying in one place. The government's been trying it for years – trying to get them to settle so they can learn

194

Indonesian and pay taxes. Hasn't worked. They trade with the farmers. Some of them do seasonal work on the plantations, but they don't ever settle down themselves. It's just the way they are. They're hunter-gatherers – like we all were once upon a time.'

Holly sighed, angered by Willis's resignation. They needed the Kubu if they were to get to Rafflesia Camp undetected; at least that was Willis's opinion. On the eastern side of the mountains the Kubu were the only people who really knew their way around the forest. Telee's knowledge became sketchy once they were over the Bukit Barisan range, and without help from the Indians he was worried they might blunder into some army roadblock or patrol. Holly hadn't been in any position to complain. She was at least drawing closer to the camp, which now lay no more than fifty miles away. Anything was better than waiting in Padang. But now, it seemed, a spell of waiting was exactly what they were in for.

'So what do we do?' Holly said, pushing the hair out of her eyes with an irritated sweep.

Willis turned to Telee and exchanged a few words in Malay.

'Nothing.'

'Nothing?'

'We go back down to the pick-up and stay put. Maybe leave them a few presents here to show good will.'

They had been travelling for five days – five days without a shower, without a change of clothes – and now he wanted to sit and wait for something to happen. Holly felt her face flush.

'Presents? What are you talking about?'

'Bush knives, tobacco. We brought them along specially. If we want the Kubu to – '

'Fuck the Kubu!'

'Holly, listen – '

'I'm not interested in your anthropological theses, God damn it. I came out here to find my children, to find the camp. You said you'd get me there!'

'We can't just – '

'They could be in danger. They could be . . . I have to get to them *now*!'

Holly's voice left in its wake an unfamiliar silence. It took a few moments for the white noise of buzzing and chirping to return. Telee looked at Willis as if surprised he hadn't shut her up already with a smack in the face. Self-consciously Willis squared his shoulders.

'Now listen here, Holly. There's no point in us charging around the bloody jungle trying to catch up with these people. We'd never find them, especially if they didn't want us to. Our best bet is to make our presence known and wait for them to find us.'

'But that could take – '

'They're probably closer than you know. Remember, this is their back yard. Anything happens round here they know about it in no time, believe me.'

'Why can't we just go to the camp? We know where it is.'

'But we don't know where the trails are. It could take weeks, and we're not supplied. We'd have to take the road, and you know – '

Willis was interrupted by Telee. He was looking up into the trees and talking. He seemed agitated. Holly turned.

'They're coming!'

She heard it first: a hard mechanical pulse from somewhere above the stream. It was a chopper, its blades beating the air, the sound echoing in the shallow valley.

'There they are!' said Willis, pointing to his right through a gap in the trees. There were two of them: massive dark green machines with long snouts, their frames pitched forwards like vultures looking for prey.

They were travelling a hundred feet or less over the surface of the water.

'Christ, I hope they don't spot the pick-up,' Willis said.

Holly looked at him.

'What if they do?'

Telee grabbed her by the arm and pulled her away. One of the choppers was slowing down. It seemed to hesitate for a moment, hanging in mid-air. Then it turned towards them, its blunt, ugly snout slowly rising, as if sniffing its way up the slope. Suddenly the noise was almost deafening. An instant before she threw herself down behind the cover of a fallen tree she caught sight of the minigun slung under the machine's belly. Willis landed beside her.

'What are they after?' Holly shouted above the noise.

'Christ knows. I just hope we're not it.'

'But we're not breaking any laws.'

Willis looked at her in disbelief.

'Well that's all right then.'

The chopper was drawing closer, the downdraught swaying the branches of the trees, shaking the leaves. Holly lay flat, covering the back of her head with her hands. Willis said something, but she couldn't hear what it was. She caught sight of Telee sliding away backwards into denser cover, his eyes fixed on the chopper that was no more than a hundred yards away now, only partly obscured by the forest canopy.

'Can they land here?' she shouted, but Willis wasn't listening. He was propped up on his elbows, pointing a small camera at the sinister machine overhead. He took two or three pictures and ducked down again.

The chopper was almost directly above them, throwing up dust and dead leaves. Where the Kubu camp had been the vegetation had been cut down or trampled, so that the soil beneath was loose and dry. In a few seconds the whole area was hidden in a red-brown cloud.

The chopper hung there for a moment, slowly turning round and round, then suddenly it lifted up into the sky and sped away towards the far end of the valley. No one moved for a while. Holly looked up and noticed for the first time a big yellow centipede gliding along the side of the fallen tree trunk a few inches from her nose.

'No wonder the Kubu moved on from here,' said Willis, climbing to his feet and tucking the camera into his top pocket. 'That's just the sort of attention they don't like. And I don't blame them.'

Holly looked up at him.

'Will they come back?'

'To the pick-up maybe, if they saw it. Maybe they'll whistle up a patrol or something. We'll have to move it, that's for sure, move it and hide it. Telee'd better get busy with that parang.'

Holly studied Willis's face. She had expected him to say that things had become too dangerous for him, that he was heading back to the coast. But he didn't look scared, he looked excited as if this was what he'd come for. Suddenly she understood. He had been lying to her from the start. His interest in the island's internal affairs was about more than resort development. Why else would he be out here, she asked herself, risking his neck? She wondered which press agency he was working for, and why he hadn't come clean. Then it occurred to her that maybe he wasn't a journalist. She had read about businessmen who supplemented their income by providing low-level intelligence in places like this. She felt like asking him about it outright, but what was the point? He wouldn't tell her the truth. And what did it matter anyway, so long as he helped her get to Rafflesia Camp? That was all she cared about. He saw her looking at him and gave a smile.

'Let's get moving, shall we?' he said.

They drove the pick-up a couple of miles further down a narrow trail and then took it off the road where the ground was hard enough to hide the tracks. Then they covered it with foliage and headed back towards the stream, taking with them all the supplies they could carry. Less than an hour after nightfall Holly lay beside the smouldering remains of a camp fire, the taste of sweet biscuits and chlorinated water still fresh in her mouth. A few feet away Willis lay asleep, snoring fitfully.

It was the first night she had spent camped out in the forest. The other nights they had always managed to reach a settlement of one kind or another, where rudimentary shelter and fried food were available for a few rupiah. But Holly found herself not minding the forest floor. Perhaps it was just the dreams she had every night, the dreams of Lucy and Emma running alone through the jungle, but she felt closer to them here. In her confused state the feeling that she was experiencing what they had experienced was relatively steady, relatively solid. It was something she could build on. When the feeling wore off she would find herself starting to panic, her heart hammering in her breast even though she might be lying quite still. Sometimes in the night she would wake up suddenly, gripped by the fear that she would never see her children again.

She worried about Jonathan too, but more than that she was angry. In her dreams she saw him as he used to be, handsome, impatient, intense. She saw him standing on a veranda, hands on hips, staring out into the twilight forest as she had so often seen him in the past. She asked herself why he had insisted that the children join him in this terrible place, a place where they did not belong – where none of them belonged? Was it just for their sake, to help give them the emotional stability he thought they needed? Or was it more than that? Was his real aim to show them the importance of his work, to fill their young minds with the same sense of outrage he felt at the destruction of the forest, the rape of nature, the indifference of the modern world? She pictured Emma and Lucy picking their way through the forest in their father's footsteps, listening to his gentle voice, explaining, defining, questioning. They would return to her converted, militants in the struggle against the industrial world. And they would hate her for abandoning their father in the midst of it, for leaving him to save the planet all alone.

And she had gone along with it! The great Dr Rhodes had spoken and she had obeyed. Of course. Because Jonathan knew what was wrong with the world; because Jonathan knew what was right. Even after all the time that had passed the conviction was hard to shake. She wondered how she had ever summoned up the courage to leave him. They had been back in the States, preparing for another long trip, and she had rebelled, refused to go. She hadn't said she was leaving him. It was never put that way. She simply told Jonathan that she was staying put and that the children were staying put with her. How had she managed to defy him, to ignore the voice of his infallible reasoning? Perhaps there was only one explanation: that he had wanted her to. He had wanted her to leave.

It was a still, humid night. Twigs snapped and popped in the fire. Holly lay on her side, staring at the dying flames through half-closed eyes. If only she had listened to Richard. If only she had been able to break free. Why hadn't she married him when he'd asked her? He was a good man, a kind man, clever but modest. She hadn't had a chance to contact him since Padang. He would have called the hotel and found her gone by now. She began to rehearse what she would say to him, how she would explain about Willis and Telee, about the Kubu and the roadblocks and the helicopters – and how to explain about Jonathan. Jonathan, that was the hardest part.

She was woken by the sounds of something moving about. For a moment she lay completely still, her eyes searching for the source of the stealthy sounds. She sat bolt upright. There were two of them. They were small, less than five feet tall, naked except for cotton loincloths, their black hair cropped short. They stood looking at her, holding their long spears, silent. A scruffy grey mongrel came and trotted up to them and sat down at their feet.

Holly slowly rolled over and grabbed hold of Willis's sleeping bag.

'Willis, wake up.'

Willis grunted and rolled over onto his front.

'Willis!'

The light from the fire was almost gone. Holly caught a glimpse of the dog sniffing around one of the bags of provisions. She jabbed Willis hard in the back.

'Uh?'

He was awake. In a moment he had grabbed a torch and was shining it all around.

'What is it?'

'Indians. They're here.'

The beam of Willis's torch swept over the spot where the two men had been: there was nothing but a handful of insects circling in the air. A few feet away Telee lay sprawled out on his back, his straw hat pulled down over his face. Willis let out a weary sigh.

'They were here,' Holly said. 'I saw them.'

'Good,' Willis said. 'They must have found the presents. I wonder what they brought for us.'

It was a honeycomb, wrapped up in vine leaves. They ate it for breakfast with more dry biscuits and black coffee. An hour later the Kubu hunters returned and, after a few minutes' discussion with Telee, led them away to their camp along a winding uphill path. It was late afternoon before they arrived.

The camp lay beside a fast-moving stream, south and west of the old one, in an area of what looked like virgin forest. A cluster of huge merantis towered over the site, making it invisible even from the air. The camp itself was made up of eight precarious-looking wood and bamboo huts, housing, Holly guessed, no more than nine or ten families. Pungent-smelling woodsmoke shrouded everything.

The Kubu themselves were small and pale-skinned with broad, upturned noses. Like the two hunters, most of them wore only loincloths, although some of the women wore T-shirts. Unlike most of the other Indians Holly had seen photographs of, they wore no body markings. Nor did she see any flower-petal head-dresses or colourful bead bracelets. Some of the children chattered and giggled, but the adults mostly kept silent, watching the strangers with a mixture of resignation and fear. Holly could understand why. According to Willis, the Kubu were Sumatra's big losers. Even the name Kubu was said to be a reference to retreat, marking some ancient time when the King of Jambi had driven them away into the depths of the forest. The name meant 'stockade', because for them that was what the forest had become.

Willis and Telee sat crouching outside the main hut opposite the elders – a group of wiry old men, whose flesh hung off their bones in loose folds. Respectfully, Holly sat a little way off, trying to get some sense of what they were saying. Eventually Willis beckoned her over. He looked pleased with himself.

'Just as well we stuck around for these fellas,' he said. 'First bit of hard information I've heard in weeks.'

One of the old men grinned at her and made a joke, showing off a mouthful of chipped yellow teeth. Holly noticed that the man beside him was blind in one eye.

'What do they say?'

'Looks like there's a problem in Muaratebo. That's what this whole thing's about, by the sound of it.'

'Muaratebo? Where is that?'

'It's on the way down to Jambi. About forty miles east of where your kids are, I think. There's some sort of emergency down there. That's why they've been keeping people away, I reckon.'

'What sort of emergency?'

One of the old men was talking again. Willis hesitated, waiting to hear what Telee said in reply.

'They don't know exactly. But it must be serious. There's a whole lot of soldiers been moving into the area, and now it's sealed off completely. Apparently some farmers from Bangko tried going down there a few days ago and couldn't get near the place.'

'Do they know about Rafflesia Camp? Do they know if anything's happened there?'

Telee turned and looked at her and then at Willis. Willis nodded back. Telee began talking to the old men again. From the slow and deliberate way he formed his words Holly realised that it wasn't Bahasa Indonesian he was speaking, nor yet Malay. It was some other dialect which he clearly didn't know so well. Willis didn't understand any of it. Holly waited impatiently for the answer to her question, ignoring the little children who kept coming up behind her now, sticking their fingers into the tresses of her long black hair and then rushing off again, giggling.

'It sounds like they know the place,' said Willis at last. 'But they haven't been down that way for a while. Because of the soldiers. Soldiers . . . in the forest. Mad men' – he looked at Telee – 'Mad men? Is that what he said?'

Telee nodded, drilling the point of his index finger into one temple.

'Mad, crazy,' he said. 'Soldiers.'

'*Nai wataan*,' one of the old men added.

Telee's expression froze.

'Dead now,' he said.

One of the elders spat out a plug of tobacco and carefully dabbed at his lips with the back of his hand. A shriek of laughter went up from one of the children.

'Dead?' said Holly. 'How? What's he talking about?'

'Wait a second.'

Telee and the old men began talking all at once. Telee kept shaking his head as if he didn't understand what they were saying; and the old men kept repeating themselves, making long sweeping gestures with their puny arms. After a while Telee gave up, summarising his findings with a burst of Malay.

'Spirits,' said Willis. 'That's what they always say when something bad happens. Evil spirits. I wouldn't worry about it. It's just hearsay.'

'Will they take us there?'

Willis nodded: 'Sure, sure. I think they're just talking the price up. Muaratebo's where the problem is. Your friends . . . They've just been cut off, that's all, I bet you. Radio broken and can't get through in the road. Best thing to do with the military on manoeuvres is to lie low. Like the Kubu themselves.'

Holly felt a little reassured. Even if there was an emergency in Muaratebo, there was no reason to believe it had anything to do with the people at Rafflesia Camp. It was probably just as Willis said: they simply hadn't been able to come and get her.

'When do we leave?'

Willis hesitated.

'We'll arrange it for you with these fellas,' he said. 'But it looks like it'll have to be Muaratebo for me. Close as I can get anyway.'

'But it's sealed off,' Holly protested.

'Oh, there are ways and means. I just wanna find

out what it's all about. Sell my story to a newspaper or something!'

'But – ' Holly looked around at the Kubu – 'you can't just leave me.'

Telee was spreading out a new array of gifts from his knapsack, including a flashlight, a penknife and a small steel teapot. Inside the teapot was a roll of banknotes.

'These fellas'll look after you,' said Willis. 'If there's any trouble you can always come and wait for me here. I'll be back in a few days.'

6

It took a moment to realise where he was. The room, the cool air, the flat grey light behind the curtains were all unfamiliar. Then, Dr Jarvis remembered: he was home.

He looked over at the electric clock beside the bed. It read four in the morning, but that couldn't be the time or it would have been dark outside. He raised himself onto his elbows and tried to read the face of his watch. Had he got around to adjusting it during the twenty-two-hour dash across the time zones? He had a faint recollection of fiddling with it while a hostess hovered over him offering tea or coffee. Half-past six p.m. If that was right he had been asleep for something like ten hours.

He swung his legs over the side of the bed and heaved himself to his feet. He felt dizzy and his head suddenly ached, a hard pressure at the temples and behind the eyes.

'Jesus.'

He sat down again and brought his hands to his face, trying to keep the pressure back. He didn't normally crash out like that after a long flight. He normally held out until evening, like you were supposed to, and then had an early night. But that morning he couldn't have done it. He hadn't even the energy to get undressed. He pulled back the curtains a few inches. It was an overcast evening, mild and still. Four floors below on the Harrington Road the traffic was moving slowly, boxy black taxis and private

206

cars with roofs that reflected the sky and the silhouettes of trees. West London: neat, solid, safe.

He had a harsh dry feeling in his mouth. He walked slowly into the bathroom and turned on the cold tap. The water tasted of mud and old copper. There was something wrong with his taste buds. He swallowed a few mouthfuls and spat out another. Then he looked up at his reflection in the mirror. His eyes were bloodshot, his eyelids puffy. He needed a shave – a shave and a long hot bath. He groped around for a razor and then remembered that it was somewhere in the depths of his suitcase.

As he was fiddling with the straps he noticed the red light winking on and off on his answering machine. He hadn't bothered to listen to the messages that morning. He hadn't announced the exact date of his return to anyone, so there wasn't likely to be anything urgent. The liquid crystal display informed him that he'd had six calls – six calls in ten weeks. He wished he'd phoned someone from Pekanbaru or even from Singapore to let them know he was arriving, but whenever he'd had a chance it always seemed to be the middle of the night, UK time. He resolved to get cleaned up and make a few calls. There was bound to be someone available for a celebratory drink in the Anglesey Arms.

He cleared his throat and felt a sharp pain shoot up from his lungs. It had been cold on that aircraft, too damned cold, and he hadn't had a sweater handy. He thought about the presentation he was going to have to make to the Research Fund Committee the following Monday. There was plenty he had to do before then: get his pictures developed and sorted, write up a report. It was going to be a very busy weekend.

'I hope I'm not going down with something,' he said to his reflection.

'Excuse me. Anyone sitting here?'

A couple of young men in suits and striped shirts were standing over him holding pints of bitter. The taller of them was pointing to the two empty chairs on the other side of the table.

'No,' Jarvis said, trying to make himself heard over the noise of a hundred hearty conversations. 'Go . . . Go ahead.'

'Sorry?'

Jarvis tried to clear his throat. The pain in his chest was bad. It made him wince.

'It's OK. Go ahead.'

The smaller man gently nudged his friend.

'Actually why don't we go out here? It's nice outside.'

They exchanged looks and the taller one shrugged. Jarvis knew that they must have thought he was a drunk or something. But he didn't care. He felt lousy.

'Take the table,' he said. 'I was just leaving.'

He got up and stumbled into the men's lavatory. He was getting sick. It wasn't just the jet lag. It was some sort of bug. He must have caught it in that damned plane. Maybe it was even something he ate. He steadied himself against the sink, breathing deeply. In spite of his weeks beneath the tropical sun he looked ghostly pale. It was just his luck to go down with flu three days before his presentation.

A man came out of the far cubicle adjusting his fly. He ran his hand under the tap and hurried out, as if afraid he might see something he didn't want to see. Jarvis belched. There were a couple of chemists' shops on the Old Brompton Road. At least one of them had to stay open after hours.

More customers were arriving at the pub every minute. The terrace was standing room only and people were spilling out onto the pavement. Jarvis found his way blocked by ranks of big men struggling to get the attention of the nearest barman. He tried squeezing his way through, but it was impossible.

'Gangway!' boomed a red-faced man as he backed past, carrying three pints of beer between his huge hands.

Jarvis pressed on. If he didn't get out of there he was going to faint. The smoke and the noise were overpowering. He heaved past people, shouldering them aside. A woman swore, her cocktail spilling over her suede shoes.

'Watch what you're doing, will you?'

He reached the doorway. The concrete ramp leading down to the street was as crowded as the pub itself. What were they all doing there, these people, packing themselves together like this, screaming at each other at the top of their lungs? Were they mad? Jarvis launched himself through them, oblivious to the protests, desperate now to get away, to breathe. He was just a few feet from the road when someone crossed in front of him, colliding head on. There was a loud bang as a full glass shattered against the pavement.

'You bloody clown! What the hell – ?'

Jarvis blinked and shook his head.

'Sorry, I've got to . . . I can't . . .'

The man was pointing a finger at him. He was young, tall.

'That was a pint of Theakstons, thank you very much. And the bar is that way.'

Jarvis turned away but the man had got a grip on his shoulder.

'Oh no you don't, mate.'

'Let go!'

The man waved his finger again.

'One pint of Theakstons, if you – hey!'

Jarvis yanked himself free and spun out into the road. He heard the man shouting after him, a woman scream and then, through both, the sound of brakes. The cab hit him on the thigh, throwing him into the gutter.

Nurse Rose Priestly sniffed her mug of Batchelor's instant

soup and picked up the report from the clinical nurse manager. Two in the morning, and the observation ward at St Anne's – or Stan's as it was known to the staff – was quiet at last. Adjusting her glasses, she squinted at the angular biro scrawl that she had come to recognise as Terry Pahadia's.

There were three cases to keep a particular eye on. One was Mrs Walden, a lady in Ward 6 who had just been operated on to remove an ovarian cyst and had reacted badly to the anaesthetic. She had vomited several times since leaving the theatre and was now running a temperature of 40 degrees centigrade. The second was a child who had been admitted through casualty with broken ribs and concussion. The third was a Dr Jarvis who had also come in from the casualty ward, victim of a road traffic accident.

The last patient was of most interest. Pahadia had noted that insect bites had been found on the legs of the patient when he was being undressed. This, taken together with the man's tanned skin and the embarkation stub which had been found in his pocket, presented the possibility that he had come back from abroad, possibly from the tropics. His fever was to be considered indicative of possible malaria or typhoid. The fractured femur had been treated immediately and had presented no complications. Several blood films had been taken for tests, and Pahadia had notified the Medical Officer for Environmental Health who had in turn contacted the Public Health Laboratory Service Communicable Disease Surveillance Centre on their twenty-four-hour hotline. The CDSC had advised that Dr Jarvis be admitted to a private room by way of limiting any risk of infection, and Pahadia had complied, putting the patient in room 23. He had even asked supplies if there was any chance of getting a flexible film isolator for him. If there had been a reply Pahadia had not noted it. Now it was a question of keeping a close eye on Dr Jarvis overnight, and awaiting the tests.

Rose was looking back through Pahadia's notes when the buzzer for room 23 lit up her panel. Rose picked up her clipboard and made her way along the corridor. She intended to take a look at him, make sure he was comfortable. If it looked serious she would contact the junior duty doctor for assistance.

The room was at the far end of the west wing of the hospital. Rose pushed through the fire doors that separated the wards, her shoes making a faint squeak on the newly waxed linoleum.

The smell hit her as she entered the room. Having worked in hospitals so long she was used to bad smells – smells of sickness and even death – but this stink came through high on her personal Richter scale. It was a thick smell of putrefaction. She dropped the last piece of muesli bar into her pocket and wiped a crumb from her lips.

'Goodness,' she said, trying to sound as cheerful as possible. She took the man's hand from the buzzer, having to free each finger separately. 'Goodness me.'

Jarvis hardly seemed to notice her. But as she took his hand, he turned his head a little. He was pulling in air as if forced to breathe through a straw. Rose pulled the cover down from his chest. She would have to call the doctor. Jarvis was in obvious distress. She pressed the pager for Doctor Stewart, punching in the number for her location, and then set about stripping the sheet from under him where he had made the mess. It would only take a second.

'The doctor's on his way,' she said. 'He won't be a minute. He'll give you something to help you breathe.' Leaning over him, she gagged on the smell, and had to stand back for a moment. 'Goodness,' she said again. It was so close in the room. That didn't help. She went across to the window, opened it a little and breathed in two or three gulps of fresh air.

Then she turned.

It was very odd. Jarvis had stopped breathing for a moment. His breath was suspended, as if in intense concentration. Rose watched, fascinated, as he tried to roll over onto his side. He was brushing at the bed behind him, brushing at the mattress. It was as if he were trying to get rid of crumbs or something. She gave herself a little shake and stepped forward.

'I'll soon strip that off. You'll be amazed by how – '

She stopped short as Jarvis gripped her wrist. She felt him tense up as he tried to draw breath, then he made a strangled sound and convulsed, retching, sending a streak of blackish sputum or vomit onto the bedclothes. Rose pulled away instinctively, stepping back across the room, wiping at the spatter on her chin and lips.

'Oh, Jesus,' she said softly. For a moment the room seemed to sway like the deck of a ship. Then she leaned forward, dizzy, nauseous with the utter vileness of the taste in her mouth, and she spat onto the floor.

7

Twenty-four hours had gone by since the batch of clean primates had been infected with the Muaratebo virus, and as yet there were no symptoms. The wrist sensor on one of the animals was registering a mild temperature, but on its own that didn't mean very much. Judging from the human cases among the quarantine workers at Marshallton, the virus incubated for four or five days before the onset of the first symptoms, but in other species the cycle might be very different. If, as seemed likely, pig-tailed macaques were a key vector from the origin of the virus to man, then it was essential to establish how and at what point they themselves became infectious.

Nine *Macaca nemestrina* were involved in the primate EPD programme at Fort Detrick. Lieutenant-Colonel Arends would have preferred a bigger number, but with the Marshallton facility knocked out, there had not been time to round up any more.

The animals were kept down in one of the BL–4 containment suites, inside airtight Perspex boxes with independent air supplies. Every few hours samples of their urine, faeces and saliva – even of breath – were taken away for analysis to check for the presence of the virus. It was unpleasant and dangerous work, especially taking the saliva samples. The animals had to be pinned by their throats to the back of their boxes, and a cotton swab stuck in between their bared teeth. They had to be held firmly or there was a risk that they would bite right through the space suits the men were wearing, and yet if the grip was too firm the animals would be throttled.

Arends was just on his way up from the BL–4 suites when a call came through from his nephew in New York. He hurried to pick up the phone.

'Hello, Stewart?'

'Hi! It's me. Were you on your way out?'

Arends could hear a lot of traffic in the background. The boy was shouting over the noise.

'No, no. Just got here. Where are you?'

'I'm outside the public library. I've just been checking on that thing you asked about.'

'About Willard?'

'Yes. I've got something, but I don't know if it's any help.'

Arends grabbed a ballpoint and a pad of paper. Something was better than nothing, and in the short time available to him between visits to the hot zone and the lab and the lengthy decon procedures that implied, nothing was about all he had. There were two places called Willard in the big atlas: one in Utah, on the north-eastern edge of the Great Salt Lake, and one in the middle of New Mexico on the Interstate about fifty miles east of the Rio Grande. Arends had been through all the registers in the Institute's extensive library, and as far as he could see there were no sizeable medical facilities in either place, still less any that dealt with tropical diseases or virology. In fact, apart from a health care centre in Austin, where the administrator swore indignantly that there had never been any hygiene problems, not a single hospital anywhere in the country bore the name Willard.

Arends must have scanned the papers Carmen Travis had given him a hundred times, searching for clues about the place it referred to, the place that received the full

214

decon treatment just nine years earlier. It occurred to him that maybe Willard was a vessel – epidemics on ships were certainly nothing new – but there wasn't a USS *Willard* anywhere in the navy. And then it struck him. Willard might be a place, but once upon a time it had probably been a person too – in some way or other a famous one.

Unfortunately, when it came to the humanities, the library at the RIID was not well stocked, and Arends was too busy on the EPD programme to get away to Washington. It was an act of sheer desperation to call up his nephew, Stewart – his flimsy pretext being that the kid was majoring in American history and culture at Brown. Fortunately Stewart was a bright and enthusiastic type, and didn't mind spending a few hours of his holiday doing detective work for his uncle in the military.

'Stew, I appreciate your doing this,' said Arends. 'What have you got?'

There was a shuffling sound, a turning over of pages.

'Well there's three Willards that seem to have made it into the history books, but I can't say I'd heard of any of them.'

'No problem. Who are they?'

'Well there was an English actor called Edward Willard, born 1853. He managed a lot of theatres in London.'

'OK. Forget about him.'

'I think everyone has already. Then there's Frances Elizabeth Willard, author, leading figure in the temperance movement. Born near Rochester, New York, 1839. Died 1898. Sound promising?'

Arends thought about it. It certainly wasn't beyond the good folks of Utah to name a town after a leader of the temperance movement. In fact, it made sense. Maybe the Willard where the decon happened really was some clinic endowed by the movement and named after one of their heroines.

'And who's number three?'

'Colonel Arthur James Willard, hero of the Indian Wars of 1885–86. Born in Texas 1838. I checked this guy out. He sounds a little more colourful, don't you think? He fought against Jeronimo in New Mexico, and apparently he developed the use of guerrilla tactics in the US army. Played the Indians at their own game, sort of thing.'

'Guerrilla tactics. Is that right?'

'Yes. Killed in battle, 1886. Fort Willard was named after him.'

'*Fort* Willard?'

'That's what it said in the book.'

'What book?'

'The name? Let me see. *Dwyer's History of the Union*. Pretty old and pretty, you know, uncritical, but thorough as hell. Maps and everything. Published in 1923, two volumes. And you know what? When I got to it, I found most of the pages still uncut. Imagine that. It's been sitting in the New York Public Library all this time and nobody took a proper look at it till I came along.'

His nephew was going to make a great historian, Arends could see that. But there was something he wanted to clear up.

'And this book said Fort Willard. I guess that's what the town of Willard was called before, right?'

'Probably. You know where it is?'

'Willard? It's on the interstate, about fifty miles south of Santa Fe.'

Stewart said something, but his voice was drowned out by the sound of a police siren.

'What was that? Stewart?'

'Sorry. Can't hear myself think. You said south?'

'South of Santa Fe, yes.'

'Er . . . No. I don't think that can be right. Fort Willard's right near where Colonel Willard was killed, over on the western side of the state. That's where the Navajo had their reservations. There were a whole string of forts down there: Fort Defiance was another one. I saw them all on this campaign map.'

Fort Willard. A military establishment. That would explain the use of military personnel in the decon operation.

'I don't remember seeing any Fort Willard,' Arends said. 'I'll have to go back and check the map.'

'I shouldn't worry,' Stewart said. 'It's probably not even there any more.'

Arends hired a pick-up in Albuquerque and drove west for a hundred miles along the interstate, before filling up in a small town called Thoreau and heading north. The unmarked asphalt road led him up into the Chacra Mesa, a rolling sun-bleached upland where nothing seemed to move except the clouds of dust kicked up by the breeze. Every few minutes he would pass a little roadside settlement: clusters of trailers or mobile homes that had lost their wheels. He hardly saw any people, just a little girl in a dirty pink dress swinging on an old truck tyre and a couple of women hanging out clothes on a line. From their dark skin and heavy black hair they looked like Indian stock. Then the settlements came to an end and there was nothing else to look at but the scrub, the shimmering, melted horizon and the blinding sky.

He drove fast, the radio tuned to a Spanish-speaking station that played salsa. He didn't like it, but somehow it was better than nothing. A map of the state lay on the passenger seat next to him, his destination marked by a circle drawn in ballpoint. His nephew had faxed him a photocopy of the campaign map from *Dwyer's History of the Union*, but he couldn't count on it being very accurate. He just hoped the road would lead him there.

Fort Willard. Seeing what had become of the Navajo made him think about the man behind the name. He was supposed to have been a hero, but what did that mean? Someone who made a name for himself riding into Indian settlements and butchering the inhabitants – women and children included, most likely. That was how they did things in those days.

Beyond taking a look at the place he didn't have any kind of plan. If Fort Willard turned out to be a functioning military facility, his only idea was to ask for directions and drive on. He might see something. And if Fort Willard turned out to be some old abandoned site, well then he was going to take a good look round all the same. Something had happened there. Something had gone wrong. You didn't order up a full-scale decon operation in 100 degrees of heat just for the fun of it. You did it because you were scared of something, of something getting out. And yet the only record that anything had happened at all was in some Special Forces report that nobody was supposed to see and which had been mailed to Lieutenant-Colonel Carmen Travis.

Ninety minutes after Thoreau and he was skirting the eastern edge of his circle. He slowed down, looking out for any turning that would lead him inside it, towards where the fort was supposed to be. The terrain had flattened out further, making it impossible to see more than a few hundred yards ahead. There was no traffic, no signposts, or power lines; nothing that pointed to any kind of military presence. The surface of the road was getting worse, the edges jagged and crumbling. Small stones bounced off the metal underbelly of the pick-up.

Arends checked his odometer: unless the campaign map had been a very sloppy piece of work he would soon be way too far north. He drove on another mile and then another, but there was nothing. He drove the pick-up onto the side of the road and stopped.

Whoever had sent the report to Carmen Travis had meant her to investigate, to uncover something. What other motive could they have? Yet the reference to Willard was the only piece of really hard information that hadn't been blacked out. That meant there had to be some way of finding it. Arends took a drink of water. Maybe the anonymous sender was a crank, or some officious junior some placc who'd come across the papers in a trash can. He looked around at the endless flat desert. It was hopeless.

He was in the middle of a U-turn when something caught his eye to the east of the road. It was a buzzard, rising up into the air, beating its big wings, a rodent dangling from its talons. Another bird was circling slowly above it, scanning the same stretch of shimmering ground.

Arends stopped the car. He sat up high in his seat to get a better look. Birds of prey liked hunting over roads because their prey was easier to spot against the flat surface.

He found the turning just a few hundred yards further back. He had been so convinced that Fort Willard was west of him that he had driven right past it looking the other way. Even so, it did not look promising: just a narrow thread of heat-buckled tarmac, wide enough for one vehicle only. Two miles on he came across a yellow sign shaped like a diamond which read: TOXIC WASTE STORAGE – KEEP OUT. It looked like someone had peppered it with buckshot.

He drove slowly now, trying to see what lay ahead of him. The radio signal was growing faint, the DJ's babble slowly sinking beneath a sea of radio-nothing. He punched the scan button but the numbers on the display just went around and around, finding the same flat hiss. Arends switched it off.

Another mile on he found a second sign, this one bigger, white letters against dark blue. It read:

DANGER

US ARMY TESTING AREA

ENTRY PROHIBITED

But there was no barrier, no gate, just the same black strip of road burning in the mid-morning sun. He came to a stop, half expecting a squad of MPs to jump out at him from nowhere, weapons raised. But no one came.

The perimeter fence lay another three miles on: wire mesh held up by concrete posts. Several sections near the road had come free at the bottom, leaving gaps big enough to crawl under. The gate was wire mesh too, topped with rusty-looking razor wire and tied to the gatepost with a heavy chain. There was a pillbox on the other side with Perspex blocks for windows.

Arends climbed out of the pick-up and walked up to the gate, blinking against the hot light.

'Hello? Anyone there?'

He felt the air move across his face like the draught from an oven. Behind the rectangular windows of the pillbox nothing stirred.

'Hello?'

He took hold of the chain. It was secured by a heavy steel padlock. He stood there for a few moments, the sweat gathering beneath his heavy cotton uniform, reluctant to take the next step, hoping he wouldn't have to.

'Is anybody here? This is an emergency! I'm trying to get to . . .'

He was wasting time and he knew it. If anyone could see him they weren't about to let on. He walked round to the back of the pick-up and stood in the shadow for a while. It took him a minute to decide there was no one there. Damn it, if there was anybody he'd just say he was curious about this empty old building. He crawled under the perimeter fence and was inside. An asphalt track ran straight ahead to the building itself.

He found the words *Fort Willard* on a semicircular brass plaque embedded in cement at the base of a flagpole. Around the pole stood two long, breeze-block huts with old-fashioned corrugated iron roofs, and a squat, windowless bunker that reminded Arends of Fort Detrick, except that it was older, judging from its stained concrete exterior, and a lot smaller. One of the huts had a narrow porch running along the front. All around the site the rocks and scrub had been cleared away to make room for a circle of lawn and even a little crescent-shaped flowerbed. But the grass and the flowers were long gone.

It was hard to tell how long the place had been empty. The edges of the doors and windows were all sealed over with silver duct tape, some of which had peeled off with the heat. Arends recognised standard decon procedure. Doors, windows and ventilation ducts were always sealed in this way prior to fumigation with formaldehyde gas. Even in the middle of this wilderness. *They'd been afraid that something would get out.*

There was no way into the bunker. The doors were iron and locked tight. A painted aluminium panel was attached to one of them with rivets. It read: IR–414 CLEARANCE REQUIRED – UNAUTHORIZED ENTRY STRICTLY PROHIBITED. Arends made a mental note of the number and went back to the main hut.

There were black venetian blinds up in the windows. He could make out a desk top upon which lay a heap of black plastic bags and a lamp on its side. A bucket and mop stood by a doorway, the sides encrusted with filth. There was a filing cabinet, the drawers all open, and the shrivelled-up remains of some big pot plant in a corner. Long, tear-shaped stains discoloured the whitewashed walls. He checked the main doors: they were wooden with square wire-glass panels at head height. He could get in there if he wanted to. *If . . .*

In the shade of the porch he climbed into the BL–3 protective gear he had brought with him: a white disposable Tyvek suit, goggles, filter mask, rubber gloves and boots. Then he picked up a rock from the flowerbed and slammed it against one of the wire-glass panels. It took a while to punch right through, but eventually he was able to reach up and retract the vertical bolt. With a little more play between the two doors, it wasn't difficult to force them apart.

The hallway had been used as a grey zone, Arends could see that at once. There was another set of doors at the opposite end and a big opaque plastic curtain strung up about a foot in front of it. The troughs where the men had cleaned off their boots with Clorox were still there, along with more unused black bags and several scrubbing brushes. The signs of haste made him uneasy. If this had been a RIID team at work, he thought, they would have bagged and destroyed everything; they would have followed procedure to the letter. But then again, in the heat, without the necessary incineration facilities on site, maybe the wisest thing would have been to kill and get clear, especially – he closed the splintered wooden door behind him – especially if the virus had been airborne. He hesitated for a moment, tempted to turn around and get out. The plastic curtain at the far end of the hallway flapped in the draught, inviting him on.

He was not prepared for the sight that met him on the other side. It looked as if someone had walked into an office and gone crazy with a water cannon, before walking off and leaving everything there to rot. The walls were all yellowed, the paint blistered and powdery. The furniture was overturned, the upholstery torn free and left on the floor. Even the covers had been pulled off the one sofa and left in a heap. The pictures – mainly colour photographs of the desert blown up large – had been torn down, leaving smeared black rectangles on the walls. Every drawer, shelf and cabinet had been cleared out and sprayed, judging from the dirt-laden residues that lay down the sides and in the corners. The only printed matter in the whole place were rows of scientific and medical texts which had been pulled down from their shelves and left on the floor.

Arends picked up a large loose-leaf volume. It was full of hundreds of electrophoresis shots: blurred white bars against a black background which revealed the sequence of bases in a section of genetic material. It was the kind of thing you could find in any medical research facility or biochemistry lab in the world. The other books were mostly standard texts, although several were in French. None of them had anything written inside them indicating to whom they had belonged. Arends looked around for photographs, of wives or children or classmates, but there were none of those either. *They'd been afraid something would get out* – several things, in fact. And one of them was the identities of the people who'd worked here. That had been as ruthlessly and systematically eradicated as anything else.

He was sweating in the suit. He went from room to room, searching for anything that would give him something to go on, give him some next step.

In all but a couple of the offices he found computer terminals. Without power it was impossible to check if anything was on them, but Arends guessed that if they had been so thorough clearing out the paperwork they would certainly have taken the trouble to wipe the hard disks. He thought about trying to get the power back on, but the generator was almost certainly hidden away inside the bunker. Besides, it was more than likely that the decon team had sprayed the inside of the computers, too; switched them on and let the fans suck the Envirochem mist right through the system. That would probably have wrecked them in any case.

Arends was in the furthest room, heading back towards the hallway again, when something crunched under his foot. Looking down he saw a flat plastic container, three and a half inches square, partly hidden beneath the carpet of blank paper which had been scattered across the floor. It was the kind used to hold portable computer disks, and it was empty except for the card inside upon which had been written *N2* in blue pen.

Arends looked at the container for a moment and then went over to the terminal. The simplest way to delete all data would have been to reformat the hard disk. It would only have taken a few minutes. But if they had been in a hurry, it was just possible they might have forgotten . . .

He reached down and pressed the button below the portable disk drive. It was very stiff. Maybe the disinfectant had corroded the mechanism – that stuff would corrode almost anything.

'Come on, damn it!'

He pressed harder, his hand moist inside the rubber glove. Then, without warning, a black plastic disk toppled out of the drive, landing with a clatter on the surface of the desk. On the label was written *N2* in the same hand as before. He reached out to take it, but then stopped. The disk would have been handled by whoever had worked there, and if the decon team had missed the disk, maybe the Envirochem and the formaldehyde had missed it too. It was unlikely that anything virulent would have survived the years of heat and desiccation, but it was impossible to be sure. He reached into his pocket for a sealable sample bag and, turning it partially inside out, carefully gathered up the disk without letting it come into contact with his glove. Then he sealed the sample bag and placed it inside another.

All the way to Albuquerque, and from Albuquerque

to Washington, the disk sat inside the sample bags in Arends's top pocket, the single tangible remnant of the emergency at Fort Willard, the emergency that had never happened.

8

Carmen Travis stood in the shade of a hangar fanning herself with a clipboard. Behind her the big four-wheel-drive Cherokees were part loaded and almost ready to go. Corporals Baker and Sarandon, responsible for the maintenance of the vehicles, including the disposition of the loads, were working through the sixty-point checklist of field equipment which Carmen had put together to cover the likely collection scenarios.

For the most part the equipment comprised basic items like whirl-pack sampling bags, strainers, forceps and adhesive tape labels, but there were also the aspirators, the liquid nitrogen used for storing insects, arthropods, and any mammalian samples they might collect; plus the blood-and-wire traps they would use to gather biting insects.

Then there were the satcom equipment and the orange Racal suits, the same as Carmen had worn back in the BL–4 labs with a basic air-cooling system added. Finally there were the rifles that Leigh had obtained – semi-automatic rimfires, firing .22 calibre rounds. Leigh had felt that given the inexperience of the team in using hunting rifles the rimfires, which had to be manually cocked after each round was chambered, were the safest choice. There was no danger of anyone spraying ammunition around and putting a hole in somebody.

Preparing for the trip, Carmen had clocked up twelve hours in the RIID library, focusing on the work done by the RIID itself, but also reviewing WHO research based on the earliest outbreaks of viral haemorrhagic fever. She had supplemented this with more recent field studies reported in the *American Journal of Tropical Medicine*, and journals specialising in epidemiology and virology.

In the welter of ambiguous and sometimes contradictory data, she had drawn up a base strategy for the mission with a view to isolating the likely vector or vectors of the disease, and their reservoir – if one existed – and thereby make recommendations to the Indonesian government to prevent further outbreaks. If the virus came from one area the authorities could try to keep people away. If it turned out that it was carried by an arthropod there was always the option of reducing the infected populations through the use of insecticides.

Preliminary reports from the WHO and Indonesian authorities suggested that Muaratebo was the epicentre of the epidemic, but that other outbreaks might have predated the Muaratebo case. There was some talk about one of the early victims of the disease having come down from the rain forest above Muaratebo. However, until the facts regarding this person and exactly where he had come from were clarified, Carmen had decided that the first ecological investigation should focus on Muaratebo itself, and should take the form of a broad study of potential vectors.

She had put together a seven-person team, comprising herself and Leigh; Dr Lennox, a RIID veterinary parasitologist; Major McKinnon, who specialised in virology; and Dr Harold Daintith the well-known epidemiologist. The other members were non-specialists: Corporal Sarandon, who, as well as driving, was responsible for telecommunications; and Corporal Baker.

Despite Carmen's initial protests, the mission was carrying an X-band special applications terminal which allowed them to complete a single thread, full duplex satellite communications link. Carmen's objection had been to burdening the operation with a second non-specialist plus all the X-SAT equipment – even though this could in fact be transported in three standard-size suitcases, and weighed only sixty kilos.

In the end it was Bailey who had convinced her of the value of the satcom capability. If the situation *vis-à-vis* the Indonesian government deteriorated – a distinct possibility if the epidemic led to a total embargo on Indonesian trade and communications – Carmen might be glad of the X-SAT, which allowed for secure voice and secure fax communication.

The X-SAT system was also compatible with government modems so that raw data could be dumped into the RIID network, thus boosting the mission's statistical/analytical capability. Finally, in the event of the mission losing contact with US military satellites, X-SAT could be reconfigured to interface a military application to the available commercial resources, both domestic and international.

Reluctantly, Carmen had given way to Bailey's arguments, consoled by the fact that Sarandon, as Major Leigh pointed out to her, was an experienced soldier and knew how to shoot straight if the situation really did deteriorate. Leigh was only joking, but the thought of a little soldierly brawn to back up their abundant brains was reassuring.

Three days into the new assignment, Carmen had longed for the preparatory work to be over. She did not relish the thought of going into what was probably a very dangerous situation in Sumatra, but anything seemed better than the endless talk and preparation. Once in the field, things would become much simpler, she had told herself.

She had turned out to be wrong.

The main reason for the continuing difficulty was now racing towards her through the heat haze in an M38 jeep. Brigadier Sutami was supposed to have full responsibility for the quarantine operation in Muaratebo, but in the few days of dealing with him Carmen had gained the impression that he was just doing as he was told, and could take few initiatives. But he was on his own. That much was clear. There had been some WHO people involved in a preliminary study of the epidemic, but they were now concentrating their efforts on dealing with the crisis in Muaratebo.

When the RIID people had arrived in Jambi it was Sutami who had explained that the team would have to carry two Indonesian observers if they were going into the interior. Carmen had objected, arguing that their transport and supplies were predicated on a seven-person team, and that observers would only get in the way. Sutami had then made it perfectly clear that the Indonesian government was ready to help the Americans only if they, in turn, showed a willingness to co-operate.

There had been a brief stand-off and then, a couple of hours later, it was discovered that the locals had yet to receive confirmation from Singapore regarding laboratory facilities which were to be made available to Carmen's team, and that the supplies – one metric tonne of them, including fresh water – had somehow gone astray. When asked about the hitches, Sutami had just smiled, pointing out that things like that happened all the time in developing countries.

Desperate to get the show on the road, Carmen had wrangled with Sutami, and had finally accepted one of the observers. His name was Sergeant Soesanto Kaoy, and Corporal Baker had spent half a day teaching him how to drive one of the Cherokees. Content with his partial victory, Sutami had promised he would look into the question of the supplies. That had been ten hours ago.

Now it was late afternoon and Carmen was still waiting for the supplies to complete the loading.

Sutami pulled up in a cloud of dust and climbed out of his jeep. He strolled towards her, looking around, obviously uncomfortable at finding her without the other high-ranking officers. It was clear to Carmen that Sutami just couldn't work out how a small woman in trousers could be in command of seven strong men. Every time she put a question to him he looked embarrassed and insisted on answering Major Leigh or one of the others. It was bad enough having the Indonesian observer attached to their group in the first place without having her authority put under this strain. Watching him approach, she decided it was time she clarified the situation for him.

'Brigadier,' she said. She waited until he was actually looking at her. His face was a dull yellow colour and there were one or two hairs on his top lip which trapped beads of moisture.

'I understood we were going to Muaratebo today.'

Sutami looked away. He cleared his throat, making his prominent Adam's apple jump.

'I have already discuss this with the Major Leigh, Colonel. He agreed with me – '

'I don't give a *damn* what you have or have not discussed with Major Leigh, Brigadier. I am in command of this unit and any information you have regarding the mission must come to me. Do you understand?'

She had raised her voice without meaning to, and now the Brigadier was sulking. He looked straight at her, pulling his shoulders back, showing that he was above such displays of emotion.

'Muaratebo unsafe, Colonel. We cannot be sure you are safe there.'

His voice was calm, as if he was trying to soothe her. Carmen felt her blood coming to the boil.

'What?'

'In Muaratebo the situation is worse. Every hour we have report. There has been civil problem. We cannot . . . guarantee safety.'

'Brigadier, we are trained soldiers. We do not . . .'

At that moment Major Leigh pulled up in a truck. He saluted as he came into the shade of the hangar. Sutami let out an audible sigh of relief.

'We've located the supplies, Colonel,' Leigh said. 'They were in a hangar covered with a tarp. Seems the quartermaster made a mistake with the paperwork.'

Carmen shot Sutami a glance, then turned her eyes on Major Leigh:

'I understand you have been discussing the situation in Muaratebo with the Brigadier, Major Leigh.'

Leigh looked at the Cherokees, and the litter of bags and boxes on the floor.

'Not really, Colonel. Brigadier Sutami told me about the situation there, that's all.'

Carmen turned back to Sutami.

'The Brigadier seemed to be under the impression that you had agreed we should avoid Muaratebo because of the danger. Perhaps he misunderstood.'

There was an awkward silence. Carmen reproached herself. There was nothing to be gained by humiliating Sutami. She tried a new tack.

'Brigadier, I have been looking at the documents you provided on the epidemiological profile of the outbreak in Muaratebo.'

Sutami straightened up, ready to go on the defensive.

'The survey of the population seems to have been very thorough in what must be difficult conditions.'

Sutami nodded, his serious eyes fixed on her mouth.

'The WHO sent advisers,' he said. 'They help us put together report.'

'But there are questions concerning the transmission of

the disease; questions raised by Dr Daintith, our expert in these matters.'

'Yes?'

'Yes. He is puzzled by the lack of entries for primary infection. The majority, in fact all of the reports, are for secondary infection.'

'Apart from the man, the monkey . . .' Sutami frowned, unable to find the word.

'The monkey hunter, yes. It's hard for me . . . for Dr Daintith to understand how one man can have infected the town so completely, so quickly. Muaratebo has a population of 40,000 people. And according to the reports as many as 5,000 are already infected.'

Sutami shrugged.

'The problem we have . . . the only explanation we can come up with is that either this disease is unlike anything we have seen before, or the survey has been mistaking primary for secondary cases. You see, the explosion of the disease might be explained by a large number of primary contacts as might be expected if the vector of the disease – '

'Vector?'

'The carrier. If the carrier of this disease were something widespread such as the mosquito for example.'

'Not mosquito. Monkey.'

Carmen looked at Leigh. She went on.

'Yes, perhaps. The trouble with a primate vector – '

'I have positive proof,' said Sutami. He removed his cap for a moment and wiped the sweat from his forehead. Carmen and Leigh exchanged a look. Sutami went on:

'The monkey trader – '

'The hunter?'

'No. Trader. The man who send the monkeys to the United States. The man who know the monkey hunter. I know where he is. You can ask him. He will tell you everything you need to know.'

They had learned about the monkey trader as soon as they had touched down in Jambi. The Indonesians in collaboration with the WHO officials had traced the supply of infected animals reported by the US back to Jambi and to one man in particular, someone well known in Muaratebo.

'He is being held at convent,' Sutami said. 'We can go there in the jeep unless you prefer use your own transport.'

Carmen sighed.

'Your jeep will be fine, Brigadier.'

Sutami was about to turn on his heels when Carmen said to Major Leigh in the most booming military voice she could muster:

'Major, I want you to instruct the men to prepare to move out today. Secure the supplies and fuel up the transport.'

Leigh snapped a salute, obviously surprised by the sudden formality, and left them. Carmen took a document wallet with a microcassette from inside one of the Cherokees and set off in the direction of Brigadier Sutami's waiting jeep.

The convent was in the Dutch colonial style and looked out of place among the traditional peaked roofs of Sumatra. Originally built for a sorority of fifty, the building now accommodated only seven, the rest of the rooms used as a mixture of hostel and clinic. As Carmen understood it, the monkey trader was being kept there in isolation, because of overcrowding at the Jambi hospital.

Carmen and Sutami were shown into a room by one of the diminutive sisters and then left alone. It was surprisingly cool after the superheated exterior and Carmen felt the perspiration on her back chill. They were standing in a stark room with crucifixes on the walls and a fan turning slowly in the ceiling. The shutters were closed against the sunlight.

There was an odd smell. Like lemons, but not fresh. Carmen stood in the middle of the room on the polished teak floor, keeping a good distance between herself and the pungent sweatiness of Brigadier Sutami. Neither of them spoke. There were flat cushions in one corner around a low table, and in the middle of the room a long table with two incongruous orange acrylic chairs. Carmen was still determined to get up to Muaratebo, but felt that a useful way to spend the time while Leigh managed the packing of the Cherokees was in talking to this man who seemed to have passed through the eye of the storm unaffected. There was even the possibility, however remote, that he carried some kind of antibody.

She was considering this when the man entered the room. Carmen felt herself break out in a cold sweat. She had expected to be led herself into an area where the man would be on the other side of a barrier of some sort. To see him walk in accompanied by one of the sisters, with no kind of barrier, not even a surgical mask, brought home to her how little these people understood about what they were dealing with. She took a step back.

'Stop right there, sir.'

He was about ten feet away. He came to a halt and looked from Carmen to the sister. Carmen turned to Sutami, the thought flashing through her mind that the whole building could be crawling with virus.

'Would you please step outside with me for a moment, Brigadier.'

She allowed Sutami to open the door for her and then walked quickly back out of the building. She waited until they were out of the shadow of the convent before she spoke. She was trembling with shock and anger, and for a moment the words would not come.

'You don't . . . you don't . . . you don't seem to realise what you are dealing with, Brigadier.'

234

'But it is safe, Colonel. The man is the same here for a long time. The sisters, they say – '

'I don't care what the sisters say, Brigadier. Until proper serological and virological tests are carried out, a person coming from an infected area must be assumed to be infected.'

Sutami looked alarmed, but he was beginning to lose his patience.

'But not sick.'

'He may be carrying the virus!'

Carmen had almost screamed. There was a moment of silence, and then both of them turned at the sound of the convent door opening. The sister was standing there in the shadow of the building.

'Explain to the sister that she must spray the walls with phenolic . . .'

Carmen felt her strength go. She got into Sutami's jeep as an alternative to swooning in his arms – he would probably have fallen under her weight. Then, furious at her own weakness, she turned the key in the ignition and roared off down the road.

She arrived at the base covered in a fine film of white dust which made her look even worse than she felt.

Leigh and Sarandon were standing over one of the X-SAT cases. They looked up as she pulled the handbrake. By the expression on their faces, Carmen could tell she looked bad.

'Don't worry. I'm OK. Just had a little surprise is all. They have the guy from Muaratebo walking around in his pyjamas down at the convent. He was about to shake my hand, I think.'

'Jesus Christ.'

Leigh came forward as she stepped out of the jeep. But he didn't try to support her.

'You sure you're OK, Colonel?'

Carmen brushed at her uniform, and went directly to the back of one of the Cherokees.

'I'm fine,' she managed to say. She knew it looked bad. How could the men have confidence going into a hot zone with her when she got into a panic in what was, after all, a low-pressure situation? She had been right to come out of the convent. She was right to get suited up before going back. But there was no reason to get emotional, goddammit! She was a soldier, a professional. She had the expertise and the back-up – the best in the world. She would take charge and deal with the problem. *Find out how we put the stopper back in the bottle*. That was what she was going to do. She would not give in to the fear. They were counting on her for that.

Carefully she unpacked one of the Racal suits reserved for her use. It was smaller than the men's suits. She felt self-conscious clambering into it, but was glad to feel a steadying anger starting to warm her cheeks. The men watched her clamber back into the jeep. Neither of them said a word.

He was enormous. And he was smoking a cigar. Carmen was pleased none of the smell got in through her fine-pore filter. She had explained to the sister and Sutami that the man was to be totally isolated until she had carried out serological tests. And now she was sitting alone with him in a room with white walls, breathing safe air through her mask. The guy could sneeze or cough, and she was in no danger at all. The cooled air pumped through by the new pack was delightful after the heat and humidity.

'It's quite ridiculous,' said the fat man. 'They treat me like a leper but I'm perfectly fine. No headache, no fever.' He sucked hard on his cigar and blew smoke up into the roof. He considered Carmen for a moment, taking in her impassive face through her visor. Carmen gave herself a little shake.

'I'm Lieutenant-Colonel Travis of the United States Army,' she said. 'We are here to trace the source of this disease and to advise the Indonesian government as to how they might deal with it. I appreciate your finding time to talk to me, sir. I apologise about what happened earlier. I'm afraid my work here is too important for me to take any unnecessary risks.'

The man smiled and held out a plump hand.

'Bacelius Habibie. Pleased to meet you, madam.'

Carmen looked at the extended hand and then reached out her own gloved one.

There was an awkward silence and then Carmen set her tape running. She took some papers out of her document wallet.

'Mr Habibie, I – '

'Are you recording this?'

'Yes. Is that a problem?'

'No, no. I just hope I can say something that will justify your going to all that trouble.'

'Mr Habibie, I understand you deal in monkeys trapped here for export to the United States.'

'Until recently I did, yes. Now I spend a lot of time looking at the wall in my room.'

'And that among the last supply you sold to a Mr . . .' Carmen consulted her notes.

'Sudirman.'

'Mr Sudirman, yes. Among those monkeys, the last you brought down from Muaratebo, there were animals that were marked with a red dye.'

'Ahmad's animals, that's right.'

'Who, sorry?'

'Ahmad. He was the hunter who brought those monkeys to me.'

'Directly from the forest?'

237

'Yes.'

'When did you see him this time? When was it he came out of the forest?'

Habibie blew smoke up at the rafters, considering.

'It's difficult to . . . I would say perhaps around the 26th.'

'Of last month?'

'Of July, yes.'

Assuming a cycle similar to Marburg – an incubation period of around seven days to the onset of symptoms and death in the following week – Habibie had had plenty of time to develop the disease and die; if the disease had been transmitted on the 26th. Of course, Ahmad might have been infected at that time through contact with the monkeys without himself being infectious to Habibie.

'Did Ahmad show any signs of sickness?'

'Well Ahmad always looked a little unwell, especially on his visits to town. He stayed at a rather seedy establishment – Madam Kim's.'

'Seedy?'

'Yes. A brothel, a whorehouse.'

Carmen sat back from the table for a moment, remembering the circumstances of other outbreaks in which sexual promiscuity had played a key role in the spread of the disease. If Ahmad had brought something into Muaratebo he might have spread it through contact with the prostitutes, who would in turn spread it to their clients. It was a worst-case scenario. It might go some way to explain the rapidity of the epidemic's development.

'So are you saying he looked unwell?'

'When I last saw him . . .' Habibie mused for a moment, sucking at his cigar. 'Those horrible yellow eyes of his and his brown teeth. He looked horrible but I would say no worse than usual.'

'No bites?'

'Sorry?'

'He didn't complain of any bites? Monkey or insect bites. Presumably he got bitten from time to time in his line of work.'

'There are few things in the jungle nasty enough, or hungry enough to want to take a bite out of Ahmad, I can assure you. Except . . .' He held up his hand, showing Carmen a small red mark: 'When we were transferring the last batch of animals, one of them did bite Ahmad, and me too.'

Carmen frowned.

'The same animal bit you both?'

'Yes. Very quick. Like the lightning.'

It seemed incredible that Habibie hadn't developed the disease.

'And when did you last see him?'

'That would have been the following day, the 27th. I went to his . . . er, hotel.'

Carmen looked hard at Habibie. It seemed like he had been very lucky. Unless of course he had picked the virus up through contact with one of the prostitutes Ahmad had used.

'Mr Habibie, I don't mean to be offensive, but did you ever visit Madam Kim's – as a client, I mean?'

The fat man threw his head back and laughed, his enormous trunk joggling with mirth. Eventually he wiped his eyes, and took a gentle suck at his cigar.

'Certainly not,' he said.

'And when did you actually leave Muaratebo?'

'I came down the river at the beginning of the month. The third or the fourth.'

Today was the 16th. Carmen felt fairly sure that Habibie had escaped untouched.

'Mr Habibie I believe you have nothing to worry about,' she said.

Habibie smiled.

'That's what I keep telling them, madam.' He slapped his chest. 'Never felt fitter in my life.'

'I would like to do some tests on you to be absolutely sure, but you will probably be able to leave here quite soon.'

Habibie looked satisfied. Carmen continued.

'Have you had any news from Ahmad since?'

'News, no.'

'Any reports of his whereabouts? Perhaps he went back into the jungle?'

'The last I knew about it he had left Madam Kim's. He usually stayed there until he had spent all his money.'

'Then what?'

'He'd go back into the forest. Catch more monkeys. He'd stay up there maybe three or four weeks at a time. He was a very simple man. Then again . . .'

Habibie turned the moist end of his cigar in his red lips. 'What?'

Habibie was clearly hesitating to talk in the presence of the tape recorder. Then he leaned forward, smirking horribly.

'Well I know he was hoping to transact some business in Muaratebo.'

'Business?'

'Ahmad traded in all kinds of things, you know. Not just monkeys. I believe when he came to Muaratebo this time he had something he wanted to sell me. Something special. Not monkeys. Not monkeys.'

Carmen frowned.

'What then? Drugs?'

'One time he came down the river with a gun. You know, a big machine-gun. Turned out that it belonged to the military.'

And he told the story of Ahmad's crimes and misdemeanours. The anecdotes seemed endless. Carmen could see that what she had been able to tell Habibie had come as a great relief, despite his bravado. He relaxed in his chair, asked for the sister to bring them water and sucked at his smouldering cigar. It was all very disagreeable, but Carmen wanted to get to what business Ahmad had sought to transact. It was unlikely that whatever it was held the key to the epidemic, but she didn't like not knowing a detail that he obviously considered important. She pressed him several times and eventually he made a confession.

He was leaning forward, his hands spread apart on the rough wooden table, smoke rising from the last inch of his cigar.

'It's difficult to understand, for an outsider I mean,' he said.

'What is?'

'How things like that happen.'

'Things like what? Are you talking about Ahmad? What he wanted to sell you?'

Habibie looked at Carmen over the glowing end of his cigar. His eyes were very serious now.

'You come here from your country and you judge us. I feel it.'

'I'm here on the invitation of the Indonesian government. I'm here to try to stop what is happening in Muaratebo happening anywhere else.'

Some ash dropped onto the table and Habibie brushed it away.

'Of course,' he said.

It was quiet in the room. Carmen breathed her purified air, relieved not to be smelling Habibie and his cigar.

'What did Ahmad want to sell you?'

Habibie wasn't looking at her now. He went on as if talking to himself.

'Two hundred million people,' he said. 'Not as many as in India perhaps, or China, but a lot of people. Millions and millions of people. Very poor, some of them. Millions and millions of children born with empty stomachs. They crawl from the cradle to the scrap heaps outside the cities, looking for chicken bones, for empty water bottles to sell to the recycling plants. You see them here in Jambi. No social welfare here, you see. Not like in the USA. Parents think that by having many children they will be supported in their old age. Sons and daughters.'

'What has this got to do with Ahmad?'

Habibie seemed to become aware of her again. He took in the orange Racal suit and Carmen's face looking out at him through plastic.

'Sometimes, you see, Ahmad would come down from the forest with friends. People think the Indians are noble. But it is not true. They also burn the forest to cultivate. They also pollute. They also drink. They become blind drunk. Get reckless. For the right price they will sell you anything.'

He looked at Carmen, no longer smiling. He looked immensely sad.

'I'm not sure I understand you,' said Carmen.

Habibie looked at the stub of his cigar and sighed.

'Some people say that what is happening in Muaratebo is a judgement,' he said gravely. Then he was smiling at her. 'But how can that be unless I, for some reason, have been pardoned?'

9

She thought she'd lost them a hundred times. The three Kubu tribesmen moved fast through the forest, their small, sinuous frames dodging through the chaos of vegetation. Crashing and stumbling after them Holly felt like she belonged to a different species, a clumsy, brutal one that had long ago traded grace for size and weight. Every few minutes she had to stop and catch her breath, and then suddenly she would find herself alone. The men were following pathways – there were thousands of them, Willis had explained, crisscrossing the jungle from one end of the island to the other – but to her those pathways were invisible. The Kubu left no tracks. She would grow frightened and hurry on, hoping she had the right direction, and just when she was growing desperate she would blunder into one of them as he stood there waiting for her. And then she would realise that she had not been alone after all. The tribesman had been standing there, waiting patiently. She just hadn't been able to see him.

They didn't speak to each other, or to her, at least not during the first day. But neither were they completely silent. On the rare occasions when she was up close to them she noticed that they were muttering or humming as they walked. It sounded like a chant, a prayer. Willis had said the Kubu believed in evil spirits. Maybe the chant was supposed to keep the evil spirits at bay. Once a monkey went by overhead, leaping from one tree to another, shaking the branches. One of the Kubu, the youngest, pointed to it and said something. That was the only time he spoke.

Holly had set out hopefully. Normally she would have called it madness to put her life so completely in the hands of utter strangers, men she knew nothing about. Yet she felt safer with the Kubu than at any time since her arrival in Sumatra. This was their country, their land. For them the forest was not an inconvenience, an impediment to development. It was part of them. If anyone could guide her to Emma and Lucy, they could. For them roadblocks and checkpoints were obstacles as easily avoided as the trees themselves, and every hour, every step brought them closer to Rafflesia Camp. That thought made it easier to ignore the blisters on her feet, the insect bites, and the sticky, stinging sweat that seemed now to envelop her entire body. The only thing she could not ignore was the dizziness that overtook her sometimes, accompanied by a wrenching pain in her gut.

At the end of the first day with the Kubu they slept beneath the huge twisted limbs of a strangling fig. Holly ate the stale dried biscuits that Willis had left her, and pieces of fruit wrapped in leaves which the Kubu gave her. She tried to return the favour by offering them the chlorinated water from her canteen, but they spat it out at once as if it were poison. That night the dysentery began. She was beginning to feel weak, but struggled to conceal the fact. She was afraid the Kubu might take her back to their village if they saw that she was getting sick. They would probably do it without even telling her, and there was no way she would know until it was too late.

Willis had said it would take about two days to get to the camp. As she lay on her side at dawn, listening to the forest awakening, she imagined how it would be when she arrived. Jonathan had described the camp: a semicircle of wooden huts painted white and grey standing in a well-kept clearing. There would be fruit trees and flowering shrubs. Jonathan would be standing on the veranda just as he had been in her dreams, looking out into the wilderness that he loved. And maybe Emma and Lucy would be playing outside – except that they were getting a little too old for play. They would all get the fright of their lives when their mother stumbled out of the forest, ragged and filthy, with three Kubu tribesmen for an escort. Perhaps Jonathan would even be impressed at her initiative, but next to Christina she would look a very sorry sight. At the first opportunity Holly resolved to clean up as much as possible, to at least wipe the grime off her face.

The going had been slower that day. Much of the time they were going steeply downhill. The tribesmen skipped and bounded down the narrow defiles, but Holly had to scramble, hanging onto whatever she could find to keep from falling. Often hidden thorns tore through the flesh on her soft palms, and the blisters on her feet burned. Twice she fell, and although she was not badly hurt, the dizziness that followed made it hard to get up again.

It was early in the afternoon, when the jungle heat was at its worst, that the tribesmen began talking among themselves. As she caught up with them Holly found the oldest of the three – to Holly he looked easily fifty, although she knew he was probably younger than that – explaining something to the others, his skinny brown arms making wide gestures across the horizon. Holly wanted desperately to know what he was talking about, how close they were to the camp, but it was no use. There was no way she could make herself understood. After a few moments they set off again, this time, it seemed, more slowly, more cautiously. Maybe, Holly thought, they were just trying to make it easier for her to keep up. Or maybe there was some other reason.

She began to think about what she had heard back at the village. The Kubu had said there had been soldiers in the forest near Rafflesia Camp, that the soldiers were mad, but that they were now dead. And there was talk of evil spirits. Did they mean that there were ghosts in the forest, the ghosts of soldiers? Willis had told her not to worry. Anything unusual or unexplained the Kubu put down to spirits, he had said. It was part of the primitive fatalism that had contributed to their inexorable decline.

They reached the banks of the great river about three hours before sunset. Holly did not notice it until the last moment, a wide expanse of deep green water, slipping silently by, its banks invisible beneath the overhang of thick green vegetation. Jonathan had told her that the camp was close to the river – just a few miles. They would be there before nightfall!

Then suddenly the oldest tribesman was talking to her, gesturing just as before. She struggled to make sense of what he was saying but the words meant nothing. It seemed to be important. He was pointing up along the side of the river, towards the south.

'The camp is there?' she asked. 'There? We go there, yes?'

The man kept talking. All the men were watching her. The young one waved his arm from side to side, a gesture of denial. Holly grew alarmed.

'You have to take me there. To the camp.'

Still talking, the older man placed the palm of his hand heavily against her shoulder and then pointed up river once again. Holly thought she understood: that was where she was to go, but they would not go with her.

'But how will I find it? How will I know . . . Please, you have to take me there!'

But they were already moving off, the dappled yellow light flashing across the skin of their backs.

'Wait! Wait, please!'

One of the men, the youngest, stopped and looked at her. There was something in his face – was it pity, curiosity? Maybe he would take her to the camp, Holly thought, even if the others wouldn't. Maybe he was too young to be frightened of ghosts. She ran to catch up with him, scrambling up the steep root-tangled incline, but in a moment he was gone. Holly stood there listening for the sound of him moving through the forest, hoping to find him again. But he made no sound.

'Come back!' she shouted. 'Come back!'

Her voice was weak; it barely seemed to penetrate beyond her own skull. She felt dizzy, nauseous. She steadied herself against the trunk of a tree.

'What are you so scared of?' she said, but her voice came out as no more than a whisper. 'What in God's name are you so scared of?'

10

London. August 17th

A police helicopter was pounding the air a few hundred feet overhead as the last convoy of ambulances turned out onto Stanley Road and sped away towards Northwick Park Hospital eight miles away. Ken Lyall, deputy director of the Communicable Disease Surveillance Centre, took a deep breath and walked towards the forecourt of Accident & Emergency where a marked police car stood waiting. Detective Sergeant Stevens opened the door for him. Both men wore white disposable Tyvek suits.

At five o'clock that morning the CDSC had reported the Jarvis case to the WHO in Geneva. Confirmation that the symptoms matched those of the Muaratebo virus followed in less than an hour. At ten o'clock a team had arrived at St Anne's to transport Peter Jarvis to the Hospital for Tropical Diseases in Camden Town, where proper isolation facilities existed. The team wore pressurised suits and were equipped with airtight bubble-stretchers. Nurse Rose Priestly, Dr Terry Pahadia and the ambulance men who had arrived at the scene of Jarvis's accident were also taken to Camden for observation and tests.

The Accident & Emergency Unit was sealed by a second team from the London Fire Brigade at twenty minutes past eleven. At the same time, the evacuation of the adjacent wing of the hospital began: 140 patients, some of whom had only come out of surgery the previous night, were loaded onto ambulances one by one and dispersed to other hospitals in and beyond London. Just assembling the ambulances proved a logistical nightmare, and in each case an individual room had to be found and round-the-clock observation organised. All leave for Control of Infection Officers at London hospitals was cancelled. At four o'clock a decontamination team from the Royal Army Medical Corps was due to arrive at St Anne's, although there had apparently been problems with their suits and this was holding them up. Their work inside A&E would take around three hours. When that was completed then, and only then, would Lyall have a chance to grab some sleep. Meanwhile he had another task to attend to.

The voice coming through the entry-phone had a strong foreign accent. There was loud music in the background. Detective Sergeant Stevens leaned in towards the microphone.

'This is the police. Could you let us in, please?'

'*Quoi?*'

'The police,' said Stevens. 'Can we come in please?'

Lyall looked up the outside of the building. On the third floor he saw a curtain being pulled back, a silhouette. They must have looked like a bunch of pest exterminators, Lyall thought, standing there in their suits with respirators tucked under their arms. At least the double-parked patrol car was unmistakable.

'Hello?'

Stevens pressed the buzzer again. The door responded instantly, the electronic bolt retracting noisily. Stevens, together with a constable and Dr Lyall, went inside and began climbing the narrow stairs towards the top floor where Peter Jarvis was supposed to have lived. They were two floors up when a head appeared over the top of the banisters above them. It was a man in his late twenties with short black hair and round glasses.

'*Allo?*'

'Evening,' said Stevens and carried on climbing. When he was level with the other man he added: 'We're looking for Dr Jarvis's flat. Top floor, is it?'

'Yez,' said the man. 'But 'e is not in.'

'Yes, we know that. Do you know where he's been?'

The man shook his head.

'Is not 'ere a lot. He go . . .' He made an aeroplane shape with his hand and made the aeroplane take off.

'Do you have a key to his place?'

'No. Is it a problem?'

'No. But we're going to have to force an entry up there. We'll leave a notice. OK?'

They marched past and up the next flight of stairs. The door they found was plain white with one deadlock and a latch. The deadlock had not been turned, but even so Lyall was surprised at how easily the policemen managed to shoulder their way in. The latch offered little resistance.

Lyall put on his respirator and waited for the others to do the same. It was probably an unnecessary precaution – Jarvis was unlikely to have left much in the way of infected material at the flat, and in two days any aerosolised particles would have dried out – but then again they could not be sure. Some viruses could survive for years outside the benign environment of living tissue, floating through the air like particles of dust, enduring temperatures no organism or micro-organism could survive. The respirators were a precaution worth taking.

It was a small two-bedroom flat containing a mixture of plain, unpretentious western furniture and items from Africa and Asia. A huge wineskin hung up on one wall, an elaborately printed rug on another. Between a plain blue sofa and a creased leather armchair lay a patterned mat made up of reeds of different colours. As he crossed the main room Lyall could not help reflecting that the man who had lived here would never see it again. It seemed wrong somehow to come and disturb it, a little like defacing a memorial – except that this was far more personal than any monument carved in stone.

'Suitcase,' said Stevens, his voice constricted, nasal under his mask. There was a battered brown bag in one corner. He crouched down and examined the luggage tags and labels on the handle.

'Flew in on Singapore Airlines,' he said. 'And Garuda some time before that. Probably a connecting flight from somewhere.'

Lyall went into the bathroom and started taking swabs from around the sink and the lavatory. These he sealed inside small plastic phials which he marked with a China-graph pencil. Then he took all the toiletries – soap, flannel, razor, toothbrush and toothpaste – and placed them in resealable plastic bags. Meanwhile Stevens went through into the main bedroom.

Lyall checked through the suitcase. It was mostly full of clothes, all of them dirty except for one pristine silk shirt, which Jarvis must have been saving for a special occasion that had never come. There was a pair of walking boots, a safari jacket, a Swiss army penknife, a torch, an alumin-ium water bottle, a portable short-wave radio and several paperback books, one of which, *A Handful of Dust*, was inscribed 'To Peter, Bon Voyage from Francesca'.

It all fitted what they already knew of Jarvis's trip, but added nothing. According to his family he had been on some sort of research project for the Natural History Museum. Apparently he was an entomologist, and had done his doctorate on a family of parasitic wasps. They had tried to raise someone at the museum that afternoon, but no one had been there who could help them. It would have been easy enough to assume that Jarvis had been in Muaratebo and had picked up the virus there: but they could not afford to make that assumption because there was always a chance he had come from somewhere else. If that proved to be the case they had another line of investigation to follow, or perhaps another epidemic.

Stevens came back into the room.

'Is this what we're looking for?'

In one hand he held a bundle of maps, in the other a black, hardbacked exercise book. The pages were crammed full of dense longhand. Jarvis had kept a log.

PART FOUR

Exposure

1

Carmen waited twenty-four hours for Sutami to change his mind, but it made no difference. Muaratebo might be important to the RIID investigation – Sutami was ready to concede that – but it was too dangerous for them to go there. Sensing the presence of an immovable obstacle higher up – some politician trying to save his ass, was Carmen's guess – she decided to throw in the towel. And besides, she was unwilling to wait any longer. After a long discussion with the rest of the team, she decided that the only thing for it was to make for the second most likely focus of the epidemic, a settlement near Muaratebo where trouble had been reported around about the same time as, if not just before, the Muaratebo outbreak.

The settlement, some kind of camp, was supposed to be located above Muaratebo on the Hari river, and so there was always the possibility that the hunter, Ahmad, who was known to have used the river to bring monkeys down from the forest, was the link between the two places. If they could pick up news of Ahmad in connection with the camp they would probably have a place to start looking for a vector, even a source of the virus. Other than that they could at least start collecting samples from the field not too far away from Muaratebo itself.

It was difficult to get any hard facts, but apparently a detail of soldiers from Padang had gone to the camp after a radio call for help on or around July 24th. Sutami was confident that the military had been able to secure the area, and so the RIID team started out.

They were obliged to take the road north-west out of Jambi, which skirted the seemingly limitless eastern salt marshlands for two hundred miles before turning west at the sleepy town of Rengat. They then followed the road west along the Indragir river, making good progress and reaching the Trans-Sumatra Highway at the foot of the Pegunungan ridge on the afternoon of the 18th.

It was eerie travelling along the empty roads. Muara-tebo was a hundred miles away to the south, and though they kept a constant lookout there was no sign of anything wrong. It was hard to believe that thousands of people might be dying in agony from the disease or simply being beaten to death in riots there. They tuned into various television and radio channels, but so far the world's media seemed to have little of substance to say about it.

Carmen sat in the lead vehicle, enjoying Leigh's company, getting to know him better. They talked about their families, and work; they talked about the crisis, discussing possible epidemiological scenarios. They went over the question of Habibie, and Leigh reassured Carmen that he thought she had acted prudently in going back for the Racal suit.

'Looking at Marshallton you have to say there's a chance this thing might get airborne,' he said. 'As an aerosol maybe, but I reckon an infected person would have to cough or sneeze to be a hazard. It's unlikely that simply being in the same room as a sick person would lead to infection.'

'What about dust, though?' Carmen asked. 'You could sweat into clothing or bedclothes. The sweat evaporates, leaving dust which you then inhale.'

Leigh laughed.

'Not with the known viral haemorrhagic pathogens.

But if you're worried, just don't go sniffing anybody's sheets is my advice.'

And Carmen laughed too. But there was something about Leigh's levity in the face of what she considered real risks that worried her. He was good for the team, though. There was a tendency for some of the others to clam up when they were anxious. Daintith was particularly bad. If Leigh could keep everyone relaxed, he would already be making a big contribution.

It was hot and humid, and even when they stopped to stretch their legs, they stayed close to the Cherokees, ducking inside to take gulps of conditioned air. Only Sergeant Kaoy, the taciturn Indonesian driver, who it turned out was a reluctant though proficient English-speaker, would walk off into the forest, smoking his clove-scented cigarettes.

It was when they reached the Trans-Sumatran Highway that they got an idea of the problems gripping the region. There were military everywhere. Camouflaged lorries lined the road, and bored-looking soldiers sat polishing their rifles or talking in small groups. They turned to stare as the RIID Cherokees rolled by. They didn't look particularly friendly.

Carmen had documents from Sutami, giving them access to the restricted areas – excluding Muaratebo – but Kaoy had to intervene occasionally with money or cigarettes or just a joke for the little convoy to keep rolling. It was that kind of culture. Carmen wondered if they were still passing bribes in Muaratebo.

At four in the afternoon they left the highway, turning back east on what was little more than a dirt track.

It was harder going now. Foliage whacked the windscreen and stones kicked up into the wheel arches like gunshots. Carmen gripped the dashboard as the Cherokee bucked and lurched. It seemed to go on and on.

'How much of this do we have to take, Colonel?'

Baker wrestled with the wheel, squinting ahead through the fly-spattered windscreen.

'According to the map, we follow this track for another thirty clicks.'

'Great,' said Leigh, who was jammed in next to Carmen on the front seat. 'Well I guess it'll save us having to shake the Martinis this evening.'

'I don't think they have Martini in this part of the world,' said Baker.

Carmen looked at Leigh's face. In spite of the air conditioning, he was sweating profusely.

'Think we'll make it by nightfall?' she asked.

'I think we should try. This camp's gotta be more comfortable than stayin' out in the woods, what with the military already there and everything.'

'Sure hope so,' said Baker. 'I could use a shower and a cold beer.'

He put his foot down a little harder and the Cherokee surged forward, lurching back and forth on the rough track.

'Just don't roll us into the ditch, soldier,' said Leigh.

The jolting ride seemed to go on for ever, although they were actually travelling for no more than two hours.

Just after six o'clock the track broadened out and the gradient decreased. The air was noticeably cooler.

'I think we're getting near the river,' said Baker. 'Should be about there, going by the odometer.'

They rolled on a little further, slower now, not wanting to miss any turnings. Then Carmen slammed her hand against the dashboard.

'What's that?'

Baker brought the Cherokee to a halt. There was a moment of stunned silence, and then Leigh opened the door. After the noise of the engines, the silence was oppressive. They sat for a minute looking forward along the track, listening to the engine tick as it cooled.

It was a pick-up. Parked next to the track. And, now that they were all looking hard, they could see beyond it a low mesh fence. The light was beginning to fade, but Carmen thought she could make out shadowy blocks of buildings about seventy yards away.

Kaoy went past the passenger door, a freshly lit cigarette burning between his fingers.

'Not so fast there, Sergeant Kaoy.'

It was Leigh who had spoken. Kaoy turned to look at them through the windscreen. Leigh climbed down from the cab. He was smiling, but he could do nothing to lessen the implicit authority that went with size.

'It may be dangerous, my friend. We're going to take things very slowly, and as a team.'

'OK,' said Kaoy, raising his hands in mock surrender. He allowed Leigh to go past him on the track as the others came up from the vehicles behind.

Leigh walked over to the pick-up. The only sound was the incessant sawing of insects. He looked over the truck, not touching anything. It looked as though it had been pulled out of the scrub, and then left there. There was no sign of damage. Putting a Kleenex over his mouth, Leigh looked inside the cabin. Nothing. Except for a brown smear on the inside of the windscreen about eighteen inches above the top of the wheel. There were small granules in the smear which made him think of the clots thrown in blood infected with Ebola.

'Let's not get ahead of ourselves,' he said softly. He stepped back, tossing the Kleenex in through the window.

'Is this it?' asked Carmen, looking back at Baker.

'I don't see how it can be,' said Baker. 'Where are all the military?' He turned to Kaoy, who was still smoking his cigarette. 'What do you think, sir?'

Kaoy shrugged.

Carmen joined Leigh at the truck. They both looked

along the road to what looked like the entrance of the camp. There was another vehicle, a jeep. It was parked across the track, blocking the entrance.

'Is there anybody here?'

Carmen's shouted question seemed to hang in the humid air.

'Hello!'

She turned to Leigh.

'Let's take a look.'

The men were still standing by the Cherokee, waiting. Carmen called out.

'We're just – '

'What's that smell?'

It was Daintith who had spoken. Carmen felt her scalp tingle. She started to walk back towards the men. They were all looking at Daintith.

'What smell?' she asked.

'Just caught a smell of something. Something rotten. Gone now, though.'

Carmen walked right up to Daintith. She could see how scared he was. And Daintith could see she saw. He set his jaw, blinking behind his thick glasses.

'Colonel,' he said, 'I think something may have happened here. I think you should be very careful, going in there. If this thing is airborne . . .'

Carmen turned and looked back along the track to Leigh.

'What do you think, Major?'

Leigh came back towards them, hands on hips.

'No point in taking risks.'

'OK. We'll put on face masks. But I think this place has been deserted for a while.'

'We're going to run out of light in another thirty minutes,' said Leigh. 'It'll give us time to have a look round, but I think we should set up camp out here.'

*

Carmen and Leigh put on white polyester overalls, gloves and respirator masks, while the others started unloading equipment. Daintith watched them as they went back towards the camp, testing their flashlights against their gloved hands.

The light was fading fast, colour bleeding out of the air. They got as far as the jeep inside the gate. Then Carmen stopped in her tracks. She was looking at what must have been a banyan tree. All that remained was the stump in the middle of a litter of branches. Twenty yards to the right of the tree there was a series of mounds. The earth was slightly darker where it had been disturbed. Rafflesia Camp had become a graveyard.

Leigh was shining his flashlight into the jeep.

'Look.'

He lifted up an AK47 assault rifle. Putting the flashlight on the hood of the jeep, he took out the clip. It was empty, and there was nothing in the chamber.

'Do you think that made those?' asked Carmen, pointing back at the mounds.

'Could be. Could be they died of the disease. My guess is the first detail came, found the cadavers humming with virus, and got infected themselves. See the Landcruiser and the M38?'

He pointed towards the buildings. Parked against the north side there were two vehicles, and next to them a grey four-man tent, collapsed on one side. 'I think the first detail came in those. This arrived later, with back-up. Maybe some expertise. See the equipment?'

There were boxes of basic medical supplies, and drums of what looked like disinfectant. The disadvantage of the respirator masks was that you couldn't smell things to tell what they were. Carmen unscrewed the cap on one of the drums and poured out a little pinkish, viscous fluid.

'Hold it,' said Leigh. He walked away from the jeep towards the fence. 'Something here.'

He picked up what looked like a respirator mask with the barrel of the AK47. Carmen shone her torch on it. There were bullet holes through the filter and faceplate, and the rubber webbing was black with dried blood.

'What the hell happened here?' said Carmen. 'It doesn't make sense. The first detail arrives. They call in support and then everybody starts shooting.'

Leigh dropped the mask and then turned back to the jeep. They walked forward side by side, the beams of their flashlights roving over the ground.

'Anyway, why do you think there was a second detail?' asked Carmen.

Leigh stopped, and looked straight at her. In the poor light it was difficult to see his eyes. His voice sounded different coming through the mask.

'The base in Padang gets a call around the 24th, right? It's just a call for help. They send some soldiers across. How many are they going to send? Three vehicles? I don't think so. I think one vehicle, maybe two. Two at the most. We have three here. I think those two over by the building brought the first patrol. They saw the bodies, realised something was up and called back for some expert support. Probably hung around for a couple of days, waiting for the guys to arrive.'

'But why the shootout? The second detail had come to help.'

'You're assuming the soldiers were shooting at each other. It may be there was something else. Maybe Indians. If they had rifles . . .'

Carmen shook her head.

'I don't think so.' She looked at the graves again, thinking. 'The first detail may have felt they had done their duty, and were ready to move out. They were probably delighted when the relief detail came up. Then . . .'

She looked around at the deserted camp. The last of the light was dying in the treetops. The darkness came so fast. It seemed to swoop in. She looked back towards the gate where the men had lit a fire and turned on the searchlight of one of the Cherokees. She imagined how she would feel if they weren't there with their generators and food.

'Then,' said Leigh, taking up Carmen's idea, 'the second detail told them they would have to wait for a few days. Make sure they hadn't picked anything up. Maybe the first bunch had touched the bodies. Done something they shouldn't have.'

'Quarantine.'

'Exactly. My guess is the second detail blocked the entrance, took all the weapons and then waited for things to develop.'

'That would explain the tree.'

'Yes. They had to have wood. They wanted to make fires, boil water, cook food. They couldn't leave the compound so they cut down their tree.'

'A banyan. It's a sacred tree to them. It shelters powerful spirits. They grow them in the precincts of temples. Big ones. And in their domestic compounds. They couldn't have cut it down unless they'd had to. Then they started to die.'

Leigh said nothing. He shone his beam at the mounds of earth by the banyan. It looked like there were ten graves, maybe more. Carmen imagined the soldiers developing the first symptoms. They had already seen the corpses. They knew what was coming to them. Sitting there in the heat, waiting. At some point they would have tried to get away, blind panic making them run for the entrance, where the other men, also terrified, were waiting. The threat of a gun would have seemed like nothing next to the sickness. You would take the gun any time. Maybe one of them grabbed a weapon, shot a guy wearing the mask. But if so, where was the body?

'What happened to the guy wearing the mask? He would have been with the second detail, right?'

Leigh stirred the earth with the toe of his boot.

'Things got out of control. The guy with the mask gets shot. The others, thinking maybe they're next, they get the hell out. Take the wounded man with them.'

'Dead. Looking at the mask, you would say he'd have to be dead.'

'So they took his body. I don't know. Anyway they took off. Maybe in another vehicle. Or maybe they just decided to make the hike back up to the Trans-Sumatra.'

Or maybe the jungle took them, thought Carmen, looking around the compound at the pale forms of trees in the black foliage. It was so weird. She had always thought herself close to nature – a nature person. The sight of a tree, any time of the year, usually lifted her heart, but here – maybe it was because there were so many trees, so few people. Looking at the pale trunks, twisting this way and that, the clouds of leaves, the black shadowy depths, it reminded her of an experiment she used to do with her chemistry set as a child. You took crystals of cobalt or copper sulphate and you put them in a solution of sodium silicate and waited. After a while the crystals started to form like threadlike limbs. These then became branches. After a day you had a forest – a dead forest growing purple and blue branches in a transparent, airless medium. It was such a strange thing. And the forest was heliotropic. You stood it by a window and the branches started to grow towards the source of light. Alive in a rudimentary way. She would stare at the forest for hours, and feel like she was suffocating. She had the same feeling now. She knew the forest was natural, followed natural processes that were generally harmonious, but it was alien too. And living within it, in harmony, naturally, was something that inside her would split open cells, rupture organs. For no reason at all. Just doing what the cobalt forest had done, living its life on its terms. In spite of the heat, she shivered.

Leigh was walking towards the building.

'What are you doing?'

He turned and shone his flashlight back at her.

'It's OK. I just wanted to take a look inside.'

'Why?'

'What do you mean?'

'I mean why not wait until morning?'

'Well there's no point wasting any time. Supper won't be ready for a while. Might as well take a look. First thing tomorrow we can start collecting samples.'

Carmen could think of no reasonable argument to prevent Leigh from going on, so she followed.

'Just don't touch anything,' she said. 'This place is probably hot as hell.'

They approached the buildings in silence. There were three separate units surrounding a lawn which looked as though it hadn't been cut for a month. In the middle of the lawn there was another tree stump and scattered branches. Carmen didn't like the idea that the smell Daintith picked up might be overpowering here and they wouldn't notice. She had an urge to take off the mask.

Leigh went up some steps onto the veranda that ran along the front of the central building. His white overalls appeared to glow in the dark. He stood for a moment, shining his flashlight back and forth. There were blackish stains on the floor which might have been dried blood. In silence he pointed at two expended shells on the wooden floor. Carmen stood next to him for a second and then went inside.

She was standing in what looked like a living room. There was a wall hanging in orange and brown on the wall opposite a window. A rug on the floor had been kicked to one side. There were more smears and dry splash marks. Leigh came in behind her.

'Very few insects around,' he said. 'Mosquitoes, mostly. Moths.'

He followed the floorboards with the beam of his flashlight until he reached the far wall in which there was a doorway leading through to a passage.

'What's up there?' said Carmen, feeling nervous in the enclosed space, which was made sinister by the disturbed furniture and black stains. Leigh looked at her and she saw his eyes smile.

'Let's take a look.'

Carmen followed him across the room, her flashlight pointed down at the floor. It flickered off for a second and then on again. She gave it a shake.

'This is where a body falls out of a cupboard and your flashlight goes off,' said Leigh, chuckling in his mask. Carmen tried to laugh, but all that came out was a scared little gasp.

There was an opening to their left. Carmen tapped Leigh on the shoulder.

'Let's swap flashlights,' she said, wanting to show him that she could kid around too.

But Leigh didn't answer. He had come to a halt in the doorway, looking into what must be a bedroom.

'What's up?'

'Jesus Christ.'

Carmen tried to see past him into the room, but he was blocking the doorway.

'What is it?'

'Oh Lord.'

He stood aside so that she could see. Carmen brought her hand sharply up to her mouth, hitting her filter instead. For a moment she closed her eyes.

It was one of the soldiers. In his stiff left hand he was holding an automatic. By the explosion of blackish debris on the wall it looked as if he had blown his own brains out. But the dark tracks of blood that striped his face had streamed from his eyes and ears and nose and were consistent with the agonal stages of viral haemorrhagic fever. His tunic looked stiff and black. The floor around him was covered in a dark crust of mingled blood and excrement.

Suddenly Carmen felt very exposed in her polyester overalls. She tried to keep a grip, reasoning with herself. Most haemorrhagic viruses were poor survivors outside the living blood of their host. It was true that Ebola and Marburg in high concentrations could survive in sealed containers for up to two weeks at room temperature, but they didn't last long when dehydrated. However, she couldn't be sure that what they were dealing with would behave like Marburg or Ebola. Standing in a dirty room splashed full of infected blood and bodily fluids was no way to find out.

'I think we should leave this till morning,' said Leigh. 'I'd feel happier in a full suit with proper – '

Carmen stopped dead. A floorboard creaked behind her. There was someone there. Slowly, holding her breath, she turned. Shrieked. There followed a moment of confusion as Leigh pushed past her, his flashlight beam jerking on the ceiling and walls. Then they were still, breathing hard in their masks.

It was a woman.

Carmen and Leigh stood there, their trembling flashlights pointing like weapons. She was filthy, her matted hair falling across her face. There were marks of blood where she had wiped her fingers across her grimy T-shirt. Her hands looked swollen, the finger-ends blackened. Her left hand was badly cut, and she had applied a makeshift bandage which was filthy too. Underneath the T-shirt she was stark naked, the V of her pubis dark against her pale flesh. Her legs were streaked with brown fluid. Neither Carmen nor Leigh could move or speak.

'Please,' said the woman, taking a step towards them.

Carmen looked down at the floor at her blackened bare feet. 'Help me. My name is Holly . . . Holly Becker. I'm an . . .' But she didn't finish. Her eyes rolled up as she fainted, pitching forward, knocking Carmen back against the wall.

2

Ken Lyall rubbed his eyes and turned to the pile of papers lying in his lap. They were copies of Peter Jarvis's log, together with the notes he'd made during the course of the day. Now he was in the CDSC communications room, waiting to be patched through to Sumatra via Washington, DC. Opposite him Moira Tenniel, his assistant, sat listening on her headset, motionless but for the faint drumming of an index finger.

Lyall was glad he didn't still have the original log. Looking through it in the hours after its discovery he had experienced the same uncomfortable feeling as he had rummaging through the man's apartment, sifting through his suitcase. It was a feeling of intrusion. He felt better with a copy: there was more distance. Given the seriousness of the situation he knew such sensibilities were trivial, even foolish – he had certainly never owned up to them – but he had insisted nevertheless that the original be returned to Jarvis's parents as soon as possible. He hoped it would make the whole thing a little more bearable for them, especially the way things had happened. Only once had they been able to see their son, and that only briefly, from behind a layer of glass and another of plastic at the Hospital for Tropical Diseases. A few hours later he was dead. At least the log would help them share his last few days and weeks.

For the research effort now being spearheaded by the US military Jarvis's log had the potential to prove of even greater value. The entomologist had documented his thoughts and actions since leaving the United Kingdom with remarkable thoroughness, in part, Lyall suspected, for lack of anything else to do during the long evenings. By the time someone had been found at the British Museum who knew about Jarvis's project Lyall had been able to piece it all together for himself. Jarvis had been interested in establishing a field station to study the effects on biodiversity of logging and clearance on the rain forest. The station would serve as a permanent base from which botanists, entomologists and zoologists of all disciplines could operate, offering basic laboratory and storage facilities, long-range communications, medical supplies and decent accommodation. It was a bold idea, not only because of the logistics involved but because of the degree of co-operation needed with the Indonesian authorities: the Forestry Department, whose land it was, the regional government and a host of ministries in Jakarta, all of whom had their right to a say. And yet it had looked as if Jarvis might actually have pulled it off. Somehow he had managed to get almost everyone on board. All he needed was a viable site, and he had spent the last two months of his life looking for one. What he had found, somewhere, was the Muaratebo virus.

And yet Muaratebo itself was not mentioned anywhere in the log. Jarvis's base of operations had been Pekanbaru in Riau province, north of Jambi. From there he headed due south towards the upland forest, drawing nearer to Muaratebo, but never getting closer than 130 miles. The possibility existed that Jarvis had stumbled upon the true centre of the virus, the location where it existed naturally in whatever rare species of tick, mite or biting fly it was that constituted its natural reservoir. Lyall had passed this information to the World Health Organisation and it was then that he had learned about the USAMRIID expedition. The WHO had already sent word of the London outbreak to Fort Detrick and now they were trying to communicate directly with the RIID people on the ground, only someone somewhere was having trouble making a connection.

'What time is it in Sumatra?' Lyall asked.

Tenniel looked up at the big clock.

'It's 0600 hours, almost. Dawn, I expect.'

The door opened and Bernard Warner came back in. He was the Medical Officer for Environmental Health with responsibility for the Borough of Westminster where St Anne's Hospital was located.

'Sorry about that,' he mumbled. 'Almost got lost on the way back.'

Warner had come by a couple of hours earlier to go through the results of the lab tests from Colindale and to pick up any new information that might be available on the virus. The news of Jarvis's death had shaken him up quite a bit. Lyall picked up a pencil and began to draw a grid at the corner of his notepad.

'What the hell's taking them so long?' he said. 'This is ridiculous.'

Suddenly Moira Tenniel was talking. 'Yes it is . . . Yes I will, thank you.' She looked at Lyall: 'It's USAMRIID. They're . . . Yes, hello General Bailey. I'm putting you through to Dr Kenneth Lyall, deputy director of the Communicable Disease Surveillance Centre.'

She tapped a string-on number on her computer console and the telephone by Lyall's right hand chirped once.

'Hello?'

'Dr Lyall. This is Major-General Robert Bailey at Fort Detrick. I trust you're well?'

'I'm very well, thank you,' Lyall found himself saying.
'How are you?'

'I understand there's some information you want to
pass on to our team in Sumatra. Is that right?'

General Bailey's voice was loud and hard, almost
aggressive. It occurred to Lyall that maybe the Americans
didn't welcome the British involvement. They were military people, after all. They probably thought they could
handle the whole thing on their own. Or maybe it was
just that the man had been up all night like the rest of
them and the strain was beginning to show.

'We've had a death here, as you know,' said Lyall.
'But we've hard information as to where the infection
may have occurred. It could narrow the search for the
reservoir considerably.'

'So I understand. And my apologies about the delay
patching you through. But there have been some . . .
developments. A lot of priority traffic.'

Just the word filled Lyall with foreboding.

'Developments, General?'

'Yes, I . . . Can you wait just one moment?'

There was a click and the line went dead. Lyall sighed
and pushed a hand through his hair. *What developments,
for Christ's sake?* Warner was looking at him anxiously.
Lyall shrugged helplessly.

Then there was another click on the line.

'You'll be hearing it in an hour or two through your own
channels,' came Bailey's voice, 'if you haven't already.'

'Hearing what?'

'I'm afraid the diplomatic situation appears to be dete-
riorating. Our sources say the Singapore government is
threatening to exclude all Indonesian ships and aircraft
from its waters or airspace, unilaterally. They want the
whole of Sumatra quarantined or they'll close the Malacca
Straits. The Malaysians may be following suit.'

'Jesus, I bet they're happy in Jakarta.'

'Far from it, I'm afraid. They're claiming an exclusion would be a violation of international law and an act of economic aggression. Most of their trade goes via Singapore or the Straits, apparently.'

'It does seem a little premature. I mean – '

'That's not the worst part, I'm afraid. The worst part is they're blaming us.'

'*Us?* What do you mean?'

'The Americans, the West, you know. They say we're scaremongering. We've exaggerated the problem deliberately so as to damage their interests – because they're a Muslim country. That part's aimed at the Malaysians, of course. Next they'll be saying we manufactured the damned virus and dropped it on them, I wouldn't be surprised. It's going to be a busy few days at the UN.'

'But have they had an outbreak? I mean in Singapore?'

'No data on that yet. We'll be making enquiries. The point is, all this could make things more difficult for our people on the ground. We were planning to put in some more back-up for them, but that might be difficult now. I hope it doesn't come to this, but if the Indonesians withdraw co-operation then we may have no choice but to evacuate.'

Bailey's position was clear now. He wanted his team to do whatever they could and get out of there before they found themselves hostages in some messy diplomatic crisis. He didn't want their task complicated by anyone, unless it was strictly necessary.

'I understand,' said Lyall. 'We'd better hope sense prevails.'

Bailey laughed, a single gruff laugh.

'Don't count on it. We should be able to patch you through now. Lieutenant-Colonel Carmen Travis is the commanding officer. She'll be waiting. Thank you, Dr Lyall.'

3

It was so hot she had hardly been able to sleep. Then she was awoken at first light by Leigh shoving his head into her tent, looking combat-ready like regular army with his unshaven chin. A satellite transmission had come through on one of the RIID channels – a Dr Lyall wanted to talk to the head of the expedition.

Three hours later, Carmen was sitting in the shade, a cold bottle of water pressed to her forehead, trying to think. The virus had reached London. Carried by Peter Jarvis, an entomologist who had been working north of Rafflesia Camp, perhaps as little as sixty miles away.

There was no reason to be particularly surprised, Carmen told herself. Sumatra was a day's flight from any of the world's capitals with their teeming populations. She tried to picture London for a moment, but all she could envisage was the Palace of Westminster and a soldier in a bearskin hat. Londoners would be intent on their business, meeting their deadlines, caring for their loved ones, thinking about what to have for supper, unaware of the microscopic organism which had left the Sumatran rain forest and made the brief journey across the time zones in Jarvis's bloodstream. Dr Lyall had insisted the outbreak had been contained, but who knew what might have been liberated in the airports and stations through which the man had passed? Maybe somebody, somewhere, looking

into their bathroom mirror at a sudden flare of conjuncti-
vitis, someone with a throbbing headache and the beginnings of a fever, had already found out. For the first time
it had come home to Carmen what they might be facing.

And there were reports of the row flaring up between
Singapore and Indonesia over restrictions on flights and
shipping from the area. Malaysia was likely to get drawn
into the argument, and then Iran leading the Middle Eastern Muslim nations. Press attention was beginning to turn
to Muaratebo. Diplomatic relations between Indonesia
and the West were under strain. It all seemed hard to
believe. Here they were sitting in the very core of a great
storm, the very source of all the suffering and destruction,
going about their business with their traps and monitors
and clipboards as if nothing dramatic was taking place.
They carried on their work in a humid, airless calm, like
the stillness in the eye of a hurricane.

Lyall had faxed through several pages of the log which
Jarvis had kept in the months leading up to his death.
The uniform slanted handwriting had been broken up,
bounced off satellites around the globe and then reinte-
grated in the X-SAT receiver, but it had lost none of its
immediacy through digitisation, and it felt odd to be reading something which, though neutral enough, had been
written in privacy and quiet; written by someone with no
immediate plans to die.

Carmen tried to concentrate on the information the log
contained, some of which promised to be of great value.
Among Jarvis's orderly notes were several references to
a freshwater source, which Jarvis had hoped was going to
make his projected research station viable. On one page
there was even a specific map reference. These caves were
not in the immediate vicinity of Jambi or even of Rafflesia
Camp, but they were in the neighbouring province. The
virus could have travelled between the two areas inside
flying insects, bats or birds. If evidence of the virus was

found at the caves it would narrow the range of potential host species considerably. At the very least Dr Jarvis's log suggested a specific place where the turning over of a few stones might be helpful.

There was a clatter away to Carmen's left. She removed the bottle from her forehead and turned to look. Corporal Baker was setting up the portable shower unit they were going to use to disinfect the Racal suits at the end of each day. It looked flimsy and the colours were garish next to the subtle greens and browns of the forest. Baker had to read from the instruction manual that came with the kit. It was not a particularly reassuring sight even for Carmen, who had a deep and, as far as life had tested it, unshakeable faith in the technology that surrounded her.

A shot rang out, followed by another. All the resonance and power of the explosion was sucked out of the air so that it sounded like a cap gun. Leigh had taken McKinnon into the forest with the rifles and Chauvency traps in the hope of trapping rodents and bagging some primates. Dr Lennox, the parasitologist, was working with Harold Daintith setting up traps for the collection of *culicidae* and *cimicidae* inside the Rafflesia Camp buildings. Gnats and mosquitoes were caught in glass tubes from resting sites inside the houses. Bedbugs were aspirated from the raffia slats of the beds or, after shaking, from the ground. They were then slightly anaesthetised with ether and introduced into Nunc tubes which were put in liquid nitrogen. It was slow, painstaking work, made all the more difficult by the clumsy gloves, and the oppressive heat which caused the sweat to run into your eyes despite the air conditioning in the suits. Daintith, perhaps wanting to prove his courage after the night before, had insisted on going into those sinister rooms where she and Leigh had found the dead soldier and the woman.

The woman was Carmen's present preoccupation. She had stayed at the camp with Corporal Baker and Sergeant

Sarandon, while the others had gone off. She wanted to be there when the woman came round.

She turned now and looked into the tent they had set up to isolate the woman. The assumption was that she was infected even though there were no indications that she had developed the disease. There was a chance that she had arrived at the camp after the virus had ceased to be active, but the cut on her hand, and her complete lack of protection, did not bode well. She was suffering from diarrhoea and was badly dehydrated. They had sedated her and got a saline drip into her arm before leaving her for the night, with Sergeant Sarandon on watch.

Carmen looked at the sleeping face. With her eyes closed she looked older. When she had stepped into the beam of the flashlight her big dark irises had blazed with fear, but with colour and vitality too. She was a beauty. There was no doubt about that. Once they had washed her hair and cleaned her face, she would be bound to make quite an impression. Carmen frowned at the thought of the woman's danger. No believer in a supreme being, she nevertheless said a small prayer.

The sound of the mumbled words drifted through the haze of Holly's drugged sleep. She opened her eyes and saw friendly blue eyes over a surgical mask. There was a voice too.

'Morning,' said Carmen, adopting a breezy, efficient tone. 'My name is Lieutenant-Colonel Carmen Travis of the United States Army Medical Research Institute for Infectious Diseases. We found you last night and you are now in our care. You may be feeling a little woozy. We gave you something to help you rest.'

Holly stirred and felt the tube tug at the back of her wrist. There was soreness there.

'That's a drip,' said Carmen. 'You were badly dehydrated. You lost a lot of fluid with the diarrhoea. We gave you something for that too.'

Holly smiled weakly. Things were coming to her with a blurred, overlapping quality. She blinked up at the canvas. Small tremors plucked at the edge of her vision. Then the events of the past few days started to flow into her opening mind. She closed her eyes.

Carmen was quiet for a moment, wondering if the woman had drifted back into sleep. There was another stifled gunshot from the forest. She didn't want to overtax the woman, above all she didn't want to give her any cause for worry, but she felt it would be necessary at some point, sooner rather than later, to tell her about what she might be carrying. She thought for a moment and then decided that the best way to proceed would be to find out exactly how the woman had come to be in the camp.

'I know you must be very tired, but I have to ask you some questions.'

The insistent, slightly formal voice came to Holly through images of the forest, moving shadows, the sound of water. It sounded institutional. It seemed to promise help. Holly wondered why the woman sounded American and thought perhaps she was dreaming.

'Perhaps you could start by telling me your name?'

Without opening her eyes, still seeing the forest, seeing the abandoned camp now through trees in the early morning light, Holly answered.

'Holly. Holly Becker.'

'How come you're here, Holly? What brought you to the camp?'

The images of the forest seemed to fold away, and all Holly could feel was anxiety, like a balloon in her chest, swelling and swelling. She raised her head again to see the masked face.

Carmen saw the woman struggle. There were chalky marks at the corners of her mouth.

'What happened to them?' said Holly.

'Pardon me?'

'To the people in the camp. What happened?'

Carmen swallowed. The woman clearly knew something about what had gone on there. She would have to come straight to the point.

'Holly, before we get on to that . . .'

'Please. I have to know.'

Holly tried to support herself on her elbows, but she didn't have the strength.

'They're dead, Holly. There has been an outbreak of a disease here, and in Muaratebo, the town downstream from us about fifty kilometres away.'

'Dead?'

Holly felt herself falling. Black emptiness rushed up like the floor of a lift shaft.

'We think so, Holly. It's very difficult to be sure. But the disease – well, it doesn't seem to spare anyone.'

'Dead.'

Carmen watched as a spasm of grief racked the woman's body. She made a harsh keening sound in her throat. Her face twisted, her eyes screwed tight to trap the sudden rush of tears. But there were too many. They streamed along her dust-covered temples and into her matted, filthy hair. For a long time Carmen watched the woman cry, patting her leg, trying to reassure her. Eventually Baker came and stood behind her.

'Is everything OK, Colonel?'

Carmen squinted up at him. He was holding a page of the manual for the shower unit. She shook her head, and motioned for him to leave them. The silent weeping continued. Behind her Carmen could hear Baker moving around. Daintith and McKinnon would be back soon. There was another burst of fire from the forest. Carmen hoped there would be no accidents.

Eventually Holly opened her eyes. She stared in silence at the canopy over her head.

'Do I have the disease?' she asked. 'Is that why you're wearing that mask?'

'There is a risk,' said Carmen. 'That is why I wanted you to tell me about your coming here. It's possible you arrived after the virus had died. Haemorrhagic filoviruses – this kind of virus, normally it can't live long without a living . . . host. We have to establish exactly when you arrived.'

Holly braced herself, actually clenching her fists by her sides.

'Did you find them?'

Carmen stopped short.

'Who?'

'My daughters, Emma and Lucy. Did you find them?'

There was a moment of complete silence. Carmen brought her hand up to the face mask, unable to believe what she was hearing. She hadn't been prepared for such a possibility, that there might be children among the corpses in the shallow graves outside. It was supposed to be a research post. She had assumed the woman was some maverick journalist who had lost her way in the forest. She struggled to steady herself.

'Holly, we only arrived last night. We aren't clear what happened here yet.'

Holly looked at the woman's face. The open pores gave it an unnatural grainy appearance. The blue eyes seemed alarmed.

'You said they were all dead.'

'There are a number of . . . of graves. I'm afraid it would be inadvisable to open them. The risk of infection would be . . .'

Holly closed her eyes again, pressing them tight shut and for a moment Carmen could think of nothing to say.

'They can't be dead,' Holly said, through clenched teeth. 'They're just children. They don't . . . they don't belong here. They're . . .' The dark eyes snapped open. 'You must look for them.'

Carmen reached out and touched Holly's wrist with her gloved hand. She wanted desperately to say something that would give hope.

'We will, Holly. We will. But . . .' she struggled for some way out – 'are you sure your daughters were here?'

Holly watched the blue eyes. The anguish seemed to be streaming from her, leaving her to breathe for a moment.

'I had a letter,' she said. 'But it was sent weeks ago. Do you think they could have left?'

The woman in the mask nodded, but the eyes remained serious.

'It's quite possible. Someone could have taken them out when the problems started, don't you think? I mean, what were they doing here in the first place?'

Carmen watched Holly Becker's face change. She was looking at her now. However misguidedly, she had found a reason for hope. The slimmest possibility that her daughters had not been caught in the disaster was all she required to start building her optimism. Even the simple, insignificant act of asking the question offered hope.

'They came here four weeks ago,' said Holly, 'to spend time with their father, my ex-husband, Jonathan Rhodes. We divorced a few years ago, but we've always stayed in touch. We both wanted things to be . . . to be as normal as possible for the children. That's why they . . . that's why the children came. That's why I let them come. We were going to be together, you see. We wanted the children to understand that everything was all right now – ' Holly put her hands to her face – 'Oh God.'

Carmen was determined to keep her talking.

'Jonathan is a scientist?'

'What?'

'Jonathan, your ex-husband. He's a scientist.'

'Yes. A botanist. He was working on a project, looking for new medicines in the forest. That's always been his thing. He always says that's the only way big business will ever be interested in preserving the rain forest, if they see it's worth more standing than cut down.'

Carmen nodded.

'How did you get to the camp?'

Holly's face seemed to go dead. She was remembering, the forest rushing back into her head, the interminable nights, her fear. The sickness shaking her until she had to kneel on the forest floor.

'What day is it?' she asked after a moment.

Carmen checked her watch.

'The 19th.'

'I said goodbye to Willis – he's a guy who helped get through all the military – I think it was the 15th. Then we were a couple of days in the forest – '

'We?'

'Local people . . . Indians helped me. Kubu.'

'And where are they?'

'They brought me within a few kilometres of the camp and then stopped. The Kubu know what is going on. They know something bad is happening in the forest. They won't come here.'

'So how did you find it?'

'They showed me. I followed the river, the Hari.'

Carmen pressed her lips together. The woman had been wandering around in an area which seemed the most likely focus of the disease.

'Then I got lost, I guess. My water ran out. But I had tablets for water from the river, so I filled my canteen with that. I ate some fruit. Papaya I think. I guess that's what upset my stomach. I washed my clothes in the river.' She stopped talking for a moment, and shot

282

Carmen a glance. 'I was drying stuff when you came into the compound. That's why I was . . .'

Her face went blank again. Carmen could see her thoughts turning back to her daughters.

'How long were you lost in the forest?'

'I don't know exactly. But I'm pretty sure I arrived here . . . at most two days ago. It's all a blur.'

Maybe there was reason for hope, Carmen thought. The most important thing was to keep the woman thinking positively.

'OK, Holly. It seems to me that there's every chance that your children – maybe your ex-husband too – may have left here before the trouble started, or got to a hospital somewhere. We certainly can't assume that they just sat tight throughout. Now things have been pretty chaotic around here – I've seen that for myself – and it's quite possible that your ex-husband has simply been unable to contact you.'

Holly looked at her pleadingly. Carmen would have given anything for her words to be true.

'Now we're here – I mean the RIID – we're here to find out where this disease is coming from, and how it started. We're going to find out what carries it and then we are either going to destroy that thing or, more likely, we are going to set up a no-go area, so that people can avoid coming into contact with it. There is a danger that you may have already come into contact with this patho . . . with this virus. You have none of the symptoms even though you have been here for long enough to develop them. So that looks good. But this disease is so virulent, so deadly, we have to be extra careful. That's why I have to see to it that you're flown out of here as soon as you're strong enough to – '

'No.'

Holly tensed up. She pushed herself up onto her elbows again, beads of sweat running out of her matted hair.

'Holly, there's really – '

'No! I'm not – ' she caught her breath, furious at her own weakness, furious at the masked face, the level, institutional voice – 'I'm not leaving without my children.'

The blue eyes above the mask seemed to burn.

'Holly, there's nothing you can do here.'

'No. I have to look for them. I have to find them. I won't go.'

'Holly – '

'I'm not going!'

She had ripped out the drip.

'All right, all right.' Carmen held up her hands, sitting back away from the entrance of the tent. She didn't think there was any danger of the woman getting up – she was too weak for that, thank goodness, but there was no use adding to her suffering. 'There's no hurry about it. We can postpone that decision, OK? Just try not to get too worked up.'

Holly looked at her, her eyes brimming over with tears.

'Carmen? Is that right?'

Carmen nodded.

'Carmen, don't make me wait someplace for news. Don't put me through that.'

Carmen nodded slowly. She was wondering how Leigh and the others would react to the idea of a civilian passenger, and a woman at that. It wasn't exactly by the book. Then again, Holly Becker was the only person who knew anything about Jonathan Rhodes's work and about life at the camp. Such information might provide vital clues as to how the virus came into contact with its inhabitants. Keeping Holly Becker among them for a few more days could be justified on operational grounds.

'All right, Holly. I'll make you a deal. It will take five days for your virological diagnosis to come through. In the meantime I need your help. Until we know, until we are one hundred per cent sure that you are free of this thing, we have to keep you isolated from the rest of the team. If there is any contact you will put us all at risk. Now we don't have the proper facilities to isolate you. But this tent and a few simple rules will be sufficient if we have your full co-operation. Is it a deal?'

The woman smiled for a moment. Then her face was sad again.

'We'll find them, Carmen,' she said. 'I know it.'

4

Powder Mill, Maryland. August 20th

The sun was going down behind a mess of power lines
and pylons as George Arends turned off the beltway and
down into the science park at Powder Mill. Light industrial units – painted breeze-block sheds with corrugated
plastic roofs – stood in three rows, each one with a six-
foot-high number painted over the front entrance. There
weren't any people about, just a handful of cars parked
in numbered bays and a pair of streetlights giving off a
sickly greenish glow. The park had only been open for a
year and most of it was still vacant.

He pulled up outside Unit 14. Saul Guthrie had
moved in with his software business a few months
before, attracted, he said, by the knock-down rent and a
special deal being offered by one of the phone companies.
He and his five staff occupied only one third of a shed but
the partitions hadn't gone up yet because nobody wanted
the rest. Guthrie met Arends at the front entrance and led
him to his office across a bare, unlit expanse of concrete.

'It's low on charm,' said Guthrie. 'But the space!
I couldn't go back to that attic in town. No way.'

Guthrie was a stout man in his mid-forties with a
high forehead and grey, swept-back hair. A one-time
neighbour in Frederick, he had kept in touch with Arends
and his wife, sending regular Christmas cards and calling
up from time to time. Arends reckoned that he was shy

and didn't make friends easily. The social schedule had always been his wife's department, but she'd gone back to San Francisco three years ago, leaving Guthrie to manage for himself. In any case, Arends had found him only too happy to help out with a little technical problem.

At the far side of the shed a sandy-haired man maybe ten years younger than Guthrie appeared, pulling on his jacket. He said good-night and went out the side entrance.

'That was Jeff,' Guthrie said when the man was out of earshot. 'Great technician, but no – ' he held up his hand and made a vague, wiggling gesture – 'absolutely no . . .'

'Imagination?'

'Right. No vision. Just can't see an opportunity till it's so obvious everyone else has got there first. Nice guy, though.'

'Been with you long?'

'Almost a year. Had his own business before, but couldn't make a profit. Well, here we are – ' he threw open a hollow plywood door – 'The new global HQ.'

The office was an L-shaped chaos of papers, cardboard boxes and portable computer technology. Even by the standards of the RIID it was functional. Everywhere there was a faint smell of wet paint.

'You want a coffee or something?' said Guthrie.

'No thanks,' said Arends. 'I just – '

'Tell you what, I got some Jack Daniels' here somewhere. 'Bout time I . . . It's after hours, isn't it?'

Arends almost never touched bourbon but he didn't want to seem unfriendly. He accepted a cup and raised it obligingly.

'Good to see you, George,' said Guthrie. 'So how's things at the Institute?'

Arends took a sip of the bourbon. It needed ice and a lot of it.

'Busy, to tell the truth. Busy as hell. Time pressure, you know.'

'Sure, sure, I know,' said Guthrie. 'Everyone these days wants deadlines. It's like being in fifth grade. No time for the unexpected, no matter if it's problems or opportunities. It's just: give me this and give it me when I say, or else. Cut and dried. I often wonder where would Leonardo da Vinci have got with customers like that? He'd have been out of business in six months.'

Arends nodded sympathetically.

'I bet he would at that. So did you get a chance to look at that disk I sent you?'

Guthrie swallowed a big mouthful of bourbon and put down his cup.

'Mmm, of course. Sorry.'

He went over and sat down at one of the computers.

'I got it here somewhere. I was looking at it a couple of days ago.'

Arends pulled up a chair beside him. He had sent the disk from Fort Willard down by courier two days earlier, having disinfected it with chlorine gas and a prolonged dose of strong ultraviolet radiation – neither of which should have harmed the magnetic medium inside. Before all that he had thoroughly swabbed down the plastic casing with distilled water, introducing the swabs into a growth medium, just to see if any form of harmful micro-organism had been present. The cultures had shown up a minute quantity of harmless fungus, but nothing more. Only when all this was completed had he slotted the disk into his computer and tried to read it. The directory had listed five files without so much as a hitch:

05GNTY4.TXT   06GNTY4.TXT   01GNTY5.TXT
PGSYS90.SIM   ANTLOG12.TXT

But that was as far as he'd been able to go. The files with TXT extensions were sure to be text – it was a standard tag used by a multitude of word processors – but though he ran them through every translator in the system all he ever came up with was a screenful of garbage: row upon row of meaningless shapes and symbols. That was when he'd decided to ask for Saul Guthrie's help.

Guthrie was rummaging in the top drawer of his desk. Arends saw a tube of microchips, stacks of paper and several plastic teaspoons, all of them dirty.

'You said you'd gotten somewhere,' said Arends hopefully. 'What did you mean?'

'I'm sure I put it . . . Thing is, it wasn't labelled and . . . Anyway I got it all on my system. Did a bit copy for safety's sake. I just thought you'd want back the original disk.'

'Don't worry for the moment. What did you find?'

Guthrie closed the drawer.

'OK,' he said, planting his hands on his thighs. 'Let me just call up the copy.'

He pressed a few keys and in a moment the same five files appeared on the screen.

'I thought same as you that the disk had gotten corrupted somehow,' he said. 'But when I checked for bad sectors it came up pretty clean. A perfectly serviceable disk, in fact.'

'So you could get into the files?'

Guthrie smiled. He was enjoying himself, mixing business with pleasure in a way that would have put a strain on any social situation.

'Well I could get into them just like normal, but I couldn't make any sense of them once I got there. Or, to be more exact, my computer couldn't make any sense of them. I'd love to know where you got this from.'

Guthrie had a cheeky grin on his face, as if this whole exercise was no more than a game to test his abilities. In fact, he probably thought that was just what it was. Arends hadn't been very forthcoming about the details.

'Someone just left it lying around somewhere. I don't know who. It's a bit of a mystery.'

'I'll say. Had me stumped for a while, I can tell you.'

'So what was it: some sort of code?'

Guthrie laughed.

'Oh no, nothing that tiresome. The data just wasn't where it was supposed to be – as far as my computer was concerned. I dare say if you went back to the computer this disk was used on you'd be able to read it without any trouble at all, provided you loaded up the right operating system. My guess is you'll find more than one on there.'

Arends frowned. Operating systems weren't something he knew very much about.

'So what are you saying? It was written on some unusual kind of computer? I saw the machine this disk was used on. It looked pretty standard to me.'

'It's not the machine that was unusual, it was the disk operating system – the DOS. Some sneaky sonofabitch customised his own. Probably messed around with the FAT file.'

'The fat file?'

'F–A–T. File Allocation Table. It's like a diagram that tells the computer where to look on the disk for each successive chunk of information – where each chunk begins and ends. Otherwise all it's got is a string of numbers: no beginning, no middle and no end. It's like trying to construct a sentence when all the words have been joined together, chopped up into little pieces and stuck together in a peculiar order.'

Arends was thinking about the books he had found at Fort Willard, the hundreds – probably thousands – of electrophoresis shots. They had been used to isolate individual genes: individual, functional chunks of data. They were parts of a map just like the one Guthrie was describing. He could see how someone who worked in genetics might be attracted to this kind of data protection.

290

It was a little like customising your very own genetic code.

'So,' Guthrie went on, 'if you tamper with the FAT file on one computer you can get all your data organised in a way which only that computer will understand. We can only read the file names because they're stored in a special sector that the FAT file doesn't cover.'

'But if you get data from outside, from other machines, you wouldn't be able to read it, surely? All *you'll* get is the file names.'

Guthrie nodded. 'Which is why I say the machine will probably have more than one DOS on it. A standard one for incoming data, and a customised one for data you don't intend to share.'

Arends could feel the frustration welling up inside him. He could see the files there on the screen in front of him. He could reach out and touch them, and yet because of some meddling, some trick he only half understood, they remained stubbornly, defiantly closed to him.

'Of course this sort of approach is really all about guarding data on a hard disk,' said Guthrie. 'Anyone on another part of a network who was trying to look at your stuff wouldn't even get to first base. Making portable disks secure – completely secure – is a pain. You gotta use proper encryption and all that.'

Arends looked up.

'You mean this disk *isn't* completely secure?'

Guthrie looked at him as if he were simple.

'Well, you can look at individual sectors – the raw data. You just can't put it all together. I mean, it would take weeks. Like a huge jigsaw puzzle with about 20,000 pieces.'

'Can you show me?'

'What, a sector? Sure, I've already taken a look at a few through the shell program. But without knowing what I'm looking for it's pretty pointless. Just rows and rows of hexadecimal numbers and a few words, if you're lucky.'

'What kind of words?'

Guthrie held up his hands.

'OK, OK. Look, it works like this. Let me just get in here.'

He reached out for the mouse and called up a complicated-looking piece of software with dozens of options and menus. It was dark outside now and the bright glow of the screen was strong enough to cast faint shadows on the wall behind them.

'OK,' Guthrie said. 'When you look at a sector you get the hexadecimal bit patterns on the left and an automatic ASCII translation on the right. When you've got any kind of text in your program or your data file this is where the words show up.'

'And you can pull these sectors off the disk I gave you?'

'Sure, and off the bit copy I made, which is this same thing. Only you have to give me either a sector number – like a grid reference – or something the computer can search for, like an individual word or something.'

Arends straightened up.

'OK, you want a word, right? A word to search for.'

'Right. And if the word comes up then you get to see that sector. But without the right FAT file you aren't gonna know where to find the next sector or the one that came before it.'

Arends tried to think. How could he get to the heart of what was written on the disk, to the heart of the secret at Fort Willard with a single word? With more time he could have arranged to have every sector pulled off the disk one by one – 20,000 screens of information in random order – but there wasn't time for that. Besides, for all he knew, the disk might contain nothing more sensitive than a laundry list – except that even laundry lists carried names.

'All right, Saul,' he said. 'I've got a word for you. Get your machine to search for V–I–R–U–S.'

A flicker of doubt crossed Guthrie's face.

'Virus? OK.'

He tapped the letters into the little grey panel on the screen.

'Case insensitive?'

'What? Oh yeah. Yes.'

Guthrie hit the return key and they waited while the computer scanned the hundreds of millions of binary switches which made up the disk's contents. After less than a minute it stopped, the screen reporting success with the word FOUND. Guthrie moved the mouse onto the EDIT key and in an instant the screen was full of numbers, symbols and letters.

```
                                    Unzoom ↑PrvFle ↓NxtFle

↑≤     Advanced Mode              PCShell                  19:47
 File  Disk  Options  View  Special  Tree  Help            ↕L
 T|^A T|^B ─┤^C ─┤^D ─┤^E                                  rr

↑≤                      Binary, BIT.
                    Hexadecimal Offset              ASCII Equiv↓
 ┃   0  1  2  3  4  5  6  7  8  9  A  B  C  D  E  F   All Characters  ↕↓
 ┃  0 6F 66 20 76 69 72 61 6C - 20 6F 6E 63 6F 67 65 6E  of viral oncogen ↕↓
 ┃ 10 65 20 69 6E 20 62 6F 74 - 68 20 53 75 62 6A 65 63  e in both Subjec ↕↓
 ┃ 20 74 73 20 52 42 31 20 61 - 6E 64 20 52 42 32 2E 20  ts RB1 and RB2.  ↕↓
 ┃ 30 20 4E 65 65 64 20 6F 72 - 69 67 69 6E 61 6C 20 64  Need original d  ↕↓
 ┃ 40 61 74 61 20 66 69 6C 65 - 73 20 6F 6E 20 72 6F 75  ata files on rou ↕↓
 ┃ 50 73 20 73 61 72 63 6F 6D - 61 20 76 69 72 75 73 2E  s sarcoma virus. ↕↓
 ┃ 60 20 20 20 20 52 2F 45 20 - 70 72 6F 74 65 69 6E 20   R/E protein    ↕↓
 ┃ 70 68 69 6E 61 73 65 20 66 - 75 6E 63 74 69 6F 6E 2C  kinase function, ↕↓
 ┃ 80 20 73 65 74 74 69 6E 67 - 20 75 70 20 6D 65 65 74   setting up meet ↕↓
 ┃ 90 69 6E 67 20 77 69 74 68 - 20 44 72 20 48 69 6C 6C  ing with Dr Hill ↕↓
 ┃ A0 69 65 72 2E 20 53 68 - 6F 75 6C 64 20 62 65 20  ier. Should be   ↕↓
 ┃ B0 61 76 61 69 6C 61 62 6C - 65 20 74 6F 20 63 6F 6D  available to com ↕↓
 ┃ C0 65 20 64 6F 77 6E 20 6E - 65 78 74 20 77 65 65 6B  e down next week ↕↓
 ┃ D0 2E 20 20 48 6F 70 65 20 - 74 6F 20 67 65 74 20 73  . Hope to get s  ↕↓
 ┃ E0 6F 6D 65 20 6D 6F 72 65 - 20 69 64 65 61 73 20 6F  ome more ideas o ↕↓
 ┃ 40 6E 20 69 6D 70 72 6F 76 - 69 6E 67 20 74 68 65 0D  n improving the  ↕↓
┣━━━━━━━━━━━━━━━━━━━━━━━━━━━━━━━━━━━━━━━━━━━━━━━━━━━━━━━━━━━┫↕
♥Help  ♦ Info  ♣ Exit  ♠Launch | GoTo
                        Viewer Search
```

Guthrie folded his arms.

'Like I said, you got the hexadecimal bits patterns on the left and, where possible – hey, you got a pretty good score. Must have all of twenty-five words there. That's the ASCII translation. And there's your virus.'

Arends moved up close to the screen, following to where Guthrie was pointing. And there it was: Rous sarcoma virus.

'Is that any help?' Guthrie asked.

Arends felt a sudden sense of deflation. Rous sarcoma virus was a laboratory favourite, something every biochemistry student came across at one time or another. It caused a troublesome disease in chickens, but was entirely harmless to almost everything else, including humans. You could be knee deep in the Rous sarcoma virus and it wouldn't merit the kind of decon job Fort Willard had witnessed – unless you happened to be right next to a major chicken farm. He scanned the rest of the short paragraph, hoping for anything that might give him a lead. Even laundry lists carried names.

And there was a name, just over halfway down: Hillier.

5

Rafflesia Camp. August 20th

Carmen waited until four o'clock before digging up the graves. McKinnon and Lennox followed. All three were wearing full suits and carrying shovels. Sergeant Sarandon had stayed behind to look after Holly and to keep an eye on Kaoy.

They worked for three hours, digging slowly, taking great care in turning over the earth, which was red and almost sandy. It seemed incredible that such soil could support the luxuriant vegetation. Every now and then they would pause, as one or the other of them found something. The bodies were blackened and rotting, the processes of decay and transformation accelerated by the extreme biochemical collapse brought about by the disease, the heat and the bacteria-rich environment. Scavenging insects and worms spilled out of rents in barely distinguishable tissue and clothing. As she turned over the earth Carmen prayed that none of the creatures would be able to carry the virus.

Despite the insulating effect of working in the suit, it was one of the worst things Carmen had ever had to do. But pretty soon there were only two burial mounds left, and they had yet to find any evidence of children. The thought that Holly Becker's children might not have been there after all, had somehow escaped the epidemic, gave her new strength. She dug and turned and sifted the red earth, totally absorbed.

Then she found it.

The body was in such a state of decay, bare bones were visible in the rubble of blackened flesh and discoloured clothing. Standing still, breathing loudly in her partially misted mask, Carmen looked at the distinctive femur of a child. She called Lennox over. McKinnon stopped working too and came to look. Saying nothing, he turned over the remains with his shovel. They were all very still now, looking down at a pair of stained slippers made to look like mice. The ears and whiskers were clotted with dirt and dried blood.

6

Rafflesia Camp. August 21st

Carmen was dreaming about home when her alarm went off. In the dream she was wearing Joey's baseball mitt, catching and returning the ball with high looping pitches. Then she was in her damp tent in the cold dawn light listening to the jungle. It was incredible that the alarm with its familiar peep-peep-peep should wake her in the midst of the honking, buzzing, whining dawn chorus that was surging all around. Incredible that the chorus itself hadn't woken her half an hour before. She was getting tired. It was the heat and the bad food. The mission was beginning to drag, and the strain of having to deal with someone directly affected by the tragedy was taking a heavy toll. After discussing the matter with Lennox and McKinnon she had decided not to tell Holly Becker that they had found a child's body in one of the graves. While the quarantine was still in effect they could not risk pushing her over the edge. For the sake of the mission Carmen was obliged to lie. She hoped it would be the last time.

She lay there looking at the digital alarm for a while, enjoying the familiar beeping, a noise which she normally found disagreeable. It came to her that the reason the relatively small sound woke her when the jungle couldn't was because she didn't want to hear the jungle; her mind cut it out, while the beeping of her alarm was like word from home. Her tiredness wasn't so much physical as emotional. She listened to the men moving around the camp outside her tent. They were probably feeling just as homesick. She wriggled out of her cotton sleeping bag. She had a duty to them to be a leader; so she would lead. The sooner they wrapped things up, the sooner they could all get back to their families.

She found Sergeant Sarandon sitting by Holly Becker's tent, sipping at a cup of coffee.

'How is she?'

Sarandon looked up. Once again he had been up most of the night, keeping watch.

'Sleeping like a baby. I guess rest is the best thing she can do right now. Seems like a shame to wake her.'

Carmen shook her head. The loss of her children would certainly wipe out any relief she might have felt at her continuing recovery, and the incredible luck that implied.

'It's going to be a hell of a day for her,' said Carmen, keeping her voice down. 'Let her wake in her own time.'

Carmen couldn't face breakfast. She sat at the back of the Cherokee with McKinnon and Lennox, drinking coffee. Her appetite seemed to have taken a nose dive as soon as she touched Sumatran soil, and she was beginning to worry about not eating properly. A poor diet meant poor performance. But no matter how she tried, the only thing she desired, the only thing she *wanted* to put into her body was coffee. They had yet to start work but were all perspiring heavily. They reviewed the plan of action for the day. The sampling would continue, but they were reaching a point where there was little left to be tested. So far everything they had pushed through the various analytical processes in the field laboratory had proved virus-free. None of the insects, mammals or reptiles seemed to be carrying the thing that, only a few weeks before, had wiped out a small community. Whatever had carried the disease to the people here seemed to have moved on.

'I'm not entirely surprised we keep drawing blanks,' said Lennox, looking into his plastic cup.

'You thinking about the single primary contact reported in Muaratebo?'

It was McKinnon who spoke. Carmen was looking across to where Sarandon sat next to Holly Becker's tent.

'That's right,' said Lennox. 'If there was only one primary infection then we can probably discount insects as far as our main vector is concerned.'

'But if the sole vectors are primates why aren't we picking it up in the monkeys Leigh bagged?'

Lennox thought for a moment. Carmen looked back and took in McKinnon's shiny face. Unlike the others who were letting things slide a little, McKinnon was still making an effort with his appearance, but it was a losing battle. His red hair and pale skin were ill-suited to the tropics and he had gone a bright pink colour in spite of the factor 20 suncream he applied every few hours. He looked more like a fish out of water than any of them. When he reached across for the coffee pot there was a faint smell of coconuts that reminded Carmen of holidays on the beach.

'Monkeys are gregarious and territorial,' Lennox said. 'There's no reason one group should come into contact with another unless confrontation was absolutely unavoidable. If there is an infected group of monkeys, they might have moved on without passing the virus into the environment.'

'You still think it was the monkey hunter who brought the thing out of the forest?' asked McKinnon.

Carmen dipped to her coffee and took a sip.

'It looks likely. But it can't be the whole story because Jarvis picked up the virus well outside the hunter's territory and he never went near Muaratebo. I wouldn't be surprised if Leigh and Daintith come up with something at those caves Jarvis talked about in his log. If so, we have to find the link between the two incidents.'

'And this incident,' said Lennox. 'Don't forget what happened here.'

Carmen looked along the track towards the silent camp. What had happened? Something in the jungle had turned over. Something in the biochemical depths had flashed into spurious life for a moment then disappeared, drawing with it a dozen people. Carmen looked at Lennox and shook her head.

'Somewhere there's a link,' she said. 'We just haven't seen it yet.'

At four in the afternoon a call came through on the X-band. It was Arends. Sarandon, woken from heavy sleep, took a message and gave it to Carmen when she returned just before sundown. She called straight back. Arends was working in level 4 and wasn't able to come to the phone immediately. Carmen ate a bowlful of rice at supper, preoccupied. Arends's message said he had some news, and she was curious to find out what it was. She had completely forgotten about the anonymous letter in the weeks she had been in Sumatra. There were so many other things to think about for one thing, and it was hard to see how the mysterious document had any bearing on what was happening in Sumatra.

When Arends called back she took the call in the Cherokee, surprised as always by the quality of the digital transmission. It sounded like Arends was in a nearby town.

'Just thought you'd like to know how my enquiries are going.'

Carmen sensed that Arends was pleased with himself, although he wasn't the type to shout about it.

'Have you got anything useful?'

'I'm not sure. Yet. I have a lead, though. I might

have some more information in a couple of days.'

'So what's it all about?'

Arends went into a long explanation of how he had found the name of a laboratory at Fort Willard, how he had gone down there and gone inside and found a computer disk. Carmen closed the door of the Cherokee.

'Wait a minute, George. You don't mean you broke in?'

'No, not exactly. Well . . . Is this line secure?'

'Absolutely.'

'Then yes. But the place was abandoned. There was nobody around, and I just had this feeling.'

'A feeling like you just had to break in,' said Carmen.

Arends was quiet for a moment.

'I just got the feeling it was worth doing. That there was some point to it, the letter, I mean. When I went down there I didn't expect anything really. I mean I didn't expect to find anything, but then there was this abandoned lab. It must have been closed down years ago. There were biohazard stickers everywhere, and tape. You know, to make the place airtight? They'd fumigated the place, nuked it and then closed it down.'

'So what did you find?'

'The whole place had been *nuked*, Carmen. I still have no idea what happened there, but something very unwelcome turned up, I'd bet on it. I've been trying to find out more about what they might have been working on, but it's not easy. I still don't know who *they* were. But I did retrieve a computer disk, and that could be a start.'

'You took it out of the lab?' Carmen sat back against the side of the Cherokee. It was incredibly hot and stuffy, but she was glad nobody could hear. 'Well I suppose if you're gonna break in you might as well take something as well.'

'What did you expect me to do?'

Carmen said nothing. When she had given the package to Arends she hadn't really given any thought to the potential developments. But all this cloak and dagger stuff made her feel very uncomfortable. Arends had gotten way out of line, and she was an accomplice. In fact she was the one who had set him on the trail in the first place. She hoped she would never have to explain the incident to General Bailey. Arends went on.

'Anyway, all I found on it was garbage, at first. I put it on my machine at home and the thing just went crazy. All I got was a screenful of junk.'

'Was it coded?'

'Not exactly. A friend of mine said he thought it had been used on a customised operating system. Something to do with the FAT file, I don't know exactly.'

'Somebody else knows about this?'

'I didn't tell him where I got the disk.'

'So what happened? Was your friend able to do anything with it?'

'All he could do was get the thing to dump screenloads of hexadecimal numbers with bits of ASCII tacked on.'

'And?'

'Well we did a search using VIRUS as the tag.'

'Virus?'

'Yeah, the word virus. And straight away we get a screenload of numbers and some text. Not much information, but enough to tell me that the work that was going on at Willard was essentially biochemical. Virology may also have been involved. There was a reference to work on Rous sarcoma virus. Remember that one?'

'Sure,' said Carmen. 'Causes sarcomas in chickens. Oncogenes and all that stuff.'

'Right. Anyway, at the end of the text there's a reference to a Dr Hillier. Does that name ring any bells?'

Carmen thought for a moment. Nothing came.

'Sorry, no,' she said. 'You?'

'No. Anyway, I'm gonna do some more checking, and my friend's still scanning through the disk. Most of it's empty, unfortunately, but maybe if we can turn up another name . . .'

'You do that. Only try and keep it discreet, OK? Sounds like we've cut too many corners already.'

'Understood. Oh Carmen?'

'What?'

'There was something else. It was at the top of the text, a reference to subjects RB1 and RB2.'

'What kind of subjects?'

'Doesn't say. Could be anything. I thought maybe R could stand for *Rattus*, like these were lab rats, but I can't find a species where the second word starts with a B. So then I thought – '

'Rhesus?'

'Right. As in monkeys. *Macacus rhesus*.'

The possibility that primates from the macaque family had been used at Willard was the first tangible link with the Sumatra outbreak to emerge. It was tempting.

'One problem though,' Carmen said. 'Rhesus monkeys are natives of northern India. You don't find them down here.'

'Maybe our source didn't know that. Maybe he made a link between Willard and Sumatra which is in fact spurious. Maybe there is no link.'

Carmen looked at the boxes of equipment crammed in the back of the Cherokee. There were already so many different pieces to the puzzle, she didn't want there to be any more.

'Anyway,' Arends went on. 'I plan to track down this Dr Hillier. Maybe he'll have some answers.'

'OK, George. Just don't break into any more buildings.'

7

All the evidence pointed to the caves. Major Leigh had not been too enthusiastic about dividing the RIID team, especially when there was talk of recalling the whole expedition, but that was before he had read the fax of Jarvis's log. Now, like his companion Harold Daintith, he was convinced that the information it contained was too precise and potentially too important to ignore. If Dr Jarvis really had become infected with the Muaratebo virus through contact with the primary reservoir, rather than through some unrecorded encounter with an infected human, then the caves were where it happened. And they were not so far away.

The most persuasive evidence as far as Leigh was concerned was the timing. To judge from the Marshallton outbreak, and from the accounts given them by the WHO in Indonesia, the Muaratebo virus had a relatively predictable pathogenesis, at least as far as humans were concerned. In all cases infection to death took a total of nine days, with the first symptoms appearing midway between the two. The virus was, as Sergeant Sarandon had once remarked, *a nine day wonder*.

Nine days before his death Jarvis had been looking for a freshwater source twenty miles north-west of a village called Muaralembu in the foothills of the Barisan range. Jarvis's log was very precise, not least because he clearly planned to return to the same spot. He had found water in several caves, although some were inhabited by bats, which meant there was a high risk of contamination. His descriptions were accompanied by painstakingly recorded grid references.

As Daintith confirmed, the bats were another promising indicator. Association with various species had been loosely implicated in past haemorrhagic fever outbreaks. In one index case, at a cotton factory in southern Sudan in 1977, bats of the species *Tadarida trevori* had infested the roof of the building and their urine and faeces had fallen onto the work surfaces used by the victims. Here, just as in the Sudan case, if the bats had been feeding off insects which carried the virus, then the virus would probably be found in their droppings. Alternatively the bats might play host to a virus-carrying species of tick or mite. In either case the bats' habitat would have become lethally hot. A cut or a graze could have been enough for a human – or a monkey – to become infected.

Except that there were no monkeys on this particular escarpment, at least no *Macaca nemestrina*. Jarvis had been precise about that, as about everything else. Instead there was a vociferous colony of baboons. This presented a problem. Baboons were fiercely territorial. Like human beings they were not good at peaceful co-existence, and would have attacked or seen off any other primates that tried to move in on their part of the forest, certainly smaller ones like *Macaca nemestrina*.

This mattered because the one species, besides man, known to have carried the Muaratebo virus was the pig-tailed macaque. It was macaques who had brought the virus to Marshallton. That was a fact. And macaques were traded in the town of Muaratebo, where the virus had descended upon the population like an exterminating army, spreading out, it seemed, from a single point, probably a single primary infection. All of which meant that if macaques never went to the caves then the caves were effectively ruled out as the epicentre of the disease. That there could be two such centres in the same area, both emerging quite independently at the same time, was not a credible hypothesis.

Leigh had read and reread the parts of the log that referred to the baboons, and he noted that Jarvis never claimed to have actually seen them: he simply claimed to have heard their calls. Jarvis was an entomologist. Wasn't it more than possible that his knowledge of primates was not as solid as he'd thought? If the calls Jarvis heard had come not from baboons but from macaques, then the location of the caves might prove a real breakthrough. They would have the chance they were looking for to put the stopper back in the bottle.

They took the Trans-Sumatra for fifteen miles and then headed north-east into Riau province. The roads were almost empty and they reached the eastern extreme of the escarpment at Muaralembu an hour after dawn the next day. Leigh could see why Jarvis had chosen the area for his field station: although there had been sporadic logging during past decades the terrain was too uneven for cultivation, and human settlements had not endured for long. Up ahead they caught glimpses of the bare limestone crags jutting up through the dense mantle of the rain forest, yellow in the morning sun. They looked inviting, beautiful.

They managed to drive further up the ravine than Jarvis had done because the ground was firmer, and because the Cherokee didn't have a broken shock-absorber as the Englishman's Land Rover had done. They pitched a tent below the escarpment's widest east-facing slope and unloaded the equipment. The operation would proceed in three stages: first, Leigh and Daintith would make a reconnaissance of the cave system to get some idea of the range of fauna that used it; second, they would set up blood-and-wire traps inside the caves to get as big a sample of the caves' insect life as possible; and third, they would kill and bag any mammals in the immediate vicinity of the cave, so that they could be dissected later at the main base and their tissue checked for evidence of infection with the Muaratebo virus (as the best marksman of the three, Baker would do most of the shooting). If any of the tests proved positive then they would return to the escarpment with a bigger team later – provided the necessary back-up arrived.

For the reconnaissance Leigh and Daintith wore two of the pressurised Racal suits that they had brought with them from Fort Detrick. Besides the battery-powered pump and filtration units, which had to be carried in a backpack, the suits were also equipped with two-way radios which the men checked before sealing their visors.

'All set, Major?'

Baker was tuned in too, although he was standing only a few yards away with a handset. His voice sounded so clear and loud Leigh felt like it was coming from inside his own head. He raised his thumb and then remembered that he could talk back. It was amazing that they hadn't got around to fitting these things back at the RIID.

'Turn your volume down a little, can you, Baker?' he said. 'I could go deaf.'

'Sorry, Major. How's that?'

'Better. OK, let's go.'

Carrying ropes and torches, they climbed carefully towards the face of the escarpment along a steep and stony path that looked like it had been made by water running down to the bottom of the ravine. They headed for a deep crag to their left from which the vegetation seemed to burst forth with unusual vigour, just as Jarvis had described it in his log. It was there that he had found the first entrance. Through the radio Leigh could hear

Daintith's breathing. It mixed with the sound of his own in a funny kind of counterpoint, except that Daintith's was more uneven, heavier.

'You heating up in there, Harold?' he asked.

'A little. Be better when we get out of the sun.'

Leigh stopped and looked up. The escarpment towered above them, the upper half of the face leaning out to meet them, vines hanging all the way down from the top. Against the shadows he could see insects moving, a swarm of mosquitoes probably. Everything about the place seemed sinister, and yet Leigh realised that was only because of what he knew – or rather what he suspected: that the last man to see it was dead.

'Shit!'

Leigh turned. Daintith had lost his footing and was stumbling backwards.

'Take it easy there.'

Daintith landed heavily on one knee.

'Just can't see my feet so good,' he said. He stood up again carefully. 'And these boots don't grip.'

'We're almost there now,' said Leigh. 'Better check your suit.'

Daintith brushed the dirt away from his knee and squeezed the suit to see whether there was any loss of pressure.

'No problem, Major,' he said.

They found the first entrance a few minutes later. It was big enough to climb through but there was a drop on the other side of about four or five feet. Shining his torch into the interior, Leigh caught sight of something shining on the floor of the cave. It was a coin.

'Can you hear me, Baker?'

'Loud and clear, sir. I could even see you till a minute ago.'

'Good. I think we're at the narrow entrance Jarvis talked about. There's a kind of antechamber and then

. . . A pretty narrow-looking opening going deeper.'

'OK.'

'There are some animal droppings in here. Don't know what kind. Birds maybe.'

'You going in, sir?'

Leigh moved his torch around, trying to get a better view.

'No. Not yet. Looks like you'd have to crawl. I don't think the suit'll take it. We'll set traps here later.'

'OK. There should be another way into the same system higher up and to your right.'

There was no path this time. They stayed close to the rock face, edging their way around, scrambling over the vines and the short twisted trees that clung to every available patch of broken ground. They had to go slowly for fear of catching the suits on the twigs and branches. The sun was well up in the sky and Leigh could feel the heat of it through his orange suit.

After fifteen minutes they reached the top of the escarpment. Above them they could see the forest canopy begin again, carpeting the landscape as it did on the other side of the ravine. Down below they could just make out the corner of the tent where Baker was waiting. The cave was hidden in shadow and lay at right angles to the main face, but it was easy to spot: Jarvis and his guides had got busy with their parangs and cleared away the vegetation from the entrance.

The entrance was shaped like an open mouth, and was tall enough even for Leigh to walk through without bending down. The torches seemed dim after the brilliance of the sun. They shone them upwards, searching for the bats that Jarvis had encountered, but there were none to be seen. They went forward slowly.

'Baker?'

'Yes, sir.'

The voice sounded weaker, and there was a fuzzy edge

to it. It was hard to make out over the steady hiss of the ventilation system.

'We're inside the first chamber. Are you still picking us up?'

There was a moment's silence. Leigh stopped.

'Yes, sir, but you're getting faint. It's all that rock in the way.'

'OK. There's plenty of flying insects; so we'll want blood-and-wire traps here too. No bats as yet, but we got some guano. What does the log say about the cave structure? It descends from here, right? To a pool.'

There was another pause. Leigh had read it all for himself, but he still wanted to hear it again.

'The cave narrows and then opens out into a big gallery. He descended about forty feet and found a stream feeding a freshwater pool. All you gotta do is follow the sound of running water.'

'I can't hear a thing,' said Daintith, his voice edgy. 'Just the sound of my own breathing and you, Baker.'

'What was that, sir?'

'Never mind,' said Leigh. But then something occurred to him. 'Hey, Baker?'

'Yes, sir.'

'Can you hear anything out there?'

'You mean water, sir?'

'No. I mean monkeys, baboons, whatever. They're meant to be around here. I hope we haven't scared them off.'

The radio buzzed.

'I'm boosting your signal, sir,' said Baker. 'Just a second here. Yes . . . OK.'

'You heard what I said?'

'Yes, sir, monkeys. I'll listen out for them.'

Daintith's torch beam had come to rest on the far end of the chamber, a confusion of sharp-edged boulders and pale grey stalactites. It looked like the only way forward.

'We're going to try and find that gallery,' said Leigh. 'We're sure to lose radio contact so expect to hear from us again in fifteen minutes or less.'

'Otherwise suit up and come get us,' said Daintith.

'Understood,' said Baker. 'Fifteen minutes.'

They secured a rope near the cave mouth and edged their way forward. It looked as if part of the chamber had collapsed, to judge from the size of the boulders and their sharp unweathered edges. They climbed carefully over them and discovered a wide archway formed from two more stalactites, huge ones this time and smooth as marble. The ground fell away steeply beyond them. Leigh went first, keeping a firm grip on the rope to stop himself from slipping. Daintith tried shining his torch into the void beyond but all he could see was the smooth roof.

'Can you see what's down there?'

Leigh found a secure foothold and slowly turned around. The torch threw long vertical shadows across a wasteland of broken rock. Small insects danced in the beam.

'Wait a second. You hear that?'

'Hear what?' said Daintith.

'There. Water. You hear it?'

The sound of Daintith's breathing stopped.

'Yes, I think so. Seems it's just like Jarvis said.'

'Baker?'

There was no answer.

'Baker, you there?' said Daintith, but they were already too far from the cave mouth.

'Never mind,' said Leigh. 'Let's keep going till we find the pool.'

The floor of the cave levelled out about twenty-five feet further down. There were more insects here. They bounced off Leigh's visor again and again as if trying to get inside. They were feeding on something, most likely animal faeces. But where were the animals?

They used the second rope to go deeper, crouching low for stability, easing themselves down between the fissures of rock. The walls above them were smooth and shiny, and tinged with a dark pink like the colour of living tissue. The roof of the cave, about thirty feet above them now, was covered in a forest of white stalactites. Leigh jumped as a grey shape cut silently across his torch beam.

'Bats,' said Daintith who had been watching too. 'I reckon they've got their own way in somewhere.'

Another pair streaked by, then a third. Their tails were long and their bellies a pale grey. They looked a lot bigger than the bats you saw back home. Leigh felt the urge to duck.

'Care to guess the family?' he said.

'*Molossus*, possibly. See the tails? Rat-like creature, scurry about on all fours, some species.'

'Great.'

'Insect-eaters with big appetites.'

They had descended something like eighty feet when Leigh saw the reflection from his torchlight thrown up against the rock walls. In front of them lay a broad expanse of black water, fed at one end by a small stream. As he drew closer he saw his own image on the surface, a ponderous, bloated figure, brilliant orange like a child's toy. Around the edge of the pool he saw sharp crystals protruding from the rock. They glistened in the beam of his torch like spring snow.

'Take a look at this.'

Daintith was behind him, staring at what looked like a heap of rocks above them on one side.

'I think this is the remains of a wall or something. You see?'

He shone his torch along the length of it. The regularity of the rocks was unmistakable, even if the intended structure was not.

'Human settlement. Who knows how old. Thousands of years, I'd bet.'

'A settlement down here?' said Leigh. 'There's no light.'

'They could have lit fires. No shortage of wood. Maybe it was just used for ceremonials.'

'Or as a burial chamber. That pile of rocks could be a burial mound.'

Daintith looked round. There was a sudden noise from the radio, a tearing sound, and then a click. It was Baker. For a second or two Leigh could hear him: '. . . quite a few . . . all around the face . . .' His voice sounded excited, anxious. But already it was gone.

'We must be near another entrance,' said Leigh. 'Maybe that first one.'

They both shone their torches away to the left, towards where the entrance ought to be. Slightly above them was a long dark fissure in the rock walls, but it was impossible to tell if it led anywhere.

Baker's voice surfaced again, more urgent this time: '. . . into the caves, sir . . . dozen maybe . . . if you can . . .'

'What's he talking about?' said Daintith. 'It's not fifteen minutes yet. He must know we can't hear him.'

Leigh didn't answer. The beam of his torch had come to rest on a pale brown heap of fur on a rock ledge just a few yards away. He stepped closer.

'We've got something here. Looks like a primate.'

Daintith followed him. The animal was on its side, lifeless, its head turned away.

'One of Jarvis's baboons?'

Leigh climbed up a couple of feet to get a better look. Scores of small flies rose up to meet him.

'No,' he said, unable to contain his satisfaction. '*Macaca nemestrina*. The pig-tailed macaque' – he was level with it now, close enough to reach out and touch it with his

313

outstretched hand – 'And there you see the pig-tail itself, just like at Marshall— Jesus!'

The fur of the animal was stained with dark blood. Standing over it now Leigh could see the mass of bite-marks, a huge laceration under one ear. The animal had been fiercely attacked. Daintith struggled slowly up onto the ledge and knelt down to examine the corpse.

'Looks like it crawled in here to die,' said Leigh.

Daintith shone his torch into the creature's face. The lips had curled back from the dark yellow fangs. The eyeballs had turned to a milky purple.

'Been dead about three weeks, judging from the state of it.'

Leigh took a step back. If his theory was correct the animal could still be red hot, its remains humming with the virus. The same thing went for the flies that had fed off its corpse and, very likely, whatever it was that had attacked it and drawn blood.

'We'll bag it when we get back, OK? Let's not take any chances here.'

'Wait a second,' Daintith said. 'Take a look at this. Here.'

He shone his beam just above the animal's left hind leg: on its fur was painted a brilliant red circle, lighter than the bloody bites.

'You said this animal was just like the ones at Marshall-ton. Didn't they have this kind of mark too?'

Before Leigh could answer the radio snapped back on.

'. . . of baboons in the caves, sir. They look . . .'

'Baboons,' said Daintith. 'That's what killed our *nemestrina*. It strayed into their territory.'

The two men looked at each other for a moment.

'Like we have,' said Leigh.

From his position below the escarpment Baker saw them streaming into the first entrance to the cave.

There were perhaps fifteen of them and they were big enough to cause problems. Now there were maybe ten more, running in the same direction. Baker gave up trying to get through to Leigh and Daintith on the radio. He picked up the hunting rifle and hastily snapped in a cartridge.

'Get the hell outa there!' he yelled, firing off a shot.

A flock of birds took off from nearby. By the cave mouth a large male baboon stood up on his hind legs to see what was happening and then vanished. Something nearby went crashing away through the trees. It sounded big enough to be a buffalo. Baker snapped another cartridge into the breach and stood ready, silently cursing his commanding officer's decision not to bring regular assault rifles. They might be on a peaceful mission, but already the jungle felt like an enemy. You only had to take a look at Rafflesia Camp to sense that.

He loosed another shot into the trees.

The cave exploded with noise. There were baboons everywhere, pressed close together by the cave walls so that the darkness was full of gleaming eyes and bared fangs.

'Jesus Christ!'

Daintith jumped to his feet, colliding with Leigh, who stumbled, pitching off the ledge. He landed badly, a wrenching pain shooting through his left ankle. His torch fell to the ground and rolled away towards the water. He tried to stand, but lost his footing again.

'Harold? Damn it, where – ?'

Then Daintith was beside him, helping him up, gripping him by the arm so tight the air ballooned up around his wrist. Their visors smacked against each other. Daintith's eyes were wide and staring.

'Come on! Let's get out. We're not – Jesus!'

Instinctively Leigh swung around. It was a male, a

big one. It was just a few feet away, lit from beneath by Leigh's fallen torch, showing the taut snarling face, the staring eyes, the sharp yellow fangs. It barked, jerking back and forth. Then leapt. Leigh lashed out with his fist, connecting with nothing. Then Daintith was screaming, the noise distorting through the radio link.

'Leigh, get it! Help me! Leeeeigh!'

In the jumble of shadow and light Leigh saw Daintith stagger backwards, the weight of the animal throwing him off balance. Leigh forced himself up.

'Help me!'

He was screaming with pain. Leigh lashed out again with all his strength. He felt his glove graze something and then he was looking at Daintith. He was propped up against the foot of the ledge, clutching his right forearm. The animal was gone.

'My suit! My suit! It's bitten right through. Jesus, Jesus.'

'Let's go! Come on!'

Daintith didn't move.

'It bit right through to the skin. I can feel it. God damn it, look!'

The whole of the right sleeve of the suit was deflated, clinging to his arm. If the virus had passed from the dead macaque into the baboon population and survived there, then a bite would be as lethal as an arterial injection. Virus particles from the animal's saliva would already be drifting through Daintith's bloodstream, carried through the blood vessels into the lungs, the spleen, the liver, the brain. The virus would feed on him as it had fed on Reiner and Jarvis, other men of science protected, so they thought, by their knowledge and their technology. Leigh grabbed his torch, and shone the beam up towards the entrance.

'We've got to get out of here, Harold.'

'Blood contact, Leigh! Blood contact. If it was infected – '

'We don't know – '

'It's the virus that makes them aggressive. At Marshallton they became aggressive. It was the brain haemorrhages, it made them – '

'Come on!'

'If the bite went through the . . . Oh Jesus, no. No!'

Daintith began to tug at the zipper on his Racal suit, frantically trying to unsuit to see if the bite had drawn blood – right there in the cave, with a hot cadaver a few feet away and blood-feeding insects all around them.

Leigh seized him by the shoulders.

'Not here, Harold. We've got to – '

'Get off me!'

Daintith pushed him away and reached up to the top of the ziplock zipper.

'Harold – '

'I have to – '

'No! We get out first. You know the procedure.'

Leigh pressed Daintith back against the rocks using all his weight. He felt the smaller man relax.

'Procedure, Harold.'

Daintith swallowed and nodded. The white mist was already climbing the inside of his faceplate as the suit lost pressure. He looked like he was drowning. Leigh shone the torch around. A dark shape streaked out of the beam.

'I'm OK,' Daintith said. 'I'll follow you.'

They hurried back up the narrow pathway, blundering against the rock walls, scrambling on all fours as it grew steeper. Daintith was talking to himself, chattering, trying to keep himself under control. Sometimes he would shout out for Leigh to slow down because he couldn't see through his visor. High above them they glimpsed the light of the cave entrance. Then the radio crackled again and Baker was talking to them. He sounded closer than before.

'Can you hear me? Over.'

317

'Got a problem here, Baker,' Leigh said. 'A baboon bit Harold. We have possible exposure.'

There was a pause at the other end.

'Baker?'

'Yes, sir. Copy that.'

Daintith was staring down at his sleeve. Two small rips were plainly visible.

8

The rubbish tip lay beside the river on the western side of town, near the raft houses of Solok Sipin with their rickety verandas and pointed roofs. The authorities had closed it two years before, but trucks still came down at night rather than pay to use the municipal site three miles out, and the children from the shanties still appeared every day at sunrise sifting through the garbage they left behind. The pickings had been poor lately. The trucks were wary about coming because of all the soldiers that had arrived in town. They were worried about being spotted. But there was always something to be found.

Bottles were what the children mostly looked out for. A batch of six Coca-Cola bottles could fetch two hundred rupiahs, and even plastic ones were of use to the men who hawked home-made drinks by the side of the airport road. But occasionally something more valuable would turn up – a piece of machinery that could still be cannibalised, old clothes or shoes – and that was when the fights broke out. The older boys always kept watch over the younger ones to see if they turned up anything special, and if that happened they would go over and take it by force. It was rare for any of the smaller kids to keep anything good, unless they carried a knife and were prepared to use it, although that had been known to happen as well. There was a teenager called Suli with a jagged scar right across

319

his cheek where some ten-year-old had opened him up with a cut-throat razor. The ten-year-old hadn't been seen since, and no one knew whether he had just taken off or if Suli had killed him somewhere.

At first they thought it was a tyre, bobbing up and down in the water about a hundred yards upriver, close to the near shore. Suli and a couple of the bigger boys raced off up the bank, slipping and sliding on the heaps of refuse, much of which had rotted down to a black mush, peppered with old bits of paper and plastic bags. A tyre was a major find, even an old one, because there were men in the shanties who could patch it up, no matter how many punctures it had. The trouble was, none of the boys were good swimmers, and the river was moving fast, swollen by the recent rains. It made big eddies as it swept past the tug-boats and raft houses, some of which were built as much as forty yards from the shore. Even a strong swimmer could be dragged under and drowned.

The tyre disappeared for a moment and then resurfaced, closer to the tip. Although most of it was submerged, it looked big enough to be a truck tyre, judging from its width. That meant it was even more valuable. In the window of one of the raft houses an old woman appeared, shouting. A bunch of small kids were crowding onto her narrow veranda with a long bamboo pole. They had run up along the top of the bank where the ground was firmer, leaving Suli and the others struggling along the bottom. One of the small kids danced up and down triumphantly waving a fist. They had got there first.

The old lady was still shouting, telling the kids to clear off, but no one was taking any notice. A boy in a filthy white T-shirt jumped into the water, hanging on to the foot of the veranda, not daring to let go in case he was sucked under. The other kids swung out the bamboo pole as far as they could, hoping they could catch the tyre before it drifted past. It was only ten yards away now, slowly rotating as the current caught against the shoreline. Everyone was yelling at once, trying to give instructions about what to do, where to position the pole. People started coming out of the surrounding houses to see what all the fuss was about. Up on the road a scooter and a battered red pick-up stopped to take a look.

The boy in the water saw it first. It surfaced for a moment and then disappeared again, a foot or so from the smooth black arc that everyone thought was rubber: a human jaw, the lower front teeth sticking up in a neat row. The body lay on its back, bloated almost beyond recognition, the head thrown back, the limbs submerged.

The boy yelled and pointed, but no one took any notice. The end of the pole slapped against the black arc, making a big dent in it. The water all around was suddenly coloured with swirls of dark purple fluid. Then, slowly, the head dipped forward, rising three or four inches out of the water, as if to discover the cause of the disturbance.

The blackened flesh was mostly eaten away, revealing a full set of grinning yellow teeth. One eye was closed, the other a gaping hole. At the back of the head the hair was tied back with a knot of cloth. As the head slipped back again one of the teeth glinted in the sun. It was made of gold.

The children and the old woman screamed, the child-dren dropping the pole and scrambling way to the far end of the veranda. Up on the road the man on the scooter stood tall to see what was going on. The boy in the water struggled to get onto the raft but slipped and fell back again, disappearing beneath the water. The body rolled onto its side and drifted past, leaving behind it a blackish-purple trail. A skeletal hand slid out of the water and came to rest against its hip.

The children ran away up the bank, shouting about the body and the plague that spread on the air. Everyone had heard about the epidemic at Muaratebo, not from the newspapers or the radio, which had said almost nothing, but from the tug-boat crews who came downriver dragging their great hauls of logs to the sawmills at the far end of town. From all around people came running, some of them carrying armfuls of possessions, some of them carrying babies hastily bundled up in the first piece of cloth that came to hand. The man on the scooter kick-started his engine and raced away towards town. The driver of the pick-up gunned his engine so that the wheels spun in the dust. Two of the children managed to jump onto the back; a third tumbled off again, landing in a heap by the side of the road. The pick-up almost collided with a truckload of soldiers coming the other way.

Down in the water the boy in the white T-shirt was struggling to reach the shore. Like the body, he was being carried downstream. He could see it over his shoulder, turning around and around in the current. It felt as if it was chasing him, trying to enfold him in its skeleton arms. Frantically, he splashed and heaved his way towards the edge of the rubbish dump, spitting out the foul water, choking.

He was almost there when he felt something grab him by the leg. He screamed and struggled, not daring to look back at the rotting eyes and the bared teeth. Then he heard a laugh. It was Suli. He swam past and scrambled up onto the bank, holding a knife in one hand and in the other a single gold tooth.

'Ten thousand rupiahs!' he shouted, holding it close to the other boy's face so that he could see it. 'Twenty thousand! Thirty!'

9

Major Leigh was fifteen minutes late calling in and he sounded exhausted. Even funnelled down a field transmitter and the headset, the strain in his voice was unmistakable.

'We have a positive result on one of the Elisa tests. Just one. From the macaque we found in the cave. It's pretty marginal, though. I think there's been substantial molecular decomposition since the animal died. Over.'

It was the first time they had found any trace of the virus in the field and yet Carmen felt no closer to her goal. That Ahmad's macaques had been infected at some time or other had already been established. Besides, there was a more pressing concern.

'What about the baboons? Over.'

'Negative so far, thank God. None of the specimens we've bagged have shown signs of infection, and the Elisa kits are showing nothing. If the virus got into the baboon population through the macaque we found I don't think it stayed there. With any luck Harold'll be OK. Over.'

Carmen felt her shoulders relax.

'Jesus. Am I glad to hear that. How's he doing? Over.'

'A little jittery. But OK otherwise. Over.'

Jittery. Carmen remembered George Arends's words when he picked her up off the floor: 'It's just the fear.' They all had a right to be jittery.

'What's the progress on the other sampling? Over.'

'It's going slowly. It's these damned suits. They can deal with the heat, but the humidity must be choking up the filters. Either that or the batteries are shot. After half an hour you're cooking. Harold almost passed out on me this morning. Over.'

Even with the back open it was hot inside the Cherokee.

'I don't like the sound of that,' said Carmen. 'I don't want you taking any chances with dehydration. If in doubt, unsuit and drink. Over.'

'Will do. We're almost done here anyhow. Baker bagged us some rodents this morning and we took some samples of animal faeces from the cave this afternoon. We've just got the blood-and-wire traps to check tomorrow. Once the samples are stowed we're out of here. And I'm not gonna be sorry, I can tell you. Over.'

'What about bats? Can you bag me some of those? Over.'

There was a pause. The sun was going down behind the forest canopy and the insects were already homing in on the points of light around the camp. Sergeant Sarandon lit a cigarette and leaned against the side of the Cherokee. The smell of tobacco smoke was familiar, comforting.

'Negative, Colonel. We haven't found the roost. It must be deeper inside the cave network than we can go. Besides, I don't think the bats are our vector here. I think they're irrelevant. Over.'

There was a grimness and assertion in his voice that Carmen had never heard before. Working inside that suit all day had knocked the jokiness out of him, for the time being at least.

'Want to share your thoughts with me? Over.'

A large flying cockroach thwacked against the window at the side of the Cherokee, attracted by the dim interior light. It clung to the glass, its long antennae swaying from side to side as if trying to eavesdrop on the conversation.

'I reckon we're on the right track with our macaques, just like we figured at the start. I'm certain that the dead animal we found here in the caves was responsible for bringing the virus here. Over.'

'OK,' said Carmen. 'What's your hypothesis? Over.'

'This macaque had been captured – we know that from the red marking – and very likely by the same hunter who brought the other infected animals to Muaratebo. Only somehow this one escaped. Maybe the hunter let it go because it was already getting sick. Either way this might explain it getting so disorientated. It got displaced and couldn't find its way back home. It travelled for days and ended up straying into baboon territory. The rest is simple. The macaque was killed. Its blood got into the water here, and maybe into the insect population too – although my guess is the insect samples will show negative just like the baboons. Anyway, Jarvis had the bad luck to go into the cave while it was still humming with the virus. Maybe he drank the water or cut himself nearby. End of story. What do you think? Over.'

Carmen caught sight of Brigadier Sutami's observer, Soesanto Kaoy, hanging around outside the tent where Holly Becker still lay isolated. Her shadow could be seen moving against the canvas. She would be thinking about her children, about their fate, still hoping – perhaps believing – that they were still alive. It was a hope Carmen dared not dispel. It was probably the only thing that was keeping the woman from going crazy. Carmen could not bear to think ahead to the moment when the truth could no longer be kept at bay. She had thought of her own children, Oliver and Joey, and asked herself if she would have the strength to go on living without them. Before Holly came along it had been the thought of her own death that she had found most difficult to shut out.

'You seem very certain of all this,' she said. 'Though all it's really based on is a circle of red dye, right?

That the macaque you found was one of Ahmad's. Over.'

'It all fits. We have three sets of primary infections involving humans: one set at Muaratebo, one here, involving Jarvis, and the Marshallton cases. *Macaca nemestrina* are implicated in all three. Whatever the exact permutations, we have to concentrate on that species. My suggestion is we try and locate the late Mr Ahmad's happy hunting grounds. That's where this thing came from, I'm sure of it. Somewhere 'round there is where we'll find the source. Over.'

Carmen thought about it for a moment. Nothing Leigh had said was new to her. The presence of the macaque in the cave was a clear explanation for the anomaly Peter Jarvis's infection represented.

'I kind of came to the same conclusion,' she said. 'Ahmad worked the banks of the Hari river. That's where we should go next if we can. Only there are some parts to all this that don't feel right. In the first place, you said there were three incidents of primary infection. You're forgetting this one right here, which was the earliest as far as we can tell. We've been at this place a week and we haven't seen a single macaque. That's odd, don't you think? Over.'

'They're easily missed. Anyway, all the activity might have scared them off. I'm not – '

A crackle of interference made Carmen wince. It was followed by a high-pitched metallic whine. Leigh's voice was lost for a moment.

' – with humans, it's true,' he said. 'The symptoms set in four to five days after infection. But with macaques it may be different. It may take longer. That reminds me: when are we going to get the results of the primate EPD programme from Fort Detrick? Over.'

'Any day now. Maybe tomorrow. Over.'

'The sooner the better. Anyway, we should be with

you in a couple of days. Will you be ready to move on by then? Over.'

'Maybe. I have to make a decision about that. Whether to continue, I mean. Assuming Colonel Bailey doesn't make it for me. Over.'

Sergeant Sarandon threw his cigarette away and moved around to the back of the Cherokee. He was trying to look casual, but Carmen knew this was something he wanted to hear.

'I don't understand,' said Leigh. 'Why shouldn't we continue? We've only just started to make sense of this thing. Over.'

'There are problems at Jambi. They've closed the airport completely and there are rumours that the virus has reached the town. Nothing's confirmed, but it doesn't look good. Sutami and his people are getting very jumpy. Over.'

'How are we for supplies? Over.'

'We're OK for now, but if we need more we're going to have to go all the way up to Pekanbaru to get them. All airports south of there are closed. It may be just a matter of time before Pekanbaru closes too. Over.'

Leigh swore under his breath.

'I say we go on while we can. Maybe the eye of the storm is the safest place to be anyway. I mean who's gonna want to head our way? Over.'

'Well, we can leave that decision until you get back here. We can't move until we know about Mrs Becker anyhow. Over.'

'How is she? Over.'

Kaoy was still standing outside Holly Becker's tent. Suddenly he realised that he was being observed and walked away, fishing in his top pocket for a cigarette as he went.

'She's fine. Clean, I think. No symptoms at all. Over.'

'Well, well.' Suddenly Leigh sounded his old self.

'Considering what she's been up to that's one lucky lady. Over.'

Carmen looked at the shadow cast against the inside of the tent. Holly was sitting on the edge of her bed, hunched over, motionless.

'I'm not so sure about that,' she said.

10

Brigadier Sutami looked at the tiny black flag, twirling it
between the finger and thumb of his right hand. On the
wall the green and grey map of Sumatra fluttered under
the ceiling fan. Dotted here and there other black flags
marked confirmed outbreaks. Sutami squinted through
the eddying smoke of his cigarette and smiled at the
futility of it all. The flags were there to make him feel
like he was in control; as if each tiny pennant marked a
unit of some invading army; an army that he could meet
with his own machines and men. But this enemy was silent,
invisible, lethal. Utterly ruthless. Indifferent to suffering.
Feeding on the population it subdued. It had no need to
occupy high ground, or strategic river crossings. It moved
wherever it pleased, but always along the line of least
resistance. It had reached the mountains to the west and
was reported as far north as Medan, but it was along the
Hari river that the flags clustered closest, at Muaratebo,
Muarabungo, and Muaratembesi.

Two days before, a body had been pulled out of the
water just above Jambi's main dock. Hairless, bloated,
black. When the boy who had found it, one of the village
children that worked the rubbish tips, had tried to pull it
in with his boathook, the body had started leaking like a
rotten wineskin. Death was flowing down from the jungle,
turning the Hari into a sewer. The one comforting thought

for Sutami was that the Americans were standing in the middle of it. The Travis woman, the Lieutenant-Colonel, with her high-tech equipment, her satellite communications and her expertise, was standing in the middle of the putrefaction and soon – it could only be a matter of time – it would be up to her neck, up to her big Yankee mouth.

Sutami had been drinking steadily since midnight, and was now a little unsteady on his feet. Despite the fan he was perspiring heavily, beads of moisture trapped in his scrappy moustache. He followed the course of the Hari south-eastward with his outstretched hand and then, placing the black flag against the red spot that marked Jambi, pushed it in.

The report had come through to him just after eleven o'clock. A scared-looking sergeant had almost fallen over running into his office. There was no doubt about the diagnosis. A twelve-year-old girl. At the small civilian hospital. Headache and fever. Inflamed conjunctivae. Rash of small granular blisters. She was in the first stages.

Sutami had ordered the immediate closure of the hospital, and imposed a curfew. It had meant a degree of brutality. But only violence or at the very least the threat of violence was enough to make civilians stay in a hospital where death was making the rounds. It was something he had wanted to do days ago, but his orders had been to avoid alarming the population. The generals, under pressure from the politicians in Jakarta, were angry with the way the army had reacted in Muaratebo. Had the army been less quick to occupy the streets, they argued, less quick to show their weapons, the situation would never have escalated in the way it had. Sutami laughed, a dry, silent laugh. Despite the generals' caution, the population of Jambi was about to become very alarmed.

For weeks they had been feeding hungrily on the

rumours trickling out of Muaratebo. There were those who said that the horrible death was a punishment for the wickedness of the people. There were those who said Jambi would not escape the same judgement. He would be surprised if the whole of Jambi didn't already know every detail of the girl. People would know her family, her home. Left to their own devices they would have burned the house down already, and the family inside, more than likely. But there would be no escalation. The army was in the street. The main routes out of town were all blocked. The disease might have reached Jambi, thought Sutami, but it would go no further. He took another shot of *arak* and sat down, his eyes still on the map.

He would sit tight until dawn. If the generals had something to say, they would say it to him, directly. He imagined the politicians and foreign diplomats asleep in their air-conditioned rooms in Jakarta and he raised his smeared glass.

'Damn you all,' he said.

'They are occupying the market area,' said the soldier, pointing to a map of the town. Sutami leaned forward on his hands, and breathed deeply. He needed more coffee. Dawn was still a couple of hours away and he felt monumentally tired.

'How many of them?'

'There are just a handful. Mostly young men. One of them has a weapon, a handgun, I think.'

'Anything else?'

'No. I think they expected to be able to leave unseen. They were stopped on the northern road, and they made for the market – to find cover, I think.'

'No, I mean are there any other incidents?'

'A fire. In the southern district. And some looting, but I think the armoured cars and the troops are making them think twice.'

Sutami stood up straight, his head swimming. He walked across to his battered metal desk and snatched up his gun belt. He took his automatic from the holster and checked the clip. As he was putting the belt around his waist he caught the soldier's eye.

'What's the problem?'

The soldier shook his head vigorously.

'I just wondered . . .'

'Wondered what?'

'If there had been any word from Jakarta.'

Sutami smiled, and put on his peaked cap. His face was shiny with perspiration. More than anything he wanted a cigarette, but it was too late for that. Now was the time for action.

'They are all asleep, Corporal. They will give their opinion in good time.'

'So what are we going to do?'

Sutami stood to attention, and gave a mock salute.

'We are going to take control,' he said.

PART FIVE

Carriers

1

Rafflesia Camp. August 25th

Returning along the path from the abandoned camp carrying a box of unused Nunc tubes, Carmen was pulled up short by the sight of Holly Becker standing in the mess area with Sarandon preparing lunch. And had to remind herself that there was no reason for alarm. Holly was fine – physically at least. And even mentally she was proving surprisingly resilient. When they had told her at first light that morning that the Elisa immunofluorescence test had proved negative and that her period of quarantine was over, she had insisted on contributing something to the mission, and had suggested helping Sarandon with the cooking.

For her part Carmen had been encouraging. Active, Holly would be less likely to brood. And the ploy seemed to be working, although every now and then Holly would stop and look towards the camp, and you could see she was struggling with strong feelings. Not yet grief, thought Carmen, because at a certain level she would not accept that her children were dead; it was more like anguish at not knowing.

Carmen came under the awning they had rigged up at the back of the Cherokee.

'Hi!'

'Ready for some lunch?' asked Sarandon, perky in a grey T-shirt rolled high on his tight biceps, his dog tags dangling, catching the light. It was clear he had taken quite a shine to Holly. Carmen had to stifle an impulse to tease him about having had his first shave in four days. She sat down in one of the uncomfortable folding chairs, and smiled at Holly.

'Sure am.'

'Here.' Sarandon handed Holly his steaming wooden spatula with a boyish smile. 'I'll go call the others.'

Carmen looked around at the site. The sullen Sergeant Kaoy was smoking one of his endless supply of clover-scented cigarettes, staring at the floor. Lennox and McKinnon were in the forest dismantling traps, washing them down with Clorox ready for repacking. Once Leigh and Daintith returned, they would be moving on to a stretch of the Hari river where Ahmad had hunted, an area where the links with the earliest outbreaks seemed strongest.

Though she had told no one, Carmen was dreading the move. The constant fear of infection was like a kind of background noise, a restlessness in the pit of her stomach that helped explain her almost non-existent appetite. The growing certainty that the virus had moved on from Rafflesia Camp had provided some respite, but now the thought of beginning again, of probing into the living heart of the disease, filled her with foreboding. They were getting closer to the virus, she sensed it, but the desire to get the job done – a desire which in Carmen's case was almost a compulsion – was dwarfed by a deeper instinct. She thought of the doctor who had refused to fly out to Zaire after the Ebola outbreak. She understood now how it must have been for him. Her instincts told her to get away while she could. To go back to her family and put as much distance between them and the virus as the Earth allowed. The sound of Holly humming softly as she worked broke Carmen's train of thought. She considered the other woman for a moment.

'Did Sarandon tell you about Richard Meyers?'

There had been a series of fax transmissions from the RIID concerning Richard Myers, who had apparently been bombarding the US embassy in Jakarta with phone calls, trying to get information regarding Holly's whereabouts. He had reported that she had been heading for Rafflesia Camp and so the enquiry had bounced back and forth across the Pacific, finally reaching Carmen. She had reported back immediately, saying that Holly Becker had been located, and was in good health. Security considerations made it impossible to say anything more about the developing situation at the site.

'Pardon me?'

'I said did Sarandon tell you about Mr Meyers?'

'Oh. Oh yes.'

Holly went back to stirring the food, thinking of Richard now, frowning. Sarandon had told her about Richard as soon as she had come out of her tent that morning, and for a moment she had been unable to understand what he was talking about. Richard seemed so far away; not just geographically but emotionally. In the last few days she had been lost in thoughts of Emma and Lucy, and of Jonathan, remembering years they had lived together, all the extraordinary things they had done. In this long stream of recollection so little of the bad times seemed to have remained that it was hard for her to recall why it was she had finally decided to leave Jonathan. She could remember the circumstances, and considerations that had led to her breaking off, but it was much harder to get back to the negative feelings she knew she had lived through. Because of that she wondered now if she had ever really understood her feelings, asked herself if she had ever stopped loving Jonathan, and was alarmed to find she didn't have the answer. When she had heard Richard's name, when Sarandon had said his name, it was as if she was being dragged up out of deep water into the light. Now, with Carmen's question, she had the same feeling. It was a disagreeable sensation. However much she wanted to be back in the light, she knew that as long as her children, *and* Jonathan – as long as her real family – was lost, she would be held down, stuck in what felt like the deep reality of herself.

'Have you known him for long?'

Holly looked at Carmen's friendly face, felt the tug of her polite question. She decided to make an effort.

'I guess it's two years now. Seems less, though.' She frowned. 'The girls really like him.'

'What does he do?' asked Carmen.

'He's an investment banker.'

Carmen inclined her head deferentially and smiled.

'That's nice. My mother always told me to choose a man with money of his own or a handle on other people's.'

It was Holly's turn to smile.

'So your husband's a banker?'

'No. No, unfortunately, I never listened to my dear old mom. How else does a daughter end up in the army? It certainly wasn't what my mother had in mind.'

There was an awkward silence.

'So – so how come you did?' asked Holly. She watched Carmen think of a reply. When she had first seen her wearing the mask, had first heard her voice, she had thought Carmen very much the soldier, but she could see it wasn't a role she played easily.

'Well, you make it sound like . . .' Carmen shrugged, looking around at the forest, 'you make it sound like an unusual choice. There are lots of women in the army.'

'I didn't mean to. I was just curious. I wondered what would make you, I mean what would make a woman put on a uniform, carry a gun.'

Carmen laughed.

'I didn't join the Marines, Holly. No I . . . I was trained

as a scientist and the army offered lots of possibilities in the areas that interested me.' Carmen could see Holly was still unsure. 'It's just like any other corporation, really. And as for the uniform – ' she looked down at her T-shirt and baggy combat trousers – 'if I was in a corporation I'd be in a white coat, and if I was in an office I'd be in a jacket and skirt – so what's the difference?'

Holly watched her for a moment and then nodded.

'You have children?'

Carmen nodded.

'Sure. Two boys. Five and eight.'

'What are their names?'

'Joey. He's the youngest. And Oliver.'

'Must be hard, being away from them for so long.'

Carmen had the familiar impression that her feelings as a soldier and mother were under scrutiny now. It was not unusual for other women to find her something of a freak – did she breastfeed her babies in uniform? They always wanted to probe a little.

'It's not always easy,' she said.

'I know Emma and Lucy always found it hard when Jonathan – my ex – was away. And he was away a lot.'

'I'm rarely away from home,' said Carmen, a little too quickly.

'It's difficult though,' insisted Holly, 'when you do an interesting job I mean, to take an interest in raising children.'

Carmen was silent for a moment under the other woman's steady gaze. She had plenty to say on that score, but she was nervous of such frankness. Clearly Holly Becker was a plain speaker and the circumstances had probably stripped away any last layer of caution *vis-à-vis* opening up to strangers. Holly lowered her eyes, conscious of the other woman's sensitivity. She went back to opening more of the ready-to-eat food.

'With me it was the other way round,' she said. 'I

mean I think I tended, I mean I *tend* to spoil them. I was just so pleased when they arrived all healthy and strong. When they were born, I mean. I never really got over that.'

'It is a wonderful thing.'

Holly looked at her, emptying food into the pot.

'I don't just mean . . . giving birth, though I guess that's a miracle enough in itself.'

'What do you mean, then?'

Holly stirred for a while, considering. It seemed as if they had got onto very personal terrain. It was the circumstances, but it was the woman too. Holly decided she liked her. She gave a little nod of decision.

'Well I needed a little help.'

'Oh?'

'There was a worry I might pass something on to my children. I have this heredity thing that can flare up as an illness in my . . . offspring – I always think that makes them sound like puppies or something – anyway something my babies can suffer from even though I don't myself. It's a defective gene.'

'I see,' said Carmen. She waited for a moment. 'You had to have treatment?'

'That's right. They were able to screen my ova, but that meant all kinds of tests and procedures. I tell you there were times when I felt like giving up.'

'I can imagine. A friend went through fertility treatment for years. She did give up in the end. She got divorced in fact.' Carmen gave a little shake of her head. 'But in your case it all turned out OK.'

'Yes. They came through just . . .' Holly paused for a moment, stirring, 'just perfect. Like I say I never really got over it. How lucky I was.' Holly's mouth set and she stirred more vigorously. 'This stuff looks awful.'

Carmen sensed she wanted to change the subject.

'We started out, when we first got here I mean, mixing

340

it up with some fresh ingredients, but everybody's getting a little tired now.'

'I guess you all want to go home.'

'No.'

Carmen shrugged.

'I mean yes, sure. What we want is to nail this virus to the floor, and put a big fence round it so nobody else can get hurt.'

Holly looked up from the saucepan. She had heard something rock solid in Carmen's voice, something that wasn't there all the time. Carmen saw her look and lowered her eyes.

'The tiredness just comes with fieldwork,' she said. 'Day after day performing simple repetitive tasks and you can't make any mistakes. You can't allow any errors to creep in. Inevitably it's tiring. Food tends to come last on the list of priorities.'

'I've noticed you don't eat much.'

Carmen slapped her hips.

'I've been trying to shed a few pounds,' she said, although the truth was she reckoned she had already lost nine or ten pounds, maybe more. She did her belt up at the tightest notch now, something she had never been able to do since she put on the uniform.

Holly smiled and peeled back another foil lid.

'And how close are you to finishing – to finding the virus? It's here, right? In the camp, I mean.'

Carmen sighed and looked away towards Rafflesia Camp.

'I don't believe it is any more. All our samples have come up negative. It *was* here, I'm sure of that, but I don't think this is where it came from, in the first place.'

'So why are you still here?'

'We have to finish our study of the site before moving on. There are two other members of the expedition who will be returning some time tomorrow. When we are all

341

back together I'll take a decision about where to go next.'

Holly looked over at Sarandon, who was putting out plates and cutlery.

'So you're in charge?'

'That's right.'

'How do you keep them in line? Bunch of guys out here in the jungle.'

'I don't have to. The army keeps them in line. It's called discipline. They owe respect to my rank.'

'But they have to respect you too, right?'

'Yes. But it's all fairly collegiate, you know. We have to work as a team, especially being so specialised. Everybody has to feel they can contribute. They don't wait to speak their mind.'

Holly took a canteen of water from the back of the Cherokee and came out from under the awning. She drank, holding the dark curls away from her forehead. Carmen liked the way she held herself. There was something straightforward about her. It was nice the way she said *bunch of guys*. There was something homey about that. Then she turned towards Carmen, her face a mask of suffering. It was like the weather had changed.

'I keep getting this feeling they're still alive.'

It happened so quickly it took Carmen by surprise. Holly's eyes were brimming with tears. Carmen went across to her. She was holding the canteen to her chest as if it were a baby. Carmen put her hand on her arm.

'Holly,' she said. She didn't know what else to say for a moment. 'It's like that when you lose someone. I remember when my . . .' Carmen struggled for a moment, was on the point of talking about her own dead daughter, then thought better of it, 'when my parents died, first my dad and then a year later my mom, there was a period afterwards where I just couldn't accept it. It seemed impossible that their things could still exist – an armchair or, I don't know, a sewing box that I had seen my mother

342

use for years – that these things still existed and yet *they* didn't.'

Holly drew the back of her hand across her face. She was frowning, her whole face puckering in the effort not to cry.

'But at least you knew . . . for sure, I mean.'

Carmen still held Holly's arm. She squeezed gently, trying physically to transfer some strength to the other woman. She asked herself if the moment had come to give Holly that certainty.

'This disease is a killer, Holly. Everybody dies who gets it.'

Holly's face went blank. It was something Carmen recognised instantly as denial. It was as if she had switched off.

2

Rafflesia Camp. August 26th

Just after midday a Cherokee came nosing along the track, pushing aside the huge ferns and overhanging branches. Carmen saw Leigh's long face squinting through the dust-smeared windshield. She would never have guessed how pleased she could be to see someone she had only known for a month.

Both Leigh and Daintith looked exhausted, Leigh particularly was scrawny around the neck where he seemed to have shed weight. His eyes seemed deeper in their sockets. Baker smoked grimly behind the wheel.

Leigh was first out of the door, and he was carrying an assault rifle.

'We miss lunch?' he said, forcing a smile, his eyes taking in Holly Becker and the remains of the meal: 'I was counting on getting a little of Sarandon's home cooking.'

Despite his wasted appearance, his voice sounded strong and full of good humour. Carmen and the others stood up, all of them looking at Daintith, the first and only member of the mission to be seriously exposed so far. It was Carmen who spoke.

'*What* is that?'

She took the rifle from Leigh.

'An AK47. Loaded. We picked it up on the road. There's junk everywhere. The military don't seem to be too attached to their equipment.'

'What's going on?'

'Did you hear about Jambi?'

Carmen nodded. They had been tuning into the World Service and forces networks all morning, catching scraps about a 'situation' in Jambi, which seemed to be becoming another Muaratebo.

'Well it looks like they've lost control of the situation,' said Leigh. 'I think they've been trying to establish some kind of cordon sanitaire around this thing. With each new outbreak they pull back and draw another line in the dirt. We're inside the line. In fact, given our epidemiological assumptions, we're somewhere near the centre of the storm. There are refugees on the road, some of them armed, but no military.'

'Well that's something to be thankful for,' said Lennox. Carmen looked at his scared face. It was a moment before she realised he was making a joke.

Slumped in the debilitating heat, Carmen debriefed Leigh and Daintith on their findings at the caves. A fax had come through in the middle of the night from the RIID laboratories. The primate EPD programme revealed a twelve to thirteen-day cycle of infection in macaques from infection to death or recovery, with extreme amplification – a surge in virus population – on the ninth day when the subject became infectious. The cycle took four or five days longer in macaques than in humans, a finding consistent with the lower mortality rate. The virus could replicate inside some monkeys but human beings were its preferred food.

Despite the overall state of the mission, and the possible threat of danger to them all. Carmen could tell that both Leigh and Daintith were excited.

With Leigh the excitement was intellectual. What he had seen at the caves had raised all kinds of questions regarding the epidemiological assumptions they were working on, and now he wanted to test his own ideas to

345

bring the mission to a successful conclusion. The discovery of the hard cycle from infection to death was going to be a big help. Daintith's excitement was qualitatively different. He was like a zoologist who had discovered a new kind of big cat. Perhaps, after his narrow escape in the cave, he felt safer from the virus than the rest of them. Perhaps he felt that to be the disease's victim was not his destiny.

Speaking into a Dictaphone which he had produced from his carefully organised kit, he speculated as to the reasons for the regularity of the cycle, making lengthy comparisons with the pathogenesis of Ebola and Crimean haemorrhagic fever. Carmen could picture him giving his first lecture at Harvard. His perspiration was no different now to what it was when he had first arrived in Sumatra, but to Carmen the beads of moisture on his forehead and upper lip were suddenly expressive, and she found herself having to look away.

Both men were anxious that the mission continue.

'The next step has to be Ahmad's hunting grounds,' said Leigh for maybe the twentieth time. 'The key to all this is the monkey hunter. You look at the timing for Jarvis, and you see that he almost certainly picked it up in the caves. Where from? We didn't find any virus in the environment. Mammals, arthropods, primates, *culicidae*. Clean. Same as here. But we did find the remains of a monkey marked, we have to assume, by Ahmad. Based on what we know about Ahmad's work, the monkey was probably caught close to the river where we know Ahmad habitually hunted. That makes two outbreaks with Ahmad or his work as the common denominator.'

'But we don't know how long the cave monkey had been there or how it had come to be there in the first place,' said Carmen, going over ground she had already covered in her thoughts a hundred times. 'Why assume it was part of the catch that infected Muaratebo?'

'It has to be,' said Leigh, though it was clear he could

see there were reasons for doubt. 'How many times did Ahmad come down the river? I mean how long did he spend in the forest before going down to Muaratebo to sell his catch?'

'Habibie said it varied. But he was never away less than three weeks.'

Leigh looked to Daintith.

'What do you think, Harold?'

'I don't think it had been there too long. I think it's fair to assume Jarvis picked up the virus either from the carcass or something infected by the carcass. The monkey comes into the cave, maybe drawn by the smell of fresh water. It gets attacked, almost torn to pieces. Its blood and bodily fluids are probably scattered over quite an area in the cave and maybe some of the baboons develop the disease and then die themselves.'

'But the baboons you bagged tested negative.'

'True, but it's possible I was bitten by a survivor who had beaten the disease or never came into contact with it.'

'Or maybe the sick animals left the troupe,' suggested Leigh. 'It's not uncommon.'

'But how does the infected monkey get there in the first place?' asked Carmen, still testing, probing.

'It escaped,' said Leigh. 'Or maybe Ahmad released it. He may have seen it was developing symptoms of some kind. A nosebleed maybe, or it might have become listless. Ahmad figures he won't get a good price so he lets the monkey go free. That way he can bag a healthy animal in its place.'

'The trouble is,' said Carmen, 'the monkeys Ahmad brought down the river did not become infectious in the US until around the 2nd or 3rd of August, when Carl Reiner came into contact with them. The earliest possible date they could have been infected was July 25th, given that the virus incubates in macaques for nine days before extreme amplification. Any other way and Habibie would have been dead for sure. He was bitten, for Christ's sake, and by a monkey that also bit Ahmad. His monkeys weren't hot when they passed through Muaratebo, only later.'

'It needn't have worked that way,' said Leigh. 'Suppose Ahmad had a full load of healthy monkeys and he's getting ready to head home. But then he stumbles on a sick one, what looks like a lucky bonus. Maybe it was too sick to get away, a lucky find. Once he realises that it's sick he releases it, of course, but not before the rest of the catch, or some of it, has been infected. Your sick monkey, disorientated, ends up straying into baboon territory and pays the price.'

There was a problem with this hypothesis and Leigh knew it. He looked down at his dusty boots, looking for an answer.

'That idea just creates a new problem, an even tougher one,' said Carmen. 'If Ahmad released the monkey because he knew it was sick, if that monkey did infect the others then it had to be at least in the ninth day of infection or it wouldn't have shown symptoms and it wouldn't have been hot. From the river to the caves is at least ninety miles. So how does a monkey make the trip in that time when it's sick?'

'Suppose it was a survivor?' said Leigh. 'It beat the disease like some of the Marshallton macaques did.'

'In which case, however long it took to get to the caves, it wouldn't be hot any more by the time it got there. Five days after the first symptoms it would be clean again, and Peter Jarvis would still be alive.'

'Which leaves us with only one explanation,' said Daintith, checking to see that his Dictaphone was still running. 'The animal was infected about the same time as the others and simply escaped. It made the journey while healthy and only fell sick when it was near the caves.'

'Which brings us back to Ahmad's hunting grounds again,' said Leigh.

'More than that,' said Daintith, 'it brings us back to Ahmad's hunting grounds around July 25th. And that's . . . Carmen, when is Ahmad supposed to have fallen ill? When did the chain of transmission in Muaratebo begin?'

Carmen frowned. What was Daintith driving at?

'Habibie said it was July 26th or 27th that Ahmad returned to the town. He died around the August 2nd or 3rd, according to the WHO.'

'Which means he was infected around the same date as the monkeys,' said Daintith. 'You see? We've always assumed that the macaques were a vector here at Muaratebo just as they were at Marshallton. That the virus got into the monkeys and that the monkeys infected the men. But it could just as easily have been the other way around. Monkeys *can* be vectors to men, but equally men can be vectors to monkeys. It's a two-way street. In fact, neither seems very likely in Ahmad's case. Monkeys and man picked up the virus more or less simultaneously, from something else. Something they met on the banks of the Hari river.'

'Something that passed through here first,' said Leigh, 'and then moved on. With a bit of luck it hasn't moved on again. It could just be waiting for us to sample it. We have to take a look.'

Carmen kicked at the dirt. She couldn't equate finding the virus at home with good luck. It was powerful, this thing, ruthless, a perfectly honed survivor for who knew how many millennia? Perhaps it was as old as life itself, a malevolent offshoot from the first sapling of creation. Yet Leigh and Daintith thought they could track it to its lair and swat it like some bothersome insect.

'We'll see what Bailey has to say this evening,' Carmen said.

Both Daintith and Leigh sat up straight. They were looking at Carmen, who was standing a little way off now, gazing towards the deserted camp. She turned.

'It may be that he wants to pull us out. We talked about the possibility last night. If things got worse here – if something bad has happened in Jambi – he'd have no choice.'

Leigh got to his feet.

'He can't pull us out. We're too close.'

'Without proper military protection from Jambi we're on our own out here,' said Carmen. 'It's not safe.'

'This is a once-in-a-lifetime thing,' said Daintith, raising his voice. Then uncomfortable under their stares, he switched off his Dictaphone and said: 'If we don't get on top of it here, on this island, we may not get another chance.'

The afternoon dragged on into a short gloomy dusk and, abruptly, darkness. Not even Leigh was able to lift their spirits. Another meal was taken in virtual silence, with the exception of Daintith who had some points about the pleomorphism of filoviruses he wanted to air with McKinnon and Lennox. Despite the fact that he was the only one talking, he finished eating before the others and then left them. They scraped at their empty plates listening to Daintith's Dictaphone. He had gone to sit in the front of the Cherokee, making notes, his pale hand flipping irritably at the moths and mosquitoes.

'Do you think we're going to be called back?' asked Baker after a while. By his tone Carmen could tell that that was what he would like. She put down her plate and then looked straight at him, her hands planted on her knees.

'I guess we'll be asked to do our duty,' she said.

At 2100 the call they were all waiting for came through.

General Bailey's voice was reproduced on the X-band loud and clear, bringing a sense of the calm and comfort of Fort Detrick's air-conditioned offices. Carmen took the handset from Sarandon, watched by Daintith and Leigh.

There were a few preliminaries, with Bailey expressing encouragement and sympathy with what he realised must be 'rugged' conditions. Then he said: 'What's the situation with supplies, Colonel?'

Carmen had a feeling he was building up to something. She imagined him sitting in his office and then had a flash of Oliver and Joey on the back lawn.

'We're OK for maybe another week. There's no problem with water. We're purifying the local brew.' Bailey said nothing. 'Did you have any further clarification from the Indonesians, sir? Regarding Jambi?'

There was another silence. Carmen could feel there was something wrong now.

'Our people confirmed the outbreak in Jambi,' said Bailey. He had nothing else to say. Carmen checked Leigh's face. He was frowning, listening hard. She went on.

'There seems to be a decrease in military activity in the area, sir. Major Leigh has been out on the road on a collateral mission and he says there is a lot of abandoned equipment. The Indonesian military seem to have withdrawn from the area.'

'Interesting,' said Bailey. 'But I'm afraid I can't be of much help there, Colonel. What the Indonesian military is doing is anybody's guess. I'm watching CNN like everybody else. Malaysia and Singapore have asked for the Malacca Straits to be closed to Indonesian shipping. I think the UN is going to take a vote today. All airports in Sumatra are closed, and KLM, Singapore Airlines and British Airways have stopped flights into Jakarta.'

'Jesus Christ.'

It was Baker who had spoken. And, looking around at

the anxious faces Carmen could see they were all alarmed. So focused on the jungle, they had forgotten about the world. It seemed incredible that the virus could be having such a devastating effect. For Carmen the news increased her sense of being in the centre of a hurricane.

'What's the situation in London?' she asked, lamely.

'It seems like the thing has been contained there, though some of the hospital staff that handled Jarvis died. We'll have to wait and see what develops.'

'What about the politicians?' asked Leigh. 'What's Jakarta saying?'

'The Indonesians are none too happy, as you can imagine, and Iran is trying to make an Islam-against-the-West thing out of it.'

Carmen looked at Leigh, and posed the obvious next question.

'Where does that leave us, sir?'

'I don't think you are in any danger, Colonel. If there's one place you're going to be left alone, it's where you are right now.'

Carmen wondered if the safety of the team was Bailey's prime consideration. She couldn't resist pushing a little.

'But things are getting a little hairy, sir. I mean how are we supposed to get out in an emergency?'

There was a pause.

'You can still rely on the Indonesian military for support. I don't think Jambi has made any difference to their commitment.'

Carmen thought of Brigadier Sutami's commitment and pressed her lips together. Sutami would be just as happy if they all died pissing blood was her guess.

'Besides . . .'

Carmen heard Bailey sigh.

'Besides what, sir?'

'Well frankly, Colonel, the Administration is worried about sending the wrong signal to the rest of the world.

We're trying to lower the temperature at the UN. We don't want open conflict down there. Things are . . . well I guess you could say delicately poised with respect to the Indonesians. If we sent a frigate out of the Indian Ocean to pick you up, while telling everybody this thing is under control, we'd be giving out a contradictory kind of signal.'

Leigh stood up from where he had been crouching and walked away towards the camp. Bailey ran on for a while.

'That's not to say we don't value what you're doing down there, Colonel. You're doing a good job, and I think your being there is . . . useful. And this thing is under review the whole time. Now I don't want you taking any unnecessary risks, Colonel. As for the suits, I'm going to get straight on to logistics and see if we can't get some through to you with the help of the Indonesians. It may take a day or two, though.'

Bailey had more to say. About Marshallton and about news they'd received regarding the situation in the UK where the outbreak seemed to have been contained. But Carmen was no longer paying attention. She was thinking about Tom and Oliver and Joey with his chef's hat on, and wishing she were home.

3

St Petersburg, Florida. August 26th

Two small white figures appeared at the far end of the eighteenth fairway, walking towards the clubhouse. Lieutenant-Colonel Arends put down his glass and went over to the edge of the veranda, sheltering his eyes from the sun. He hoped one of the figures would turn out to be Dr Alfred Hillier. They had arranged to meet at twelve noon and it was already after quarter-past. He was beginning to worry that his man wouldn't show.

'Can I get you anything, sir?'

One of the bar stewards was standing in the doorway with a cloth over his arm. He was Hispanic, with a square, brown face, his colour accentuated by his bleached-white jacket.

'No, thank you.'

The steward nodded and turned. They had them well trained in this place. As Arends had driven up to the front another attendant had appeared from nowhere to open the car door for him. The attendant had held out his hand, and there had followed an awkward moment in which Arends had fished in various pockets for a dollar bill, only to discover that what the attendant wanted were his car keys. The tip, of course, was payable on departure.

'There is one thing.'

'Yes, sir?'

'Do you know Dr Hillier, by any chance? I mean, by sight.'

'Yes, sir.'

Arends gestured towards the eighteenth.

'Is that him over there?'

The steward took a couple of steps, squinting into the distance.

'I think so, sir, yes. The gentleman on the right. He plays most mornings, nine holes. Eighteen at weekends.'

'A real enthusiast, huh?'

The steward returned him an empty smile.

'Nothing more to drink, sir?'

'OK, yes. Another club soda please.'

The steward disappeared and Arends sat down again. He didn't much like golf courses. You took a nice piece of countryside or wilderness and turned it into a kind of suburbia without the houses – that was how he saw it. Golf was a country sport for people who didn't like the country, or who preferred it carpeted. Even now someone wearing a striped green apron was kneeling on the eighteenth green trimming the grass around the hole with what looked like a pair of nail scissors.

Arends felt out of place in his plain army uniform, but he had worn it deliberately. His first instincts had been to dress in civilian clothes, just in case things didn't work out and Hillier turned nasty. Out of uniform he might have been able to disguise his connection with the RIID and keep himself out of trouble. But with the latest bulletins from Sumatra he had changed his mind: things were going badly there, and if Hillier knew anything useful, however small, then this was the time to start talking. If it became necessary to try and force his hand then Arends would do it, if he could. The uniform might help him do that. Dr Hillier was a civilian, after all.

Finding him had proven easier than Arends had expected, thanks to the disk he had retrieved from Fort

355

Willard and his friend Saul Guthrie at Powder Mill. Guthrie had pulled off more than a hundred sectors from the disk, using a string of search terms dreamed up by Arends. Apparently 95 per cent or more of the disk was empty, but the short bursts of text he was able to recover contained two names, one of them belonging to a company called Gensystems Inc., the other to Dr Alfred Hillier.

The two white figures were closer now, just fifty or sixty yards short of the eighteenth green, towing their golfing trolleys behind them. Hillier was the taller and slimmer of the two and walked with quick, regular steps. The other man was fat. He waddled, struggling a little to keep up. Hillier wore dark glasses and a sunshade that threw a green shadow over his face. He looked in good shape for a man his age.

There wasn't much information available about Gensystems Inc. in the public records. The company had been registered in Palo Alto, but it had been wound up more than nine years earlier. Arends had hoped that, like many young biotechnology ventures of the time, Gensystems had gone after equity capital, which would have meant a detailed prospectus explaining its actual and planned activities. Unfortunately it turned out that Gensystems had never taken that route because its capital was all supplied by a big parent company: Westway Pharmaceuticals. He recalled that in those days it had become the norm for corporations like Westway to spin off certain research and development operations into separate subsidiaries so as to reduce the potential liability. Patent infringement actions were one of the main worries, because however brilliant your research people might be, you could never be absolutely certain some of that brilliance hadn't been borrowed from someone else – until it was too late and your product was about to hit the market. On the other hand, sending your scientists to work at an old army camp in the uplands of New Mexico was surely taking the point to extremes. Arm's length was one thing, internal exile another.

Arends did not like the idea of making his enquiries through the official channels at Westway. He was not going to get the information he wanted without explaining why he wanted it, and who he represented and what it was all about. Even then he could expect a delay of several weeks while his request was processed. So the only thing he had asked for when he called was Dr Hillier himself. He was transferred a couple of times, and then a helpful lady had come on the line to explain that Dr Hillier had retired from Westway the previous Christmas. The woman, it transpired, had been Hillier's PA for seventeen years and was coming up for retirement herself in a matter of months. Hillier had apparently been a senior research director at Westway. Arends lied: he said he was calling from the biology department at Amherst College and was thinking of inviting Hillier to speak at a conference. By the end of the discussion he had all the information he needed to reach him.

On the phone Hillier had seemed friendly, even helpful. Arends had responded by being truthful, up to a point. The RIID was doing some important research which they thought Hillier could help them with. Unfortunately it was too complex to go into over the phone, and, regrettably, a violation of military procedure. Hillier had seemed flattered by the idea that his name had reached government circles. He had agreed to a meeting. Why he had chosen his golf club as the venue was hard to say. Maybe he saw the interview as an opportunity to show off to his friends.

In the last few moments Arends had time to ask himself once again if he was doing the right thing – by which he meant the smart thing. He had toyed with the idea of putting up some harmless bluff and avoiding the subject of Fort Willard altogether, of just getting out of there before Hillier figured out that something was wrong. Arends had only heard of Willard through what had clearly been a classified document. He had only seen Willard as a trespasser. He only had Hillier's name off a piece of stolen property that was most likely protected by the privacy laws. If anyone pieced together his actions over the last few weeks they would have enough for a court martial and a mandatory jail sentence. And now he was about to risk putting someone on the scent, someone who might turn out to have friends in all kinds of high places.

So why was he taking the chance? The question had been lurking in his mind for days, but only now did he fully grasp the answer. It was this place, this clean, sunny, get-away-from-it-all paradise, that brought it home to him, this retreat from the messiness and filth of the non-exclusive world. Why? Because he, George Arends, did not belong here. The non-exclusive world was his world, and always would be because, uniform or no uniform, he was still a doctor. And in the non-exclusive world people were dying from a hideous disease that no one had ever seen before – not people that he knew, not people he had ever even seen, but still people. That was one reason why he had taken to Carmen Travis from the start, why he had gone so far in carrying out her request. Despite all the years of military discipline the focus of her loyalties was unchanged from her first year in med school. It wasn't the flag, or the Constitution or even the Institute. It was a more generous loyalty than that.

Hillier tanned well. His skin colour was even and he had managed to avoid the boiled lobster look that many Florida retirees never seemed to get beyond. His short hair had mostly turned silver, but he could have passed for fifty, at a pinch. By the time he appeared on the veranda his sunglasses had been swapped for discreet bifocals with fine golden frames. In fact, gold seemed to be his colour, gold and white.

'I'm sorry to find you in uniform, Colonel Arends,' he said as they sat down. He spoke slowly, his words almost too carefully articulated. 'I hope that doesn't mean you won't join me in a drink.'

'No problem in principle,' Arends said, 'but it's a little early for me.'

Hillier laughed.

'Bad habits. One gets into them so quickly. At Westway there was a strict no-alcohol policy. The president of the company had a genuine Queen Anne drinks cabinet full to the top with cartons of apple juice.'

The steward reappeared carrying what looked like a whisky soda on a tray. Hillier took a moment to register that it was there.

'Are you sure you won't have anything? An hors-d'oeuvre, perhaps?'

Arends declined. The steward left.

'So. You head the veterinary medicine division, I understand. I'm intrigued. It doesn't sound like my field at all.'

Arends let Hillier take a drink.

'Your field being precisely what?'

Hillier looked troubled.

'Well, cell biology, primarily – I assumed you knew that. I assumed that was why . . .'

'Please forgive my ignorance, doctor,' said Arends. 'It's just that my interest in talking to you is a narrow one and I haven't had time to check out your wider qualifications.'

'I see,' said Hillier, taking another sip. 'I think. And what *is* your interest in me, may I ask? Or are you going to tell me that's classified information?'

'You've heard about the epidemic on Sumatra?'

Hillier looked puzzled.

'Yes, I've seen the papers. What of it?'

'We have a team out there trying to trace the source

of the virus and in the meantime here in the US we're anxious to gather together all the comparative data we can that may be relevant.'

Two men came walking out of the bar, one of them Hillier's golfing companion. He was carrying a glass of white wine and a plate piled high with elaborate appetisers.

'Getting some strategy tips from the military?' the man called over as he sat down at a nearby table.

Hillier smiled back: 'You bet, Don. Hello, Pete.'

When he spoke again his voice was quieter.

'Frankly, I don't think I'm your man, Colonel Arends, although I'm flattered by the idea that I could help you. You see, I'm *not* an epidemiologist. I'm just a biochemist, and a retired biochemist at that. In fact, I'd love to know how it was you got the idea – '

Arends interrupted. He did not want to get onto that ground, not yet. There was still a good chance that Hillier would help him willingly once he knew the nature of the problem the RIID was up against. He wanted to concentrate on that.

'What we have in Sumatra is a filovirus, an airborne filovirus. In humans it causes a violent haemorrhagic fever and kills in nine days. We have no documented cases of recovery. Not one.'

He stopped, hoping for a reaction. Hillier simply nodded slowly, and raised his eyebrows as if to say: *well?*

'The action of the virus is unique. It begins by attacking the respiratory system, the lining of the lungs and the bronchus in particular. The victim develops a cough which serves to propagate the virus. Then it spreads to the other internal organs and the brain. We know of no other viral epidemic where the pattern of symptoms matches this one. It's a virus that we've never seen before.'

Hillier glanced down at his drink and began to swill the ice-cubes around in the glass.

'I'd heard it was pretty unpleasant,' he said after a moment. 'Are you sure you won't have a drink? Your soda looks pretty warmed up.'

'No, thank you. What I need to know is whether you ever encountered such symptoms during your time at Westway.'

'Dr Arends, as I've already – '

'Or more precisely at Gensystems Incorporated.'

Hillier fell silent. At the other table Don paused to look at them, a forkful of potato salad suspended an inch from his gaping mouth. Hillier sat back in his chair. He smiled again briefly, then his expression changed.

'Now what *are* you talking about? I've never worked at Gensystems, you must know that. I've always worked exclusively for Westway, and not in any medical capacity. Gensystems was quite a separate operation and it was wound up years ago.'

Arends felt an urge to back off. There was seriousness in Hillier's voice that verged on the threatening. That there had been a full-scale decon operation at Fort Willard was beyond doubt, but Arends was painfully aware that the circumstances of this discovery had led him into a host of hypotheses all pitifully short of evidence to sustain them. He was about to say something apologetic, but Hillier wasn't finished.

'If you want to know about Gensystems then you should talk to the people who ran it. I never had anything to do with them, or next to nothing. Why are you people dredging it up now, anyway?'

You people. What did Hillier mean? For the first time, Arends sensed it, just a glimpse of it: fear. Like Westway itself, Dr Alfred Hillier was anxious to put as much distance between himself and Gensystems as possible, even ten years on. Arends was holding only one card. He decided to play it.

'Dr Hillier – ' he leaned forward and lowered his voice

361

– 'you were called in by the Gensystems research team at Fort Willard, New Mexico nine years ago, a matter of weeks before operations there ceased. We have documentary proof of that. We also know that operations ceased at least in part because some sort of contamination occurred. Now our objective in all this is to find out what took place, not to look for culprits. I want you to understand that. Now, if you prefer not to co-operate with these enquiries, that is up to you. All I can say is that, given what may be at stake, and the likely public interest, it may not be a position that's easily defended.'

Hillier was staring down at the table. He seemed to be thinking hard. As he looked up Arends saw him swallow.

'It's true, I . . . I was called in as a consultant right at the end, but that's all. I mean, I was still on my way when it . . . when all the problems began. If you have the records you must know that. In any case I really don't see what those problems have to do with the Sumatra epidemic. I mean, this was nearly ten years ago.'

'All the same, I'd like to hear about them. The details.'

Hillier looked over his shoulder at Don and the other man. Neither of them was talking.

'Do you mind if we go somewhere more private?'

Arends nodded and followed Hillier back into the clubhouse. It was light and airy inside, the walls painted off-white with dark green trimmings. A couple of middle-aged men were drinking at the bar, but otherwise the room was empty. They took a table in the far corner beneath an array of black-and-white pictures, each one featuring a different professional teeing off. Arends thought he recognised Gary Player.

'The first two were already in hospital by the time I arrived,' Hillier said. 'The labs were already sealed off. I suppose I was lucky.'

'How so?'

'Well if I'd gotten there sooner I might have been infected too. A few hours earlier and I probably would have been.'

'I see. And how many people were infected?'

Hillier frowned.

'Three, I think. There was a scare about a fourth – a lab technician, Lucas his name was – but that turned out to be bronchitis. That's right. There were only three fatalities.'

Fatalities. Arends struggled to contain his surprise: three fatalities and nothing in the medical journals. What had they been trying to hide? It had to be more than sloppy laboratory procedures. Hillier was still talking.

'I stayed there – a kind of self-imposed quarantine, in effect – and helped supervise the remedial measures. There wasn't much else I could do by that time. There wasn't much anyone could do.'

Arends nodded. He couldn't let Hillier see that any of this was new to him.

'So it was you who supervised the clean-up?'

'The initial stages. The quarantining, the screening of water supplies and so on. Of course the final decon of the site was organised higher up. I don't know anything about that, although I assume there was a decon.'

The bar steward was coming towards them. Hillier waved him away.

'But you were called in because of the contamination, I assume.'

'No, not at all. No one was aware of it then.'

Arends frowned.

'But I thought – '

'That all happened just afterwards. In retrospect there may have been some connection, but I was called in to advise on a different problem entirely.'

'What sort of problem?'

Hillier hesitated.

'I do want to help you, really, but . . . I don't see how this has anything to do with the Indonesian virus. I mean – '

Arends interrupted: 'When we have all the facts, Dr Hillier, then we can decide if there's a connection. What we can't do is guess.'

Hillier avoided Arends's stare.

'It has to be strictly off the record, or I . . . I can't say anything. This was proprietary research. Intellectual property. I signed things, and I cannot jeopardise – '

'All right. It's off the record. I'm looking for answers, not a Pulitzer Prize.'

Hillier nodded slowly.

'The people at Willard had observed something in some of their cultures that they weren't sure how to interpret. I think it was my work on cellular oncogenes that interested them. That was what Dr Irwin said, as I recall. Of course, I never got a chance to talk it over in detail with him.'

From Hillier's tone of voice Arends knew why. Dr Irwin had been one of the three fatalities.

'Let's go back a little,' he said. 'What were Gensystems doing at Willard? I mean their research. What were they looking at?'

Hillier folded his arms.

'Well, as I recall, the company was formed on the back of some advances Irwin and others made at Berkeley. They identified the defective genes responsible for a group of inherited diseases – you've heard of Methuselah Syndrome?'

'Causes glandular malformation and effectively accelerates ageing.'

'Right. Well Irwin and his team pinned down the likely culprit. Somewhere on chromosome twelve, I think. Of course, we're talking about a pretty rare complaint. Not much money to be made in treating it. But Westway were interested in studying the action of the disease because it was thought that this might shed light on the ageing process generally, at least the genetic components of it – perhaps a rather naive idea in hindsight. But you can see the attraction from the commercial point of view. If you really could come to grips with the ageing process there'd be no end of products you could develop to retard it. Back then, you see, people thought genetics held the answer to everything.'

'So Westway set up a subsidiary and gave Irwin and his pals a slice of the equity.'

'Of course.'

'And then packed them off to the middle of nowhere. What were they afraid of, industrial espionage?'

Hillier's eyes narrowed for an instant. Arends got the impression that he was expected to know more than he did. Perhaps his bluffing had worked a little too well.

'That's what you're interested in? All that?'

Arends tried to sound reassuring.

'I don't think so, but – '

'Well I had nothing to do with that. I mean you have to know that: I was not involved in any of those decisions. I didn't have the seniority in those days. I didn't even know what the deal was until the crisis hit.'

'OK, I understand. So what of it?'

A loud burst of laughter came through from the veranda. Hillier bridled as if someone had just poured a glass of water down his back.

'Well, there was a lot of excitement in the early stages. And concern.'

'Concern? About what?'

'About all the potential of Gensystems' work being realised by other people first, other countries. The company, I mean Gensystems primarily, felt that our ethical restrictions placed the United States at a disadvantage to other countries, and that the result might be that our pharmaceuticals industry would fall behind. So they approached the government. Who did exactly, I don't know. Westway must have played a part, I suppose.'

'What ethical restrictions are we talking about?'

'Human embryo experimentation. Irwin just wanted a little more leeway. So that they could get a clearer view of the effects of the gene therapy they were developing. Sometimes you can only get so far with rats and pigs, you know.'

'And the government agreed to waive the rules?'

'They drew up guidelines, new guidelines, for a limited period.'

'Which they never published, I suppose.'

Hillier shrugged in a helpless kind of way. No one could blame him for the duplicity of politicians.

'There was one condition: Gensystems had to come and do their work on federal property where the government could supervise it. That was the deal. Fort Willard had been a biological warfare research facility. The Pentagon no longer had any use for it. It was well equipped and very isolated. Perfect.'

Arends tried matching Hillier's account of things with what he had learned on his own, and the fit was good. The cover-up and the use of military personnel at the decon now made sense, and that was something that had been puzzling him from the start. But he had the feeling that Hillier was still being careful, guarded. Maybe he had played a bigger role in the whole thing than he cared to admit.

'So how did it all go wrong? In your opinion.'

Hillier pushed his glass clean away from him and locked his hands together on the surface of the table. He had been a medical man too. Outwardly he resembled the classic, reassuring family doctor. And yet there was something else there too: a shrugging equivocation, a worldly, resigned manner. It was tempting to think that the money had done that to him, but maybe it was more complicated than that. Maybe the man had just been too long away from the sick and the maimed in the non-exclusive world, too long in the company board room.

'I honestly don't know. The company never came up with a product, but then they weren't really expected to in their first few years. They were close to developing a gene therapy procedure to deal with Methuselah Syndrome itself, but before they could make it generally available the virus showed up and killed half the team.'

'A filovirus.'

'Yes. Yes, and the symptoms were similar to the ones you described. I give you that.'

'Similar? How similar?'

'From what you've just said, pretty similar. I mean it all happened so quickly we couldn't be sure about the early stages. I believe there was some talk about bronchial infection.'

Arends forced himself to keep his voice down.

'But you had no idea where this virus had come from?'

Hillier pushed his fingers up behind his glasses, massaging the flesh between his eyes.

'Ideas, yes, we had ideas. But no way of testing them. You see, with Irwin dead and the lab off limits we had no way of finding out what had happened.'

'But all the other known filoviruses come from the tropics. Were Gensystems working with monkeys?'

Hillier shook his head.

'There was a reference in some notes I read to Subjects RB1 and RB2. Could they have been monkeys, rhesus monkeys?'

'No.'

'What about rodents of some – '

'No.'

'Then it must have been people. Someone must have

come back from the tropics. We've just seen a case in London where – '

'No one. We checked all that. Irwin's number two had been to Mexico – Cancun, I think – about three or four months before. That was the closest we got. We went as far as to cross-check the symptoms of Guanarito and half a dozen other pathogens, but none of them matched.'

'What about lab supplies? Is it possible that your nutrient solutions were contaminated off-site?'

'Possible, but extremely unlikely. All the nutrient solutions were irradiated before use, and besides, they were kept in cold storage for months beforehand. It's hard to see a virus surviving that. We checked with the suppliers anyway, and they reported having no problems at all.'

'Then it's simple: there has to have been some local reservoir or vector. Sand flies maybe, or black fly.'

'At Fort Willard? There are no sand flies and no black fly either. There's no ground water, no fauna of any size round there and absolutely no evidence of infestation. We sucked up every damn insect we could find – which wasn't many – and they all showed up clean. I don't think this was some nasty local feature.'

Arends could feel his colour rising. Three people had died from infection with a previously unknown virus, but rather than publicise the fact it had simply been swept under the carpet. He wondered who had been more anxious on that score: the company with its fear of lawsuits or the government with its fear of the voters. The decision to cover up must have been a tough one for both of them.

'So where the hell did it come from? It had to come from somewhere.'

Hillier sighed.

'We talked about genetic pollution. Just speculation, of course, but there was always the possibility that the genetic alterations they made to chromosome twelve were responsible.'

Arends stared.

'What are you talking about?'

'The possibility that the virus arose from the cell cultures themselves.'

'Human cell cultures?'

'Yes. Like I said, they were close to developing a gene therapy treatment for Methuselah Syndrome. They had to monitor the effects of that therapy on human cell cultures in case it produced some undesirable side-effect. We weren't quite as alert to the interdependency of genes then as we are now, but even so, Irwin would have wanted to do culture tests before attempting a genetically altered baby.'

'So? You're saying that this virus was – what? – *made* through this process?'

Hillier raised a finger.

'Not made, *expressed*.'

Arends folded his arms. Viral expression was a concept he had read about, but in his work for the RIID it had never come up. He had assumed it was a phenomenon confined to the realms of theory. What was Hillier trying to do? Did he think that if the problem at Fort Willard was more inexplicable that it would make the company's subsequent actions – or lack of them – more excusable? It seemed an unlikely tactic.

'What makes you say this, Dr Hillier?'

'Only one thing, really. You see, Irwin had two sets of cultures, half with the altered gene and half with the gene as it was. In the former he and his team began to detect an abnormal shortfall in the production of a particular enzyme, a protein kinase. The enzyme's function related to the regulation of inter-cellular signalling, somehow, although nobody knew exactly how. Perhaps it acted as a kind of fail-safe that would cancel certain harmful signals from reaching the genes in the nucleus. Anyway, Irwin thought that the enzyme shortfall was the direct result of the genetic alteration he had made to tackle Methuselah Syndrome. It was a fair hypothesis. Genes are so complex, there's always a possibility that if you go chopping a bit out of them and substituting another you'll change more than you mean to.'

'And Irwin called you about this. Why?'

'Well, as I said, I'd done a lot of work on cellular oncogenes. These genes are often responsible for producing protein kinases. That's what they do more often than not, you see. That's why Irwin wanted me to work with him. He thought he might have quite inadvertently altered an oncogene that was supposed to code for his missing enzyme.'

Another burst of laughter came from the veranda, followed by Don and his companion. Arends shot them an unfriendly look. He might never get Hillier back on track if he were interrupted now.

'You mean Irwin didn't know his Methuselah gene was an oncogene?'

Hillier held out his hands helplessly.

'Genes overlap. They're multifunctional. They interact. And besides, the gene splicing techniques Irwin was using back then were quite probably not one hundred per cent.'

'I still don't see – '

'For every cellular oncogene there is a *viral* oncogene. That's how the very first oncogene was discovered: not in a human or an animal at all, but in a virus – rous sarcoma virus, to be exact.'

'Rous sarcoma virus,' Arends repeated. 'That was mentioned in the log.'

'But there are others. Identical genes found in both living cells and in viruses. The point is, in some cases it's not just *one* viral gene that's present in the nucleus, but a full set: the genetic blueprint for a complete virus. As time goes on we're finding more and more of them.

It seems that the evolution of viruses and animals is more intimately connected than we imagined.'

'And all that's needed – ' Arends found himself stumbling over the words – 'is the right signal . . .'

'Or the *wrong* signal, for those genes to be expressed *as a virus*. Precisely. And just such potential signals are exactly what Irwin would have been trying out, you see? He would have wanted to see what difference not having enough of that enzyme would make to the cells. He would have been chucking every antigen at it, every chemical signal he could find, just to see what particular, primaeval eventuality that enzyme was supposed to deal with. It's perfectly possible that he found what he was looking for. The wrong signal got through to the nucleus because the enzyme wasn't there to filter it out. And the consequence was viral expression.'

Arends tried to picture Irwin and his team at the moment of discovery. The presence of the virus would have eluded them completely at first. What they would have seen using Northern analysis was a sudden flurry of biochemical activity around the nucleus as the transcription factors went to work. They would have been excited, elated. It would have felt like a breakthrough, like opening a door that had been locked for centuries.

'The individual viruses would have been secreted from the cells into the liquid growth medium,' he said. 'And then . . .'

'Inhaled, almost certainly. Pipetting would have been especially hazardous. Lots of tiny fluid particles. That's how Irwin and the others would have become infected, if this is really where the virus came from.'

'Just like that virologist at Marshallton.

Hillier frowned.

'I'm sorry, who?'

'Marcus Gaunt, that was his name. You didn't know him.'

Hillier fell silent. Don was waddling towards the table, a full wineglass in each hand. His curiosity had got the better of him.

'Ah, the conspirators,' he said. 'You putting your friend up for membership, Alfred?'

Arends ignored him.

'I have just one other question for the present, Dr Hillier.' Hillier looked over his shoulder at Don. Suddenly he was self-conscious. 'You're quite sure that no altered ova were ever reimplanted? Gensystems never offered this type of gene therapy to the public?'

Hillier shook his head.

'The public? Of course not. They were a long way from that. A very long way.'

4

Jambi Province. August 27th

Things changed after Bailey's communication. The mission changed. What had started out as a carefully planned investigation, with projections, goals, targets – specific tasks for everyone in the team – was becoming less focused, and somehow more vulnerable, more apt to break down. Bailey's reminding them of the world outside, of its posturing and politics had made them all feel different about what they were doing, had made them all feel in some indefinable way subtly compromised. The mass of broader considerations seemed to press down on the mission, exposing weakness.

Lack of results was a factor. Day after day they fed data into the hopper of the sophisticated analytical apparatus they were carrying, and day after day the computer readouts came up blank. It was as if they had come to the wrong island. Daintith and his Dictaphone constructed detailed theories explaining why the Muaratebo virus, while so patently active in the dwindling population of Sumatra, was nowhere to be found in the area where logic demanded it must have first emerged. Major McKinnon, with his superior virological knowledge, picked holes in Daintith's reasoning. Intellectual dispute spilled over into their increasingly sordid daily life. There were rows about whose turn it was to sterilise lab equipment or protective clothing, or who was using too much detergent to wash their sour-smelling clothes.

Corporal Baker, who made no secret of his desire to go home, was no longer pulling his weight, allowing Sergeant Sarandon and Holly Becker to do most of the mess duties, while he kept his head under the hood of one or other of the Cherokees, claiming repair and maintenance were more important than cleaning dishes. Carmen did her best to encourage and cajole, resenting the whole time Leigh's lack of participation. Leigh was no less committed, no less focused, but he worked silently at the various tasks in hand, hardly ever speaking. It was as if he wasn't there.

Bickering and sulking they moved into the margins of Ahmad's hunting ground.

The jungle had changed too. Now that the shine had been knocked off their original purpose, it seemed more forbidding than ever, more of an obstacle. They had to crawl along the overgrown tracks, pushing back the tangle of vegetation which immediately closed behind them. When one of the Cherokees got stuck, they all climbed out into the heat and humidity and watched Baker attach the steel cable of the winch to a nearby tree. The constant stopping, the constant need to literally drag the big vehicles forward weighed on their spirits.

They were getting nearer to Muaratebo, nearer to the river, the confluence of all their theories about how the virus had come out of the jungle. They had become accustomed to the area around Rafflesia Camp, and felt more vulnerable in the denser, darker jungle which bordered the Hari. Jostled by the poor tracks, Leigh, Lennox and McKinnon worked at the filters on the Racals, replacing the micropore cartridges which had been invaded by a tiny blue-grey fungus. The time was approaching when they might need some protection. The possibility that some localised pocket of insect life might be humming with Muaratebo was their big unspoken fear.

Just after 1600 hours on the 27th they pitched camp half a mile east of the Hari river. Carmen and Daintith started the painstaking task of unpacking and checking the laboratory equipment while Leigh looked over the rifles. Primates were still top of their most wanted list and Leigh intended to start collecting samples straight away. At five, with an hour of decent light left, Leigh and McKinnon went into the forest.

They had stopped the Cherokees on a slope where the vegetation was sparse enough to pitch camp, but it was still necessary to hack away the undergrowth before being able to erect the tents. Holly Becker watched Baker work his way across the slope, grunting with the effort, the back of his T-shirt blackened with perspiration. Sarandon was carefully unpacking the X-SAT, opening the umbrella of the satellite dish. Holly watched him check the different units, keying in instructions, adjusting the pitch and direction of the antenna. He was more careful now than he had been back at Rafflesia Camp. Their one link with home seemed to have become more precious.

Holly had been reluctant to leave Rafflesia Camp. It felt like she was giving up, finally accepting that her girls were dead. Just before pulling out she'd suppressed an urge to go back into the abandoned compound. Then, as they left the familiar territory she was overwhelmed with a feeling of anxiety bordering on panic. The girls would now never be able to find her. That was the thought that came into her head. She had said nothing, realising that her worry was absurd. The children were long gone. Even if they were still alive – it was still impossible for her not to feel that there was a chance of that – they would be far away. She tried to imagine them arrived somewhere, in some town, tried to imagine their faces. But it was impossible to think of them outside the perimeter of Rafflesia Camp, and in her head she could only see their faces sprinkled with earth, the eyes closed. Now, looking at the man cutting a hole in the hillside, she had a feeling of emptiness as sharp as the first pang of grief she had experienced when Carmen had told her that everyone at Rafflesia Camp had died. There was a difference, though. Things had changed for her since the news about Richard in New York. And in the midst of all the emptiness, she felt a knot of anxiety – like a soreness in the midst of anaesthesia, a proof of vitality. The fact that he was unable to be with her physically, but was thinking of her, loving her, experiencing the same frustration and confusion as her, made his presence somehow more pervasive. It was as if he had been pulled into the depths she now inhabited

'Worried about Richard?'

Holly started at this piece of clairvoyance and turned to see Carmen Travis's friendly blue eyes.

'I just hope he's OK.'

'He'll be fine. The embassy guys will keep him informed as far as possible.'

Carmen smiled, and despite herself, Holly felt reassured. She had been watching Carmen over the last few days. Watching how she coped as the mission slowly turned brown at the edges like the fallen forest leaves. For Holly it was clear that the RIID's investigations had been overwhelmed by events. Men and machinery were showing clear signs of fatigue, and it was only a matter of days before they had to turn to the Indonesian military for help. But here was Carmen standing before her with a smudge of dirt on her chin, as operational as ever and reassuring *her*. Suddenly it all struck Holly as very funny. She looked around at the endless vegetation. Here they were standing in a seething mass of life, a green cauldron, bubbling too slowly for their human eyes to see, metabolising, synthesising, a super-complex ecosystem predating their own version of life by millions of years – the jungle here went back at least one hundred million – and Carmen was about to get her tweezers out again to start her sampling.

'What's so funny?'

Holly hesitated to speak, but then just had to say it.

'It's all so . . . it's all so futile,' she said, and she walked away down the slope towards the Hari river, laughing.

Carmen, without moving, called after her.

'You don't believe that, Holly.' Her voice sounded almost bitter.

Holly paused and looked back up the slope. Baker had stopped working for a moment and was cleaning his machete against a stone. Holly watched Carmen's face. She regretted what she had said. Despite Carmen's tough professional manner, Holly could see that she was struggling a little here, feeling vulnerable.

'Oh no?'

'You mean our search, right?'

'Sure. This whole thing.'

Carmen started towards her.

'It's a chance we're taking, Holly. No guarantee of success. If there's a reservoir, a source anywhere on this island, it'll be in this area.'

She was near to Holly now. Holly smiled again.

'I'm sorry,' she said, and she touched Carmen's arm. She gestured to the surrounding vegetation. 'It's all this . . . all these trees. It's sending me nuts.'

'Need a few skyscrapers to calm you down? Missing the midtown traffic?'

Holly didn't have the strength to think of home. She was blank for a moment, looking for something to hold on to. Jonathan seemed to come to her. She felt an acute need to see him. Then she thought of Richard, sitting in his office or at home, worried to death.

'I just need to see him,' she said, her voice coming out small, confused. 'I need to talk to Richard.'

Carmen took her in her arms, and for a moment they held each other. Holly was surprised to find that Carmen was quite a lot smaller than her, smaller and frailer.

'I need to talk to Tom,' said Carmen, 'and Joey and Oliver. I need to sit in the garden with my family.'

They looked at each other for a moment.

Holly was about to say something, when she was brought up short by Sergeant Sarandon, calling down from where the Cherokee was parked.

It was a call on one of the RIID secure channels, and had started to come through as soon as the system was up. Carmen took it in the back of the Cherokee, through the headphones. She didn't want to have any more morale-sinking calls from Bailey being broadcast to the troops.

But it wasn't Bailey, it was George Arends. Even through his calm, steely voice, she could tell he was excited.

'It's not what we thought, Carmen. At all. I spoke to Hillier. The man mentioned on the disk, remember?'

'Sure. Arends, what time is it? At your end, I mean.'

'Wait . . . it's . . . What difference does it . . . ? It's six o'clock, almost. I wanted you to know as soon as possible. I've been thinking about this thing all night. It's so . . . I don't know. I can't make head or tail of it.'

'What did Hillier say?'

'Well at first he was pretty unhelpful. Didn't really want to admit that he was involved with Gensystems at all. Then I bluffed a little, made out I knew more than I did, and he got kind of nervous. He said first he'd been called in as a consultant just before they closed the facility at Willard. He said that two of the people working on the project were already in hospital when he went in, and that the labs were sealed. Carmen, three people *died*.'

'So how come . . .'

'Wait. Their symptoms were very similar to the ones we saw at Marshallton – inflammation of the bronchus, etc. So I asked him where he thought the virus had come from. I asked him if anyone had just come back from the tropics. He said that one of the guys had been to Mexico – no mention of Sumatra. And he was adamant they'd used no monkeys, rhesus or otherwise. No rodents either. Then he says – and this is the thing – he said he'd considered the possibility of some kind of genetic pollution.'

Carmen straightened her legs and sat back against the side of the Cherokee. She didn't know what to make of it.

'OK,' said Arends. 'Let me put you in the picture. They were working on the genes responsible for a group of inherited diseases. Irwin, the doctor leading the research, one of the men who died in fact, he thought he'd isolated a gene that had something to do with Methuselah Syndrome.

'Right.'

'Apparently Westway, the mother company, wasn't happy funding the research into something that wasn't going to pay off commercially, but they were interested in tinkering with Methuselah because they thought it might give them some insights into the ageing process generally. And Carmen, they didn't fool around. They made a deal with the government. Special guidelines were drawn up for Gensystems to be able to work on human embryos.'

'Jesus.'

'Right. Anyway, Hillier thinks it's possible that the alterations they made to chromosome twelve might have been a factor, I mean, in the course of their work.'

'Alterations? You mean gene therapy?'

'Yes. Hillier said that Irwin had two sets of cultures for the chromosome twelve work – subject and control.

In the altered sample they started to see an anomaly, a shortfall in the production of an enzyme, specifically a protein kinase. Irwin figured that he might have altered an oncogene that coded for the protein kinase. Hillier thinks that this was a distinct possibility, but he believes the alteration to the oncogene in the subject cultures did more than just affect the enzyme level. Now I don't know how much of your histology you remember, or your genetics for that matter, but the thing is that for every cellular oncogene you have a viral oncogene. In fact the first oncogene was actually discovered in a virus. Hang on to that idea: identical genes found in living cells and in viruses.'

Carmen could hear Arends's excitement. It was a line of enquiry no one at the RIID had ever considered.

'In some cases, in some cells there isn't just one viral gene, but a complete set, everything required to make a complete virus. Now, I've thought this through a little, and I think it makes sense. Imagine that somehow, perhaps during the earliest phases of evolution, some virus incorporates itself into the DNA of some ancestral species of ours. Perhaps the virus even came first, the cell developing, making use of the virus's replicating skills for its own purposes.'

'Cells exploiting viruses? It's a novel concept.'

'Not so novel as all that, given the interdependence of the two.'

'All right. Then what?'

'Well, whatever the origins of the situation, the cell has an interest in ensuring that the virus isn't expressed or replicated, unless it's in some way the cell can control. Otherwise the virus could take over. Inclusion bricks busting through the cell wall – all that. So it evolves a mechanism for suppressing the biochemical signal that would normally cause the virus DNA to be expressed. In this case, the mechanism is an enzyme. Figure it as a little neighbourly dispute between two sets of DNA strands that was settled half a billion years ago, with the cellular oncogene winning out.'

'So you're saying Irwin's work enabled the virus to come out, to be expressed.'

'Exactly. They knew the enzyme was there for something. So what they were doing was exposing the cultures to different antigens to see what would happen. At some point they must have shown the culture something the cell, in the absence of the enzyme, couldn't deal with. The wrong signal got through to the nucleus and kaboom. Suddenly they have a Petri dish full of virus, a virus that has been dormant on chromosome twelve since . . . well, like they say, the dawn of time.'

'It's . . .'

'I know. Scary as hell.'

'But I still don't see how this . . . accident at Gensystems ten years ago has any bearing on what's happened here.'

'I know. That's what has been keeping me awake all night. Whoever it was put us on to Willard must think there's a link. But there's no guarantee they're right.'

Arends was quiet for a moment. Carmen heard Leigh's voice outside. In the time she had been speaking night had fallen. She was sitting in the dark.

'All I can think of is the fact that they were working on human embryos. Carmen, imagine if they screwed around with chromosome twelve and then fertilised an egg, implanted it, made a baby.'

Carmen drew her legs up against her body. She felt the hairs stand up on the back of her neck.

'The kid wouldn't necessarily know anything was wrong. Nothing would be, really. He'd be short a few million of this protein kinase that has no particular function in the normal run of things. Maybe he'd suffer some obscure side-effect. A small deformation of the cuticles, who knows? Or nothing. Then along comes the antigen. Florists in Chicago start stocking a new South American cactus, whatever. It flowers once a year. Kid walks by the florist, catches a whiff of cactus pollen. A chemical signal on the pollen surface is recognised. Suddenly the genes coding for the virus light up, and half the population of Chicago dies of a viral haemmorrhagic fever.'

'But, at Gensystems . . .'

'No, thank God. I made a point of asking Hillier if any of the gene therapy being developed there was ever offered to the public. He said they were a long way from any human trials.'

'Thank God.'

There was a long silence. Carmen listened to McKinnon and Leigh talking. They had bagged a macaque and were deciding on whether to cut it up under the electric lights or wait until daylight.

'The whole thing is so . . . it's a mystery,' said Arends. 'And it's driving me crazy.'

That night Carmen lay awake long after everyone else had turned off their lights. She had been listening to the tape she had made of her interview with Bacelius Habibie, trying to see if there was anything that offered a clue, anything that might seem different to her now. But the whole gloomy mystery seemed just as obscure as when she had first arrived. In the dark the cell kept coming back to her, the idea of the cell trying to make its way in the world at the beginning of everything, the idea of the protein kinase blocking the signal the virus required to replicate. She imagined the seas back then, and a kind of gloomy light over everything. Thick, turgid sea and sky. Then she thought of her home, and the avocado plant growing in the kitchen window, grown from the stone Joey had taken from her as she prepared guacamole, standing at the kitchen table.

Someone went past outside with a flashlight, bringing her back to full consciousness. She heard a zipper pulled and then the sound of somebody taking a leak. She switched on her own flashlight, and picked up the tape recorder.

She listened with the earphones so as not to disturb anybody. Habibie's voice droned on, and she felt herself slipping away again, her mind coming back into focus every now and then, as she heard herself ask a question. *Those horrible yellow eyes of his and his brown teeth. He looked horrible but no worse than usual.* She wondered if Habibie's luck had still held out once Jambi started to fall apart. Knowing Habibie he would have paid the bribes necessary to get out before the rioting started – *was hoping to transact some business . . . traded in all kinds of things, you know. Not just monkeys. I believe when he came to Muaratebo this time he had something he wanted to sell me. Something special.* Carmen opened her eyes and looked at the roof of her tent. She switched off the flashlight and continued to stare at the darkness. It was oppressively hot, and the T-shirt under her head was already wet. What was so special?

Carmen wound back the tape and listened more attentively. But there was nothing new. She let it run on. *People think the Indians are noble. But it is not true. They also burn the forest to cultivate. They also pollute. They also drink. They become blind drunk. Get reckless. For the right price they will sell you anything.* Had Ahmad bought something from the Indians, something special? *Sometimes Ahmad would come down from the forest with friends.* What friends? What use would Ahmad have with friends? It was all getting jumbled up in her head. Carmen stopped the tape and wound it back to the very beginning. Then she played it right through. There was the vague shadow of something behind Habibie's words, something he had been ashamed of. *It is difficult for you to understand how things like that happen.* Ahmad had come down from the forest with something special to sell, something illegal, it sounded like, something he had bought from the Indians. *Muaratebo is a judgement. But how can that be unless I, for some reason, have been pardoned?* Wasn't that an admission of guilt?

Carmen woke up with the hiss of empty tape in her ears. She unplugged the earphones, and tried to get comfortable on her side. She listened to the jungle all around her, as old almost as the seas she had pictured before. Almost as old, growing out of the same gloomy prehistory. The forest had gone on evolving, chanting its endless mantra, interrupted for a few million years by armed and plated giants, then, after their passage, resuming its ceaseless chant as if they had never existed. She thought about the way the thick foliage let the Cherokees through, closing again behind, more like water than foliage. She thought of the little bare patch their temporary camp had made at Rafflesia, how the grasses would already be pushing out of the trampled ground, so that the mark they had made seemed in her half-sleeping mind like the mark left on glass by warm breath, receding and shrinking until it disappeared altogether.

5

Jambi. August 28th

Brigadier Sutami cursed through gritted teeth and pressed the telephone to his ear with both hands. Outside the window another Puma was taking off, its huge rotors kicking up a storm, shaking the whole flimsy edifice of the terminal building. On the other end of the line General Rana was actually screaming – not shouting, screaming – his voice rising to an alarming, strangled falsetto. It sounded like someone had their hands around his throat, which wasn't far from the truth. If things didn't improve, heads were going to roll: that was very clear.

Sutami had already heard part of the news, thanks to a satellite dish which the engineers had rigged up on the terminal roof. According to CNN, the isolation of Indonesia had intensified with the news that the plague was spreading beyond the interior of Sumatra towards the cities on the coast. Most countries in the region, including Malaysia and the Philippines, had closed their airspace to flights from any part of Indonesia, and all over the world Indonesian vessels were being turned away from port, their cargoes left to rot in international waters. The Jakarta Stock Exchange had been shut down after five hours of free-fall in which $40 billion had been knocked off the value of shares and three exchange employees shot dead by an hysterical investor. The bulletin was accompanied by an interview with a smooth-faced westerner in a hand-tailored suit who opined that Indonesia could withstand about three weeks of international isolation before the onset of complete economic collapse.

That night the President had gone on national TV to reassure the people that the Sumatran crisis was being brought under control. As an extra measure, he announced that three battalions of the Presidential Guard were being dispatched to the island immediately. This was not welcome news to Sutami. The Presidential Guard would probably bring Lieutenant-General Iskandar with them, and as the senior ranking officer he would take command. Sutami would have no opportunity to rescue the situation on Sumatra and with it his standing.

Sutami had argued. What were needed more than soldiers was protective clothing and medical supplies. More than half the men under his command had nothing to protect them from infection except surgical masks. There were not even enough rubber gloves to go round, let alone goggles and respirators. But Rana was in no mood to listen. The first elements of the Guard would be arriving in thirty-six hours. Unless they could report to Jakarta that the situation had improved, Iskandar would assume formal command. The implication was clear: Sutami's chance had all but come and gone already.

The operations room was still being set up next door in what had been the cafeteria. With the riots in Jambi they had been forced to evacuate the operational headquarters to the airport seven kilometres away. From the narrow cement control tower a plume of black smoke was still plainly visible rising from the town. The big map was laid out on tables in the middle of the room with the radio sets arranged untidily around it. The voices of the operators echoed loud in the room as they talked with one forward command position after another. Empty Coke bottles and plastic cups still lay strewn across the floor. Flies buzzed lazily from one to the other. There had been no time to clear up.

As Sutami entered the room one of the staff officers, Major Tanjung, came hurrying up to him.

'The southern perimeter of the town is secure, sir,' – more hope than certainty in his voice – 'we have tanks at the roadblocks.'

Sutami grunted and went over to the map. Two weeks earlier the black pins that marked the progress of the epidemic had been strung out in a line, shadowing a fifty-mile section of the Hari river. Now they reached out in every direction: north and south to villages on the Trans-Sumatra Highway, west towards the Minang Highlands and now east as far as Jambi. Sometimes they represented only isolated cases, sometimes a handful, sometimes cases that were probably not cases at all, only scares – but scare or not, every reported outbreak unleashed another wave of refugees. If the roads were blocked they took to the rivers, if the rivers were impassable they picked up their belongings and headed into the forest on foot. The helicopter patrols reported seeing bands of them moving through the plantations north and west of Jambi. Every time he drew up a line of defence as General Rana instructed, another rash of cases sprang up behind it. Even the sight of the cordons themselves could set off a panic as people fought to reach the other side before it was too late. And so the area that he was supposed to quarantine grew larger and larger, the perimeter more and more difficult to hold, his soldiers more scared and demoralised. From the beginning the strategy had been defensive – with foreign medical teams and scientists at work inside the cordon it had to be – but that strategy was not working. With the whole future of the country at stake it was time to change it.

One of the radio operators, a corporal, was shouting louder than the others. Sutami guessed that he was speaking with one of the outlying positions in the west where the hills obscured the signal. Then suddenly the operator yanked off his headset and stood up. He was sweating heavily, his shirt clinging to his chest. He swallowed hard.

'Padang, sir,' he shouted. 'Colonel Azwar's command reports outbreak in Padang.'

For a moment the room went quiet. One of the other officers looked at Sutami and then slowly reached out for one of the black pins, planting it deliberately on the map. It was the only one west of the Minang Highlands, the first coastal city.

Sutami felt the blood draining from his face. He had family in Padang: a sister, a brother-in-law, two nephews. He had thought about getting them out somehow, but only as a precaution, later on, if things really got out of hand. Besides, the only way he could have organised it would have been through Colonel Azwar, and that would have sent all the wrong signals at just the wrong time. He had thought the Minang Highlands would act as a barrier. You could only cross by road and the roads were all closed. He'd been wrong.

'How many cases?' he demanded. 'Confirmed cases.'

The operator looked down at his pad of paper.

'Three cases, maybe four. They said they've heard – '

'Confirmed cases, damn you! Don't give me rumours.'

'I . . . I don't know, sir. At least one death. They're pretty worried. There's been shooting. And some men have gone missing, they said.'

'Run away, you mean. Damn it! Get Colonel Azwar on the set right away.'

'Sir, Colonel Azwar is still sick, sir. With dysentery. He's – '

'I said get him on the line, Corporal.'

The operator scrambled to put on his headset.

'Yes sir!'

Sutami turned smartly to Major Tanjung.

'What combat aircraft do we have at Medan?'

'They've a squadron of Hawks, sir. And there's another at Palembang in the south. They've some F–14s, too.'

'All equipped for ground strikes?'

'I think so, sir, but – '

'Good. I want them all armed with incendiaries and ready to go at thirty minutes' notice.'

'Sir, with all due respect – '

'Order all foreign and medical personnel out of the cordon area. We've pandered to their selfish demands long enough. We shall adopt a more proactive strategy.'

'Sir?'

Sutami looked down at the map. Each black pin was a token of backwardness and failure, stains upon his country's honour and his own. He wanted to tear them out and fling them away.

'This thing isn't spreading on its own. People are spreading it. Frightened people. And is it any wonder they're frightened when their army is not permitted to do its work?'

6

Jambi Province. August 29th

The problem was knowing where to look. Ahmad could have hunted anywhere in an area covering seventy square miles on the eastern bank of the Hari where the habitat supported several species of primate including macaques and gibbons. But, according to the military maps they were carrying, an erratic springline followed the Hari river two miles to the east about thirty kilometres north of Muaratebo, with narrow, fast-moving streams breaking up the jungle every couple of miles. In one place a larger tributary stream emerged from a system of caves.

'Shelter and fresh water,' said Major Leigh tapping the map with a grimy forefinger as they stood around the back of the Cherokees in the dawn light.

'He was up here for weeks at a time, so he must have had some kind of camp,' said Carmen.

So the caves and the tributary stream became the focus of the second phase of their search for the virus. If Ahmad had used the caves for shelter, there was a chance that was where he'd picked up the disease; caves, with their blood-heat symbiotic fauna, were prime sites for both infestation and the transfer of pathogens.

The approach to the caves was going to be made difficult by the broken, variable terrain which was covered in a dense mantle of vegetation. Moving on from what had become their base camp, they would be able to drive to within three miles of the caves, but no further. Their idea was to establish another camp at the caves with two men to monitor the site. It wasn't the best use of manpower, but logistically it was the only workable option. A group of five people would be able to carry enough supplies for a two-man camp to be able to run for seven days without resupply. The plan would mean carrying the rifles, traps, sampling equipment and supplies on foot in the intense heat and humidity, a task none of them relished. The two-man team – Leigh and Daintith were again designated – would stay in contact with the base camp by radio. They would take two of the better Racal suits – filter replacement on an ongoing basis over seven days was only feasible for two because of the unforeseen fungus problem they were getting – and would only use them in extreme circumstances.

Carmen, Leigh, Daintith, McKinnon, Lennox and Baker were to set out just after 0800 hours taking a mud track due west. Kaoy and Sarandon would remain at the base camp to look after the X-band and radio telecom links. Very much against her will, Holly Becker would stay with Sarandon.

Holly was bored with sitting around doing nothing, and felt she could be helpful in some of the more straightforward sampling and collection. Although Carmen was sympathetic, realising that what Holly needed above all was something to take her mind off the children, she nevertheless insisted that she stay, reminding her of the dangers involved in hunting BL–4 pathogens in open country.

'This thing won't be in a test tube,' she said as they prepared the second Cherokee for departure. 'It'll be in a bug or an animal that may not like being disturbed. And if it tags you, Holly, you're it.'

The mud track very quickly petered out into a trail choked

391

with vegetation. If anything the atmosphere had become even more oppressive, and it was uncomfortably hot and sticky. Through breaks in the canopy they could see dark clouds rolling in from the eastern plain. After two hours of fitful progress with constant interruptions to clear the path of fallen branches, they came up against a tumbled ketapang tree, the roots growing out of the trunk like the tailfins of a rocket. Everyone got out.

'The Europeans used to use them to make the rudders for their big boats,' said Leigh contemplating the fallen tree, his hands on his hips.

They were all drenched with sweat despite the Cherokee's air conditioning.

'We'll have to go on on foot,' said Baker, coming round from the other side of the massive trunk. 'There's no way we're going to move this.'

'How far are we from the caves?' asked Lennox.

'The odometer makes it twelve miles from our starting position so I figure we have another four to go,' said Baker.

They sprayed their boots with insecticide to discourage leeches and then shouldered their packs – Leigh carrying a full pack plus the two rifles, and Baker the field radio. They moved on in Indian file, Leigh taking the lead.

Old watercourses cut across the track and soon there was no track at all, just a suggestion of an opening in the vegetation. From time to time there was a rumble of thunder from the east, but around them the air was still and warm as if they were in fact in an enclosed space. Following the compass, they continued to move north-west climbing the tight-woven mesh of roots and vines to the top of small inclines and then slipping into the next declivity, struggling for purchase in the heavy red earth that seemed too poor to support such abundant growth. McKinnon cut notches in the trunks and branches of trees as they went, marking a trail. It was hard going, and twice

Daintith fell, his big boots getting caught in the tangle of roots. The second time Daintith slipped Carmen called a halt.

'Let's take a breather,' she said. 'We're not trying to set any records.'

She could see that Baker was forcing the pace in his soldierly way. Leigh's ankle was bothering him after his fall in the cave a few days earlier and he was getting left behind. Daintith flopped back against a bank of earth and shrugged off his pack. His face looked pouchy from the heat and he was streaming with sweat.

'We need to be there by midday,' said McKinnon.

'We get tired, and someone sprains an ankle,' said Carmen. There was a moment of silence as she took a drink from her canteen and offered it to Daintith. 'Then we'll be carrying them back, and that *will* be hard, apart from being a waste of time.'

Leigh wiped his mouth on a hairy forearm.

'I'm sorry to hold you guys up,' he said, glancing irritably at Daintith. 'Only this damned ankle's killing me. I thought it was OK, but . . .'

'We can't be more than a mile away now,' said McKinnon.

Baker took out the map again, spreading it out against a tree, and following the line of a contour with his fingers. Lightning flickered away to the east and there was another shuddering roll of thunder.

'The next chance we get to move down I think we should take,' said Baker. McKinnon went over and stood next to him. Baker showed him where he thought they had got to and the two men talked for a moment, considering their options. Then McKinnon looked over his shoulder at Carmen, who was drinking again, sitting next to Leigh.

'What do you think, Colonel?'

'I trust you guys to get it right. Next gully we fall over

in, we'll go down like Baker says. At least it'll be easier sledding.'

Suddenly Daintith snapped out an arm, pointing sky-wards.

'What's that?'

They all looked up. Carmen felt her scalp tingle as she tried to follow Daintith's trembling finger.

'I see it,' said Baker.

They were all looking up at the canopy, which was about forty feet above them. To Carmen it was just a mass of green; then a slight movement caught her eye and she was looking at the pale face of a macaque. The animal watched them for a moment and then was gone, leaving behind a swaying branch.

'One of Ahmad's friends,' said Daintith.

They moved on for about twenty minutes, making their way up an incline which was completely covered in tree roots and ferns. Water was coming down from their right, spilling across the slope in a shallow wash making the red earth between the roots slick and slippery. They had to watch where they were putting their feet the whole time even though the temptation was to look up to see if there were any more watching faces. Carmen had taken the lead in the hope of slowing things down a little, but despite her efforts, Leigh kept being left behind, and every few minutes they had to turn to watch him pick his way up the slope.

Then they were at the top of the incline in a cloud of flies. Ahead of them the ground fell away and between the dense foliage Carmen could see the silver ribbon of a stream moving from right to left down towards the Hari. The flies buzzed in the air, spinning in pairs and swooping back and forth. Harmless, by the look of them. They seemed delighted to have found some big hairless primates to work on. As they stood there more and more of the flies gathered in the air, seeming to condense until there was quite a swarm. Carmen brushed them away from her face.

'We'll make our way down here,' said McKinnon going past her. 'It should bring us out above the caves.' He was gone, moving swiftly down through the thickly growing plants, a few flies in pursuit. Baker followed him, swatting his hand back and forth. Carmen wiped her face with a drenched bandanna, her right hand keeping the flies from her face. Then Daintith was at her back, breathing heavily.

'I wonder what the flies are feeding on?' he managed to say. It was even hotter standing still. A fly settled on Carmen's mouth and she brushed it away.

'At least it's all downhill now,' she said and she moved on.

From where he stood, Major Leigh could no longer see the others. He steadied himself against a tree trunk and looked up towards the top of the incline. The pain in his ankle was getting worse and he could feel it swelling up inside his boot. He unlooped his pack from one shoulder and took his water bottle out of a pocket. Without the sounds of the others, the jungle noise was more noticeable, an incessant sawing and calling. Again he looked up the slope, struggling to get his breath back, blinking the sweat out of his eyes. He decided that they were probably waiting for him on the other side of the slope. He took a long drink, then replaced the bottle and started to move on.

He had gone three paces when he heard the sound. It was a faint buzzing, so faint at first that he thought it might be inside his own head – his biosystems telling him to slow down. But then, as he stood there, the buzzing seemed to increase.

'Flies,' he said to the trees all around him.

The sound was coming from his right. And there was

something else: a smell. A smell of decay faintly tainting the humid air. It was impossible to see anything because of the dense foliage. Careful where he put his feet in the tangle of slippery roots, he made his way across the slope. It occurred to him that he might be near a nest of some kind, and so he moved forward cautiously. He pushed aside a large fern and reached to get a foothold on a thick, glistening root.

'Where's Major Leigh?' said McKinnon as Carmen and Daintith came to the bottom of what was in fact a little gully cut by a muddy stream. They all looked back up the slope and waited. They waited for about a minute and then McKinnon shrugged off his pack.

'I'll go back up. Probably having trouble with his ankle.'

There had been a moment of flailing panic and then he had found himself looking up at ragged tree roots, his head full of the heavy buzzing sound. Leigh tried to move his arms, but his shoulders seemed to be wedged between the earth and something harder, a stone or a tree root perhaps. The hole was no more than a couple of metres deep, ripped out of the earth by a fallen tree, and he had plunged into it head first. He tried to move his right arm; he wanted to get a grip on something to lever himself out. But his hand was trapped underneath him. He made a fist and felt it somewhere in the small of his back. There was no pain, no apparent injury, but he was stuck. The buzzing increased. It was distinctive now. He must be very close. Then the first fly settled on his face. At first there were only two or three flies. They bumped against his eyes and nose. Then they started to settle. Leigh pressed his lips together and tried to shake them off but he couldn't move his head. They were all over his face now, avidly sucking at the perspiration and grease, working at the trembling seams of his closed eyes. With his mouth clamped shut Leigh tried to breathe through his nose. But they were crawling into his nostrils, into his ears. He began to suffocate. The panic welled up in him, his inverted torso jarred by his pounding heart.

He was screaming when McKinnon pulled him out of the hole and continued to scream, eyes staring, gasping for breath until McKinnon had him on his back in the mud, and was sitting astride him telling him it was all right. Breathing hard, Leigh looked up at McKinnon's sunburnt face.

'My God I was – '

'It's OK. You're . . .'

McKinnon was looking away, looking at something beyond Leigh's field of vision. Slowly he stood up, his muddy boots either side of Leigh's supine body.

'What is it?' said Leigh. But McKinnon wasn't listening.

'Jesus Christ,' he said.

He stepped away from Leigh, abstractedly reaching out a hand to pull him up. Leigh struggled to his feet and turned to see what it was that held McKinnon's attention.

They were in a hollow, a bank of twisted roots and vegetation to their left and the fallen tree to their right. It was airless and hot and the dead air was full of the flies. Over their heads another huge tree was tilted at a dangerous angle and a strangling fig had twined itself around the trunk, sending down roots which hung in a curtain of feathery ropes. Neither of them spoke for a moment. Then Leigh took a step forward to get a closer look at what at first sight appeared to be a nest on the other side of the fallen tree.

It wasn't a nest. Smothered by the seething mass of flies, five dead macaques were twisted together on the ground. They looked as if they had been there for no more than a day or two. The heads of two of the macaques were twisted skywards, the exposed eyeballs as yet uneaten. The distinctive light brown pupils were barely visible in the film of burst blood vessels. There was dried blood on the snouts and around the open mouths.

It rained briefly after their midday meal. They had pitched camp at a sheltered site about a hundred yards from the caves. After Leigh's inadvertent discovery, they had found a number of sick animals in the forest, and two more cadavers. There was no way of telling if they were infected with Muaratebo or not, but to Carmen and Leigh, the symptoms they showed correlated strongly with those observed at the Marshallton primate centre. The mission was back on track, but nobody was cheering.

They came back along the trail at four in the afternoon, Baker in front followed by Carmen and Lennox, and a few yards behind them Daintith. Carmen had taken the decision to leave McKinnon with Leigh at the camp. Leigh's ankle needed resting, and there was the possibility that he had picked something up by ingesting flies. After his fall Leigh had put his fingers down his throat and forced himself to vomit, in the hope of getting any insects out of him before they started to break down in his gut. Carmen and McKinnon had emphasised how unlikely it was that the virus was still active in the cadavers, if indeed it had ever been present. And he had not been bitten.

They had removed material from all of the dead macaques, and were able to get good samples from the spleen and liver of two of the better-preserved cadavers. Baker shot another animal which they had discovered sitting on the ground, swaying back and forth, blind, spots of blood on its trembling forelimbs, and this too had provided them with samples of damaged tissue. They had also trapped a number of flies live. All the material

398

was to be tested at the base camp for the presence of Muaratebo.

It was easier going without the supplies and equipment, and they were making good time, following the trail marked by McKinnon in the morning. They reached the Cherokee just before six with the light starting to fade fast. Apart from the brief shower the storm had held off all day, although thunder continued to rumble along the eastern plain. Baker cursed, sweeping animal droppings from the roof and hood. Carmen could see that the jungle had pushed him to his limit. They threw the packs into the back and then climbed into the cab.

'We'll have to turn the thing round,' said Carmen looking out of her window.

Baker sat back against his seat.

'What's the problem?' said Carmen.

He turned and looked at her for a moment.

'We're crazy,' he said. He looked back at Daintith who was slouched against one of the back seats. 'We're completely crazy. We're out here . . .' He slapped his hands against the wheel and stared out at the fallen tree which had blocked their path in the morning. 'We're out here with no proper protection. The suits don't work. And now . . . things are starting to go wrong. We're – I mean, what are we supposed to do if one of us starts to . . .'

He stopped talking and looked in the rearview mirror at Daintith.

'Major Leigh's going to be fine,' said Carmen. Then, looking back at Baker, her expression hardening, she added: 'Now are you going to start this bus or do I have to put you on a charge?'

For a second Baker returned Carmen's stare, and she feared he was going to say something he might regret. A breakdown in discipline was all they needed – would in fact be disastrous. Time seemed to slow, the endless zip and rush of insect noise intensifying. Then Baker faced forward and turned the key in the ignition.

7

Jambi Province. August 30th

There were three candles high up on the whitewashed wall, fluttering in the draught. It was night-time in the convent, and as she crossed the room Carmen remembered that she had forgotten to close the shutters. She could hear them rattling and banging as the storm drew nearer. Soon the candles would all blow out and she would be in darkness. She went back towards the door and it was then that she saw him, huddled in the corner: it was Habibie, the trader from Muaratebo. On the wall above him hung a crude iron crucifix. She walked towards him. He was busy at something, humming to himself. Carmen thought he might be praying. *Muaratebo is a judgement. But how can that be unless I, for some reason, have been pardoned?* Then she saw that he was not praying, but writing – writing in one of the log books they used to record the results of their fieldwork. He looked over his shoulder at her and grinned. *How can that be?*

He had no business writing in the log. It was a classified document. She wanted to take it away from him but something held her back. He might be infected. The epidemic had reached Jambi. Perhaps it had reached him. Habibie held up the book for her to see. She could not read the writing but she knew they were names, names and dates. The wind blew the pages over one by one. There were hundreds of them, thousands. The dead. Outside she could hear the wind in the trees. She had to close the shutters. She had promised Tom that she would do it. The storm would wake Oliver and Joey and then they would never get back to sleep. As she hurried from the room she saw Joey at the far end of the passage, walking sleepily towards the kitchen in his oversized pyjamas. She called to him but he just kept on walking – unsteadily, his feet slapping against the stone floor. She reached out and put her hand on his shoulder, but as she did so she noticed a dark stain spreading out beneath the cotton, from his arm to his neck and down the length of his back. Blood. *Muaratebo is a judgement.* She turned him around, calling to Tom for help. Joey's face was deathly pale and shiny like a china doll's. *Joey!* She called his name once, twice, three times.

And then he opened his eyes.

Carmen lurched into consciousness. She was sitting upright, her body bathed in sweat. Distant thunder rolled, echoing in the far-off uplands. She took a couple of deep breaths, trying to calm her heart, then opened the flap of her tent and went outside.

'Can you hear them?'

Carmen gave a start. It was Holly. She was sitting on one of the boxes a few feet away, the outline of her head just visible against the faint light of the sky.

'Jesus, Holly. You scared the hell out of me.'

'There. You hear them?'

Carmen listened. There came another roll of thunder followed by a long whooping call from somewhere up in the canopy.

'It's just a monkey,' she said. 'Maybe a gibbon. They're supposed to be around here. It's nothing to worry about.'

The call came again, this time from further off. It was a lonely, mournful sound. Carmen took another deep breath. The nightmare had shaken her badly.

'I've been listening to them all night,' said Holly.

'Listening to that sound . . . I think they're searching.'

Carmen looked out across the tiny clearing around which the Cherokees and tents were huddled. Everything was dark and still. Her heart would not slow. Maybe it was just the nightmare or the thunder, but she had a bad feeling inside. She reached down for her flashlight and switched it on.

'Searching for what?' she said.

'For their dead,' Holly said, her voice oddly flat, emotionless. 'The ones we killed today.'

Carmen let the beam of the flashlight come to rest on the jumble of cases and bags stacked up along one side of her tent. By the reflected light she could see Holly's eyes watching her.

'It's probably just food they want,' she said gently. 'They can smell it. Either that or the thunder's upset them.'

'The Kubu say if a *bilou* is slain then a man must die. Otherwise evil befalls the tribe. Willis told me that.'

'A *bilou*?'

'A gibbon.'

'Well the Kubu are entitled to their opinion, of course. Anyway, we haven't killed any *bilou*. This is the first time we've come across them.'

'So you'll kill them tomorrow. If you find them.'

Carmen sighed and pushed her hair away from her forehead.

'Maybe. We have to take specimens. That's the only way we can track this thing down. I'm sorry if it upsets you.'

She saw for the first time that Holly had been crying. For an instant it occurred to her that she was maybe beginning to crack. God knew, she was close enough to it herself.

'We don't belong here,' Holly said, and when she said it it felt as if something that had been tight inside her, something that had been drawing tighter and tighter for weeks, had suddenly come loose. 'We should never have come,' she said, softer now, as if reading from a book. 'We're the disease here. We're the virus. The forest knows that. And it wants to destroy us. If we hadn't come, if we hadn't . . .' – she closed her eyes – 'my children would still be alive.' Carmen watched Holly's head fall forward. Her shoulders shook as she wept. 'If we hadn't . . .'

Carmen put her hand on her shoulder. So she saw it now. The belief that had kept her going these last ten days was finally gone, overwhelmed by the evidence of her own eyes and ears. There was no word from the Indonesians that any children had been picked up from Rafflesia Camp, and the pretence that somehow they might have survived unaided in the forest was increasingly untenable. They were dead. Faced with Holly Becker's despair, Carmen felt helpless.

She squatted down and took Holly's hands, fighting back her own tears. She looked into Holly's beautiful face and tried to think of something she could say to give her a little more hope, a reason to go on, to get out of the forest; a reason to go back. She pushed the tears out of her eyes with the heel of her palm.

'Holly I . . . I know how . . . I know what you are going through.'

Holly pulled herself free and dragged her hands across her face, trying to clean it, trying to stop the tears. But the grief was too much for her. She was shaken by another sob, but despite her anguish her eyes remained fixed on Carmen's.

'Do you?' she said then, struggling to control her voice. 'How can you?'

Carmen closed her eyes, forcing herself to recall. In the first years it had come to her often, memory just pulling apart like a wound that could never close. Only with resolution and devotion to all the other things in her life had she managed at last to mask the pain. She never talked about it any more, not even with Tom, although once she had found him sitting huddled beneath the shower jet, sobbing. It had come as a revelation to her more than two years after the event that he could feel the pain as intensely as she did.

'A long time ago, I lost . . . my . . .' It felt like she was drawing something out from inside, something physically attached. 'My daughter. Our . . . my first child. Only eighteen months old.'

Holly brought a hand to her face.

'It was just one of those things,' Carmen went on. 'An embolism, a blood clot in the brain. She went to sleep one night just like normal and the next morning . . . Tom found her. That was the thing I was spared. But when I held her body in my arms, when I knew she was dead, I thought my life was over. I couldn't see any way out of the . . . well I guess it was despair. I despaired.'

Holly was shaking her head, staring.

'Carmen,' she said. 'I'm so sorry. I had no – '

'Five weeks after she died, I found that I was pregnant again.' Carmen thought back for a moment, remembered being alone in the bathroom looking at the spatula from the pregnancy test on which a blue line had magically appeared, remembered her utter confusion. She looked at Holly. 'I still worry that for the first two years of his life I was only half a mother to Oliver – my eldest boy. I mean it took that long.'

Holly looked at the ground.

'My God.'

Carmen brushed the tears from her cheeks. She took in a deep breath and slowly let it out.

'The thing is – ' she had to breathe again for a moment, trying to say it straight, wanting to be clear, 'the thing is you don't know that your girls are . . . dead. I know it looks bad, but until you see . . . until you see with your own eyes, you can't know. And until you know, you can't let go.'

Holly looked up at her. She was silent for a long time, taking in Carmen's round face, the big eyes, reddened with crying.

'But you think they're dead,' she said. 'So do all your men. I can see it in the way they look at me. Why do you pretend?'

'I'm not pretending, I'm just . . .'

Carmen struggled for the right words. Was it kinder to let Holly despair and mourn? Her children were dead. Surely. How else could you explain the remains at Rafflesia Camp? Even if it turned out that what they had found was someone else's child the odds that they had somehow escaped the virus before the outbreak were so small, they bordered on the infinitesimal. And yet a mother's love, a mother's hope, what had that got to do with the odds, with logic?

'Holly, all I'm saying is . . . your suffering, it . . . You are suffering because you're caught between hope and grief. Grief, letting go, finally, is easier, believe me, than the uncertainty. But you can't let go, can't really grieve yet. Just because we haven't heard from the Indonesians doesn't mean a thing. We don't know what went on at that camp, not even after the soldiers turned up there. The military, they've bungled this thing from the very beginning. And now there are refugees all over the place, complete anarchy probably. Sutami's not going to make locating your kids a priority, not now. They could have been taken anywhere: Medan, Padang, even Jakarta. It could be weeks before someone actually works out who they are.'

Holly closed her eyes. The hope was almost as painful as the despair.

'As soon as we're out of here,' Carmen said, leaning forward slightly, 'I'll organise a search at every hospital and refugee camp and orphanage from one end of the country to the other. And we'll get a proper search done around Rafflesia Camp too. I promise you that. One way or another we'll find out what happened.'

Holly nodded agreement, but it was her inner voice that she was hearing.

'If I lose them I won't be able to go on living,' she said quietly.

'You say that now. I felt the same. But you're young. I know it seems unthinkable now but you could . . . there will be other children.'

Holly shook her head firmly, compressing her lips.

'No,' she said. 'You don't understand. You're forgetting what I told you. I *can't*. There's the . . . there's the thing in my family. I had to go through all that treatment the last time to be sure I didn't pass it on. I couldn't go through all that again and anyway I don't think the treatment is even available.'

Carmen frowned. The air was still and heavy. It felt as if the pressure were dropping.

'What was it you had exactly?'

'Gene therapy. A kind of gene therapy.'

'But surely if it was available all those years ago it must be available now. Research has come a long way since then. It's probably even better now.'

Holly pushed her hands down between her knees. She stared down at the trampled earth.

'No,' she said. She sat like that for a long time, slowly shaking her head. 'It was a special . . . case. It was exceptional. If it hadn't been for Jonathan I wouldn't even have had the chance. It wasn't available generally, to the general public I mean. Jonathan set it all up.'

'Jonathan? How? Wasn't he, I mean isn't he a botanist, a pharmacologist?'

'He is, but the company, his company, they didn't

just do pharmaceuticals. They were big on all sorts of healthcare. Huge. Still are. To tell you the truth . . .' She shook her head again. 'To tell the truth I wasn't keen, really. On the idea. It all seemed too – ' She looked up at Carmen for a moment. 'I was really scared, Carmen. Unless Jonathan had been there, pushing me, I don't think . . . It was too, I don't know, *experimental*. But Jonathan was convinced it was the right thing to do. He was really . . . convinced. Enthusiastic. He said it was up to me, of course, and that he would go along with whatever I decided, but I could see he was terrified of the idea of bringing up a handicapped child, really terrified. And when I hesitated, because I just didn't know very much about it, about the risks, he started talking about our *responsibility* to the child, to give it the best possible chance. And I knew that if I refused the treatment and the child was born with the syndrome that it would be the end for us. He would have always blamed me.'

'So you went along with it.'

'Yes, and it turned out fine. I have my . . . I have my beautiful girls, but I was right too, about the work they were doing, about the techniques they had developed.'

'How do you mean?'

'Well they never took it any further.'

'How do you know?'

'I know, because I asked a couple years ago, this was after I met Richard. They said, the people I spoke to, people I knew through Jonathan, they said it was impossible.'

A dull flicker of lightning lit up the clearing. The storm was getting closer. Carmen felt movement in the heavy air.

'Who did? Who said it was impossible?'

There was the sound of a tent opening. Daintith and Baker were out, stumbling around. Sarandon was shouting something about covering up equipment.

'Holly, who? Who said they couldn't treat you?'

'Like I said, people Jonathan knew. I should have asked Jonathan to arrange it, I suppose, like before. But I didn't want to. I didn't want him to know I was thinking of having more children. I didn't know what he'd think, and I hadn't known Richard very long then anyway. So I approached them myself, or I tried to. Hardly any of the people I remembered were still there. In the end only one, in fact.'

There were torch beams moving around outside. Lennox was shouting something about the traps. Carmen watched Baker hurry past, swearing as he stumbled on the uneven ground. Suddenly the headlamps on one of the Cherokees were switched on.

'Colonel?'

It was Sarandon. Carmen squinted into the headlights.

'Colonel, we better get everything we can back in the vehicles. We got weather comin' in.'

'Be right there,' she called back. A thought was looming, a possibility, half-formed. She kept her eyes on Holly's face.

'Holly, who did you speak to? Who are you talking about?'

Holly stared back at her, trying to understand what it was that was so important.

'His name was Hillier, Dr Alfred Hillier. He was the only one who was still at the company. All the others were gone.'

Sarandon went by again, carrying one of the big X-SAT cases. He stopped and shouted something, but Carmen was not listening. Her skin pricked into bumps as a terrible, horrible idea came to her. As Harold Daintith had pointed out, it was just as easy for macaques to be infected with the virus by humans as it was for humans to be infected by macaques. But what if the reservoir itself, the source of the virus, were a human being? Or two human beings, RB1 and RB2. And then she understood: *Rhodes/Becker 1 and Rhodes/Becker 2.*

Somehow she got to her feet. First the camp, then Ahmad's hunting grounds, then Muaratebo. *They were a long way from any human trials.* That was what Hillier had said. But Hillier could have lied.

'What is it?' asked Holly.

Carmen looked down at her.

'Your husband's old company, the one that helped you, what was it called?'

Holly hugged herself against the rising wind.

'Westway,' she said. 'Westway Pharmaceuticals.'

8

What other explanation was there? Again and again Carmen asked herself the question, staring into the pre-dawn darkness, listening to the last of the rain which had fallen steadily through the night. Her body ached from lack of rest. After Holly had told her about Westway and Dr Hillier, she had returned to her tent with its damp bedding and scattered notebooks, but there was no question of sleep. Again and again she went through the sequence of events, starting with the elements she was sure of: the symptoms and the timing, the unexplained package containing classified documents; picking her way through the past six weeks, trying to come up with a scenario which did not have Holly Becker's dead children at its dark heart.

But it was impossible. It was the only explanation that tied all the elements together. The documents were the key. Unless she discounted their appearance as purely fortuitous she had to assume that someone had seen what had happened, had been privy to the Marshallton outbreak and had felt compelled to act; someone who knew the disease well enough to see the parallels with what had happened at Willard; maybe – and this had made Carmen's scalp tingle – someone who knew that the children were visiting Jonathan Rhodes at the time of the Muaratebo outbreak, someone who had remained

411

in touch with Rhodes after he had left Westway, someone who, perhaps, had feared such an outcome. It had to be someone who had access to classified military documents related to the Willard incident, someone who did not themselves want to come forward – maybe because of their involvement in the Gensystems project – someone close enough to the RIID to know she was looking at the Marshallton case and might be expected to run with the ball. General Bailey? Carmen hadn't known him long enough to be able to rule him out. His unnamed contact at the Pentagon? – the man who had wanted the Marshallton facility nuked, no questions asked.

The last of the rain eased to fitful spatterings and then nothing at all. Carmen threw an arm across her face and the darkness was immediately replaced by an image of Holly Becker's brimming eyes as she talked about her inability to have any more children.

'Sweet Jesus,' said Carmen under her breath. How was Holly going to take it? It was almost too much suffering to contemplate. Then it came to Carmen that it wasn't something she could delay. She sat up, her head brushing against the side of the tent. In a couple of hours they would be starting the day, and it was her duty to the rest of the team to share what she knew. Was there some way it could be kept from Holly? Carmen lowered herself back to the ground and closed her eyes. The sound of the rain had been replaced by the steady dripping of the forest all around them. *Holly, your children are the source of all this. Holly, they weren't the victims, they were the cause.*

If true, it would explain why the outbreak at Rafflesia Camp came first. Just as Arends had figured, the carriers of the altered genes must have come into contact with an antigen that triggered the production of a virus, until that moment dormant in their DNA. Even now, now that she had all the pieces, Carmen could still hardly believe it. It was too terrible, too cruel. It made no difference to the children's suffering – they would have succumbed immediately, passing the virus onto the others before they died. Holly was the one who was going to suffer. She would see it as her fault: the direct consequence of her desire for healthy offspring. All that terrible suffering, all that black putrefaction and agony flowing from her loins.

Suddenly the tent was intolerable. Carmen unzipped the flap and clambered out into the darkness. The warmth surprised her. It was as if the storm had never happened. She walked away from the tents towards the hole the Cherokees had made in the vegetation, deep in thought.

Now that she understood Rafflesia Camp's place at the beginning of the epidemic, placing Ahmad in the chain of events had become problematic. How had Ahmad picked it up? Perhaps, as Daintith had suggested, macaques had been near Rafflesia Camp at the time the virus became active. If that were the case, all that was required was for the infected macaques to be then taken by Ahmad. It was a tenuous link, but perfectly credible. Rafflesia Camp was only thirty miles from the edge of Ahmad's hunting grounds. Once Ahmad had the infected primates or had caught the disease himself, the spread to Muaratebo was as inevitable as his routine trips downriver to Habibie.

Carmen stopped at the edge of the camp and checked her watch. It was just after five in the morning, only an hour before dawn. And then Carmen was remembering Habibie, remembering what he had told her at the convent and it was as if the darkness was pressing in on her from all sides.

The tape recorder was by her canteen. She grabbed it, and, stuffing in the earphones, stabbed at fast-forward and then rewind, trying to find the words she wanted to hear. Then she stood up, letting it run, hardly aware of the first glimmering of dawn above the surrounding trees. . . .

traded in all kinds of things, you know. Not just monkeys. I

believe when he came to Muaratebo this time he had some-
thing he wanted to sell me. Something special. She played it
once, twice, three times as if something new would come
out of Habibie's words, something that would mean she
was mistaken. Then she took out the phones, and shut
off the machine.

A figure loomed up at her out of the dark, making
her start. It was Daintith in a T-shirt and shorts holding
a pencil flashlight. He put his finger to his lips, and
whispered an apology.

'I heard you moving around,' he said, his voice a
low growl. 'I wasn't able to sleep myself.'

They walked away from the tents, following Daintith's
faint beam of light.

'How are you feeling, Harold?'

'OK. What were you sneaking around for?'

Carmen looked at Daintith's pale face in the first
glimmerings of light. There was no time to think, to
consider her next step. The stakes were too high for
her to be withholding what might be essential information. She had to tell him her deepest fears about what
had happened. How Holly took it was something else,
something that would have to be dealt with later.

'Harold.'

Carmen stared for a moment, hardly knowing where
to begin. Then she told him the whole story, standing
in the dawn light, starting with the arrival of the classified documents, and Arends's research, and finishing
with Holly's story about receiving a genetically altered
ovum at Willard as part of the Gensystems programme.

Daintith just stared. From time to time he shook his
head. When Carmen had finished, he looked down and
saw that his flashlight was still lit. He switched it off.

'How long have you known?' he said eventually.

'Arends told me about Gensystems' work a couple of
days ago.' Carmen looked across to Holly's tent. 'Holly

414

told me about her link with Gensystems last night.'

Daintith put his lips together and blew a low whistle. Then he was frowning at Carmen's exhausted face. The sky above them was tinged with green. All around them insects began to whir and zip as circadian timers clicked into the new cycle.

'Which would explain Rafflesia Camp,' said Daintith. 'Its precedence.'

Carmen blinked, realising that for Daintith the problem remained a scientific rather than a human one. Holly Becker's tragedy did not figure in his thinking. She looked away from Daintith at Holly's tent again, expecting to see her emerge at any moment.

'But there is still the problem of how the virus leaped from Rafflesia Camp to – ' Daintith looked around at the forest – 'to here, and into Ahmad.'

'One of Holly's children brought it,' said Carmen flatly.

For a moment neither of them spoke, as though trapped in the thick gauze of jungle sound.

Then Carmen went on, speaking in a low, urgent monotone: 'When I interviewed Habibie in Jambi he as good as admitted that Ahmad brought children down from the jungle from time to time to sell at Madam Kim's. He told me that the last time Ahmad came down the river he had something special he wanted to sell. Harold, I think he wanted to sell Habibie one of Holly Becker's children. Why else did Habibie say it was so special? If it had been one of the Indian children what would have been so special about that? Habibie said that Ahmad brought them down the river only occasionally. An Indian child would have been unusual, yes, but special? A twelve-year-old white girl. That was special. That was merchandise Habibie or Madam Kim, the owner of the brothel, might have paid a lot of money for.'

'Twins,' said Daintith. 'That would have been even more special.'

'I thought about that,' said Carmen. 'But if the children were the source of the disease it would have been impossible for them to become infectious in Rafflesia Camp and then come into contact with Ahmad, then make the journey down to Muaratebo.'

'So you're saying only one of them met Ahmad?'

'I'm saying that it's possible only one of them came into contact with the antigen, developed the symptoms, and then passed the disease to the rest of the camp. The sister could have fled the camp or been driven forcibly from the camp by someone trying to save her. She was then taken by Ahmad: maybe he found her on the Hari, the two sites are linked by the river and the child could have used a boat.'

'Of course all that's required is for the child to infect Ahmad. There's no reason for the child herself to enter Muaratebo.'

'You're right,' said Carmen. 'I just get the feeling that Habibie . . .'

She left the sentence unfinished. In a way it was easier, less onerous, to believe that the child reached Ahmad in the agonal stages of the illness. The trauma of seeing everyone around her at the camp dying in such horrible circumstances, and then succumbing herself, was nightmare enough, without adding the journey downriver with the monkey hunter, trader in prepubescent girls, and then the arrival at the brothel itself – the pawing hands, the lecherous smiles.

Carmen shuddered at the thought that maybe Habibie himself had . . . But then she realised that Habibie could not have come into close contact, certainly not of an intimate sexual kind. If he had, he would certainly have contracted the illness. Perhaps the girls had died in the jungle after all.

'I still can't take it all in,' said Carmen. Then, paying no attention to Daintith any more, who was himself lost in thought, she went back to the beginning, going over the different elements as if they were the beads of a rosary, and as if by counting them often enough some good, some Grace, would intervene and make everything less horrible. Maybe she had it all wrong. After all, the idea that the children were the source was too far-fetched, too . . . it was almost unthinkable. She brought her hands together and actually wrung them, half praying that everything she thought might be mistaken.

Then Holly was there. Standing in the dawn light, her back to them momentarily, stretching, brushing the hair from her face. She turned. She saw them standing together and was obviously a little taken aback.

'Hi.'

She came towards them and then stopped. It was Carmen who found something to say: 'Did you manage to sleep?'

'Sure. I don't think the storm's made much difference, though – to the air, I mean. I sure could do with some Manhattan smog.'

'At least there you can see what you're breathing,' said Daintith, and the moment, the moment in which Carmen felt she might have to tell Holly everything, passed.

Baker hardly said a word at breakfast. Carmen tried to talk about the day's work, and the chances of finding a reservoir of some kind at the new site. She avoided Daintith's eyes.

'We can probably complete the setting up of the traps today. Maybe investigate some of the less accessible areas.'

'Am I going to have to sit around here again?' asked Holly. Carmen could not bring herself to look at Holly's face.

'What's the matter?' said Sarandon: 'Don't you enjoy my company?'

'I just want to do something useful. Help bag a few specimens, maybe.'

Carmen turned to Daintith now, who was pouring himself the last of the coffee.

'Harold, would it be OK by you if Holly came up to the site in your place? I'd sure appreciate it if you could work on the samples here with Dr Lennox; prepare some stuff for moving out.'

There was an uncomfortable silence. Everybody knew Carmen wanted to minimise the group's contact with Daintith after his bite, even though he had shown no signs of developing the disease. Having him stay at the field laboratory was the best way to achieve that.

'We moving out?' asked Baker sullenly.

'We're not going to be here for ever,' said Carmen, trying to sound cheerful. 'There are samples to fix and stain. Material to freeze.'

'Sure,' said Daintith with a shrug. 'There are a few things we can be getting on with.'

'Great,' said Carmen. 'Sergeant Kaoy can lend you a hand.'

Holly got to her feet. Carmen watched her go across to her tent. She looked more in control now; still grieving, but trying to be positive. It occurred to Carmen that it might not be necessary for her to know about the children's role. At least for the time being. Once back in the US, things would be different. There was no way she could imagine Daintith publishing research that omitted key facts. But it was going to be difficult to let the others know without Holly getting wind of it.

They followed the same track west. Leafy branches thwacked against the mud-spattered windshield but Carmen hardly noticed, her mind still churning with epidemiological permutations. She was trying to decide what difference it made to the mission if she was right about the children. In the first place it was clear that, while they might be finding infected animals in Ahmad's old territory, there was no question of them locating a reservoir, a population of animals or insects that could sustain the virus without succumbing to it. If Muaratebo had originated through a chance coming together of an antigen and an altered gene, it would hopefully burn itself out in the population of Sumatra. Viruses that killed too ruthlessly, as Muaratebo clearly did, soon found there was no host left to support them. Muaratebo needed feeding, it needed people or primates in order to replicate. In London good fortune had prevented an outbreak. If the Indonesians' cordon sanitaire was effective, the virus would eventually run out of new hosts. Without a reservoir, the virus itself would quickly disappear.

That being the case, the RIID's mission was over, and all she had to do was plan the safe withdrawal of her team from what was an increasingly dangerous situation.

'There it is,' said Baker, the first words he had spoken since setting out.

The tree seemed to have shifted a little overnight, settling in earth made softer by the heavy rains. So massive, it looked utterly immovable – was immovable to the puny forces they could bring to bear – and yet in the living tissue of the forest it shifted and turned, moving a couple of feet in a matter of hours. Despite the settling, there was still no room for the Cherokee to get past. They climbed out of the air-conditioned cab into the wet heat.

'We walk from here,' said Carmen in answer to Holly's questioning expression.

Baker led the way, following the trail, referring in moments of doubt to the cuts made by McKinnon in the trunks of trees and on prominent branches. In two hours they had reached the second camp.

Leigh and McKinnon had pitched their tent on an escarpment which pushed out of the surrounding vegetation above the level of the Hari two miles to the east. The gently sloping eastern face was covered in a meagre fuzz of vegetation which gave it an almost naked appearance seen from a distance. Leigh and McKinnon were hard at work on samples gathered from the traps that morning, and didn't notice their approach until they were on the escarpment itself.

'We talked to Harold on the radio,' said Leigh, nodding a greeting to Holly Becker. 'Says his temperature's normal.'

Carmen unclipped her pack and lowered it to the ground. It was even hotter out of the woods, despite the partial cloud cover.

'He seems fine. He's working up some samples at the camp with Lennox so Holly's going to help us today.'

Carmen could see Leigh was uncomfortable having a civilian working with them. But he relaxed a little when, in discussing their plans for the day, Carmen assigned her to labelling and packing samples that had already been bagged. It was a task Holly had already carried out at the other sites, and though boring, it kept her away from any possible exposure to infected material. Holly was less than thrilled, but she accepted the drudgery with a shrug.

McKinnon took Baker into the forest below the escarpment to tend traps they had set for ground-feeding mammals the night before, while Carmen and Leigh set out for the tributary stream which emerged from the caves nearby. They hoped to find signs of Ahmad's presence there that would serve as a guide for their trapping and sampling.

It was noticeably cooler out of the sun. Carmen followed Leigh down through the trees, a hunting rifle slung over her shoulder. Leigh had taken to wearing a bandanna around his head to keep the sweat from running into his eyes. It gave him a tough hombre look and made Carmen think that he was probably enjoying all the jungle hardship. He was quieter now than when they had first arrived, taciturn almost. The last of the jokiness had evaporated after Rafflesia Camp, and Carmen wondered if what she had at first taken to be signs of displeasure were not in fact the opposite.

'Mark.'

He stopped and turned. Carmen stood her rifle against a tree and mopped her face with her own blue bandanna.

'What is it?'

'We have to talk. I have to tell you something.'

Leigh came back up the slope, his head tilted slightly to one side. And for the second time that day Carmen went through the whole Gensystems story.

Like Daintith, Leigh could at first do no more than stare.

'I waited till we got out here to break it to you, because I think it's better if Holly doesn't know. I've already told Harold, so she'll probably find out sooner or later; if he goes ahead and publishes, I mean. But I think we stand a better chance of tying this thing up and getting out cleanly if Holly is kept in the dark.'

Still Leigh stared. He seemed unable to take it all in.

'You're sure?' he said finally. 'About the viral expression, I mean.'

'I've been through it in my head a hundred times. It has to be true. We'll only know after a proper investigation into what was going on at Gensystems and what happened to Irwin and the others.'

Leigh smiled. It was a cynical, unamused smile.

'Well I wouldn't hold out too much hope about that,' he said.

'What do you mean?'

Leigh unshouldered his own rifle and put it next to Carmen's.

'Well I figure it took a breach of security ten years after the incident at Willard to bring this thing to light because Gensystems, Westway, the government, whoever, didn't specially want it in the public domain.'

'But with all this – ' Carmen gestured at the forest, at the island and its suffering people – 'the pressure to come clean will be too great.'

Again Leigh smiled. He said nothing for a moment, letting Carmen think it through for herself. A ray of sunlight like a needle filtered down through the leaves and touched Leigh's shoulder. After a while he went on.

'The pressure to keep the lid on Willard will be greater. And it won't be the people linked to Gensystems that are covering up, it'll be Uncle Sam himself.'

Carmen felt sick suddenly. She could see where Leigh was going with this, but she didn't want to accept it. If he was right then they were all going to come out of Sumatra compromised, sullied, soiled. For a moment all she could hear was the noise of the forest. Except that it wasn't noise, but system. Carmen looked at a drop of water on a leaf which was condensing light from somewhere, throwing out a little tongue of prismatic colour. Life is too complex, was the thought that came to her. Despite the fortune cookie simplicity of the idea it seemed incontrovertible, immovable, like the fallen tree on the trail. Life was too complex for them, for the scientists. Leigh was talking again.

'Disclosure of the full story would be an admission that what has happened here, what is still happening, is the fault of the United States of America, the government of which sanctioned experimentation on human embryos.'

'Muaratebo was made in the USA,' said Carmen.

'Precisely. And the Indonesians would want reparation.'

'They'd be right.'

'Maybe,' said Leigh, 'but consider something else for

a moment.' He looked down at his muddy boots for a second before going on. 'We're still here. The mission, I mean. Us. Now, if what you say is true, our being here looking for a reservoir is pointless. There never was a reservoir; the source of Muaratebo died with the kids. So our next step is to get out. To do that we have to explain to Bailey why we think the mission is at an end. And despite the fact that the Indonesians are more preoccupied with keeping their people from dying at the moment, I dare say they would also be curious to know about what exactly we found out here.'

'Right.'

'Especially as we are probably going to have to rely on the Indonesians, maybe that son of a bitch Sutami himself, to extricate our sorry asses. Now, that being the case, I think our first consideration in explaining why we are ready to go home is what effect any given explanation might have on the locals.'

'Right.'

'We wouldn't want to find ourselves being used as a bargaining chip in any political stand-off that might arise as a result of our telling the truth.'

'You're saying we should lie to Bailey and to Sutami?'

'If Sutami asks us what we found here, yes. Bailey is another question, but I think that given the nature of your source, and the vested interests Stateside, it might be wise to keep this whole thing under our hats for the time being, maybe for ever.'

'Jesus.'

'You only told Harold, right.'

'Yes, but I certainly didn't get into the political implications of all this, and by this time Harold may well have told Sarandon, Lennox and . . . God forbid – '

'Sergeant Kaoy.'

Carmen, drenched in sweat, nevertheless felt a chill go through her.

'Oh my God.'

Leigh spat and drew his foot across it.

'Well maybe not. He might talk to Lennox, scientist to scientist, but I can't see him shooting his mouth off indiscriminately.'

Leigh turned his back to her and walked a little way along the trail. 'What worries me is Sutami,' he said. Then he turned, his face as serious as Carmen had ever seen it. 'The thing is, if we were taken as a bargaining chip in some indemnity row – here in Sumatra.'

He didn't need to finish.

'You don't think Sutami would . . .'

'Maybe not deliberately, but let me ask you this. How would you like to spend the next month in Jambi, for example, or Padang? Because I don't think they'd be shipping us off to Jakarta. They'd consider it too risky.'

Carmen shuddered. Leigh was right, of course. If the US team did become infected in Jambi or any of the other Sumatran towns it would only bring home to the great American public the tragedy, the enormity, of Uncle Sam's blunder. It would guarantee the Indonesians prime-time exposure. It was clear to her now: they would have to lie their way out of Sumatra. It was the only option.

'OK,' said Leigh, pulling off his bandanna and wringing it dry. 'The bad news – all things considered – is maybe a few thousand people have died horrible deaths, but the good news is at some point it'll stop.'

'We hope.'

'It'll stop. It's killing people too fast. Holly Becker was wandering around Rafflesia Camp with a cut hand and she didn't pick it up. And I'd bet money on Harold pulling through too. Outside the body, after the death of the host, this thing can't survive. It's like the other filoviruses. It cools down, it dries out, it's finished.' Leigh nodded confirmation, wanting to believe his own reasoning. 'OK, OK. There's no reservoir. We can be pretty sure of that. All we have to say to General Bailey, to the world, is that we found no reservoir, no source. The same as with Marburg outbreaks in the eighties. They were up there at Mount Elgon in that cave . . .'

'Kitum.'

'Right. They worked Kitum cave, trapping everything that moved for weeks and they found nothing. OK, this mission turned out the same way.'

They looked at each other for a long time then. Carmen had made a close study of the Kitum survey prior to shipping out. The RIID had set cages around the cave containing guinea pigs, baboons and green monkeys in the hope that they would develop the disease which had killed a French engineer in 1980 and seven years later a Danish boy on holiday there. The caged animals had remained healthy. Then they had trapped everything in sight – rodents, bats, insects. They found nothing. Like Leigh said, it had happened before, it could happen again. With all the heat and the noise and the deceit Carmen felt stifled. She picked up her rifle.

'But we'll have to complete the day's work,' she said. 'We can't just say to the others, it's all over, there's no reservoir. After all, we've been finding infected animals.'

'Sure,' said Leigh. 'You're right. I think we should work the area for another couple of days, then clear out.' Carmen watched Leigh walk away through the thickly growing vegetation. 'Let's just hope Daintith kept his mouth shut,' he said.

They had gone another hundred yards together when Carmen's walkie-talkie spat and crackled into life. It was Baker; he sounded out of breath.

'Colonel, there's something we think you should see. Over.'

'What is it? Over.'

'We're just below the camp, not too far from the river. McKinnon saw it first.'

There was the sound of McKinnon's voice, then it was McKinnon himself on the walkie-talkie.

'Carmen, we think it may be Ahmad's camp. There are tins and stuff, some wire traps. But someone was here. Refugees, maybe. Baker says they could be looters. Over.'

Carmen looked at Leigh.

'Lennox ran into some on the road a few days ago and they were armed,' he said.

'I don't see why they'd be down there, McKinnon. Maybe it's just Indians. Over.'

'Whoever it was I think we scared them off. They were cooking something – it was the smoke that caught my attention – and we disturbed them. When we reached the shelter, they'd gone. They tried to kick the fire out, but there's stuff that's still warm. Over.'

'How do we find you? Over.'

'Go up to the camp and then follow the trail I cut. Major Leigh knows the way down. We'll watch out for you. Over and out.'

'It'll take us about half an hour,' said Leigh, turning to go back up the slope. Then, seeing the expression on Carmen's face, he paused. 'What's up?'

'Holly,' said Carmen. 'She's on her own up there.'

By the time they got back to the top of the escarpment they were both drenched in sweat. Holly stared, open-mouthed as they came blundering through the scrubby vegetation, their rifles at the ready.

Leigh went to the edge of the escarpment and looked over towards the area where he and McKinnon had set the traps the day before.

'Holly, we just got a call from McKinnon. He says he surprised somebody down there in the woods. It may be OK, but I'd rather you stuck with us for

426

a little while. We're going down to find McKinnon now.'

Holly stood up, a black marker pen and a crumpled checklist in her left hand. She was halfway through labelling a rack of cryovials which were in an insulated case at her feet.

Leigh came back from the edge of the escarpment.

'I don't like leaving all this stuff up here unattended, but I guess we don't have a choice. At least we can take the radio down.'

He shrugged off his field pack and clipped on the harness for the big field radio.

The trail down towards the river was much steeper than the one going across towards the caves. Leigh led them down, pointing out footholds in the tangle of mud and roots, followed by Holly and then Carmen. They went quietly, not wanting to alert any looters there might be to their presence. After fifteen minutes of steady progress, the ground levelled out. They could hear the sound of the river, a distant rush underpinning the constant chirring of insect sound.

Suddenly Baker was there.

'I think whoever it was took off,' he said. His voice seemed to break a spell. 'We've been taking a look around, but there's no sign of anybody.'

Without a word they followed him into thick vegetation, stumbling over ridges and hollows.

It was no more than a grass and palm roof, supported by two crudely hacked bamboo poles, the whole thing leaning against exposed rock that had the brown, dullish look of bauxite. The recent rains had dragged part of the roof down, and it looked like a stiffish wind would have pushed the whole thing over.

'Not much of a shelter,' said Carmen, squatting down to look at the bundle of traps McKinnon had found nearby. There were tins of tuna stacked in a hollow in the rock, but no sign of an opener. A battered tin cup was on its side in the middle of the trampled earth floor. Carmen tried to imagine the monkey hunter living there alone, but it was hard. What did he do through the long hours of darkness? Sit and dream?

'The remains of the fire's out here,' said McKinnon. Carmen stood up and went out through the other side of the shelter. There was a bad smell in the air, a buttery, rancid smell. Leigh and Holly Becker were already looking at the little bundle of partially burned sticks, over which some of the red earth had been kicked. There was a smell of ash mixed with the other bad smell.

'What is that stink?' said Carmen. Several mango stones were littered on the floor about six feet from the fire.

'I don't think they were looters,' said Leigh looking down at the dead fire. 'There'd be more garbage around.'

'Wouldn't be out here anyway,' said Baker. He was standing several feet away, his back to them, looking at the forest. 'It's too far from the road.'

'Somebody trying to escape the plague, maybe,' said McKinnon.

'Why'd they light a fire?' asked Leigh, squatting down and turning over one of the half-burned sticks. He looked at Carmen's frowning face. 'What were they trying to do? Cook something, maybe. But I don't see any kind of spit, anything like that.'

Carmen looked around at the trampled earth. Then she saw it. She stood up and went across to where the flat mango stones were scattered. A foot beyond them, half hidden by a small, leafy shrub, there was a piece of fruit of a sort she had never seen before. It looked like the fruit had been hacked in half with a small knife, a knife that was too small for the job. The fruit had a thick, horny rind, and inside, the flesh, some of which had been gnawed at, was a creamy white.

'This is what smells,' said Carmen, dragging the fruit out into the light with her foot.

'It's a durian,' said Holly in a voice that brought Carmen slowly to her feet. She watched Holly bend down and pick up the fruit. 'In Singapore you can't take it into public places because of . . . the smell.'

Holly was holding the fruit a foot from Carmen's face. Held up to the light you could clearly see where the flesh had been gnawed at, and in one place there was a clean bitemark, too small for a man. The exposed flesh had hardly oxidised. Whoever had been eating the fruit must have abandoned it when Baker and McKinnon arrived. Carmen looked from the fruit to Holly, and she could see the belief in Holly's face, in her brimming eyes.

'They're here,' said Holly in a whisper. 'I can feel it.' She was trembling all over. The men turned to look. Carmen slowly shook her head, though her heart was quickening. She took the fruit from Holly and tossed it into the bushes.

'No, Holly. It's impossible.'

She was on the point of explaining: *your children cannot have escaped the disease, they were the cause*, when it came to her, the idea rushing into focus like an oncoming truck – *they are immune.*

'What is it?'

It was Holly. She had seen the change in Carmen's face. Seen something more than just change. Suddenly she was against her, her fists twisting in her clothing. Leigh and McKinnon were trying to pull her off. Again Holly shouted.

'What is it? *What do you know?*'

Carmen backed away, watching Holly struggle against the restraining hands.

'Nothing,' said Carmen. And it was true: she knew nothing for sure. It was the horror of the idea that had shaken her, not its validity, not its truth. 'Nothing,' she repeated. But she was shaken nonetheless. The idea that the children might be generating the virus without themselves succumbing – it was too horrible; wandering through the towns and villages, angels of death, watching each place they entered bubble and blister into disease. Instinctively Carmen looked over her shoulder at the forest. Holly was shrieking now, despite Leigh's gentle reassurances.

'Tell me! Tell me!'

The forest seemed to stare back. Not malignant, Carmen had never felt that, but indifferent, the rush of insect sound like the noise of a machine grinding out versions of itself, grinding out more self in senseless repetition like the mindless replication of the virus. With Holly's panic-stricken cries filling her head, Carmen prayed that the children were not out there, prayed that they were indeed in the ground at Rafflesia Camp. Because if they were there, out in the forest, frightened, hungry, perhaps watching her through the leaves at that very moment, then the question of their immunity and of the danger they embodied would have to be answered.

Then Baker stabbed out an arm and Carmen felt her heart jolt like a doubling amoeba.

'Look,' he shouted.

They looked away towards the river. Emerging from the thickest foliage only fifty feet away, two children became visible, their clothes hanging in shreds, their bodies and faces blackened with grime. But it was their eyes that seemed to enter Carmen's soul, it was their eyes she could never afterwards forget, holes drilled into unimaginable darkness, the blackness of them, the terror, the hunger as they sought out the source of their mother's voice in the group of soldiers.

For a moment there was complete silence, as if even the jungle held its breath. Then Holly was staggering forward, weeping, her voice broken, joyous, deranged.

'My . . . Lucy, Emma . . . my babies. I can't – '

Carmen couldn't move. It felt like she was spell-bound, suddenly stone. She watched in horror as Holly blundered across the broken ground, staggering against bushes, pushing back fronds and branches. The children didn't move, holding hands now, watching their mother come on. Then Carmen was freed.

'*Stop!*'

She rushed forward, grabbing Holly by the arm. Aston-ished, Holly gripped Carmen's hand and tried to twist it free of her sleeve. For a moment the two women struggled, grunting with the effort.

'Holly, Holly you have to listen.'

Then Leigh was there, pulling Holly away, but tripping, falling, bringing Holly down with him. She struggled to her feet, kicking at Leigh's clutching hand. Carmen got a grip of her shirt, which tore as the woman twisted, and pulled.

'Holly!' Carmen was shrieking now, desperate. 'Your children, they have the disease! It comes from them. They are the source.'

It was as if she had received a blow in the face. There was a breathless silence as Leigh got to his feet. Holly blinked, her mouth opening, her tongue moving across her lips. Carmen gripped her tighter.

'It happened at Gensystems. The treatment you had. It made the virus.'

Holly's eyes rolled upwards and for a moment Car-men thought she was going to pass out. Then a spasm of rage shook her body and she was shrieking, screaming, twisting, clawing at Carmen's face.

'Lies! *Lies!*'

Leigh got an arm around her throat, but she bit down, her teeth meeting in the flesh, sending Leigh backward, yelling, clutching at his arm which was suddenly bright with blood.

Only now did the others move. Everyone was shouting at once, rushing forward, but it was too late. With a final wrench, Holly freed herself from Carmen's grip and careered off through the trees towards where the children had been.

9

Dr Lennox watched Sergeant Sarandon's eyes widen in astonishment as he listened to the transmission. He came into the shade of the Cherokee, no longer listening to Daintith's virus talk, realising that something was happening. Seeing him approach, Sarandon flipped the speaker button so that everyone could hear what was coming over the air. Kaoy stood with a cigarette between his lips, squinting through smoke.

'They're alive,' said a breathless man's voice. 'The children, they're still alive.'

Daintith stood up, sending over the little camp table with the remains of their meal. The urgent voice went on.

'We need you to call the Jambi headquarters – call Sutami and get a Puma sent out here immediately. Over.'

'McKinnon, can you repeat that? We're not clear – I mean, why don't you just bring them in? Over.'

'Look Sarandon, we don't have time to get into this; the Colonel believes the children may be infected. They need to be hospitalised straight away.' Daintith took the headset from Sarandon. 'We also need you to come down with Daintith to help us look for them. Over.'

'McKinnon, this is Harold Daintith. Look for who? Over.'

'Harold' – it was Carmen now, she sounded agitated,

barely able to control her voice – 'we spotted the kids and Holly took off after them. Now they're all . . . we have to find them Harold. Over.'

'OK. Do we call for back-up? Do we call Sutami? Over.'

'Yes. Tell him . . . tell him we've got some US citizens here and we believe they may be carrying the virus. Call General Bailey too – I don't care if you have to get him out of bed – call him and see if we can get some kind of support from our people, at least some pressure. Over.'

'Do you want us to come down? Over.'

'Yes. I mean . . . no, the best thing is – can you come down with Lennox? I'd rather Kaoy stayed up there, Harold, and I want Sarandon on the satellite link. Over.'

Lennox gave Daintith a nod, and mouthed the word *where*.

'What's the rendezvous position? Over.'

'At the camp. McKinnon will be waiting with the radio. Over and out.'

Daintith took off the headset.

'Jesus Christ.'

He wiped the perspiration from his face with the back of his sleeve. The children were alive. He couldn't believe it. They were still alive and yet Carmen suspected they were carrying the virus. Did she mean they were carriers? Not developing the disease itself? But there was no time to think. Daintith stood up.

'Raise Jambi.'

It took Sarandon two attempts to get an answer on the frequency he had been given, but then he was immediately through to Sutami. Sarandon identified himself and gave longitude and latitude for the ground position of the base camp.

'At Muaratebo?' snapped Sutami. There was a burst of Indonesian at the other end and then Sutami barked: 'Over!'

'Maybe thirty kilometres above Muaratebo on the east bank of the Hari river. We need assistance, Brigadier. We have picked up two US citizens, children, who we believe are carrying the virus and require your help to effect their immediate hospitalisation – '

'Tell him we've already spoken to Washington,' nudged Daintith.

'Washington has advised us that we can count on your assistance, sir. Over.'

There was a long pause. Daintith leaned forward, straining to hear. Indonesian was being spoken in rapid bursts. Sergeant Kaoy came forward, listening. Then Sutami was back, sounding calmer now.

'So sorry, soldier, but we have crisis here too. Hundreds of citizen dying every day, and we are already . . . stretched. Unless we get the official confirmation of the Washington's request it is impossible to redirect resources. I have asked for all foreign teams to be withdrawn from the area. You should be on you way out already. Over.'

Daintith snatched the headset from Sarandon.

'God damn it, listen to me. These children are the carriers. They may well turn out to be the source of the whole damn thing.' Daintith looked at the astonished faces surrounding him. Then, remembering himself, he handed the headset to Sergeant Kaoy. 'Explain, Sergeant Kaoy. Explain the situation. We have to get them isolated, in a proper hospital. Over.'

Kaoy leaned forward and started talking into the mike. It seemed to go on for ever. There were a number of exclamations at the other end. Then Kaoy handed the headset back to Daintith.

'They want precise co-ordinates for the pick-up,' he said. There was a half-smile on his lips. Daintith reached for the map and Lennox put his hand on Daintith's bare arm.

'What did you tell them?' he said to Kaoy.

'I can't believe you didn't tell us,' said Baker. He gripped the hunting rifle as if he was ready to use it. Carmen looked up from Major Leigh's arm. She had dressed the bite with a strip torn from her shirt. They had proper field dressings at the second camp, but no time to get back up there.

'There wasn't time,' she said, 'and we didn't know – that they were alive I mean.'

'But you're sure they're carrying it?' asked McKinnon.

'They have to be. They're the only link with Rafflesia, Ahmad, Gensystems. It has to be them.'

'So how come they're not dead?' said Baker.

Carmen stood up, brushing leaf mould and dirt from her knees. She knew that if she looked at Baker's face, she'd lose it. She was at the end of her rope with him.

'I don't know,' she managed to say. Then, to Leigh: 'How does it feel?'

Leigh opened and closed his fist. He shrugged. Then he looked across at Baker.

'They're alive is the main thing, soldier. Just about. And if we don't get after them straight away we don't stand a chance of picking them up before nightfall.'

'OK,' said Carmen. 'This is what we're going to do. Now, there's help on its way, OK? But as Major Leigh says we can't let them get too far or we'll never find them again. Now, the important thing is to stay in touch. I want you Baker, and Major Leigh to take walkie-talkies – '

Baker started to back away, clutching the rifle.

'Man, I ain't going anywhere close – '

Carmen went for him, grabbing the rifle from his hands.

'*Dammit!* Dammit that's an order, Baker. And you don't have to get close. You just have to find where they went.' She pushed the rifle back at him. 'McKinnon I want you to go back up to the camp and get the suits.'

'It's too hot,' said McKinnon. 'They're no good out

here. You're safer just keeping your eyes open.'

'Get the damn suits! I'm not suggesting you run around in them. We'll get close first. Talk to them. Tell them we need the suits to protect ourselves. These kids may be humming with this thing.'

'What about Holly Becker?' said Leigh. Carmen turned and looked at him.

'We just have to pray she doesn't reach her kids before we do.'

Sutami felt drunk. He stared at the co-ordinates in his hand, his head swimming. He hadn't had a decent meal for two days, keeping going on eggs and rice, Javanese coffee and cigarettes. It was 4.30. In another hour the commander from Jakarta would be arriving to take control and his career in the army would come to an abrupt end. He considered the piece of paper on which he had scribbled the numbers, the words of the American going round in his head. It felt like a moment of destiny. They had been delivered into his hands – the ones responsible. He blinked and drew the back of his fist across his mouth. It felt like a turning point in his life, a moment in which things could go either way, depending on the choice he made.

He raised the garrison that had been established east of Muaratebo to discourage the flight of refugees. Two short exchanges got him through to the head of the airborne unit they were using to watch the roads. The officer, Lieutenant Sumendap, sounded young, ambitious. Sutami listened to the rustle of a military map as the young soldier checked the co-ordinates.

'Twenty minutes from here, Brigadier. We have a slight westerly above two hundred feet, but otherwise conditions are perfect.'

'Good. Now listen carefully. A team of US scientists has picked up two American citizens, two children, who are known to be the carriers of the disease. Our own man on the ground has confirmed it.' There was a sharp intake of breath. Sutami nodded: 'Yes, Lieutenant. After a long struggle we are finally gaining the upper hand. They are the cause, the origin of what happened in Muaratebo, what happened in Jambi. Americans. *Children*. These specialists want us to pick them up, take them to a hospital. But they must not . . .' Sutami's anger tightened his throat: 'they must not leave the area. It is too dangerous. Do you understand? For national security.' Sutami waited for a moment, his eyes on the second-hand of his watch which seemed to hurry between the numbers. 'We will put an end to this suffering today, Lieutenant Sumendap. You will put down a unit on that spot. They will find the children. I want these . . . these *carriers* killed. Do you understand?'

'Yes, Brigadier.'

'I want you to come back, I want you to tell me you saw their bodies burn.'

She was mad for a while. Raving. Blundering forward, trying to run, getting snagged in branches, tripping, crying the whole time, her body racked with sobs, her eyes stinging, blinded. Leaves and branches struck her face, cut her. Then she could run no more. Gasping for breath she fell against a tree. The bark was smooth, flawless, like something manufactured. She blinked the sweat from her burning eyes, drawing breath in long, shuddering gulps. Then her strength drained away and she was sliding down the tree, the smooth bark cool against her face.

She lay on the ground for a long time, listening to the pulsing rush of the jungle all around her. Ants followed an invisible line just a foot from her face, paying her no attention. She thought she heard a shout, but then there was nothing – just the jungle. She pulled herself up until she was sitting against the tree, blurred vision riven by a glittering band of light which seemed to float above the ground, winking and flashing through dark foliage.

She had reached the Hari river. Watching the stream of light, her mind drifted back and she was remembering the birth of her children, remembering the fear and the pain and then the infinite relief, the joy of having them healthy in her arms, warm parcels of life; remembering Jonathan, his worried face relaxing into a smile, so much younger then. It seemed like another lifetime, almost another period of history; it seemed impossible that that time was connected to this terrible moment, that the same hearts had continued to beat through the intervening years. The tears welled up in her again, but she had no strength left to cry. She was remembering their last farewell, JFK at 8 a.m. Emma's down jacket with the peacock motifs. Her worried eyes. *Don't worry, Emms.* Emma had told her she couldn't help it. *What are you going to do for two weeks?* she said, and Holly had realised that Emma was worried not about the trip, not about leaving, but about leaving her mother at home alone. It had been a funny moment, a moment in which she saw how fast they were growing up.

She looked at her filthy hands, at the filthy army pants she had been given, all torn and stained. She saw her hands close into fists. And it was as if her mind closed too, closed against Carmen and her reasoning. How could treatment given thirteen years ago in the US produce a virus here, now? And if her babies had got the virus somehow, how had it not killed them? It was ridiculous. Carmen was wrong. But – Holly's hands opened again as the thought took shape – if they took them back to one of the filthy towns, to one of the miserable hospitals, then they *could* catch it, probably would. To have them die a second time would finish her. They might as well just roll her into the same grave. She climbed unsteadily to her feet. She had to reach the children before they did.

On their own the children would not be able to argue. They were tired, scared. They were only children. She had to protect them, prove to Carmen that she was wrong. Then, from nowhere, she found herself laughing. *They were alive. Alive!* She clapped her hands against her mouth, and pressed her eyes tight shut, waiting for the feeling of joy to subside. It was too big, too much after long weeks of misery. She didn't feel strong enough for it – felt like she could go crazy. Then she was suddenly hungry for them – it made her head swim – she had to have them in her eyes, in her arms, she had to have the smell of them, the sound of their voices.

Suddenly there was the sound of a walkie-talkie. Holly froze. It was away to her left.

'I'm almost at the river,' said a man's voice, and Holly recognised Baker. 'Still no sign of anything.'

The walkie-talkie spat something back, but Holly couldn't hear what was said. She kept absolutely still as Baker's footsteps passed. He was trying to be quiet, stalking her children. From behind the tree Holly peered through the vegetation but she couldn't see him. Then something moved and she saw a booted foot, perhaps thirty feet away. He became very still, listening for something. Then Holly heard it too: a distant throbbing, building rapidly into the distinctive thwack-thwack of a helicopter. The jungle seemed to erupt with animal sounds as it swept overhead clattering up towards the escarpment, stirring up the canopy as it went. Monkeys screeched and whooped, birds skimmed between the branches. Holly saw Baker's foot turn as he followed it with his eyes. For a moment there was only the helicopter, and then out of the diminishing noise, Baker's angry voice:

' – should pull us out and napalm the whole fucking jungle.'

Holly pressed herself against the tree, praying he wouldn't come any nearer. It had never occurred to

440

her that they might mean actual harm to her children. Was he armed? She was straining to get a better look at Baker when a movement to her right caught her attention.

She turned.

Emma's dark eyes stared out of leafy shadow, the beginnings of a smile twitching the corners of her mouth.

Daintith's thighs trembled with the strain as the Cherokee bucked and dipped. The only way he could stay on the seat was to lock his legs against the bench opposite. On the floor beneath him a petrol can and Leigh's captured rifle slid back and forth in a piece of filthy green canvas. He tapped Lennox on the shoulder.

'Why d'you bring the rifle?' He had to shout above the noise of the Cherokee. Lennox looked at him in the rearview mirror, his hands braced against the wheel.

'Did you see that look on Kaoy's face? When he'd finished his little speech, I mean. I didn't like it.'

'He was calling for support,' said Daintith, his eyes on the rifle now. 'You don't think – '

'Hey Harold, carrying a gun doesn't mean you have to fire it.'

The trail levelled out, something banged against the underside of the Cherokee, and for a moment the going was smoother. Daintith was about to say something when Lennox gave a yelp. The Cherokee hit a patch of wet leaves and slewed round. There was a sickening moment of weightlessness cut off by a jolting crash and a shower of glass.

Daintith struggled up off the floor. The Cherokee was almost wedged underneath the fallen ketapang tree.

'Nice parking,' he said. Lennox kicked open the buckled door.

McKinnon squinted into the driven dirt and leaves as the chopper hovered over the escarpment. A rope dropped and six armed soldiers came sliding down like something out of a manual. McKinnon watched each one of them hit the ground, the sight of them looking so mean and lean giving him a bad feeling. Almost immediately the chopper veered off to the south-east in the direction of Muaratebo. When the noise had subsided one of the soldiers came across to where he stood next to the field radio. He was a powerfully built man with a pock-marked face.

'Lieutenant Sumendap, 8th Airborne,' he said, with a snappy salute. Then, looking around: 'The children, where are they?'

McKinnon looked past him at the other soldiers who were checking their packs and rifles. One of the men had a canister on his back, like an oxygen bottle, with a line going down into a funny-looking rifle. They were all clipping on masks. There was no isolation equipment.

It seemed to take for ever for Baker to move off. He went right past where they were crouching and on down towards the banks of the Hari. All the time Holly watched her children's faces. Lucy's hair was matted and held back with a piece of rag, showing a partly healed cut on her forehead. Their fingernails were chewed and black with grime. Finally, when she could bear it no more, Holly stood up, her arms held wide, her eyes brimming with tears. She took a step towards them.

'Don't come any nearer, Mommy.'

It was Emma who spoke, keeping her voice down, backing away a little. Then Lucy, in a simple matter-of-fact way, said: 'Everybody who touches us dies.'

It was all true. Holly didn't know what to say. She stood there, staring at two girls who looked like what they needed most in the world was a hug. This is the end, she thought.

'What . . .' For a moment there were no words, then: 'What happened, Emms?'

Emma put her arm around Lucy and gave a little shake of her head.

'We don't want to talk about it,' she said.

Lucy brought her grimy hand to her eyes, her shoulders beginning to shake. It was too much. Holly blundered forward and grabbed them, pressing them against herself, hard. They were all crying now – desperate, almost hysterical tears. Through sobs Lucy said: 'Are you going to die too, Mommy?'

Holly squeezed her tight, kissing her filthy matted hair. She kissed Emma's frightened face, kissing her eyes, her nose, her mouth.

'No, darling. No, I won't die. I'm not leaving you now. We're gonna stick together.'

They were all skin and bone. Holly held them away from her, wanting to see. Lucy's bony shoulders showed through rents in what was left of her dress.

'She's been sick,' said Emma, reading her mother's expression. 'She just kept coughing the whole time. It isn't so bad now. But she can't run.'

'It gets kind of tickly in my chest,' said Lucy, showing her the spot. 'Then I cough and cough and I can't stop.'

Holly looked at her daughter, trying to put together everything she had been told. But it was impossible. All she knew was that her children looked starved and she had to feed them. She looked up at the sky. In another couple of hours it would be getting dark.

'He's coming back,' whispered Emma, pointing through the trees towards the river.

'They're all armed to the teeth, Carmen. They're wearing masks and one of the guys has what I think is a flamethrower. Stank of kerosene, anyway. I asked them where the bubble-stretchers were, but they just ignored me. All they wanted to know was where the kids were. Over.'

'What did you tell them? Over.'

'I said I didn't know. But I think he guessed, the leader, I mean. I kind of gave it away, when they first arrived. I was looking over to Ahmad's shelter, seeing what I could see. They took off down the escarpment about five minutes ago, and I heard them shout. I think they found the trail I cut on the trees. Over.'

'OK, McKinnon. This sounds . . .' Carmen didn't know what to say for a moment. She couldn't believe Sutami would send executioners. She took a deep breath: 'I want you to call Sarandon on the radio. Get him to notify Fort Detrick of what we think is going down here. As soon as Lennox and Daintith turn up I want them to come straight down. If we pack this area with enough uniforms maybe they'll think twice about getting rough. Over and out.'

It sounded like a cough. Baker froze, listening hard, trying to cut out the buzz of insects. Then someone, a child it sounded like, was coughing hard. He turned, trying to pinpoint the sound, and out of the corner of his eye saw a flash of pink. The coughing continued, and now he saw all three of them, trying to move away from him, stumbling, plunging forward through the bushes.

'Mrs Becker! Mrs Becker you shouldn't get too . . .'

They disappeared from view. Baker started forward, shouting into the mouthpiece, pressing the walkie-talkie to his ear. Leigh answered immediately.

'I have them,' shouted Baker: 'They're maybe fifty yards from me, moving in your direction. Holly Becker is with them. Over.'

'What!' Leigh cursed, and for a moment Baker thought he had thrown down the walkie-talkie, but he was straight back, shouting now. 'Jesus Christ. Did you try talking to them? Over.'

'They just moved off as soon as I opened my mouth. They're running scared. Over.'

'OK keep following them. That was the Indonesian military just now, so all we have to do is contain them in this area until the support arrives. How far are you from me now? Over.'

'No idea, sir. With all the trees I . . . I could try shouting. You might be able to hear my voice. Over.'

'Fire your weapon. I'll hear that.'

The shot brought Lieutenant Sumendap's head round. He listened for a moment, his whole body tensed in readiness, his breathing loud in the face mask. It came from away towards the river. He hadn't realised they were armed. He looked back at the men, who had come to a halt behind him. They'd heard it too. He held up a hand, and then pointed in the direction of the shot. He was about to move into the bushes when a woman suddenly appeared, standing in front of him, her hands on her hips. She didn't look like a soldier, but she didn't look exactly like a scientist either. She saluted, and stepped forward to shake his hand.

'Lieutenant-Colonel Carmen Travis, RIID expedition. Pleased to meet you, sir.'

Sumendap, thrown by the sudden politeness, came to attention. He pushed his mask up and introduced himself with an answering salute.

'Can I ask you what you've come here for?'

The woman looked scared. Her face was streaming with sweat.

'There was a call for assistance to Jambi HQ.'

'But we asked for medical support,' said Carmen, improvising – with no real idea of what she could achieve, except perhaps give Leigh enough time to get to the children. 'I don't see any medics, or any medical equipment for that matter.'

Sumendap smiled.

'We have orders, Colonel.'

'What do you mean?'

'Talk to Jambi,' said the man and he pulled his mask back down. He turned and waved his men forward. Carmen stepped in his way, so that for a moment she was looking at her distorted reflection in his faceplate.

'Lieutenant Sumendap, if any harm comes to the American citizens there will be a – ' But she was unable to finish. The soldier pushed her hard in the chest so that she fell back into the bushes. Then they were gone. She ran back to the shelter where she had left the radio and the walkie-talkie. She was about to call Leigh, when the thing was suddenly alive.

'Carmen? This is Major Leigh, are you receiving me. Over.'

'Go ahead, Mark. Over.'

'Baker spotted them down by the river, but they ran off. He's on their tail. Holly Becker is with them. He's pushing them in my direction and if I'm guessing the distances right they're going to be on top of me in another few minutes. What do you want me to do? Over.'

'Mark, the military just showed up. The bastards are here to kill the children. I tried to stop them, but they actually pushed me out of the way. I think if you get in their way they'll shoot you where you stand. That's the situation. Over.'

'What? You have to be . . . Those fucking inhuman . . . Wait a second. I can hear them coming. Jesus, sounds like one of the kids is coughing her lungs out. Listen, Carmen. Seems to me the only thing we can do is put ourselves between the kids and the soldiers. If we raise the stakes they may back off.'

And he signed off. Carmen stared at the walkie-talkie, blinking the sweat out of her eyes. They were helpless. Leigh would stand in the way. If he was carrying the rifle they'd put him down. She called McKinnon.

'Any sign of Lennox? Over.'

'Nothing. I called Sarandon, and he's getting on to the X-SAT. Did you see our support? Over.'

'They stomped me on their way to the kids. This is for the record, McKinnon. They used violence. I think they're planning on worse for the kids. Major Leigh is going to try to stop them. I'm going after them myself.'

Holly didn't see Leigh until the last minute. They blundered through a patch of young bamboo and he was there right in their path no more than twenty feet away standing under a brilliant red heliconia which came down out of the branches like a chandelier. She pulled up short, spreading her arms to protect her children. Lucy let go her hand, coughing, whooping, trying to get her breath, sinking to her knees. Keeping her eyes on Leigh the whole time, Holly gathered her up, lifting her into her arms. A month ago and she would have been too heavy. Now she was just bones. Emma clung to her legs, whimpering.

'Holly. We're not going to hurt you.'

Leigh took a step forward, but Holly could see he wasn't going to grab them. He was scared. Scared of the virus.

'So why'd you take a shot at us?'

Leigh shook his head.

'That was Baker. He fired a round into the air so I could tell where he was.'

'He said he wanted to napalm the forest.'

Leigh took another step forward, still shaking his head, still denying everything.

'Holly, I don't know anything about that. Holly listen to me.'

Lucy twisted in Holly's arms, coughing, still gasping for breath. Holly held her tighter, whispering close to her ear.

'It's OK, honey, just breathe, just try to . . . just breathe easy. Nobody's going to hurt you.'

Emma squeezed against her legs, hiding her face. Suddenly Baker emerged from the bushes on her right, pushing through foliage, his eyes scared. He stopped a few feet from them, still gripping the rifle.

'She has the virus, Baker. My baby's coughing and the air is full of it. You want to die, just keep coming.'

Baker looked across at Leigh, and then, carefully, watching where he put his feet, moved away towards where Leigh was standing. Leigh couldn't take his eyes off the woman and her two children. It was the saddest thing he ever wanted to see.

'Holly, for Christ's sake, we only want to help.' Lucy was breathing easier now, whimpering a little, her face pressed into Holly's throat. 'The chopper you heard? That was the Indonesian army. They've sent men here to kill the children.'

'What?' Baker snapped a round into the chamber of the rifle, his eyes everywhere, watching for this new threat.

'That's right. Guess they decided they wanted to put an end to this thing.'

'You're lying,' said Holly. 'It's a trick. You just want us to come with you so you can throw my babies into some Indonesian refugee camp.'

'Holly, McKinnon calld down from the camp. When Carmen tried to stop them they just pushed her out of the way.'

'Liar! If the soldiers are here – '

She stopped, astonished to see Leigh drop to the ground under a shower of splinters. At the same time the air exploded into hammering automatic gunfire. Holly, Lucy still in her arms, threw herself to the ground, pulling Emma down with her. Baker shouted something, screaming against the roar of the guns, and then stopped. Holly saw him jerk up straight, as if pulled on a string, the hunting rifle held in front of him as if to return fire.

Suddenly there was total silence, broken only by the fall of cut foliage. Even the insects were silent. Baker tried to say something, his mouth moving, but no sound coming out. Then Holly saw the blood in his hair. Snaking out of his hairline, it was suddenly abundant, splashing down onto his surprised features and trembling naked arms. He pitched forward out of sight.

McKinnon ran to the edge of the escarpment. The short burst of gunfire had been followed by total silence. The jungle looked unchanged, the canopy a solid field of green. A solitary heron flew low over the trees and then dipped out of sight as though diving into water. McKinnon stared for a moment, unsure of what to do. Then he turned back to the radio. He had to call Sarandon, let him know what was going on.

'Mac!'

McKinnon looked up. Daintith and Lennox carrying an assault rifle shambled into the camp. They looked like they'd just run the New York marathon. McKinnon pushed a canteen into Lennox's hands, and for a moment neither man spoke, just gulping down the warm water, getting their breath back.

'We've got to get down there,' said McKinnon, looking out towards where the shooting had come from. 'We've got to get to the kids.'

'What's up?'

'The Indonesians sent some military back-up. But they're not here to help. They're executioners. It's a fucking commando unit.'

Lennox snatched up the rifle.

'Fuck it. I *knew* it. That was them shooting?'

'Well *we* don't have any automatic weapons.'

'We do now,' said Lennox, slapping the barrel of the gun.

McKinnon looked at Lennox's streaming face, and for

the first time felt genuinely scared. He had the feeling he was looking at a man who was about to get shot.

'Now don't get excited, fella. You've been in the forest too long. There's no way we're going down there with that thing. Colonel Travis wants us there to calm things down. She figures they might not pull the trigger with us watching. You go in there like Rambo and they might pull the trigger anyway.'

'Sounds like they already did,' said Daintith.

'You coming or not?' said Lennox, looking more keyed up than ever.

They were already walking away, without even knowing how to find the trail down. McKinnon tried to spit but his mouth was suddenly dry. Then he came after them, pointing to an opening in the scrub, the beginning of the path.

Baker's eyes were fixed under motionless lids. Leigh tried to wipe some of the blood from his face, but it was already beginning to coagulate. He detached Baker's warm fingers from the hunting rifle, and then took the remaining ammunition from his pants. There were four rounds, plus one in the rifle. Peering forward through the jungle, Leigh crawled into the cover of a small tree. His guess was the soldiers had gone as soon as they saw Holly Becker take off. He listened for a moment longer. Then, taking a last look at Baker's dead body, he moved into the tangle of lianas and branches where Holly Becker and her children had disappeared.

Almost immediately the ground fell away to the left and he found himself up to his elbows in dead leaves. There was a soft, bad-smelling mulch underneath the leaves and he guessed he was in some kind of choked stream bed. He crawled for about twenty yards before risking getting to his feet. Even for the forest, the stream bed was stifling. Leigh waded forward through the leaves.

It felt like his head was being cooked. If Holly and the children had stayed in the stream bed, they were heading straight back for the escarpment.

At first he thought it was part of the insect noise. But standing still, up to his ankles in dead leaves, he could hear coughing. It was the girl, Lucy, coughing again. They could only be a matter of yards ahead of him. He imagined the frantic mother trying to make the girl stop, knowing that the sound would draw the soldiers to them. He listened for a moment longer. The coughing had stopped. All he could hear now was the zip and rush of the insects. Then something else. To his right. He squatted down, his heart starting to thump hard again.

They hadn't seen him. There were two of them, both carrying assault rifles. Their sweating limbs looked like polished bronze against the camouflaged weapons, their heads hidden by leaves. They moved forward in a half-crouch, their pace quickening even as he watched. They weren't worried about being heard, closing in now, the distance judged, the kill all but in the bag. Leigh raised his weapon and got the sights on the man in front, aiming at the armpit. He squeezed the trigger.

Suddenly the air around him was full of zipping impacts, kicking up leaves and mud. A branch burst open like a firecracker showering down yellow woodchips. Leigh threw himself to the ground.

'Run! Holly! Run!'

He rolled onto his side, forcing his shaking hands to push another round into the rifle.

'Get back up to the others!'

There was another volley of fire. Leaves over his head seemed to explode into green confetti, filling the air with a pungent smell of sap. Leigh tried to think. They were on his left, stalking him probably, waiting to get a clear shot. Or maybe his own fire had drawn them onto him. It was only a matter of time before they realised he had a single-shot weapon. When they did, they'd stop treating him with such respect.

He wriggled forward, pushing hard with his elbows and knees. They continued to empty their magazines into the foliage over his head, but they were way off target, and it looked to Leigh like they were raking the jungle, hoping to get lucky. He realised with a sudden surge of exhilaration that they hadn't yet figured out the terrain. The only way they were going to nail him was if they got into the stream bed.

Daintith slipped and fell with the first volley of shots, bringing down Lennox with him. It had seemed so close. But then when he heard Leigh's voice shouting Holly's name, he realised they were at least fifty yards away from where the shots were fired. He clambered to his feet.

'I lost my footing.'

From above and behind him, McKinnon said:

'That sounded like Major Leigh's voice. He must be trying to draw their fire.' He came down the slope. 'Did you hear? He fired off a shot with the hunting rifle before the Kalashnikovs started.' He looked at Lennox's rifle: 'Does that thing work?'

'I guess.'

'Fire off a few rounds.'

'What?'

'Fire off a few round. Give these fuckers something to think about.'

Lennox looked around him.

'Where?'

'Into the air!'

Lennox closed his eyes and squeezed the trigger, firing off five rounds in a deafening burst. McKinnon pulled on his arm.

'OK, OK. Damn thing only holds thirty pops. Now listen.'

It had become very still, with a tense, listening silence as if the forest had gone up on tiptoe. All of them realised at once that any soldiers out there were now looking in their direction. A single gunshot split the silence followed by another burst from the Kalashnikovs.

'We'd better keep moving,' said McKinnon, going down in front of them now: 'Don't want to give them a stationary target.'

They had reached a part of the slope which was so steep it was necessary to use the tangled tree roots as steps. They went down one by one. At the bottom of the slope, the ground levelled out and twisted away to the left. McKinnon crawled under the low branches of a juniper tree and found himself staring at Carmen, who stared back, a finger to her lips. She was carrying the other hunting rifle. Seeing Lennox with the assault rifle, she gave a grim nod.

Holly pushed the children forward, running bent double, keeping low under the overhanging branches. She had heard Leigh's shout. *Get back up.* He must have meant to the camp. The path seemed to be rising, twisting back and forth. Then Lucy fell, rolling over on her back, struggling for breath. Holly was nearly frantic, shaking Lucy, trying to revive her. She looked deathly pale under the grime.

'Come on Lucy, come on, darling. We can't stop.'

Emma put a hand on her mother's arm.

'Give her a minute. When she gets like this, it's the only thing that works.'

Holly forced herself to be still. The jungle around them seemed full of furtive noises, whispers, stealthy footfalls. The ends of Holly's sweat-drenched hair trembled with her beating heart. She watched Lucy revive, coughing fitfully, crying a little, obviously weak. But they had to keep moving, it was their only chance.

'Lucy, come on darling. You have to try.'

Something stirred on the track behind them. Emma and Holly turned, their eyes searching for movement.

It was Leigh, about thirty feet away. They both saw him at once, inching towards them, crawling on his belly, his pale eyes fixed on them. The air seemed to thicken, everything slowing down. Holly saw the masked soldier come into the stream bed behind him, taking for ever to emerge. At first he looked away from them, turning away towards the river, and Holly saw the canister on his back like an aqualung. Then Lucy's cough brought his head round, and they were looking at his eyes through the faceplate of the gasmask. In the same instant with the same slowness Leigh rolled over and fired, hitting the soldier in the chest, punching a small black hole in his sternum. His head lolled to one side, and the barrel of his gun described a small lazy ellipse as he tried to get his sights onto Leigh who was kicking leaves scrambling to his feet, running towards them, screaming, arms flailing wildly.

'Run Holly, run. For God's sake!'

The blast of heat was like a furnace door suddenly opened. Above them the branches burst into flame, and the ground too was burning. Screaming, Holly grabbed Lucy up in her arms, and ran, her face burning in the heat, her fist clenched in the back of Emma's dress. Behind her she could hear Leigh's strangled cry, could hear his heavy erratic footfalls and the thud as he went down. She ran screaming, sure that they would be next to burn.

Lennox saw the fireball and heard Holly scream. No more than twenty feet from them to their right. He crashed into the thickest of the vegetation, yelling, firing the Kalashnikov into the air, then stumbling and pitching forward, sliding down a steep mud bank into the stream bed. Before he could get up, McKinnon was clambering

over him, running to Leigh who was still burning, screaming, rolling back and forth in the dead leaves. McKinnon
leapt onto him, beating out the flames with his bare hands.

Lennox struggled to his feet, looking away up the slope.

'Holly!'

But she didn't hear him; she was scrambling forward,
pushing Emma ahead of her. Lennox started to run.

'Holly!'

She heard him now. She looked back. But instead
of relief he saw eyes fixed in terror. He turned. Beyond
McKinnon, four masked men were running along the
stream bed. They threw themselves down behind the
body of the fallen soldier and raised their weapons.

'Get down!' shouted Lennox, and as the soldiers took
aim, he opened up, pulling the jolting Kalashnikov tight
against his ribs. Bullets ripped into the ground, hitting
him in the legs, punching him back, but he kept on
firing, watching his own bullets cut up the stream bed
then the body of the fallen man, hitting him in the legs
and back. There was a hard metallic thwang and the
air was suddenly a brilliant roaring ball of flame which
blinded him, throwing him backwards into the dirt and
leaves.

There was a fluttering, crackling silence and a smell
of fuel. Lennox blinked up at the sky which seemed to
be raining burning leaves and twigs, his nose and mouth
full of the stink of gasoline. He tried to raise himself, but
his legs wouldn't move.

Carmen stumbled down the earth bank into the ditch,
followed by Daintith. The first thing she saw was the
twisted burning bodies of the Indonesian soldiers. Lennox
had hit the fuel flame thrower's tank.

'Look after McKinnon and Leigh,' she said, stumbling
towards Lennox, who was on the verge of blacking out.
He was losing blood through two wounds below his right
knee. Carmen ripped open the leg of his pants, and tore

strips to make a tourniquet. Suddenly he was staring at her, his hands gripping hers.

'I'll be OK,' he said. 'Look after Holly, the children.'

Carmen turned to see where they had fallen. Daintith ran past her.

'Harold, be careful. Remember the kids are hot.'

Daintith came to the bundle of bodies and looked down, hesitating to touch them. Holly Becker was on her back, her face spattered with fresh blood, her legs twisted underneath her. She had pulled Lucy against her, trying to protect her from the bullets, perhaps after Lucy had been hit. There was a blackening entry wound in Lucy's left shoulder, the only wound Daintith could see on any of them. Emma was further up the slope, her face in the dirt.

Carmen came and stood next to him.

'They're alive,' he said.

10

Carmen hadn't made it an order, but the whole team turned up all the same to see the coffin loaded onto the Chinook – all except Major Leigh, who was still too badly injured to leave the field hospital. The wind was getting up and spots of rain were falling on the tarmac as they lined up by the ramp, watching the approach of the service truck as it made its way slowly from the cargo hangar. No one spoke, the awkwardness of the silence masked by the scream of the aircraft's huge turboshaft engines.

News of the death of Baker had already been given to the next of kin by General Bailey's office, but it would fall to Carmen, as the operational commanding officer, to write the personal letter. It was something she had never had to do before and she was dreading it. She wanted to write something truthful, comforting, more than the worn-out expressions of sympathy that immediately came to mind. But it was hard to think of words that measured up. Only since his death had she come to realise how little she knew about him. Baker had a wife in Memphis called Kristie. That was about it. Carmen had wondered about her. She imagined a little driveway, a rectangle of freshly mown lawn, a neat suburban house not much different from her own, and then, from inside the house, the sound of the telephone ringing and ringing until Mrs

Baker picked it up. She imagined the polite voice of a stranger on the other end of the line, a stranger from Fort Detrick.

Carmen looked into the faces of her men. Their expressions were grim, troubled. The mood had been subdued ever since their return from the forest. Their relief at getting back alive had been overtaken by a sense of futility, even of betrayal. Baker was dead. So were six Indonesian soldiers. Major Leigh's burn injuries – especially to his right arm and hand – were going to leave him disfigured. Yet nobody could say why, or what it had all been for. There were still too many questions, and yet, in the interests of security, they were not even permitted to ask them. Carmen had been obliged to remind everyone that all aspects of the RIID's work on Sumatra were classified. In forty-eight hours they would be going home themselves, their investigation – officially – unsuccessful. What had begun in a spirit of honest scientific enquiry had ended in secrets and lies. In that sense the mission reflected perfectly the history of the Muaratebo virus itself.

Major McKinnon took the salute and the coffin was carried up into the belly of the plane. A few minutes later Carmen was watching it climb slowly into the banks of grey cloud.

Turning towards the field hospital, located in the main service hangar on the edge of the airfield, Carmen saw Lieutenant-General Iskandar and one of his adjutants hurrying towards her. Iskandar was Sutami's replacement as commander of operations on Sumatra. At least ten years older than Sutami, he was taller, with silver hair and big brown eyes that gave him an effeminate look. Although some issues remained unresolved, his arrival from Jakarta with the first elements of the Presidential Guard had probably saved the Americans' lives. Horrified at Sutami's actions on August 30th, he had ordered rescue teams to the scene of the firefight. Back at a hastily re-equipped field hospital Indonesian army surgeons, wearing pressurised suits, had operated on the wounded. Although exhausted and shaken, Carmen had insisted on being present during the operations, which were potentially as dangerous for the surgeons as they were for the patients. Fortunately there were no mistakes; the surgeons attached to the Presidential Guard were the military's best.

Since then Dr Lennox, Major Leigh, Holly Becker and her daughters had been lying in special isolation suites, tended by nurses wearing Tyvek suits and respirators. Five days had passed, and as yet none of them had shown any sign of succumbing to the disease. The Muaratebo virus had been found in Lucy's bloodstream in quantities that corresponded with the early period of the cycle of infection, but this did not square with her account of what had happened after they left Rafflesia Camp on July 24th. If Lucy and Emma were to be believed, Lucy had been carrying the virus for around six weeks.

Carmen had interviewed the girls on her own: first Emma, and then, once she was stable and strong enough to talk, Lucy herself. It hadn't been easy. It was clear that they hadn't quite got to grips with what had happened to them. Nor did they seem to grasp why the strange lady dressed up as a soldier wanted to ask so many questions. They were fidgety, sullen, sometimes dreamy. Carmen, gently probing, trying to reconstruct the sequence of events that led up to their discovery near Ahmad's camp, slowly built up a picture.

They had fled the camp after their father had gone to get help. He was, in Emma's words, very sick – *coughing all the time like Lucy and all the veins in his eyes, she said, sort of showing.* Standing on the veranda they had watched him crash his truck into the perimeter fence and then, without looking back, walk into the jungle, leaving the girls alone with what she would only refer to as *the others*. When Carmen had asked Emma about these people, she had gone very quiet, starting to hum to herself, swaying gently back and forth on her chair. It broke Carmen's heart to see her eyes fill up with the terror of those remembered scenes. It was hard to believe that such beautiful innocent eyes – dark like her mother's, and fringed with thick lashes – could have soaked up so much blood and suffering. Despite the evident upset Emma was feeling, the eyes remained dry. *It's OK to cry*, Carmen had said, hoping to bring her to some sort of release. But Emma had just looked at her for a moment, before saying: '*I already did*'.

These pauses, these brief moments of overwhelming recollection in which Emma could only hum, could only sway on her chair as though trying to rock her memory to sleep, happened again and again as they proceeded through the story. For her part Lucy, still ill, propped up on pillows, would just stare at the ceiling, her hands clenched in the bedding. But despite the gaps, Carmen learned that after the departure of their father, Dr Rhodes – out of his head, probably, the virus having eaten into his brain – the girls had themselves left the camp, heading towards the Hari river where Rhodes kept some boats. They had paddled downriver for a day or so, coming across Ahmad's camp by chance. It was the sound of the monkeys that had attracted their attention, particularly the sounds of one animal, which, by Emma's description of the 'spooky' call, Carmen guessed was probably a gibbon. After a virtually sleepless night by the river – during which Lucy was racked by a hacking cough – they were ravenous. Their hunger made them bold. At the camp they found tinned food, fruit, bottled water and, of course, Ahmad's caged monkeys. Lucy remembered how sad they had looked all caged up. She had tried to let them all go, but only one was bold enough to dart past her, giving her a bite on the way. Carmen made a careful note of the times and places, sure she had discovered the way in which the macaque that infected Peter Jarvis had picked up the virus.

Ahmad had found them in the act of liberating his hard-won catch. As Emma remembered it, the monkey hunter had made a great show of being angry when he found them in his camp. But then, with many gestures and horrible smiles, he had reassured them that he meant them no harm, even feeding them from his substantial supply of tins. He expressed concern for Lucy's attacks of coughing, holding her against him as if she were his own child. At the mention of this there was another of Emma's eloquent pauses. Carmen asked if Ahmad had done anything else. Had he tried to hold Emma too? Emma shook her head and looked down at the floor. Carmen suspected that further questioning from someone experienced in such matters would reveal a further layer of suffering. But there was no time, and, Carmen realised, no point in digging further. She might even do more harm than good. For the time being the shadowy corners of Emma and Lucy's memories would remain undisturbed.

Whatever ambiguous, incomprehensible thing had happened with Ahmad, the girls were evidently glad to have found someone to look after them. He was ugly and smelly, he wanted to hold you close, but he was after all a grown-up. And he was not afraid of the forest. They went down the river in his boat which was loaded with the funny, sad monkeys, Ahmad letting Emma and Lucy take turns at steering and, when the temperamental outboard motor stalled, showing them how to restart it. Such a prolonged period of contact, Lucy coughing virus into the air the whole time, would have been more than enough to ensure Ahmad's infection.

What had happened during their time at Madam Kim's

– Carmen's worst fears about Habibie's story were confirmed – was the biggest mystery. Neither girl wanted to talk about it. Gently inquisitive, reassuring them the whole time, praising their courage, Carmen managed to learn that they had been held prisoner for a while and then had escaped with the help of one of the girls who worked for Madam Kim. The girl, herself developing symptoms, had abandoned them in the middle of the night on a road outside the town. Hungry and afraid, Lucy worse than ever, with fits of coughing that left her breathless and lethargic, they had made their way back to the riverbank where Ahmad had tied up the boat.

It was Emma who had decided that the only thing for them to do was to go back up the river, to try to find Ahmad's camp again. This puzzled Carmen. She could understand the girls taking the boat, but why not go downstream? Why go back into the heart of all the suffering? *I just knew I could find the camp*, said Emma, simply. *There was food. There was nobody to hurt us.* Carmen asked if people had hurt them at Madam Kim's. Emma lowered her head.

What had followed was simple enough, though in some ways the hardest to comprehend. Emma had found Ahmad's camp without too much difficulty, and for three and a half weeks they had sat tight, working their way through Ahmad's supplies, foraging in the forest for fruit among which, Lucy's favourite, was the foul-smelling durian. Both girls were matter-of-fact about these three and a half weeks. There was no question of it being an adventure. Carmen tried to imagine what they had been feeling as they sat in Ahmad's hut with nothing to think about but the death of their father, of the people at the camp, of the people in Muaratebo. She pictured them stunned by all the death and suffering they had seen, folding themselves together like hibernating animals until the sound of their mother's voice, raised in desperation and hope, had caused them to come forward.

The resilience of the girls in the face of such horror was something Carmen found incredible. They had not come through unscathed, and only time would tell how deep the psychological wounds really were, but there they were still fighting for survival, eating, talking, sleeping regularly. It was the presence of their mother that made the difference. How they might have reacted to a group of strangers was, Carmen thought, probably another matter. Holly's proximity – they couldn't actually touch, because of the fear in the early days of cross-infection – the sight of her smiling face, was certainly worth any amount of sedation or expert counselling.

And if their resilience was hard to believe, the problem posed from a biochemical point of view was utterly mysterious. The fact that Lucy could sustain a substantial population of the virus without succumbing to it, the fact that Emma had never developed the disease, the fact that Holly herself, despite the final desperate hours of exposure to her daughter, appeared to be clean, were all beyond Carmen's understanding. Of course the temptation to speculate was overwhelming, and in the days of convalescence they all advanced theories that might explain why the Beckers had not died. One idea surfaced in all the argument: perhaps the existence in Lucy Becker's genes of the palaeo-virus in its dormant state somehow prevented the Muaratebo variety from replicating in sufficient numbers to be lethal. Perhaps the necessary sites on her genetic code were already occupied.

On the basis of this idea, Holly was able to add one final piece to the epidemiological jigsaw. In his last letter to Holly Becker, Dr Jonathan Rhodes had stated that Lucy had fallen ill. This, Carmen felt certain, marked the period of viral expression which would have followed exposure to the tropical antigen that triggered the reaction. It was quite possible that this would have given the child a fever, her immune system reacting to the presence of unfamiliar particles. The process of expression would have continued until the antigen began to be dissipated or broken down – long enough evidently for Lucy to pass the virus to Dr Rhodes, his wife and everyone else at Rafflesia Camp, including a young girl called Indah, the housekeeper's daughter, whose body Carmen had found in one of the shallow graves. Worst of all, she had still been infectious at the time she encountered Ahmad the hunter and his catch, through whom the virus spread to Muaratebo and the wider world beyond. After that, the virus, having no means of reproduction inside Lucy's body, had begun to fade away. She could produce the virus and transmit it for a period. Because her sister and her mother carried the same dormant virus entwined in their DNA, they shared her immunity.

This last fact was the RIID team's one cause for celebration. For fifteen minutes after the last negative test results had come in, Carmen, Major McKinnon, Sergeant Sarandon and the two of the Indonesian army doctors had stood beneath the neon lights of the hospital lab drinking warm Cokes to mark the occasion. But as soon as the Indonesians had gone, the truth of the new situation had struck home. While there was no longer any reason to fear for the children's survival, the possibility remained that the virus might one day re-emerge. Emma had never produced the virus because she had not come in contact with the antigen. But if ever she did . . . As McKinnon had pointed out, the antigen that had triggered the problem was unidentified, and would very likely remain so unless Dr Irwin's work for Gensystems could be completely reconstructed. The unavoidable conclusion – the one the authorities back home were bound to draw – was that the twins represented a serious, if unquantifiable, health risk to all those around them. The future for Emma and Lucy Rhodes would be played out within the four walls of a sterile, hermetically sealed containment suite. This was one more thing Carmen was obliged to keep secret, not only from the Indonesians, but from Holly Becker and her family as well.

General Iskandar had arrived. He saluted and offered Carmen his hand.

'Once again my commiserations, Colonel,' he said. 'If there is anything further I can do, I hope you will not hesitate to ask.'

'Thank you, General,' Carmen said. 'I think we've done what we can for the present, at least as far as Corporal Baker is concerned.'

Iskandar nodded gravely as they carried on walking towards the hangar where the hospital had been set up.

'I wanted to inform you in person that a full enquiry has been ordered by Jakarta into the incident which claimed the life of Corporal Baker. Brigadier Sutami is due to give evidence in the capital tomorrow.'

Carmen did not react. She was glad to hear that Sutami's career was as good as over but she could not afford to show any satisfaction at Iskandar's words. Her overriding priority, as she saw it, was to get Holly and her children back to the States before any more information about the origin of the virus leaked out, and for that she needed all the leverage she could get. Indonesian embarrassment at Sutami's actions, intensified by Washington's unexpected support for Indonesia at the United Nations and a promise of emergency aid, was a resource too valuable to squander.

'I shall be interested to hear its conclusions, General,' she said. 'In the meantime I'd be grateful if you would let your medical staff here know that we shall be evacuating Mrs Becker and the others as soon as suitable forward transport can be arranged to the United States.'

Iskandar came to a halt and Carmen turned to face him.

'My medical staff tell me that it would be premature to release any of our patients while any suspicion remains that they may have been infected. As for the girl, Lucy, while she may not have developed symptoms, she *is* infected. Thus far she is the only example of an immune system that resists the virus. Our doctors would greatly appreciate the opportunity to study her further.'

'General, they have all been in quarantine for five days, and none of them show any signs of deterioration. Considering what they've been through, I'm sure you can understand their desire to be repatriated as soon as possible. As regards Lucy Becker, I fully appreciate your interest in her case, but I can assure you we are as interested as you are in learning whatever we can about this disease. She will be subjected to the most rigorous scrutiny USAMRIID's technology can bring to bear. Any results we produce will be made available to you. If there's one thing this outbreak has taught us it's that Muaratebo does not respect national boundaries. Neither should science, or medicine for that matter.'

Iskandar seemed to reflect for a moment. He gave a nod.

An armed guard saluted at the entrance to the field hospital and held open the door for them. The interior was a honeycomb of partitions and heavy plastic screens. It bristled with equipment, a far more impressive facility than any Sutami had been able to command.

'Our doctors will be very disappointed,' Iskandar insisted, but Carmen sensed he had already given up. She was right, after all. The RIID would stand a much better chance of discovering what it was that stopped Lucy Becker from dying. The fact that they would never share that information with the Indonesians was something Iskandar could not suspect.

'I accept that, General,' Carmen said, though she

found it hard to believe that the doctors would have much chance to carry out any pure research in the coming weeks. The crisis in Sumatra was far from over. 'But in the circumstances I think Mrs Becker's wishes should be respected. And she wants to take her children home.'

They had been walking down the main corridor towards the far end of the facility. Suddenly Iskandar stopped. In front of him lay the entrance to the quarantine area, marked with the same bright red biohazard warning symbol as they used at Fort Detrick. It was still three doors way from the special wards where Holly and her children lay, but his reluctance to enter was obvious.

He cleared his throat.

'I feel I ought to tell you that Brigadier Sutami continues to maintain that the children were identified – by your team – as the source of the virus, as carriers. He claims he was told as much by one of your officers. How do you – '

Carmen interrupted. It was a lie she had rehearsed so many times, it came out with a naturalness and ease that surprised her:

'As I tried to explain at the time, General, that was a misunderstanding on the Brigadier's part and on the part of his observer. We had reason to suspect that the children had been exposed to the virus for a prolonged period without having succumbed. Naturally we wanted them brought out of the field to facilitate further study. It may be that Lucy and Emma Becker have some kind of immunity, that they may actually be carriers. But the idea that they are somehow the source is absurd. How could that possibly be?'

Iskandar nodded slowly. Carmen sensed that in spite of her confident performance he did not believe her. But she also sensed that it no longer mattered whether he did or not. Political considerations demanded a show of co-operation, and political considerations were the only ones that counted.

Epilogue

The swing-ball was a definite hit. Tom had brought it home the night before and screwed it into the middle of the back lawn, hoping to tempt Oliver and Joey away from the junior tennis that had already cost two cracked windows on the first floor. Now the boys were somewhere in the middle of their seventh set, hitting the brilliant pink ball back and forth as hard as they could and grunting Jimmy Connors-style.

Carmen put down her mug of coffee and watched them for a minute. Though smaller, Joey was pretty much holding his own. His favourite stroke was the overhead double-handed slam dunk, which involved hitting the ball downwards as hard as possible so that the elastic whipped it back up again on the return, right over Oliver's head. Many of Oliver's high shots had been punished this way, and he was forced to keep the ball at shoulder height rather than risk setting up a winner. For the time being Joey had found an answer to the height mismatch, and was revelling in what he clearly felt was a moral victory. Tom, who was umpiring from a safe distance, looked round at Carmen with a grin on his face.

'Thirty, forty, break point,' he said, in a corny commentator voice. 'And the crowd senses something.'

Carmen smiled and reached for the Saturday paper. On the cover of the colour supplement was a picture

469

a man inside a pressurised suit, holding a glass flask in a pair of tweezers. A lurid red light played across his plastic visor. The headline read: RUSSIA'S SECRET ARSENALS. She was just turning to the contents page when a slim grey envelope slid out and landed with a slap on the patio floor.

At first she thought it was a bill or another credit card offer from the bank, but when she turned it over she found that the address had been handwritten, in blue ink. The postmark said Wisconsin. Carmen didn't think she knew anyone there. The handwriting was unfamiliar too, slightly rounded and a little shaky in places. She tore back the flap.

September 3rd

Dear Carmen,

I hope you aren't too surprised to hear from me after all this time. I've been wanting to talk to you ever since we left, but it's been difficult, and I promised Richard I wouldn't take any chances. He's very afraid that someone will come after us and take the children away. I hope you'll understand why we couldn't let that happen. I tried to call you once, a couple of days after we left the Taylor Trust, but I heard a man's voice and I hung up. I guess it was just your husband, but I was afraid someone from the RIID was there at your house and that they might trace the call.

I worry that maybe you feel we betrayed your trust, taking Emma and Lucy out of the hospital like we did. I like to think you knew that's what we would do, and that was why you authorised the transfer out of Fort Detrick. It's just a feeling I have. Richard says it's wishful thinking, but he never got the chance to know you like I did. I hope you didn't get into trouble about it. If you did, I'm truly sorry.

I know a lot of people will say we've been very irresponsible, seeing as how there still isn't a vaccine, and that some day the virus could reappear. But those people don't care about my children. It isn't going to bother them if Emma and Lucy spend the next ten years of their life – maybe all their lives – in a glass cage, talking to people in space suits or behind screens, never seeing the outside world. I know some of your colleagues at the RIID think that way. When I asked them how long it would be before I could have my children back they just sat there and talked about the dangers involved in letting them go, because the antigen that activated the virus hadn't been identified. Some of them even lit up cigarettes while they explained about the need to minimise the health risks.

We talked about those risks once – do you remember? It was the last time I spoke to you. You said the antigen was almost certainly tropical, pollen from some jungle plant or maybe something in an insect bite, and that outside of the tropics it wasn't likely to show up again. When you said that, I finally made my mind up to get the children away. Did you know your words would have that effect? I've often wondered.

We're living on a farm now. It's beautiful country, with hills behind us and woods and a rocky stream two hundred yards from the house where Richard goes fishing sometimes. Now that Lucy's shoulder is all healed up she and Emma are going to start riding lessons soon. They're very excited about it. There's a little school nearby, nothing fancy, but the teachers seem very friendly and dedicated. There are no drug problems and none of the students carry knives. I was afraid it was asking too much of Richard to leave New York and come out here, but I think he really loves it.

He says Wall Street was sucking the life out of him.
He and the children seem much closer than before.

Carmen, I suppose you can imagine that it hasn't been easy for the girls, and I don't know if it will ever get easier. Lucy seems to suffer most with her nightmares despite all the help the RIID people tried to give, and when she is really bad there seems to be nothing I can say. But in a way I know that as long as she has Emma, she'll be OK. They went through everything together. It means they can share the load a little. Sometimes I find Lucy in Emma's bed in the morning, the two of them clinging to each other as if they were back out there in the jungle.

But what I said about Richard is true enough. The children seem to have accepted him and they are closer than they were. It feels like we're a real family at last. We are closer too. I mean Richard and myself. That probably sounds strange to you. But thinking back to that time, when I first talked to you at Rafflesia Camp, if you had asked me if I wanted Jonathan back, I would have probably said yes. Are you surprised? You see I never properly broke up with Jonathan, and when I went out to Sumatra I think a part of me did want something to happen. Maybe for us to – I don't know how to say it really – but for us to pick up where we had left off. I knew he was with another, younger woman, but I let myself believe that all his talk about the good of the children was really a smokescreen for a plan he had to get me back.

But when you told me that everything had happened because of the Gensystems treatment I felt so angry. Against you at first, as you probably remember. But afterwards against Jonathan and myself. I recalled discussions we had going back to the time when he told me to have the treatment and when, despite my own feelings, I went ahead and did it. Because I trusted him. I mean not just as a person but as a man of science. I think about the risk I was ready to take, the risk I took, just because he thought that was the best thing. When you told me how everything started at Gensystems it was like something snapped inside me. And suddenly there was room for Richard. Everything became very easy. I don't know if any of that makes sense to you, but it brings me to my other piece of big news: we went off to see a minister last week and got married. It wasn't much of an occasion, but I wish you could have been there all the same.

Of course we're very careful about the children. If either of them so much as coughs I banish Richard from the house and keep them at home to make sure no one comes into contact with them. So far we've only had one false alarm, but Richard's already equipped a habitable den over one of the barns. We're a very long way from the tropics up here, but if the virus ever does return then I know where to reach you. Our nearest neighbours are more than two miles away.

I've taken quite an interest in virology since this whole thing began, and I still visit the county library every now and again, just to see if there is anything new about Muaratebo in the medical journals. I keep hoping there'll be some breakthrough with a vaccine or a new form of treatment, but I guess that will probably be years away – even assuming anyone keeps working on the problem. If there are no more new cases then I don't suppose it will remain much of a priority.

I read Harold Daintith's paper in Science. It seemed very impressive about the action of the virus and how it spreads, but I was surprised it said so little about where it came from. Why didn't *it mention the programme at Gensystems or Fort Willard or any of that? When I read that I thought maybe the whole theory had been discarded, that it had all been a mistake, but then I thought about what it might mean if everybody found out what really happened. I thought about how embarrassing it might be to the government, and I thought about the Indonesians. It struck me that they could make a good claim for compensation from the United States for the cost of the whole epidemic. I suppose it would be more surprising if the whole thing wasn't kept a secret under those circumstances.*

I wish I could hear from you somehow, just to know that you and your family are well. Maybe when they find a vaccine, or when everyone has forgotten about Muaratebo, we can meet again. I don't think I ever really thanked you enough for what you did – not just for finding Emma and Lucy, but for getting us all out of Sumatra alive. I'm sure that without you, I would have lost my children for ever.

It was signed *with love from Holly Meyers* and there was a photograph of Holly and her daughters standing next to a barn with an affable-looking man Carmen assumed was Richard. They were squinting into bright sunlight, but behind them, beyond the barn, storm clouds were gathering. Carmen put down the letter and gazed across the lawn. One of the neighbours had a small bonfire going and the smoke was drifting past the big maple, catching the scattered rays of sunlight. She got up and went through to the kitchen. The car keys were in an empty fruit bowl on top of the refrigerator.

he drove around Aspen Hill for thirty minutes and then t onto the turnpike. She didn't know where she was ng. All she knew was she couldn't sit at home, watching her family play ball in the garden. Holly Becker – Holly Meyers now – was alive and well and living somewhere in Wisconsin, or maybe over the state line in Michigan. It felt like momentous news. It felt like she ought to do something, but, driving towards the low September sun, she realised she didn't want to do anything. Things had become too complicated, too compromised.

After the disappearance of the children from the Taylor Trust there had been quite a fuss. As General Bailey explained, the Administration was very anxious 'to keep a lid on this thing', although Carmen was never sure if he meant the virus or the truth behind it. If the virus in Sumatra hadn't started to burn itself out the RIID would probably have mounted some kind of search.

But as the epidemiological studies had shown, the primary strain of the Muaratebo virus had been a little too hot for its own god. Its replication level was such that those it infected became sick after five days and died after nine. This meant that there were only four days during which it could be easily passed on – and during most of that time its unfortunate hosts were immobilised. In the crowded and unsanitary conditions of a tropical township this four-day window was enough to create an epidemic. Blood contact with the sick and with fresh corpses had been common in the early stages, as well as aerial transmission. But where adequate medical procedures and facilities were in place the virus could be contained. Given its population density London would have fared a lot worse had not the carrier, Peter Jarvis, been hospitalised within hours of becoming infectious. But, then again, the accident that put him there had probably been brought on by the onset of the sickness itself.

More than a year after the eruption of the virus the precise number of fatalities on Sumatra was still not known. The last population census on the island was hopelessly out of date and there were still m⁣

thousands of displaced persons living in coastal shanties or with relatives in other towns. The government put the number of dead at around 16,000, but no one believed that figure. An as yet unpublished WHO report put the total closer to 40,000. The report was also highly critical of the way the Indonesian authorities had handled the situation, which it described as both complacent and heavy-handed. If they had been quicker to organise a major medical relief effort and less concerned about their international standing, many lives could have been saved.

In the months following the first outbreak the greatest fear on Sumatra had been that an insect vector, mosquitoes in particular, would carry infected blood from the dying to new hosts. The high replication level of the virus would be no disadvantage in survival terms if the rate of transmission to new hosts exceeded the rate at which the old hosts died. However, while there were some cases where this type of infection was suspected, they were few. Mercifully for the whole region, the virus called Muaratebo did not seem to thrive in the bellies of insects. As Daintith concluded in the paper he wrote shortly after his return, given its limited methods of transmission, the virulence of the virus had to be considered a major limitation on its ability to propagate – in effect, a competitive disadvantage.

Daintith's conclusion was confirmed as early as the following November, when the first documented cases had begun to appear of non-fatal infection. A cooler, less dangerous strain of the virus was easing out the other, the first step in a gradual evolution that might end in benign co-existence. The last stages of such an evolution might even see a strain of the virus incorporating itself into the genetic code of its hosts, thus ensuring replication from generation to generation. Such a thing had happened with Holly Becker's ancestors, after all. The virus had been passed down harmlessly from parent to offspring for many thousands of years. Any doubts that Carmen had about that were dispelled by the immunity to infection which Holly, like her children, enjoyed. An incoming virus particle could not take over the reproductive machinery of her cells, as it could other people's, because the site it needed for that purpose was already occupied by its benign relative. This, or something close to it, was the only convincing explanation for Holly and Emma's survival.

Yet this last part of the argument was missing from Daintith's paper, just as Holly had said. There was no mention whatever of the evidence that George Arends had uncovered, no reference to the events at Fort Willard. No sooner had Carmen arrived back in the United States than she had been reminded in no uncertain terms that all her findings were subject to the full strictures of military security and henceforward classified. She was not to talk to the press, she was not to describe her findings even to other officers. She had imagined at the time that this was standard Pentagon paranoia, expecting that in due course everything would be laid out for the general good of medicine. When, some months later, a draft of Daintith's paper was passed to her for comment, she had felt utterly sick. Corporal Baker had died, Major Leigh, though making a full recovery, had been badly burned, millions of dollars had been spent trying to uncover the source of the virus, to reach an understanding of how it functioned, to learn the lessons and assess the risks. And yet the biggest lesson of them all, the heart of the matter, was considered too dangerous to publish. The question was: dangerous for whom?

The day she saw Daintith's paper Carmen had asked herself how many other such secrets there were, locked away inside pressurised containment suites in governmer laboratories the world over, how many other projects t delicate for anyone to know about? She had put a in to Harold Daintith, but his secretary had said he was unavailable. He never got back to her. The next morning she had organised the removal of Holly Becker's children to the Taylor Trust in Baltimore. It was, after all, a small risk next to the one her superiors seemed willing to take. A few days later she put in a request for a transfer out of BL–4 work. General Bailey had been understanding about it. She had done her share in the front line, was how he put it. After two months working on some new, drug-resistant strains of tuberculosis that had started to show up in Latin America, she had left the army altogether.

She felt certain now that it was Bailey who had sent her the documents on the decon operation at Willard. He was virtually the only officer in the RIID who would have been senior enough back then to receive details about what the decon was for, about what it was they were dealing with. Carmen guessed that he had been called in to advise on the operation, which had then been handled by some *ad hoc* team of Special Forces and spooks from the Pentagon or Langley. Of course, he'd had no way of knowing if the events at Willard were relevant to the emergency on Sumatra, but in leaking the documents he was covering himself: if the whole covert programme became public knowledge he could use his action to defend himself against Congressional committees and the odium of the medical world; and if it didn't, no one would ever be able to prove that the leak came from him. At first she had felt like talking the whole thing over with Bailey. He was experienced, he knew the score. But she had long since changed her mind about that.

She was working with Tom now in his small animals veterinary practice in Bethesda. It had been wonderful to start with, wonderful particularly to be able to redis-over her husband and kids. But it didn't take long fore she was finding the work repetitive and dull. d, despite the boredom, and despite the niggling sense that she had taken the easy road, had missed her vocation, she felt more centred, more at ease with herself.

Carmen pulled off the turnpike and stopped the car. She felt the need of a cigarette. The sun was beginning to set, turning the clouds bloody along the horizon. A barbed-wire fence running along the side of the road had snagged scraps of packaging which were caught along the bottom. She looked down at the floral print dress she was wearing and could feel her depression deepening like an incoming weather system. She wanted to go back home. More than at any time in her life she needed her family. And they needed her. That was the one truth that had emerged from the whole sordid affair. And if this feeling was partly a genetic thing, something in her chromosomes which made her need her offspring, it was something else too. And whatever it was, it was a human thing, a thing she felt, something that made her more than a living, replicating machine, something more than a virus. She started the car and pulled into a U-turn, heading back to the turnpike. Tom and the boys would have finished playing tennis. They would be wondering where she was.

PATRICK LYNCH

The Annunciation

'There is nothing inevitable in decay, no corruption that cannot be redeemed. With the instruments of our own creation we can re-create ourselves!'

1995. Mendelhaus is the most mysterious cosmetics company in the world, with a covert programme of genetic research that is about to change the course of history.

Primed with inside information beautiful Wall Street analyst Cathy Ryder is the first to tip the shares as they surge from nowhere.

A revolutionary new product that reverses the ageing process throws the cosmetics industry into turmoil. Mendelhaus have found the answer to humanity's dream of eternal youth.

But the dream turns to nightmare for Cathy as she is chosen for the central role in a far more secret project that will have unimaginable consequences for mankind . . .

'Marks the emergence of a major storyteller'
Independent

PATRICK LYNCH

The Immaculate Conception

2003: The New Millenium

The Japanese military surprise the world by successfully testing a star wars space defence system using technology they were not supposed to have. With the alarm bells ringing in Washington, the president of a major US defence corporation puts a gun in his mouth and pulls the trigger.

As the tension mounts between the Pacific superpowers, the American government assigns Investigating Officer Jack Coldwell to uncover the truth.

The trail leads to Tokyo and Hiraizumi, a powerful industrial dynasty. But the threat Hiraizumi poses goes way beyond the hardware of geopolitical struggle. It is at once more profound, more terrifying.

At its heart is not military technology or espionage, but a visionary geneticist by the name of Edward Geiger. And two children. Twins . . .

The brilliant and explosive sequel to *The Annunciation*.

'Gripping'
Sunday Telegraph

JAMES HALL

Mean High Tide

Harden Winchester's a man to avoid at all costs. A government-trained killer turned rogue, he's going to unleash massive eco-terror just to satisfy a personal whim. His man-eating daughter's from the same mould – but with some special quirks all her own.

Thorn didn't mean to get involved with either. Down in the Florida Keys he was doing just fine – for once. But his girlfriend's death while diving is no accident. And Harden's obsession with changing America's eating habits for ever is less than healthy.

Taking to the back roads and swamps of the Everglades Thorn prepares to enter the Winchesters' kingdom of twisted dreams . . .

'Crackerjack tale of Florida low-lifes who believe in getting mad and then even . . . with dialogue as tough as shark skin'
Daily Telegraph

'Rich in atmosphere, wild in action and peppered with colourful characters, Hall nails you to each page until the suspense-laden climax'
Clive Cussler

A Selected List of Thrillers available from Mandarin

☐	7493 0054 X	**The Silence of the Lambs**	Thomas Harris	£5.99
☐	7493 1091 X	**Primal Fear**	William Diehl	£4.99
☐	7493 0636 X	**Bones of Coral**	James Hall	£4.99
☐	7493 1749 3	**Mean High Tide**	James Hall	£4.99
☐	7493 1398 6	**The Immaculate Conception**	Patrick Lynch	£4.99
☐	7493 1528 8	**The Minstrel Boy**	Richard Crawford	£5.99
☐	7493 1324 2	**Call of the Lion**	Christopher Sherlock	£4.99
☐	7493 1323 4	**Eye of the Cobra**	Christopher Sherlock	£4.99
☐	7493 1968 2	**The Tick Tock Man**	Terence Strong	£4.99
☐	7493 1972 0	**The Cruelty of Morning**	Hilary Bonner	£4.99
☐	7493 1713 2	**Kolymsky Heights**	Lionel Davidson	£5.99